Laura

A West of the Divide Novel

A.G. GRAHAM

Library of Congress Control Number: 2024926970

ISBN
979-8-89641-019-5 (Paperback)
979-8-89641-020-1 (eBook)
979-8-89641-018-8 (Hardcover)

CHAPTER 1

Alex

She didn't hover but watched carefully from a distance as Alex put the finishing touches on a plate of baked Pacific halibut garnished with a sprig of rosemary and lemon slices. He gazed at the presentation a second and called out, "Order up."

As the waitress took the plate away, Laura nodded and said quietly to herself, "Excellent."

Alejandro Iglesias glanced back at her, smiled, and returned to work. He was thirty-nine years old, the son of a Mexican immigrant from Guadalajara who came to the United States and worked in a picture framing factory in San Diego. His father met his wife, Renata, shortly afterward and they were married. She gave birth to Alex a year later.

Alex had no formal culinary training. He started cooking as a teenager, gradually working his way up the coast to Los Angeles, hoping to get a job in one of the trendy restaurants. The closest he ever came was two years as a dishwasher and busboy. By the time he was in his early thirties, he had saved enough money to buy a taco truck, fell in love, and made up his mind to ask the girl to marry him. When she confessed that she'd been seeing someone else, he packed his few belongings, and headed north on the Pacific Coast Highway.

Gradually he settled in San Francisco and began playing with new recipes of traditional Mexican dishes. His truck was parked by Golden Gate Park, not far from Laura's house, when she stopped on her day off to get something to eat. One bite convinced her to hire him. But he said no. A few days later, he showed up at her restaurant first thing in the morning and ordered an espresso.

Laura was formally trained as a chef in Paris and was eventually offered a job in San Francisco by Armand Moreau, the owner and head chef of one of the Bay Area's destination spots. She worked as his sous-chef for five years before gambling everything to start her own place. It was small, serving breakfast and lunch, but after three years it took something short of a miracle to get a table after eleven without a reservation.

Her business had growing pains and that led to Alejandro Iglesias; she'd been looking for someone to work under her, someone she could train the way Armand had trained her. Finding a person with experience wasn't a problem but finding someone with talent and experience was something altogether different. And she couldn't compete with the kind of salary range that high-end restaurants offered.

Laura was in the back going over the accounts, enjoying an Americano and a croissant, when Shelly Andrews, the barista who opened the café in the morning, came into her makeshift office. "Yes, Shelly, what is it?"

She smiled. "There's a good-looking guy out front who would like to talk to you. He says you offered him a job."

A grin spread across Laura's face as she grabbed her Americano. "Thanks, Shelly."

Alex had done his homework. It wasn't hard to learn about Laura Patterson and her café, Bistro at the Bay. Her reputation around the city was excellent but he'd given up trying to be anything more than what he'd become. The truck provided a good living, he had no one to answer to besides himself and he was free to try his own recipes without anyone hassling him. But after he had quickly said no, the artist within him struggled with the refusal.

Laura watched him for a moment before saying to Shelly, "Bring him a piece of the frittata we made this morning and another espresso." She walked over to his table, smiling. "It's good to see you again, Mr. Iglesias."

He stood as she started to sit. "Please, call me Alex."

She asked bluntly, "How long have you been cooking out of your truck?"

"I bought it about six years ago. The owner wanted to retire."

"Where did you work before that?"

The interview was beginning to irritate him. This wasn't what he had in mind when he decided to come and talk to her. "Coffee shops mostly," he replied defensively. And then before she could reply he continued, "Listen… I make a good living and I like having the freedom to cook what I want."

Laura sensed his discomfort. "Me too." She grinned. "My grandmother was the first person to teach me. How about you?"

"My mother."

Shelly brought the slice of frittata and his coffee, placing both in front of him and taking his empty cup away. Laura said, "I'd like to know what you think."

He took a bite, letting his taste buds linger before replying, "The asparagus is nice with the ham." Alex set his fork down. "The flavor is subtle, too subtle for me."

She appreciated his honesty and knew that his palate had probably become used to more aggressive flavor. That wasn't necessarily a negative. On the contrary, his use of spice, his artistry, was what attracted her in the beginning. You could teach anyone how to follow a recipe; that's not what she was looking for. She wanted someone who could expand on what they were taught.

Laura came to the point quickly. "Would you like to learn what I know?"

"I know?"

Alex nodded slowly. "Yes."

"Why?"

She didn't waste time and he appreciated that. "I want to be the best at what I do, at least the best I can be." He paused briefly. "Years ago I wanted someone, anyone with experience, to teach me. It didn't happen, and I gave up until you asked me to work for you." The rest was hard for him to admit and as he continued, the volume of his voice lowered. "When you offered me the job… I was afraid."

When she was a young girl, going to school at ASU in Tempe, Arizona, one of the most difficult things she had to do was tell her parents she wanted to go to Paris and become a chef. They supported her, lovingly and financially; she didn't have to struggle to make ends meet. Laura respected Alex for his persistence but she wondered if he was able to give up any bad habits he'd cultivated over the years. She took a drink of her coffee. "You'd have to start from scratch and follow my direction to the letter. It won't be easy for you. You'll want to revert to what has worked for you in the past." She shook her head from side to side. "Don't. You'll have to trust me."

Alex had to ask, "Why me?"

Laura grinned. "You have talent. That's not as easy to find as you might think. But talent isn't enough. I think you know that."

"When do I start?"

"Tomorrow. You'll help open up."

The weeks and months went by quickly after that. When Laura said he had to start from scratch, she meant every word. Alex began by maintaining the kitchen; he washed dishes, cleaned, and scrubbed every inch. He worked up to prep cook and she retaught him the simplest things. While he was cutting vegetables one afternoon she walked by and took the knife from him. She demonstrated a technique, returned the knife to him, covering his hands with hers to show him slowly how she wanted it done. These small lessons became an everyday occurrence and Alex began to feel her eyes on him everywhere. There were times when he'd dreamt of her at night and the dreams were often far from pleasant.

Spring turned to summer, then fall, and the holidays approached. Laura was showing him how to make chicken Dijon; she heated a skillet with olive oil until it shimmered before adding the seasoned drumsticks. A few minutes later after the chicken had browned she added onion and began to stir. "Don't add the garlic until the onion is softened."

Once she allowed him to begin preparing food, Alex became impatient to do more. "I don't understand why you don't want me on the grill. It's something I'm good at."

She added broth and crushed coriander to the mixture. "Are you paying attention to what I'm showing you?"

"Yes," he said with a sigh. She gave him the look; he hated the look and replied assuredly, "Sí, sí, I'm paying attention!"

Her voice was soft and deliberate. "Bring it to a boil and cook until the chicken is done." She turned to him. "There's no point putting you on the grill. It's a waste of my time and yours."

"Why?"

"Because I know you're good at it. You have too much else to learn."

Before he could reply she started walking toward her office. "What do you want me to do?"

She called back, "Watch the chicken, then do it again by yourself! Bring me a sample when you're done."

In late October she began taking him to the fish and vegetable markets with her in the early morning. She introduced him to the vendors and showed him exactly what to look for. "Everything begins here," she told him. "The quality of what we do begins with ingredients. That's the difference between us and most of our competitors."

They were at the fish market talking to Angelo Ferreira, a third-generation Portuguese fisherman, when she said emphatically to Alex, "I would rather build my menu around what looks good each day than what I've preplanned. That's why some things on the menu change daily. The crab is almost in season again, we'll watch for that, but today, the tuna and halibut look good."

Shortly before six they left the vegetable market in time to open the restaurant. When they unlocked the front door the smell of fresh bread hit their nostrils. Tony Morello was her baker and had been working since two that morning. Laura could have used a commercial bakery but one of the restaurant's signature items was fresh bread, croissants, bagels, and rolls.

Laura went straight to her office and Alex began taking the chairs off the tables. He had no idea why, but she insisted that he learn everything about the front of the restaurant as well as the back. After several months she left the responsibility of opening to him. He'd just finished when an attractive Hispanic girl walked in. "Yes," he said, "may I help you?" Alex was in the process of making an espresso for himself and an Americano for Laura.

She gripped a thermal bag in her arms and said quietly in broken English, "Perdón I have appointment with Laura Patterson."

Alex poured espresso into a cup of hot water, before adding an exact amount of cream and sugar. "Who should I say is here?"

Her eyes wandered about the room. "Isabella Perez."

He took Laura's Americano to the back and told her about the young woman. "What should I tell her?"

"Tell her to come back for heaven's sake and ask her if she wants coffee or anything."

Alex showed Isabella to the office and by the time he returned to the front, there was a customer at the counter who wanted to order coffee and a roll to go. Three more people were sitting at a table. After that he was busy and forgot about everything but the customers; he was relieved when Shelly walked in to begin her shift. The early rush had just begun to ease when Laura appeared by his side and held out a small flour tortilla. "Try this and tell me what you think."

He took one bite, thought about it for a second and said, "Excellent," then finished the rest. "What's this about?"

Laura grinned. "Your fish tacos are today's lunch special." As she walked away she said, "Use the tuna for them and the halibut for fish and chips."

This was the first time she put him in charge of preparing any dish and for a moment he was shocked, then whispered, "Yes, Chef."

The day was frantic with hardly a moment to take a break and by four in the afternoon they were closed. It had been a good day for Laura; Alex was progressing well, and she received her beer and wine license. There was a knock on her office door. "Come in."

Alex stuck his head inside. "Everything's cleaned up for the night."

She motioned for him to sit. "You did well today. The tacos were a success."

"Sí, Chef," he agreed. "It was fun being on the grill again, doing something I know I'm good at."

"You're good at many things, Alex."

He let the compliment slide. "Where did you find Isabella?"

Laura chuckled. "I never reveal my sources. How would you like to have a drink with me... not here, someplace where we're waited on for a change?"

His boss surprised him twice in one day. "I'd like that."

She considered taking him to Entretenir, it had been a long time since she'd seen Henri, the bartender and a close friend, but she knew that Chef Moreau could smell talent for miles. Laura had no intention of letting Alex get anywhere close to him. She took him to one of her favorite wine bars instead, just off Lincoln Way and close to her house.

They were seated in a quiet corner near the fireplace; Laura ordered an Italian Pinot Grigio, and Alex ordered a beer. He felt self-conscious, this wasn't the kind of place he frequented. She asked the waitress, "What are your beers on tap?"

The waitress reached for the beer and wine menu on their table, opened it and said, "The tap beers are here"—she pointed them out with her finger— "but we have an excellent selection of bottled beer as well."

Laura smiled at her. "What would you recommend?"

"The Westvleteren is very nice."

"Bring that for him please."

Alex was furious, his emotions fueled by the discomfort he felt. When the waitress was gone, he leaned across the table saying, "I can order for myself."

She could see the fury in his eyes and found it attractive. But she knew that he had a point. "I'm sorry but I didn't bring you here by accident."

"Why then?"

She leaned across the table, inches from his face and grinned. "I received our beer and wine license today."

He was confused; Alex didn't realize that she was interested in providing liquor to her customers. "Will there be much of a demand? We close at four."

"Not any more. I'll be extending our hours next month. We'll have an opening and invite all our regulars."

"Do you know anything about wine?"

"A little but not enough. I'm going to have you work breakfast and lunch. You'll oversee the kitchen. I'll be in charge of dinner." Laura had to bring up the rest of what she wanted to share tactfully. "I'm interviewing someone to manage the front during lunch and dinner. She knows wine and beer… well, more about wine really. Her name's—here she is now."

Alex watched an attractive blond in her late twenties making her way toward them. His mind was still trying to process all that had been thrown at him in such a short amount of time. She was beautiful, he thought. But it appeared to him as if she intentionally played down her looks.

The two of them stood as she approached, and Laura said, "Alex, I'd like you to meet Lorraine Strickland."

The woman embraced Laura quickly before holding out her hand to him. "Please, call me Reina."

As the three of them took a seat, the waitress came back and put Laura's wine and Alex's beer down on the table. "May I get you something, miss?"

Reina glanced at the menu knowing she wanted to impress. "Bring us a bottle of the Caymus." Once she'd gone, Reina turned to Laura saying, "I tried this Cabernet the other night and it's perfect right now. I'd like you to try it."

They sat and made small talk for several minutes; Laura listened for the most part until Reina asked her point-blank, "What is it, as far as wine and beer are concerned, that you would like to provide to your customers?"

There was no hesitation as she replied, "Quality, value, and variety. I want our customers to be able to enjoy beers and wines from around the world that they don't have access to anywhere else."

Alex was still trying his best to get his head around this new vision of Laura's. Why he wondered did she want to change the entire format of the restaurant when she was so successful?

The waitress arrived with the bottle of red wine and opened it silently. As she was about to pour a taste Reina said, "We'll let it breathe for a moment. Could we have some bottled water please?" She turned to Laura, then Alex. "This wine was bottled in 1995 in Napa. It has beautiful color and a wonderful scent with an excellent finish."

Laura asked, "You grew up in that area, didn't you?"

"My folks live in St. Helena, but I was born in Santa Rosa." She blushed. "I'm a wine brat. My dad is a vintner and has spent his life in the business."

Alex, for the first time, began to see the person behind the professional airs she put on. He didn't have a great deal of patience for pretentious people or those who hid behind their intellect or social status. And he thought she was charming.

Reina poured a small amount of the Caymus into the glass closest to Laura. "Please, try it."

Laura brought the glass to her nose and took in the scent briefly before taking a sip. A moment later, she smiled. "Delicious."

CHAPTER 2

Daniel

He'd been spending every November in the Bay Area since George W. was elected and the towers fell. These would be the last of his California shows before heading southeast to spend the winter months in Arizona selling to the snowbirds in Scottsdale.

Maneuvering the travel trailer through the city to Golden Gate Travel Park was a bit tight at times but by five that afternoon he was checked in and hooked up to his spot. It wasn't the best park he'd stayed in, not quite as nice as Andy's on the bay side or the one in Chula Vista, but it would do.

Travis, a golden retriever, watched him work patiently, waiting for him to finish. Dan sat down next to him saying, "Tomorrow we get to go to our breakfast place, get the good coffee, and set up the show. That sound good to you?" The dog picked up his Frisbee and held it in his jaws. "OK, but just for a little while and then I have to start dinner. And I'm getting a beer first."

The two of them played together for an hour. He tossed the Frisbee into the air and Travis invariably snatched it before the dilapidated piece of plastic could hit the ground. Afterward Daniel made a makeshift goulash while Travis took a quick nap. The Boss's landmark album *Born to Run* was playing on the stereo; Clarence Clemmons was in the middle of his sax solo on "Thunder Road" as he sat down at the two-foot-by-three-foot table in his trailer to eat.

He took a bite and said to Travis, "I liked *The Rising*, it was good. But you can't beat the classics. And this, my friend, is as good as it gets."

Travis had finished his dinner in seconds, looked up at him briefly, and sighed before curling up again.

Daniel Whitman was an artist; he spent six months of the year in his Southern California studio painting and the rest of the year on the road. He made enough to pay the bills. But there was always hope that one day his work would be discovered by a gallery owner. Right now, he was content. He'd traveled across several states having truly remarkable experiences. And the next adventure was always just around the corner.

It was still early by the time he finished cleaning up. Dan grabbed his coat. "I'm goin' out for a beer. Do you want to come?" Travis rolled onto his side and closed his eyes. "Suit yourself, I'll be back early."

Dan cruised the streets for thirty minutes before he settled on a suitable-looking sports bar, parked the car, and went inside. There was a decent crowd, mostly holdovers from happy hour. He found an open seat at the bar and watched the bartender while he waited; she had cute, light brown hair pulled back into a ponytail, and a very nice view from the back. She turned and gave him a professional smile. "What'll you have?"

"Corona."

"Comin' up." In one graceful movement she took the beer from the cooler, flicked off the cap, put a slice of lime inside the bottle, and set it in front of him.

Before he could use a thank-you as a reason to start a conversation she was gone, pulling another beer for someone else from the tap. He looked around the bar; it was football season and in the middle of the week there was nothing on television but recaps from ESPN. Most of the televisions were being used for a trivia game; Daniel noticed several of the people at the bar with consoles, competing with one another, each one using a game alias.

Triple X was ahead of Bambi by a hundred points and ahead of Outlaw by more than four hundred. The new category was actors and actresses of the '40s. The question on the screen asked the players to identify a B-grade movie tough guy. The first hint appeared on the screen, "Adam's sibling"; a moment later a second clue followed, "Eddie Mars nemesis." Dan whispered, "Humphrey Bogart," when he noticed the third clue come up and an attractive blond make her selection. She was sitting by herself drinking a glass of red wine.

He grabbed his beer, moved next to her, and grinned. "Let me guess. You're Bambi."

She replied abruptly without taking her eyes off the screen. "That would be me."

The next question appeared, and he said, "Bette Davis."

The blond scowled but pushed the button anyway. "I knew that." She turned to him. "If you're going to sit down, do it, but keep your answers to yourself. If I'm going to beat this guy, I'm doing it without help."

He sat down, the next question came up, and the answer flashed through his mind. And by the look in her eyes she didn't know it.

The final clue came up and she said quickly, "OK, what is it!"

"Ingrid Bergman."

The category came to an end and the scores came up on the screen; Bambi was still behind Triple X. She took a drink of her wine, turned, and said, "You're good. Why don't you play?"

"I just like to see how fast I can come up with the answer."

"Are you like that with everything or just bar games?"

He grinned. "Bar games, mostly." Holding out his hand, he introduced himself, "Daniel Whitman."

She shook it and replied, "Reina."

"Are you from here, Reina?"

"St. Helena."

"Where's that?"

"Wine country, not far from Napa."

Dan took a long drink of his beer. "What brings you into the city?"

"I applied for a job today."

"Well… good luck."

"Oh, I got the job. It's with a little bistro on Bay Street not far from Fisherman's Wharf."

He replied quickly, "Bistro at the Bay."

"That's it. How did you know?"

"I go there when I'm in town. I'm an artist and there's a show at the Presidio this weekend. It's close by. You should stop by and see it."

The two of them spent the next hour talking, and with his help, Reina's scores improved, and she began catching up with Triple X. It was getting late, however, and she had an early morning meeting with Laura at the restaurant. She paid her check and stood up saying, "I had a good time. But I have to turn in." She put her purse on her shoulder and finished the last of her wine. "I'll try to stop by your show this weekend."

"If you don't mind, I'll walk you out."

"That would be great."

When he made it back to the trailer thirty minutes later and opened the door, Travis was waiting expectantly. The retriever could tell Dan was happy as his master scratched behind his ears and said with a grin, "I met someone tonight, big guy! And she was great." He opened the door to take him for a walk before bedtime. "Come on, boy… let's go."

It was a clear night with the faint smell of the ocean in the air. Dan let the dog wander as his mind replayed the evening with Reina. It had been a long time since he'd been attracted to anyone beyond the physical. But he liked just talking to her. He thought of the last four years on the road. It had been fun most of the time, but he was no further ahead today than he was when he began.

Travis came trotting back to him and Daniel gave him a pat. "Maybe it's time we started thinking about settling down, boy. We're not getting any younger." The dog looked up at him, at the trailer, then back at him again. Dan smiled. "OK, let's go in."

The retriever wagged his tail, following Dan back through the door and into the tiny bedroom, jumping up on the bed to lie down and wait for him. Daniel kicked off his tennis shoes, stripped off his jeans, and picked up a novel he'd been reading by Michael Connelly. He fluffed the pillows and propped them against the headboard of the bed before lying down next to the retriever. "Let's see how Bosch is doin' tonight." Travis sighed, rested his head on Daniel's leg and closed his eyes.

The two of them were up by first light. The back of his Dodge Ram pickup was filled with the canopy booth, portable walls for him to hang his work, and several of his paintings ready to be hung. Dan looked at his watch; it was almost seven and time to get something to eat. He put on a clean shirt and jeans just in case he ran into Reina. After opening the driver's side door of the truck Travis jumped in. A moment later they were heading north toward Golden Gate Park and Fort Mason, avoiding the major highways.

Alex had just returned from the markets and opened the front door; Laura was already there with Reina going over a list of various vendors. The chairs were down, and Laura had already made coffee for the two of them. He nodded toward them saying, "Hola."

He hung up his coat in the back and made an espresso for himself. Tony was taking fresh bread from the oven for the noon rush. Alex watched him work for a minute before saying, "How long have they been out there?"

Tony shrugged. "Maybe an hour. Laura left the lunch menu out for you to look at. She said if you have questions, get back to her."

The dishwasher, Paul Sanders, came back to the kitchen, followed by one of the prep cooks and, a few minutes later, Shelly, who smiled at him. "Laura says you're in charge of the kitchen this morning."

Alex looked at the menu she wanted prepared; it was straightforward and basic. He grinned while putting on his chef's coat. "Let's get to work."

Laura said to Reina, "I know that most of your experience is with Northern California wines, but I want to expand our customers' choices."

"What do you mean?"

"I want to bring in wines from Europe, Latin America, and maybe Australia."

Reina nodded. "There are some nice wines for the price, particularly Chile and Argentina." She grinned. "My father would kill me if he knew I was even talking to you about this."

The restaurant was beginning to get busy, and Laura started gathering up her notes. "We better move to the back. It's going to get pretty hectic."

Daniel walked through the front door just as Reina picked up her briefcase and began following Laura. As she headed toward the back, a tinge of disappointment struck him harder than he thought it might.

Shelly gave him a second after he was seated before going to his table. "Good morning. Would you like coffee?"

He knew what he wanted when he walked in. "A large cappuccino and the Italian omelet." Dan glanced out the window at Travis in the cab of the truck. "I'll be sitting at one of the tables outside."

"You sure? It's still pretty chilly."

He nodded. "My dog's out there."

Shelly fastened her pen to the pocket of her apron. "I'll be out with the cappuccino in just a minute."

The food was just as good as he remembered, but it didn't make up for his disappointment. Dan was pretty sure that she saw him. He wondered if he'd imagined the attraction between them. He looked down at Travis on the concrete beside him and sighed as he said, "Time to go to work."

The canopy went up easily and the fog burned off by eleven. It was going to be a chilly day but with plenty of sunshine. By one that afternoon the portable walls that held his paintings were up and his stomach told him it was time for lunch. He brought the canopy sides down and zipped them shut, closing the booth.

Ghirardelli Square was within walking distance and there was a restaurant that he liked there. But thirty minutes later he was driving by the bistro looking for a place to park. It was packed. All the tables inside and out were filled. He scratched Travis behind the ears and said, "I guess it's In-N-Out Burger for us."

Reina had caught sight of him earlier that morning as she was following Laura. She wanted to say something but what could she do? She couldn't just stop and tell her new boss to wait a minute. She told him the night before she had an early meeting. Another hour went by before they took a break; Reina looked out front for him, but he was gone. She stopped Shelly. "There was a guy in here a little while ago. Did he say anything to you about me?"

"The good-looking guy, short brown hair, brown eyes, about six foot, with the dog."

"I don't know about the dog but yes that might be him."

Shelly shook her head. "Not a word." She could see the disappointment in her face. "But he'll be back."

"How do you know?"

"He comes to the city once or twice a year, stays for a few weeks, and leaves again. Eats here all the time when he's in town."

By eleven that morning thoughts of Daniel Whitman were buried in a sea of customers. Laura worked in the kitchen with Alex, and Reina did her best to help in front. She hadn't waited on tables since college, but she was able to take names for the waiting list and see people seated when there was a table ready. The staff worked well together; she noticed they were fast and efficient without rushing the customers. But it was clear to her that Laura's biggest obstacle was space. The bistro was too small to accommodate demand. If this was a problem in the middle of the day, she asked herself, what would it be like during happy hour?

Reina was exhausted by four when the doors closed. The kitchen had finished shutting down an hour earlier; Alex took a break and came to the front to make himself an espresso. When he saw Reina sitting by the window, looking out, he made her a cappuccino, took it to her table and sat down beside her.

She looked at the coffee with a blank stare. "What's this?"

He smiled. "A pick-me-up."

She chuckled weakly. "I need it."

"Long day?"

Reina nodded. "How do you do it every day? My feet are killing me."

"Good shoes." He grinned. "You get used to it." He hesitated a second, then asked, "I'm curious. What made you decide to start working here? The winery you were working for is a job a lot of people would die for."

"I don't know really. The money's good working with my parents at the hotel. And the wines in the restaurant are from my dad's vineyard. I like working with people, educating them about wine."

"Why didn't you just continue working for your parents?"

"My dad makes a great bottle of wine, but I thought it was time to spread my wings."

Alex realized he'd misjudged her. He'd assumed she was the silver spoon type. He grinned. "Good for you."

She shrugged and replied, "It's almost impossible anymore for small wineries to compete... but my mom and dad are happy. They live in one of the most beautiful spots in the country."

While they were talking, she'd finished her coffee. He pointed to her cup. "Would you like another?"

Reina shook her head, then asked spontaneously, "Would you like to have a drink with me after work?" It embarrassed her a little as she admitted, "I don't know many people here yet."

"I'll be here another hour or so... but yes, I would like that."

She smiled. "Do you like trivia?"

CHAPTER 3

Reina

They drove in separate cars and met at the bar. Reina asked for a console from the bartender and was playing by the time he arrived. Alex noticed she was drinking beer and it amused him. He sat down next to her and tapped the edge of her glass. "What would your father say?"

She pressed the button, making her selection, before the second clue came on the screen, then turned and smiled. "It's a weakness, I know. But what can a girl do?"

Dan had his show set up and ready for the next day by five that afternoon. He drove to Golden Gate Park and took Travis for a run. The retriever had been patient all day while he worked, and it was time for them to have a little one-on-one. They did the Frisbee thing for thirty minutes before stopping for a six-pack at a convenience store. His plan was to forget her, have a couple of beers at home and cook supper.

It took less than an hour for him to say to Travis, "I'm just going over there for a quick one and maybe something to eat. You can come if you want." The animal turned and went toward the back of the trailer and jumped on Daniel's bed, glaring at him as he left.

Alex and Reina were working on a pile of nachos and their second beer. It didn't take her long to figure out that he was a terrible trivia player. But she liked him. While they were between categories she asked, "When did you know you wanted to be a chef?"

He took a quick drink. "I was a teenager. My mother was a great cook, and my dad wasn't around much. I learned from her."

"Why wasn't he around?"

"He works in a factory that makes picture frames. The hours are long."

"I'm sorry."

Alex wanted to shift the conversation. "How about you? What was it like growing up?"

Reina shrugged as she replied, "I was an only child. My dad works a lot, but we've spent some good times together. He always made sure of that. And he never missed a school function or soccer practice."

"How about your mother?"

"She runs a tight ship and always kept Dad and me in line. I honestly don't know what he would do without her." Suddenly, she saw Daniel come in the front door and it felt as if her heart skipped a beat. She saw him glance her way, hesitate as if he wasn't sure what to do, then sit down as far as he could across the bar. It surprised her that he wouldn't at least say hello.

He noticed the reaction and asked, "What is it?"

She picked a chip with plenty of cheese and took a bite. "Just someone I met briefly."

Dan kept his eyes focused on the television screen, but it was hard for him to concentrate. The bartender, the same girl from the night before, interrupted his thoughts. "Corona?"

He nodded. "Please."

The bar wasn't as crowded as the night before and when she brought the beer she asked, "Do you want something to eat?"

Dan shook his head. "Maybe later."

She smiled. "It couldn't be that bad."

"What's that?"

"Whatever it was today that took the wind out of your sails." When he didn't respond she held out her hand. "My name's Jess."

Despite his irritation he grinned and took her hand. "Daniel."

"You in town on business, Daniel?"

"I'm in an art show at Fort Mason."

"Really. What kind of art?"

"I draw and paint."

"I'm off on Sunday. Maybe I can stop by."

He smiled. "I'd like that."

Reina couldn't help herself; her eyes kept glancing toward him. Finally, Alex said, "Why don't you just go over and say something?"

Her eyes snapped back at him. "Say something to who?"

"That guy."

She finished her beer and glared at the bartender talking to Daniel. "I wonder what you have to do to get another drink around here? If she would stop flirting with him maybe we could get some drinks."

Alex put a twenty-dollar bill on the bar. "I've got to take off anyway." He stood up. "It's been fun."

She said quietly, "You can't leave me here alone."

"You were alone when I got here."

"I know, but it's different now."

He sat back down. "Are you going to stay or go with me?"

Alex took out a pen and made a sketch on a cocktail napkin. "This is my address and a map of how to get there. If you want to come over, I'll fix us something to eat."

"Sounds great, let's go."

Once she was in her car, Reina had a few minutes to think about Daniel on the way to Alex's apartment. He seemed attracted to her the night before but completely ignored her tonight. She wondered if he thought she was on a date with Alex.

His address was on Third Street over by South Beach. Reina got lost for a few minutes and had to pull over to look at his directions again. It took another fifteen minutes to find his apartment, an old three-story brick building. She parked on the street, went inside, and began walking up the stairs to the top floor. He'd left the door ajar. She knocked softly and called out, "Hello."

Alex raised his voice and answered, "Come in."

The apartment was tiny but huge compared to the kitchen. He was busy shredding a leftover chicken breast with his fingers when she came in. Reina took off her jacket. "What are you making?"

"Burritos with chicken and rice." He took a jar out of the refrigerator, poured some of the contents into a pan and began to heat it slowly on the stove. "Would you like a beer?"

"Please."

He took two bottles of Negra Modelo from the fridge, opened both, and handed her one saying, "This is all I've got."

She took a sip. "It's great thanks. What's that you put in the pan?"

"Ranchero sauce. It's my mother's recipe."

"It smells great. Can I do something to help?"

"No thanks, cooking calms me."

"But you've been doing it all day."

Alex grinned. "I know. A busman's holiday… right?" As he continued working he said, "So tell me about this guy."

"There's not a lot to tell… we met last night, and I thought we had fun. But tonight, he acted as if he didn't know me. I think he thought you and I were together."

"We were together."

"You know what I mean."

He laughed. "You mean together… together."

"That's pretty much it."

"Would you mind if we were together, together?"

She took a sip of beer. "Not a good idea. I want this job to work out."

"Me too," he said with a chuckle. "Besides I have my eye on a young girl who came into the café the other day."

"Tell me," she replied enthusiastically.

"Her name's Isabella. I don't know much more than that, but I'd like to."

Reina laughed. "Did you get her number?"

"No."

"That could be a big mistake."

Alex stopped what he was doing for a second and took a sip of his beer. "If it's meant to be, it will be."

"So, you believe in fate?"

"Yes, don't you?"

"I believe in creating my own destiny."

"Hmm… let's say that you didn't go into that bar last night, that you went to a movie instead. You would never have met this guy you're so interested in. But you did and now you want to see him again."

"I meet a lot of people."

"We'll see," he replied and went back to work. "Going back to that same bar tonight wasn't random. You were hoping you'd run into him."

Reina was sitting on one of two barstools beside a countertop directly opposite him. She grabbed her beer and casually began looking about the room. "How long have you been working for Laura?"

"Just over a year," he said as he spooned the sauce over each plate. "I think that maybe fate had something to do with that as well."

She picked up a picture of a man and woman who appeared to be in their mid to late fifties. "Are these your folks?"

"Sí, and the one next to it is my sister and her family." He set both of their plates on the countertop. "Dinner is ready."

"Good, I'm famished."

Reina sat down on one of the barstools. "This smells delicious." She picked up her fork and took a bite. "Yum!"

He smiled, took a drink of his beer, and came out of the kitchen to sit next to her. "Do you want to know a secret?"

Her mouth was full, and it took a second for her to say, "Sure."

"I think watching women eat is sexy."

Her fork stopped in midair. "This isn't a pass, is it?'Cause I thought we covered that."

Alex put his napkin in his lap and grinned. "No, just being honest."

The two of them ate quietly for a moment before she said, "Do you think our lives are written in the stars?"

He wiped his mouth. "Maybe," he replied. "I've always wanted to be a real chef from the time I was little. But no one would give me a chance so I bought a taco truck and traveled all over California. One day I parked it a few blocks from Laura's home, she was hungry, and now, here I am." He shrugged his shoulders. "What else could it have been?"

Reina snickered. "Dumb luck."

"Senorita… you are too skeptical. Where is your sense of destiny?"

"I believe in doing, not wishing, for something to be done."

"So do I, Reina… but I feel the magic as well."

She asked, "Have you ever been in love?"

Alex's expression became serious, and it took a moment for him to answer. "Yes, there was someone years ago, but it didn't work out."

She sighed. "It seems like there's always someone who didn't work out."

"Who was your someone?"

"A guy I went to school with. We were going to get married but after 9/11 he joined up."

"What happened?"

"We wrote each other for a long time and then the letters from him started to taper off. One day they just stopped coming."

"Did something happen to him?"

She shook her head as she carefully put together another bite of food. "Nothing physical. He just changed. I ran into him about a year ago and he wasn't the same guy I'd been in love with. Besides, he was with someone else."

"I'm sorry."

"It's OK… I'm over it."

Alex didn't totally believe her. He knew as well as anyone how long it took for the heart to heal. He noticed her plate was empty and asked, "Do you want another?"

"No, I'm stuffed. If I start getting used to your cooking I'm going to end up looking like a blimp."

The two of them talked for another hour. She helped him with the dishes, and it was after eight when he said, "I've got an early day tomorrow."

She made a pouty face. "OK, I'll go." Reina gave him a quick hug. "Thank you for tonight."

"You going to be OK to drive?"

"Yes, the hotel's not far and I'll be careful."

Her bed was turned down by the time she got back to her room. Reina dropped her purse on the desk, thought about checking emails, changed her mind and turned on the television. She switched from channel to channel, but nothing caught her interest and the pay-per-view movies were putting her in the poorhouse. She whispered to herself, "I've got to find a place to live." Thirty minutes later she was curled up in bed after raiding the mini bar for a bag of M&M's, while watching *The 40-Year-Old Virgin.*

She dreamt of him that night, at least she thought she did. The images were an odd mixture of Daniel and Alex. And while she was in the shower the next morning she made up her mind to find a place to live and go by Daniel's art show over the weekend.

It was a little after eight by the time she got to the restaurant, but the place was already half full. Alex was busy in the kitchen, and Laura was in her office going over the day's menu. Reina knocked lightly on her door to ask, "Could I see you for a minute?"

"Certainly, what is it?"

She sat in a chair on the other side of the desk but looked as if she could spring to her feet at any moment. There was a brief pause before she said, "I've got to get out of the hotel and into an apartment. It's too expensive. I have a few appointments with vendors today, but would you mind if I spend some time looking for a place?"

Laura quickly jotted down her address, took her key out of her purse and handed it to Reina. "I have plenty of room… you can stay with me until you find something. After your meetings you can take some time to go over there and get settled. I have a cat so be careful that he doesn't get out."

Reina looked down at the key, still trying to get over her surprise. "Thank you so much."

"Go, I've got work to do."

She started to leave then said spontaneously, "I'll never forget this. And you won't regret it I… promise!"

Laura waved her hand. "Go… go! You have a meeting and I have a menu to put together."

CHAPTER 4

Daniel

It was a three-day show but even for a Friday, it was slow. He had a few lookers and sold one box of greeting cards with images of his paintings on the front, but that was all. Dan had been grumpy all morning. He stayed away from his favorite breakfast place to avoid running into her and it irritated him. His mind was made up; he wasn't about to let her ruin one of the things he liked best about this city.

He was rereading a copy of Victor Frankl's *Man's Search for Meaning* to pass the time when a middle-aged couple walked into his booth. The breakfast sandwich he'd eaten earlier was anchored in his gut as he watched while their eyes fixed on a large abstract seascape he'd painted the previous spring. He waited a moment, forced a smile, and interrupted them briefly saying, "I did that piece earlier this year."

They were from Milwaukee, visiting the Bay Area to get away from the winter cold and snow. The piece they were looking at was done in San Diego, but Dan didn't tell them that and thirty minutes later the sale was complete. He'd just marked it sold when he saw Reina walking his way.

After dropping off her belongings at Laura's house, Reina didn't think it would hurt to stop by for a few minutes and look at his paintings. She'd told him she would. As she strolled along she stopped several times to see the work of various artists; there was hand-blown glass, pottery, and jewelry in addition to the work of several painters. There was a pair of earrings that caught her eye when she noticed him a few booths away covering a painting with bubble wrap.

Reina handed the earrings back. "Thank you. I'll think about it." She saw him glance her way as she approached and greeted him cheerily, "Hi there."

Dan secured the bubble wrap with tape and set the piece aside, out of harm's way. "Hi," he said quietly. "You have the afternoon off?"

It wasn't the most enthusiastic greeting she'd ever received but she let it pass. "I checked out of my hotel this morning and had a few minutes, so I thought I'd come and take a look at your work."

He stepped aside to give her a better view. "This is it."

Reina didn't know a thing about art; she only knew what she liked. But it only took her a minute to see how talented he was. She had no idea what to expect after deciding to stop by, but any preconceptions were washed away as she went from piece to piece, studying each carefully. There were several abstract seascapes like the one he'd just sold but there were figures too; some clothed and others unclothed, each one finished in the same colorful style.

Dan watched her as she surveyed his work. She was beautiful, he thought, just as beautiful by daylight. Unfortunately, the way it appeared to him the last time he'd seen her, she was already seeing someone else. Still, he thought he'd love to paint her. After a few minutes he said, "What do you think?"

"They're beautiful." Reina didn't turn around to look at him. "These should be in a gallery."

He forced a grin. "That's something we agree on. All we have to do now is convince someone in the business and we're home free."

She was thinking of a large wall in the restaurant that faced the street and how good one of his pieces would look there. "Do you do commissioned work?"

"Sure."

"What time do you close up?"

"This time of year... I'll stay till five."

Reina looked him in the eye. "I want to bring my boss back here this afternoon to look at your work. There's a place in the restaurant that would be perfect for one of your paintings. But it has to be the right subject matter and the right size."

She'd taken him by surprise again. He picked up one of his business cards and handed it to her. "My cell number's on the card. Give me a call when you want to come over."

"Thanks, I will." She started to walk away, then stopped and turned back toward him. "I'm glad I came. It was good to see you again."

The rest of the afternoon went well; he sold ten boxes of cards at twenty dollars each and a small painting for a hundred and fifty. That, along with what he'd made from the Milwaukee couple, covered his booth fee on the first day. It was usually a good sign. His sour mood shifted, and he was just about to start shutting down his booth when his cell phone rang.

"Are you still at work?" Reina asked.

"I was just starting to close up for the night."

"We're ten minutes away. Will you wait for us?"

"Sure, but the light's getting bad. There'll just be the spotlights."

"That's fine. I'll see you in a minute."

He continued to pack his things and they arrived fifteen minutes later. Dan recognized the owner; she'd talked to him a few times in the restaurant. The guy with them was the same man he'd seen in the bar the night before.

Reina smiled as she approached. "Daniel, I'd like you to meet my boss, Laura Patterson, and one of our chefs, Alex Iglesias."

Dan shook Laura's hand briefly. "It's good to see you again."

Alex said, "Reina's told us many good things about your paintings."

Dan ignored him and kept his attention fixed on Laura. "The light's not great but take a look and see what you think."

Laura sensed the discomfort between the two men, but she was concentrating on the artist's work. Reina had already sold her on the idea, and she could see that she was right. "Can you come by the restaurant and look at the space to see what you think?"

He nodded. "I'll be there first thing in the morning."

Travis had been asleep behind the canopy; he heard Daniel talking and got up to investigate. He stretched, looked around, and knew by the setting sun it must be time for them to leave. His scent caught a familiar smell that a few nights before had been on Daniel's jacket.

Reina was just about to ask him if he wanted to come for a drink with them when she felt something nudge her leg. She looked down at a large golden retriever that was staring up at her with a look of expectation. Kneeling down she began to scratch behind his ears. "Well, hello there."

Dan was momentarily flustered and started to apologize. "I'm sorry about that. He has a schedule and I'm kind of a slave to it."

"There's nothing to be sorry about," she replied with a smile. "What's his name?"

"Travis."

Reina's attention returned to the dog as she cooed, "Are we interrupting your schedule, pretty boy? Are you ready to go home?" She gave him another good scratch behind the ears and a loving pat. "We'd better get going then."

It was Laura who said, "We're going out for drinks. You're welcome to come along if you like."

He glanced at Reina and then Alex. "I really do have to finish closing and get my dog something to eat. But I'd like to take a raincheck."

Laura shook his hand again. "I'll see you in the morning then."

As he took her hand it seemed tiny compared to his. Her personality, in contrast, always seemed larger and self-assured. After they left, the warmth of her grip stayed with him until, finally, he said to Travis, "Come on. The quicker we close, the quicker we can get out of here."

It was difficult for Laura to accept that someone with so much obvious talent had such a hard time finding the success they deserved. She said to Reina as they were walking away, "You were right about his paintings. Where did you say you met him?"

"In a sports bar a few nights ago."

With a grin, Alex interjected, "He doesn't like me."

"That's silly," Reina replied. "You've given him no reason to dislike you."

Alex chuckled. "He thinks I'm your boyfriend."

"For your sakes I hope he's wrong," Laura replied. "You know how I feel about that."

"It's nothing," he said. "We went out for a beer, and he walked into the bar and jumped to a conclusion."

"That's all it was," Reina agreed. "Daniel and I met the night before and hit it off. I think he came back hoping I'd be there and when he did Alex was with me."

The story seemed plausible enough and Laura decided to let the subject drop. But it was best, she thought, to keep an eye on the two of them. "Let's go get that drink."

Dan stayed in the trailer that night. He was lying down watching *Lost* on a small, ancient Sony television mounted on the bedroom wall. To celebrate his first big sale of the weekend he stopped on the way back to the trailer and picked up a pint of ice cream. Travis loved Ben and Jerry's.

The next morning, he was at the restaurant five minutes before it opened at seven. Shelly unlocked the door and let him in saying, "You're here bright and early."

"I have a meeting with Laura."

"She's not here yet. Do you want coffee?"

"A cappuccino, please, and the bagel breakfast sandwich."

"Do you want bacon, avocado, or ham on it?"

"Bacon please."

Alex was making himself an espresso and overheard Daniel ordering the cappuccino; he decided to take it out. A few minutes later he set the cup in front of him and asked, "Do you mind if I sit down?"

Dan looked up at him, irritated. "No, go ahead."

"I think that there is a mistaken idea between us." Alex hesitated. "Reina just started working here this week. We went out for a beer to get to know one another. There was nothing else to it."

The explanation seemed reasonable enough. "Thanks for telling me."

"I didn't get a chance to say it yesterday, but I like your work." Alex pointed to a large wall across from where they were sitting with a couple of framed prints hanging from it. "I think that's where Chef wants your piece."

Just then, Laura walked in, saw the two of them sitting by the window and said, "Daniel, I'll be with you in a minute. Alex, I'd like to talk to you." In the next instant she was gone, walking through the kitchen toward her office.

Alex finished his espresso and said as he stood, "Good luck. I hope you get the job."

Dan gave him a slight nod just as Shelly brought out his sandwich and set it in front of him. She smiled. "Is there anything else you'd like?"

It was flirtatious the way she stood and gazed down at him. He smiled back. "Thanks, Shelly. I'm good."

"Well if you change your mind just whistle." It was a line from an old Lauren Bacall movie. She grinned and said, "You know how to whistle don't you, Daniel?"

He grinned and finished the line for her. "Just put your lips together and blow."

She winked at him. "That's right," she replied and walked away.

Laura's office door was open; Alex knocked lightly. "Good morning, Chef," he said while setting the Americano he'd made for her on the desk.

"I worked on the Thanksgiving menu last night when I got home." She handed him a sheet of paper. "It's traditional, maybe a little too much so... I know that. But I want this to be special. Get with Reina and pair this menu with a wine selection. We'll stay open later and take reservations till seven."

He looked at the menu. "Is there anything else, Chef?"

Laura picked up her cup of coffee, stood up from behind her desk and squeezed past him in the small space. "Actually I was waiting for comments."

"There is one thing."

"What?"

"Why stay open on a holiday? Most people want to be home with their families."

She smiled. "When I was a girl, my grandmother would fix Thanksgiving dinner for our whole family. It was a time of togetherness."

Laura started walking toward the kitchen. "Many people don't have family to be with. That's why we stay open."

As she walked away he whispered, "Yes, Chef."

Shelly had just made Daniel a second coffee when Laura came toward him saying, "Thanks for coming." They shook hands and she showed him the wall. "I want one large painting right there. A painting of the bay, maybe the bridge with part of the city. I want it to speak of the area."

In his mind he estimated that a four-foot-by-five-foot canvas would fit nicely. His price for a painting that size would normally depend on the intricacy of the work and the quality once it was finished. But she would give him a down payment now and cash when it was complete. He decided to settle on the minimum. "I can do it for eight hundred unframed."

"Can you complete it, frame and all, by Thanksgiving?"

"I don't know. I'd have to check on frame shops in the area. I don't usually have that done here."

"If you can get it done by Thanksgiving, I'll pay you a thousand plus the cost of the framing."

"I could do a mural… it would save on the cost and be done faster."

"No," Laura replied with a grin. "You never know… your paintings might be worth a lot of money one day. Is half up front OK with you?"

"I might need a little more when it's ready to be framed."

"That's fine with me. Wait just a minute and I'll get you a check."

He was finishing his cappuccino and making a few thumbnail sketches when Reina walked in. She smiled and said, "Have you met with her yet?"

"She's getting me a down payment now."

Reina took off her coat and held it folded across her arm. "I'm really happy for you." She handed him an old business card. "I don't have any new cards yet, but this one has my cell number on it. If you want someone to celebrate with later. Give me a call."

He grinned. "I just might do that."

Laura walked up to them. "Here's your check." She held out her hand to him and he received it with a firm shake. "And thank you very much for coming in this morning. I hope you have a great weekend." She turned to Reina. "I want you to get with Alex about our Thanksgiving menu."

"Right away, Chef." She glanced back at Daniel. "I'm glad this worked out for you."

"Me too."

Later as he was unzipping the canopy to open it for the day his mind was filled with images of the two women. They were both beautiful. Reina was definitely younger, and Laura appeared to be about his same age. But Laura was a little intimidating. There was something about the latter of the two that attracted him, something difficult to identify.

It was a Saturday and business picked up quickly. Dan was finishing a sale that afternoon when he noticed the business card Reina had given him on the table where he kept his sales pad and credit card slips. He looked at his watch, picked up his phone, and began to tap in her number.

CHAPTER 5

Reina

She was slammed all day. There was the meeting with Alex to discuss which wines to order for Thanksgiving, appointments with two vendors in the afternoon, and another meeting with Laura that lasted until five. Shortly after leaving the restaurant, she heard Daniel's message and called him back; he didn't answer. Reina left a message, then thought it wasn't that far to Fort Mason, and she still might be able to catch him before he left his booth for the day. The idea of surprising him lifted her spirits.

By the time she parked her car it was getting dark. His booth was closed for the night but the jeweler she'd talked to about the earrings the day before was still there. He'd just finished with a customer when she approached him. "Is the painter in the booth next to yours gone for the day?"

The jeweler was carefully putting a gold and diamond necklace into a portable case. "For a minute I thought you changed your mind about those earrings." He paused briefly and smiled. "I think Dan had a pretty good day. He packed up right at five."

Her disappointment was evident. "Thank you."

As she started to walk away he said, "If you want to get hold of him he's staying at the Golden Gate RV Park. It's across the bridge just north of Corte Madera… you might try there."

She tried his cell number again, but it went straight to voicemail.

Daniel and Travis had a routine each day after work; it didn't matter what city they were staying in, the pattern rarely varied. They played together for an hour, usually in a park or on the beach. Afterward, they went back to the trailer to fix supper. But on this particular day, Dan was thinking of his commission and stopped at Vista Point just off the 101 instead. It was a good spot with a view of the bay, the cityscape, and the Golden Gate Bridge. He worked on some preliminary sketches until it was too dark to see. Travis sulked; missing playtime didn't work for him.

It was almost seven by the time he reached the RV park, and he noticed Reina sitting outside his trailer in one of the camping chairs. As soon as Daniel opened the car door, Travis recognized her scent and bolted out of the truck's cab to investigate. The retriever seemed overjoyed as Reina showered him with affection.

He'd just given her a few good licks across her face when Dan walked up saying sharply, "Travis, sit!" The dog did as he was told as Daniel grinned and said to her, "It looks like you've made a new friend."

"I guess so."

"I was just about to call you back. I've been doing some sketches for Laura's painting."

It had taken her over thirty minutes in rush hour traffic to find the RV park and all the charm she could muster to talk the manager into giving out Daniel's space number. She smiled up at him as she continued to pet Travis. "Would you like to go get something to eat with me? I know a great place in Sausalito."

"Sure, but I've got to feed him and clean myself up a little. Let's go inside where it's warm."

The interior of the trailer was tiny. There was a small table on one end, next to the door, surrounded on three sides by a U-shaped bench covered with cushions. The kitchen consisted of a miniature sink, stove, and refrigerator along one wall. The bathroom was opposite the kitchen. It occurred to her that she may have seen larger bathrooms on transcontinental flights.

For the sake of her own safety she took a seat on the bench to wait for him. Daniel was in the process of changing his shirt and didn't close the door all the way. He wasn't a tall man particularly but as her eyes fixed on him, she couldn't help but admire the muscle development in his arms and upper body. She noticed he'd left his sketchbook on the table and raised her voice enough to be heard. "May I look at your drawings?"

"Knock yourself out," he called back. Dan put on a fresh shirt and made a mental note to do laundry on Monday. He walked into the bathroom. "I haven't decided on anything for sure yet but it's a great view of the skyline from there."

Daniel did the drawings in Copic markers and outlined the shapes with a fine-point black Sharpie pen. She replied, "I like these, all of them really. I wouldn't know which one to choose."

"I'll do some more sketches next week when there's better light. Those are too dark." He came out of the bathroom and filled Travis's bowl with food. "I'm as ready as I'll ever be. Where to?"

Reina picked up her purse and gave Travis a final pat before opening the door. "Do you know the Spinnaker in Sausalito? It's right on the water."

He followed her outside. "No, I can't say I do."

"It's just west of downtown on a little point of land that sticks out over the water. You'll love it."

"We could go in one car."

She turned back toward him. "I'd have to come back here."

He grinned. "I know."

Reina shook her head and giggled. "That's not happening."

"You can't blame a guy for trying."

She opened her car door. "I suppose not. I'll see you there in ten minutes. Give me a call if you get lost."

It had been a good day for him financially but once he was inside the restaurant he knew this place was going to put a serious dent in his resources.

She was already there when he walked inside and Reina asked, "What do you think?"

He forced a smile and replied reluctantly, "It's nice."

Reina took his arm and said to the hostess, "Jennifer, we're ready."

They were seated at a table, next to an extensive wall of glass that looked out over the bay. Dan felt self-conscious and said in a whisper, "This place is packed. How did you get a table?"

"When I worked for my dad, this restaurant was one of our accounts. I'm good friends with the manager."

Reina ordered a bottle of wine and an appetizer for the two of them. Daniel was surveying the menu, thinking to himself that it would take most of his commission to pay for dinner. But when he looked up into her eyes he knew it was worth it, to be with her. "I want to thank you again."

"For what?"

"You know… introducing me to Laura."

"She loves your work. It wasn't a hard sell."

"Anyway, it means a lot to me."

The waiter brought the bottle of Cabernet she'd ordered, opened it, and poured a small amount into Reina's glass. She took a sip and nodded to him; the waiter poured generously for each of them and said, "Your appetizer will be right up, enjoy."

She raised her glass. "Here's to you."

He grinned. "And you."

Reina took a sip and set her glass down saying, "Tell me about yourself."

"There's not that much to tell. I grew up in Montrose, Colorado, and left home when I was old enough to study art. I haven't been back since."

"How about your parents?"

"They're still there. My stepmom sends me birthday and Christmas cards. But I travel so much it might be weeks before I finally receive them."

"And your father?"

He hesitated. "We don't get along."

She sensed the unease and reached across the table to take his hand. "It's OK. I was just making conversation."

The touch of her calmed him and he smiled. "Not all of us come from an ideal kind of childhood. Sometimes it's just best to forgive and forget. Walk on to something else… you know."

"That's difficult for me," she replied. "I have a hard time letting go and cling to things longer than I should." She lowered her head and blushed. "I'm just stubborn I guess."

"Stubborn isn't always a bad thing. Look at me, if I'd any sense at all I would have given up painting a long time ago." He chuckled. "I'm just a bear for punishment."

"I think the important thing is doing what we love to do. I'd like to think that everything else just falls into place."

"And what is it that you love to do?"

She shrugged. "I guess I haven't found my thing yet." Reina corrected herself immediately. "It's not that I don't like my job… I do, very much. But I wonder sometimes if there isn't something inside, something in me that's still untapped that could make a difference."

"What kind of difference?"

She brushed a lock of hair away from her face. "I don't know… stop world hunger, save the environment."

"You made a difference in my life. The commission means a lot."

"That's not the same thing."

"It's a start… isn't it? Maybe the best thing any of us can do is start small and work up to the big things."

Before she could reply, the waiter brought the appetizer, took their order and refilled their glasses. Once he'd gone she asked, "What's it like, moving around the way you do?"

"You have to take the good with the bad. Meeting you and Laura has been one of the good things. There are certain things I like wherever I go. But the downside is never having roots, or friends who aren't temporary. I would like to have kids one day."

She grinned. "Just kids."

He smiled. "OK, a wife too."

"That's a relief," she said laughing.

The evening went like that with them; they sparred together, each one peeling a little of the layer that unveiled what lay hidden beneath.

When the restaurant began to clear, and Daniel fought unsuccessfully for the check, he walked her to her car. She leaned her back against the door. His lips were inches away from hers, as he leaned even closer, whispering, "I had a good time tonight."

Reina kissed him softly and whispered huskily, "Me too."

He kissed her back, his tongue seeking hers. "Come back to my place."

She cupped his face in her hands, kissing him again. "Too fast for me. Besides you have to get up early and I'm beat."

A groan escaped from him, but he grinned. "Call me tomorrow."

"I'll try but I promised my mom and dad I'd drive up to see them." She opened the door to her Honda Accord, quickly slipping inside before any restraint she had left would give way. Before she could shut it, Daniel leaned inside and kissed her again. Her willpower was dissolving quickly; she pushed him away lightly and said as she closed the door, "I'll see you soon."

+++++

When Laura worked for Entretenir she was used to early mornings and late nights. After opening the bistro those hours changed dramatically; there were still the early mornings, but the restaurant closed at four. Now she was planning to change that and her feelings about the change were mixed.

The life that she'd made for herself was stable and provided a comfortable living. Why, she asked herself, was there always something more that drove her? This change, bringing in wine and beer, staying open later, hiring new people was already seriously cutting into her budget. Reina had already mentioned the biggest problem: the restaurant was too small to accommodate the customer base they had presently. What if she was wrong?

It was getting late by the time Reina turned the key in the lock and opened Laura's front door. She'd been as quiet as she could, but it was unnecessary; her boss was sitting at the table in the breakfast nook working on her laptop. Laura looked up and took off her reading glasses. "How was your night?"

"I took Daniel out to dinner." Reina put her purse on the table. "I thought you'd be in bed by now."

"Couldn't sleep."

"I'm going to go see my folks tomorrow. And if it's alright with you, I'd like to stay over till Monday and make some calls to wineries there."

"That's fine as long as your calendar is free."

"I want to thank you again, for the job and a place to stay."

"You're welcome. I've just been using that room for storage anyway," she replied. "Daniel seems like a nice person."

"He is," Reina said and then added shyly, "I think I like him."

"You mean like, like boyfriend like, or just a friend?"

"He kissed me tonight... well, I really kissed him first, but it was nice."

Laura hadn't been kissed since she'd broken her engagement with Matt Stryker three years before. She'd been sure he was the one for her, but he wanted things she didn't. And then she found out he was still in love with someone else. Armand Moreau, the chef and owner of Entretenir, told her once that there wasn't enough room for her way of life and marriage. She believed that then, but it didn't stop the desire to be held at night or for someone to share her hopes and dreams. It was hard being alone.

The thought of it made her feel weary. Laura stretched and turned off her laptop. She picked up an empty cup and saucer from the tea she'd made earlier and set it on the countertop in the kitchen. "I'm going to bed. Are you coming up?"

"In a minute."

Reina undressed in the spare bedroom upstairs next to Laura's and went into the bathroom to take off her makeup. She looked at herself in the mirror, touching her lips softly where he'd been kissing them a short while ago. Her body still ached from the desire he'd aroused. It had been a long time since she'd made love with anyone, and the thought frightened her a little. Sex always seemed to complicate things. She'd tried to be honest when telling him about clinging too long, particularly with relationships. Was it really stubbornness, she asked herself, or something else?

The next morning when Reina opened her eyes she could tell that it was late. Laura let her sleep in and had already gone to work. There was a thermos on the countertop in the kitchen with a sticky note on top that read, *"Have a good day off, drive safe, and I'll see you Tuesday."* There was an arrow pointing down— *"I left you fresh coffee, Laura."*

An hour and a half later after a nice long shower, Reina was driving over the Golden Gate Bridge heading north, then east toward St. Helena. This way was slower than taking Interstate 80, but she preferred it. The city, with its congestion, gradually gave way to rolling hills and acres of vineyards; she felt herself relax as the miles passed by bringing her closer to home.

CHAPTER 6

St. Helena

Erica Strickland married her husband, Michael, two weeks after they both received their undergraduate degrees from the University of California at Davis. Michael was there to study viticulture and enology with plans to take over his parents' vineyard. Erica was studying to become a nurse. The two of them dated for two years before he proposed.

They were wed at the Episcopalian Church in St. Helena, the same church where Michael was baptized as an infant and where his parents had been married. Erica had grown up in Pasadena; her father worked for the Huntington-Sheraton since being discharged from the army in the early '50s. Her mother was a nurse and met Erica's father while he was recovering from wounds received in Korea. The family was Presbyterian but rarely went to church and because the Stricklands were adamant about it, Erica saw no reason why she shouldn't marry in St. Helena.

Michael had been accepted to the graduate department at UCD the following fall. While her husband was in school, Erica worked in the maternity ward at Sutter's Memorial Hospital supporting the family until their daughter, Reina, was born the following year. They continued to struggle financially for another six months before he dropped out of the program to return home and work for his parents.

For years afterward, he talked of going back to finish his degree, but it never happened.

Reina and her parents had lived in a small cottage next to a small quaint hotel owned by the family. It was less than a mile from Strickland House, her grandparents' home. When her grandfather suddenly died of a heart attack in the early '90s, Michael, Erica, and little Reina moved back to the main house to stay with her grandmother Elleanore.

A few years later the family sold Strickland House and part of the acreage in order to save the vineyard. And in order to help out financially Erica went back to work in the obstetric department at St. Helena hospital.

The Oak Barrel Inn, as it was known at the time, was approximately a mile south of downtown St. Helena just off the highway. The surrounding property had originally been part of the Strickland Vineyard and it was Michael's idea to build the hotel there. The Strickland's English heritage inspired the Tudor design of the exterior; the grounds were extensive with a combination of lush gardens, lawns, and a patio attached to the restaurant. After Strickland House was sold, the family moved into the inn and were able to afford the construction of two large architectural wings on each side of the main building that doubled the amount of rooms available.

Reina turned her Honda into the driveway that led to the parking lot of her parents' hotel. It was almost noon when she arrived and as she went inside several guests were in the process of checking out. Her father and a young girl she didn't recognize were working the front desk. Michael's eyes were fixed on the computer screen as she said, "Do you have a room available?"

He looked up over his glasses, and his face came to life. "Reina," Michael exclaimed as he came around the desk to hold her. "How are you, sweetheart?"

"I'm fine, Daddy. How are you?"

"Oh, we get by. Your mother has been chomping at the bit all morning waiting for you. She's in the dining room with your grandmother helping the staff with lunch." Michael hugged her once more. "You better go see her. I'll send the bellman out to get your bags and put them in your room."

Erica had already put in sixty hours at the hospital and today was her day off. She was in the process of showing a young couple from Nebraska to a table when Reina walked in and noticed her across the room. Elleanore Strickland was working the cash register and saw her granddaughter first. She called out cheerily, "Lorraine!"

Reina turned and smiled. "Granny," she replied and hurried to her seventy-two-year-old grandmother.

As the two women embraced, Erica heard them and hurried across the dining room to see her daughter. Reina was still in Elleanore's arms when Erica pulled her away into hers, saying enthusiastically, "Tell me how it went. Do you like the new job? Have you found a place to stay yet?"

"Mama, please slow down a little."

"Goodness, child, I've been fretting about you all week."

Reina had one arm around each of them. "I'll tell you both everything but right now I'm starving."

Elleanore hugged her again. "You two go catch up. I can handle everything here."

Erica led her daughter outside to the patio; it was a nice sunny day and the chill from the night before had given way to the warmth of midday. A waiter took their order as the two of them sat together. They'd talked for several minutes when Reina said, "I like her a lot, Mama. She's an excellent chef and I think she knows exactly what she wants to be able to do… but…" She hesitated.

"But what, dear?"

A look of concern came over her. "I think the space is too small for what she has in mind. It's been fine up to now for breakfasts and lunch, but I don't think she can compete in the evening… not there anyway."

"Have you told her this?"

"I've only been there a week, Mama. But, yes, I sort of mentioned it. She listened, but maybe I'm wrong, maybe it will work."

Erica took her daughter's hands in hers. "You've got a knack for business, Reina. If you're right, maybe you should keep your options open."

"I like her, Mama; she took me in for heaven's sake." She chuckled. "I mean that literally. I'm living with her until I can find my own place. If it doesn't work out, I'll just have to find something else."

"If you want to work in the business, sweetheart, you should come back here. We need you; your father won't say anything, but it's true, we do. He's just not a very good businessperson."

After Reina's grandfather Roger Strickland died, the majority of his estate was given to his two oldest children. But Michael and his younger sister, Adriana, were left out of his will. The house and vineyard went to Elleanore. And she never contested the inequity of the will. They sold the house and part of the land to build the hotel. They struggled financially at times and yet they were always able to make ends meet.

Reina asked, "Are you in trouble, Mama?"

She shook her head. "We're fine with what I make at the hospital and the hotel does alright. But the hotel should be doing much better than it is. Your father has hired more staff than we should and spends most of his time in that damn vineyard. If it wasn't for your grandmother, I honestly don't think we would be able to keep this place going."

"Do you think it would help if I talked to him?"

"He would be furious if he knew I was saying anything to you."

The waiter set Reina's food in front of her and turned to Erica. "Will there be anything else, Mrs. Strickland?"

"No, Roger. We're fine."

After one bite Reina said, "You really need to hire a better staff of people in your restaurant."

"We afford who we can, dear."

"But, Mother, a better restaurant might improve the business."

"If you want to help, Reina, then come back here and help. Right now, we're doing the best we can."

"I'm sorry, Mama… it was just a suggestion."

Erica took her hand again. "Oh, I'm sorry, dear. I'm just tired and there's no sense taking it out on you."

"How's everything at the hospital?"

Erica's face was strained as she said, "A nice young woman gave birth to twins a couple of weeks ago. They were premature and I'm not sure both will make it."

"How are the parents doing?"

"Alright, I guess. Bless their hearts, I don't think they know how fragile the situation really is."

Reina looked up and saw her father approaching. He kissed her quickly on the cheek and sat down, saying with a grin, "Tell me what I've missed."

"I like my job," Reina replied with a smile. "Laura has given me complete authority for building an inventory of wine and beer that we'll introduce on Thanksgiving Day."

He interrupted. "You've told her of course that you have to be home for Thanksgiving?"

"Daddy, this is a new job, and you know as well as anyone that restaurants and hotels stay open on holidays. I have to wait and see if she wants me to work that day."

"But we're always together on Thanksgiving."

"The damage isn't done yet, Michael," Erica said impatiently.

Reina sensed the hostility in her mother's tone and quickly changed the subject. "I met a guy."

"What's he like?" her mother asked enthusiastically.

"He's an artist."

Michael spoke up. "In galleries and that sort of thing?"

"No, Daddy, he travels."

"You mean in those tent things… outside?"

"Yes, Daddy, but he's really very good."

His response was disdainful. "How good could he be when he's nothing more than a common gypsy?"

Erica spoke up sharply, "That's enough, Michael. If Reina likes him, I'm sure he's a very nice young man."

He snickered. "Does he have both his ears?"

"Daddy, you're a snob."

"Yes, sweetheart, and proud of it."

Erica looked at her husband sternly. "Don't you have something to do?"

He stood up and kissed his daughter on the cheek. "OK I'm going. I've been experimenting with some new samples that I'd like you to try, Reina."

"I will, Daddy, later this afternoon."

Once her husband was gone Erica said, "Tell me about this young man."

Reina missed her parents a great deal but the two of them unknowingly pulled at her. Erica wanted her to come back and run the hotel. Her father was oblivious to everything and everyone as he pursued his passion as a vintner. It wasn't just the perfect wine he was trying to create but the remembrance of something transient that slipped from his grasp. Reina sensed this, and it saddened her. But she knew that there was nothing she could do to soften the sense of loss within him.

It was her grandmother Elleanore who always wanted the best for her. She'd encouraged Reina from the time she was a little girl and acted as a kind of safety zone between her mother and father. It was Elleanore who listened without judgment and provided support when she was down.

Later that night Reina took a moment for herself, walking about the darkened grounds that surrounded the hotel, lit only by moonlight. There was an iron bench under a large oak; the tree had been there long before the hotel was built and for as long as Reina could remember. She'd played with her dolls under it as a little girl and came here to be alone when she was older.

Elleanore found her there and said, "I thought you might be here."

Reina looked up. "I thought you went to bed."

The old lady sat down next to her. "We haven't had much time together today." She hesitated a moment. "And you seemed distant at supper tonight. What have you been thinking about so hard?"

"Changes, I guess. I've been going through my share." Her grandmother listened patiently. "It's like I'm looking for something but don't know what it is or where to look. Do you know what I mean?"

"I think so."

"I thought maybe moving to the city and the new job would be a step in that direction but now I'm not so sure."

"Why?"

"I think it's the people I've met. Laura Patterson, Daniel, and even Alex are all driven by something they know they want to achieve. But for me it's just a job. I like it… I like them. But being near them has only created more doubt within myself." She gazed into her grandmother's eyes as if she might find an answer there. "I feel there's more for me, something, but I just don't know what it is yet." Reina shrugged her shoulders. "I'm just being silly."

"I don't think you're being silly, dear. But I do think you're being a little impatient." Elleanore chuckled. "If I've learned nothing else in my seventy-odd years it's that each day is precious." The image of Adrien came to her. "Moments are all too often taken for granted and in the end, believe me, they shouldn't be. Why don't you just try living for a while? Enjoy these new people you've met, your new job, and maybe somewhere along the way you'll get a piece of the puzzle you're trying to solve." The old lady took her hand. "But try not to try so hard. Give it time."

"I do that, don't I?… Try too hard I mean."

Elleanore didn't answer but gave her a hug instead. "Who is Alex?"

"Didn't I tell you about him?"

"No, Lorraine, you left him out."

"He's just one of the cooks, Laura's sous-chef."

"And you like this young man."

"Alex is just a friend."

Her grandmother smiled. "I see. He's just one of the cooks and he's just a friend. Is he just anything else?"

Reina grinned. "Well he is handsome if that's what you're getting at. And he's thoughtful when you least expect it."

"How does he match up to your artist?"

"Granny, I told you, he's just a friend."

"Yes, you told me." Elleanore got up and kissed her cheek. "I'm going to bed. But there's one more thing I want you to know."

"What's that, Granny?"

"I've always wanted you to be your own person, to be strong and independent. But I think you know that independence isn't always easy to achieve in our family. It hasn't been for your father or his brother and sisters." Suddenly she thought of Adriana and the thought saddened her. "I wanted it to be different and I failed with them. But you have choices, Lorraine… and I want very much for you to choose wisely."

Reina looked up at her. "I will, Granny."

CHAPTER 7

Elleanore

Ellie was a senior in high school the year she met Roger Strickland for the first time. It was during the spring of 1947; her father, Edward Thomas, brought him home for supper. Thomas Import-Export had been doing business with Strickland Shipping for fifty years. But this was the first time one of the Stricklands had been brought home to supper.

He sat across from her at the dinner table. Ellie listened to the polite conversation for as long as she could stand it and finally asked, "Are you married, Mr. Strickland?"

It was her father who answered. "Don't be impertinent, Elleanore."

Roger grinned. "That's alright." He looked at her. "No, Miss Thomas. I'm afraid I haven't had the opportunity."

"And why is that, sir?"

He could see the flirtatious look in her eye, and it was best he decided not to encourage her. "The war I suppose." Roger thought of Charlotte and the way they'd said goodbye in the winter of '42. She was married by the time he returned.

"But the war has been over for some time, Mr. Strickland."

Her father corrected her again. "You're being rude, Elleanore. It is no business of yours why our guest has chosen not to marry."

"Excuse me, Father," she said innocently, "I was merely curious. Mr. Strickland is, after all, eligible."

Her mother, Rosemary, finally spoke. "Our guests eligibility is of no concern of yours, Elleanore."

"Yes, Mother."

Roger Strickland was amused by her. "And how about you, Miss Thomas? What are your plans for the future."

"I've been accepted to Stanford in the fall."

"For what course of study?"

Her eyes gazed intently into his. "That is one of many things I'll have to discover once I'm enrolled, sir."

He grinned. "I wish you good luck then."

After he'd gone and Elleanore was in bed looking at the moonlight shining through her window, thoughts of him filled her head. Roger Strickland was a handsome man; he carried himself with a cool, distant, sophisticated air, as if he possessed some secret hidden from those around him. All the same, she thought, he seemed lonely and a little sad to her. His demeanor wasn't something she found unattractive, on the contrary, it lent an element of mystery that fascinated her.

As the weeks and months followed thoughts of Roger Strickland rarely occurred to her as she settled into university life. He was all but forgotten, when, in the fall of Ellie's sophomore year, at a university football game, she saw him talking to a group of men during halftime.

He was speaking with a friend he'd gone to school with when she touched his arm, interrupting the conversation. As Roger turned, he remembered her immediately. "Good afternoon, Miss Thomas. This is certainly a surprise."

She smiled. "As much for me as you, Mr. Strickland."

Roger introduced her to his friends briefly before taking her gently by the arm and moving a short distance away. "My friends and I are alumni. We played football on the team before the war. The five of us try to get together for at least one game a year."

"I shouldn't keep you then, Mr. Strickland."

He held on to her arm gently. "Please call me Roger. It would be nice to dispense with the formality."

She gently covered his arm with her hand. "I'd like that, Roger."

"Would you have supper with me tonight, Elleanore?"

She nodded toward the group of men. "How about your friends?"

He grinned. "They are all happily married men and will be home with their families."

"In that case, I'd like to very much. And please call me Ellie."

That was the beginning. The two of them saw each other regularly throughout that winter and spring. And as their relationship deepened, the restraint that each of them exercised began to fade. At the end of April, he asked her to marry him and she agreed. Her parents were overjoyed, and the wedding was held in St. Helena where the Thomas family had a small country home. Roger Lawrence Strickland the third was born less than a year later.

The wine industry in Napa Valley suffered a number of setbacks in the early twentieth century. An infestation of sap sucking insects killed the vines, then Prohibition was passed, followed by the Great Depression, and World War II. During the 1930s, Edward Thomas purchased a house and five hundred acres of prime property in St. Helena, a portion of which had been planted with grapevines, from an acquaintance who was forced to sell at a fraction of its value. There was a small winery on the property that hadn't been in operation since the Volstead Act was passed in 1920. Thomas had no intention of producing wine from the grapes growing on his property but as the industry began to bounce back after the war his profit from the sale of the grapes increased.

Many of Elleanore's fondest memories as a child were centered around the summers spent in St. Helena, which inspired Edward and Rosemary to give the property to the couple as a wedding gift. It was Roger who came to realize the potential of the vineyard; under his direction during the next ten years, the winery was modernized and by the late'50s they were producing two hundred thousand bottles of wine per year.

The majority of Roger Strickland's business was still in San Francisco and their primary residence was in the city. But Roger traveled a great deal while Elleanore was increasingly left at home with their two children. Each summer she would pack up the household and move the family to St. Helena.

Her husband hired a vintner from France, Adrien Forche, to supervise the vineyard and winery. Under his direction the quality and reputation of Strickland wines began to flourish. Ellie began to take a personal interest in the vineyard and her affection for Adrien grew gradually.

In 1956 the Stricklands hired an architect to design and build a new vacation home in St. Helena; Ellie began to spend more of her time there. The affair began suddenly with little warning. It had been months since Roger had touched her; she was lonely. The children were still in school that spring and Elleanore had left the city to check on the progress of their new home.

The day was hot for the beginning of May in Northern California; she wore a light sleeveless print dress to stay cool. Her plan was to drive up for the day in her Cadillac convertible and be back by late afternoon when the children would be home from school. It felt wonderful with the sun shining down on her as the breeze caressed her skin.

Ten years had flown by since meeting Roger Strickland for the first time and she was slowly approaching thirty. Workers were installing marble flooring when she arrived. Ellie wandered about the property, looking over the work they were doing, and wandered aimlessly from the construction site to the winery. There were times, years later, when she would ask herself if she'd intentionally searched for him that day. Maybe she did but there was never really any way of knowing.

Ellie walked down rows of stacked oak barrels; it was cool inside the winery. She'd just turned and was about to leave when she heard him say, "Bonjour, madame."

It startled her for a second. "You frightened me, Adrien!"

"Excusez-moi, Madame Strickland."

She took a step toward him. "That's alright. Have you seen the contractor this morning?"

"He was here earlier, madame, and left."

"I see." She started to turn then said with a hint of reluctance, "I suppose I should go."

Adrien reached out tentatively and gently touched her arm. "If you have a moment I'd like to show you something."

The touch seemed to burn her skin; she felt flushed but managed to reply, "Certainly, Adrien, what is it?"

When the winery was remodeled the loft above was turned into an office and living quarters for him. He led her upstairs. "I've been working on a new Cabernet, madame, and would like you to try it for me."

As she followed him up the stairs the scent of him was unsettling; it was an earthy masculine smell mixed with a hint of tobacco. Her husband continually smelled of soap and cologne. They reached the top step and stood briefly next to one another; it was as if she could feel the heat radiating from his body. Ellie intentionally stepped around him into the open space and saw what appeared to be a kind of laboratory with several sample bottles of wine, each one carefully labeled for identification. An open door on the far side of the loft led to another room; she could see a partially made bed inside.

He quickly moved around her to close the door and appeared slightly embarrassed as he said, "I am a poor housekeeper… please forgive me."

She felt herself become moist and forced herself to say, "You've prepared all of these samples?"

"It helps me pass the time."

Adrien came close, his scent lingering in her nostrils; she trembled and suddenly felt faint. The space closed in on her and the room started to spin. When she opened her eyes, moments later, she was lying down, and Adrien was sitting on his bed next to her. She tried sitting up, embarrassed by her behavior. "I'm terribly sorry." Ellie could feel herself blush. "I've never done that before."

He held out a glass of brandy. "This might help."

She took the sip of liquor from him; it warmed her and eased the tension that had taken hold of her. He reached out and felt her cheek with the back of his hand as gently as a mother might with her child. The intimacy of the touch was too much; instinctively she took his hand away, to protect herself, but rather than let go of him as she should have done Ellie's grasp lingered possessively.

She heard herself whisper, "I can't do this," and in the next second pulled him toward her, letting her lips, touch his gently. The kiss was sweet, almost innocent; Ellie started to apologize but before the words were clearly formed his lips cut them off, his tongue forcing itself between her lips. Her arms wrapped around his neck, pulling him close, kissing him urgently.

Adrien's hands roamed down her back, across her breast, then lower, under the hem of her skirt, above the knee to her thigh. Ellie began to breathe rapidly while one kiss led to another; she'd kept her legs together at first and tried to push his hand away but did so reluctantly. All sense of propriety was soon forgotten as the passion between them continued to build and her legs parted enough for him to feel the heat and moisture emanating there.

Ellie's mind tried unsuccessfully to argue for restraint as his fingers gripped the elastic of her panties to pull them past her hips. It was, she knew, the last chance for her, but another more basic need had already taken hold of her. The next instant she felt the fabric caress her legs before his fingers returned to find the sensitive exterior that seemed to blossom with his touch. He pulled his hand away, moistened his fingers, and returned them once more as her hips rotated to meet his caress. A finger slipped inside easily, curled up, and Ellie was lost now, longing for release.

The sound that came from her as she reached her peak was more a wild cry than a moan; she felt her body shiver as one wave of pleasure led to the next. Moments later she offered no resistance as he slipped the dress over her head. Ellie unclasped the bra herself while watching him, waiting, as he removed his shirt and trousers. Impatiently she reached out and softly gripped his manhood, caressing the silky feel of it briefly while he joined her on the bed once more.

Even after ten years of marriage and the birth of two children, Elleanore was still naive to the varied wonders of physical love. She expected him to mount her now, to find his own release within her, quickly, as her husband did when he was in the mood. But when Adrien returned, to lie next to her, his kisses began once more. Ellie continued to respond as his mouth bit into the soft curve of her neck then suckled her breast. She opened herself fully waiting for him to enter when unexpectantly he lowered his head instead, kissing her softly as he journeyed downward and took her in his mouth. Ellie was suddenly transported into a world of love that she had no idea existed, the pleasure he gave her intensifying to such an extent that she was literally unaware of anything but the feel of his kisses. Then, just as suddenly as he'd begun, he stopped momentarily to gaze into her eyes; she looked at him pleadingly, raising her arms, and whispered, "Please come to me."

He raised her legs slightly before slowly entering her, to give Ellie a moment to accommodate him; she climaxed again quickly and impatiently pulled Adrien into her, her hips moving faster and faster. She could feel the power of him, meeting her thrust for thrust, when all at once he cried out and she felt him empty himself into her. As she listened to his breathing become less labored, her body began to calm. But Adrien didn't pull away as she expected. He began to kiss her once more, his hips gradually moving again rather than withdrawing. Ellie's tongue sought his, her body moving slowly in rhythm to him, tenderly at first, then more urgently until both of them found release once more.

The light from the sun shifted across his bedroom as she rested in his arms. This was another first; Roger never held her afterward but rolled over quickly, silently, almost as if he was embarrassed by his need. A part of her always felt as if she was doing something wrong but she was afraid to ask, afraid of what her husband's answer might be. Ellie closed her eyes as she nested into Adrien for what she thought was only a second but when she opened them the shadows told her it was late.

Adrien felt her shift as she started to rise and said to her, "Are you alright, chérie?"

This one simple endearment pulled at her. "It's late. I've got to get back."

While Elleanore began to dress he got out of bed without bothering to cover himself and reached for his pants. He smiled at her. "You are wonderful, mon chérie."

She glanced at her watch while brushing her hair quickly, grabbed her things and began walking toward the stairs. Ellie ran down them without saying a word when suddenly she felt him pull her by the arm into his embrace. He kissed her once more and whispered, "Come back tomorrow."

"I can't. This was a mistake."

Adrien held her tight. "Non, mon amour."

Elleanore pulled away and began running to her car, running away from him. She wasn't more than a mile down the road when the guilt and shame began to settle itself inside of her. She was sure that Roger would know just by looking at her. And the children would be home from school by now. The household staff would be there, she thought in panic, and then, desperately trying to calm herself she began to rationalize; she'd been late before. These thoughts were interspersed with the memory of Adrien's touch and then suddenly the fear of pregnancy occurred to her.

Two hours later she walked into her home, expecting the worst, when the maid, a young Hispanic girl, greeted her. "Good afternoon, Mrs. Strickland."

She replied quietly, "Where are the children?"

"Your daughter is in her room and your son is watching television."

She handed the young woman her hat and gloves. "Is Mr. Strickland home yet, Sofia?"

"No, senora. Senor Strickland called to say he'd be late."

CHAPTER 8

Elleanore

She went upstairs to bathe before supper after avoiding her mother-in-law and checking on the children. While the water was filling in the tub, Ellie removed her dress and bra before slipping off her stained underwear to soak them in the sink. Her heart was beating fast as she slid into the hot water. Images of what she'd done continued to run through her mind; images of him, what he'd done and how he'd made her feel, played and replayed themselves.

Her eyes closed, and when they opened once more the water was lukewarm. She rose from the tub, drying herself with a towel before stepping out of the water onto the bath mat. Ellie gazed for a moment at her reflection and realized she looked the same outwardly. But the person she had been was gone, she could sense that. There was no going back, not after today, there was only the living with what she'd done and the belief that somehow she would be able to make up for it.

Ellie was dressing when she heard a soft knock on the door. "Yes."

It was Sofia who answered, "Supper is ready, senora."

"I'll be down in a minute."

Ellie's mother-in-law, Abigail, was sitting at one end of the long oval mahogany dining table, the children were sitting on her right while their mother took a seat opposite them. There was a place setting at the head of the table for Elleanore's husband, should he arrive.

The Stricklands had a small household staff that consisted of Sofia, the cook, Angela, and Hector who took care of the exterior grounds. Sofia had been with them for two years, but Angela and Hector had worked for the Stricklands before Roger married Elleanore.

Roger Strickland Senior and his wife, Abigail, had the house built after the end of World War I, when their son was a baby. It was considered modern for its time, a lavish three story not far from Huntington Park. The dining room was adjacent to the kitchen as was the breakfast room on the east side of the house. A spiral staircase led to the bedrooms above.

Abigail was a severe-looking woman dressed all in black; it was the only color she wore since her husband's death fifteen years earlier. She rang a small bell that sat on the table next to her right hand. A moment later Sofia entered quietly from the kitchen and began removing the dishes from their first course.

Both children were sitting stiffly, silent, not wanting to attract attention. Abigail wiped her mouth delicately with her linen napkin. "You were certainly gone for a long time today, Elleanore."

Ellie knew this was coming. "I'm sorry I was late. I went to look at the new house and lost track of time."

The old lady looked over the top of her glasses. "Your mother stopped by earlier today. She was disappointed you weren't here."

"Yes, I spoke to her on the phone a short while ago. She wants to go shopping tomorrow."

"I could never understand the interest some people have for purchasing things they don't need as a means of recreation."

Ellie was baited but refused to take it, staying silent instead. Abigail liked nothing better than to exercise her sense of superiority. When Elleanore and Roger were first married, Ellie assumed that they would have a home of their own. It never happened. And there was always a perfectly logical reason for them staying in the family home. Roger's primary argument was his mother's health; Ellie believed the old lady would outlive them all. Building the vacation home in St. Helena was offered to her as a substitute.

Abigail never went to St. Helena during the summers but preferred staying in the city close to her friends and the social life there. For Elleanore it meant a few weeks of bliss. She was able to spend time there with the children without interference and she could maintain their home as she saw fit. She worked exclusively with the architect and contractor for the new house. Her husband and mother-in-law made their attempts to influence her decisions but in the end, the choices were hers.

When Elleanore didn't reply, Abigail asked, "How is your project coming along?"

"The flooring is being installed."

"Well, that certainly explains your tardiness this afternoon."

The caustic remark was nothing new; the old lady used it as a weapon and Ellie chose to ignore it. As she was about to offer the explanation she'd rehearsed earlier Sofia entered the dining room with their salads. "Is there anything else right now, senora?"

"No, Sofia, I'll ring if I need you."

"Yes, senora." She was gone as quickly and quietly as she arrived.

Abigail shook her head. "I've tried my best with that girl. But I don't think she's working out. Her kind rarely does."

Ellie's daughter, Jane, spoke up innocently. "I like Sofia."

Her grandmother snapped back, "It's not polite to correct your elders, dear. It is still best if children are seen and not heard. And keep your left hand in your lap when you're eating, Jane. It's impolite to use your hands."

Elleanore'd had enough and challenged her. "I like Sofia too, Jane."

"It's best not to become emotionally attached to these people," Abigail countered. "They'll take advantage if you do."

Roger suddenly appeared in the dining room, kissing his mother on the cheek saying, "Good evening."

He leaned over and gave Ellie a quick peck but not quick enough to disguise the liquor on his breath. She smiled. "You've had a very long day."

Abigail rang her bell and Sofia entered. "Yes, senora."

"Please bring my son his first course." She asked Roger, "Would you like a glass of wine, dear?"

"Yes… please."

"And a glass of wine, Sofia."

"Yes, senora."

Each evening when Roger was home for supper he would carry on conversations with his mother while Elleanore and the children listened quietly. Periodically if Ellie was to ask a question or offer a suggestion it felt to her as if she was being dismissed. It irritated her to such an extent that eventually she mentioned it to her husband.

Roger simply kissed her on the forehead and said, "Mother is simply interested in the business. She is the largest shareholder, Elleanore."

Ellie was dismissed again but replied, "And what am I?"

He smiled. "My very young and beautiful bride who has no business worrying her pretty little head about such things."

That was the end of the discussion. Elleanore began to feel as if there was very little difference between her station in life as the wife of Roger Strickland and growing up under her parents' supervision.

Her husband didn't even ask about her day, and Abigail, once her son was home, lost all interest in Ellie and the new house in St. Helena.

Elleanore stayed in the city, away from the vineyard and away from Adrien while Roger went to New York on business for several days, leaving her at the mercy of Abigail. When the children were in school she had several meetings with the interior decorator in the city, choosing fabrics for drapes and picking out various pieces of furniture.

That weekend she took her children to the zoo. Outside of the monkey cage Jane looked up at her mother and asked, "Why can't we have a puppy?"

"We will, darling, at the new house," she said quietly. "Just you wait."

Jane was six years old and her brother, Roger, was eight. He was her firstborn and she loved him dearly, but he was a carbon copy of his father. The boy had the same air of Strickland superiority that defined his father and grandmother. He knew they didn't have a dog because Abigail thought they were annoying creatures.

The boy corrected his mother. "Grandmother won't let us have a dog. They're messy and cause trouble."

Ellie put her arm around her son and noticed how stiff he was. "That's true, Sonny, but we'll have one in St. Helena, at the vineyard." She wanted her son to be like other boys, to play baseball and ride bikes without keeping his head in a book all the time. As far as she knew Sonny didn't have any friends. And that would change, she thought, once they moved into the new house.

Jane was different; she reminded Ellie of her mother and it was comforting to think of her that way. When they reached the elephant enclosure the little girl said, "I think they look sad."

Elleanore thought so too; she felt the same way about herself at times—caged. The thought depressed her, and she forced a smile, suggesting, "How would you two like to go down to Fisherman's Wharf for lunch?"

Jane clapped her hands. "Yes please."

Her son sighed. "When are we going home?"

"Aren't you having a good time?"

The truth was he hated the zoo almost as much as he disliked Fisherman's Wharf. There were too many people and it was dirty. He preferred being left alone with his things, to watch television if he wanted or finish the book he'd started. Roger didn't like the vineyard either. He couldn't understand why his mother cared for it so much.

"I just want to go home."

Ellie gave him a quick hug. "We will. Right after we get something to eat." How could she explain to an eight-year-old that the home he spoke of wasn't the same for her? It wasn't her home at all. It was

Abigail's and she ran it with an iron fist; Elleanore's presence there was nothing more than it might have been for any guest.

Sunday seemed to drag by for her; she went to church with the children and Abigail in the morning. Their main meal for the day was in the early afternoon. Jane had been fussy during the sermon and her grandmother was giving her a lecture about it while they were eating. They were having fried chicken, which was Jane's favorite, but her grandmother insisted they use a knife and fork. It was hard for the little girl to maneuver the large utensils and that in combination with Abigail's criticism was upsetting.

Elleanore could see that she was barely touching her food and asked, "Would you like me to cut your meat for you, sweetheart?"

Jane answered with a slight nod of her head as Abigail said, "That's utter nonsense. How is she possibly going to learn if you do it for her?"

Ellie didn't bother to reply but got up from the table, walked around to Jane's place and began cutting up the chicken. When she finished she kissed her daughter's cheek and whispered, "I love you."

Later that afternoon Ellie began thinking about Adrien again. But her thoughts were not those of guilt or shame. She began to reflect on how he made her feel and longed to feel that way again. The next morning, she called the contractor and arranged for him to meet her at the site after lunch. As she was putting on her hat and gloves, Ellie said to Sofia, "Please tell my mother-in-law I won't be back till late."

She had plenty of time to think as she drove, mixing thoughts of desire with doubt. Twice Ellie considered turning around before it was too late; she knew that the first time she'd been with him it was a mistake, even a forgivable mistake possibly. But to return to him, to the desire she felt and want more of him was something else again. There were words, she thought, and not pleasant ones to describe her behavior.

Ellie arrived at the vineyard a few minutes before eleven but rather than going to the new house she parked in front of the older vacation home her parents had given them as a wedding gift.

She'd stopped at a small market along the way and picked up a few groceries, which she began putting away. The house was relatively clean; they had a woman come in twice a month to maintain it. It was a nice place but small; nothing more than a cottage really, built during the 1920s.

The house under construction was almost a mile away from this one, well off the highway and much closer to the winery. When she was finished with the groceries, Ellie got back in her car and drove to the site. The contractor wasn't there and the men who were working on the floor were sitting around eating lunch. She took a quick peek inside; the beauty of what they'd done was enough to take her breath away.

Ellie thought that Adrien might notice her car and come to see her, but he didn't; she went looking for him. She tried the winery first, tentatively walking up the stairs to the loft and called out, "Hello… Adrien." There wasn't an answer. The loft was neater than it was the first time she'd been there; the bedroom door was closed. She opened it and noticed the bed was made. One of his shirts was tossed over a chair; she picked it up and inhaled his scent briefly before carefully folding it.

She walked outside but there was still no sign of him. The contractor, Henry Phillips, called out, "Good afternoon, Mrs. Strickland."

Ellie turned and waved to him, saying as she approached, "I was inside the house earlier and looked at the work you're doing. It's beautiful so far."

They shook hands and he began telling her of the progress they'd made. "I'm fairly certain you'll be able to start moving in by July."

As she listened her eyes wandered, looking for Adrien. It was difficult paying attention to the contractor with her mind elsewhere. Henry gave her a tour of the interior and an hour went by before she was able to excuse herself and leave. There was still no sign of Adrien and it saddened her. After checking the winery once more she started driving back to the cottage and noticed his truck parked along the side of the road. He was checking the vines.

Ellie parked the car behind his truck and went to join him. He grinned as she approached. "Bonjour, Madame Strickland."

She was afraid to kiss him there but took his hand secretly instead and replied softly, "I've been looking for you. And why so formal?"

"The last time I saw you, you were running away."

"I was late getting back."

"Is that the only reason, chérie?"

She shook her head. "I was frightened."

"Of me."

"No, of myself."

He seemed to accept that for the moment. "I've missed you."

Ellie wanted to reach out to touch him, to feel his lips on hers. "I'm going over to the old cottage for a late lunch. Will you join me?"

"Certainement. I'll be along in a few minutes."

She squeezed his hand. "I'll be waiting."

CHAPTER 9

Reina

Reina had two days to think about what she wanted to say by the time she returned to the city on Monday night. As she walked through the front door, Laura was curled up on the couch laughing at something on television. She smiled. "What's so funny?"

Laura set her glass of wine on the coffee table. "*Two and a Half Men* is on." She turned off the set. "How was your trip?"

She left her suitcase inside the door and began taking off her coat. "My folks are my folks… not a lot of change there. I did talk to several vintners today and have some possibilities that might work."

Laura sensed there was a but coming but chose not to say anything. "We had a good weekend at the restaurant."

"That's great," Reina replied enthusiastically as she went into the kitchen to pour herself a glass of wine. "There's something I want to talk to you about."

"It sounds serious."

She came back into the living room and sat on the sofa next to Laura. "It's something I'd like you to think about."

"What?"

Reina took a sip of her drink. "You know how I mentioned that size might be a problem at the bistro."

"Yes, I remember. I've been thinking about that quite a lot."

There was a moment's hesitation before Reina continued. "I do think, with your ability and reputation, your talents would be better served in the evening, preparing dinner."

"Go on."

"Just hear me out a minute before you say anything." She paused briefly once more, taking a deep breath. "What if you didn't change the bistro? What if you kept it as it is, you could still serve a small selection of wines and beers for lunch but still keep it as a breakfast and lunch place." The next part Reina knew was going to be a hard sell. She took another sip of wine. "And you could open another place, a larger place."

Laura replied, "I thought about that and can't afford it yet."

"What if I had a way you could afford it?"

"I'm listening."

"My folks have this beautiful hotel in St. Helena. It should be doing better than it is but one of their big problems is the restaurant. The food is OK but not good enough to bring people back." She smiled. "Imagine opening a new restaurant there, using your reputation and skill to bring people in." As Laura started to respond Reina continued urgently, "I know, I know, it's not San Francisco and this is your home. But there are a lot of people who vacation in Napa Valley. And you could still keep the bistro going."

The idea was tempting; Laura had to give her that. But her plan had always been to build a restaurant here, in the city she loved. She asked, "How do your parents feel about this?"

"I haven't said anything to them yet. I wanted to suggest it to you first."

Laura finished her wine and got up to get another glass; she brought the bottle back with her. "I'll think about it. But don't get your hopes up."

Reina spontaneously gave her a hug. "That's fair. Thank you."

The idea kept running through Laura's mind, interrupting her sleep. She'd already gone through the numbers at the bistro several times, thinking that somewhere she could find a way to make it work. But Reina's analysis appeared to be right. There were simply not enough tables to justify the additional expense of keeping the bistro open in the evening. It would mean a lot more work for her with failure built in from the beginning.

After tossing and turning most of the night, Laura got out of bed at four that morning and went for a run through the park with only the sound of her feet hitting the ground and Bruce Springsteen's *Born in the USA* coming through her earbuds. She gradually began to feel invigorated; after three miles she slowed to a walk by the de Young Museum and started toward home.

After opening her front door, she could smell coffee and heard the shower running. Reina was up. Laura poured herself a cup in one of the stoneware mugs she'd purchased at an art fair on Union Square when she first moved to the Bay Area from Paris. She heard the water turn off, fixed another cup for Reina, and took both to the bathroom knocking lightly before opening the door. "Good morning. I brought you coffee."

Reina was drying her hair with a small towel. "Thanks."

Laura stood just inside the door and took a drink. "I've been thinking about what you said last night. And I think it would be a mistake for me not to look into it."

A grin spread across Reina's face as she said excitedly, "That is so cool. I'll call my grandmother tonight and see if she'll talk to my parents."

"Why don't you talk to them?"

Reina gave her a devilish grin. "Because they just might listen to her. They need this even if they don't know it yet."

"If they like the idea, set up a meeting and I'll look the location over."

It seemed to Reina that this idea might be the answer for Laura, her parents and maybe for herself. She was still thinking about what she was going to say to her grandmother when she walked through the doors of the bistro. Shelly was waiting on a customer and Alex was cooking in the back. Tony Morello was just bringing out a fresh batch of croissants from the oven.

There was a new girl, not much over five feet tall with long dark hair, helping Alex. He looked at Reina and smiled. "Back from your holiday already."

She countered quickly. "I was visiting my parents. And I worked yesterday."

He grinned and introduced the girl helping him. "Reina, this is Isabella. She's our new prep cook."

"What happened to Bobby?"

"Didn't show up for work on Saturday. Laura hired Isabella yesterday."

The girl was pretty, and Reina felt a tinge of jealousy, but she smiled just the same and held out her hand. "I'm glad to meet you, Isabella."

The young woman wiped her hands on her apron. "Hola."

Reina picked out a croissant and began to nibble on it as Shelly came into the back and said to her, "That artist friend of yours is out front." She smiled and gave her a playful nudge. "He's asking about you."

Daniel had a good weekend and a great start to the trip. But he'd gone to the restaurant on Monday and was disappointed that Reina wasn't there. When he saw her come from the back toward his table he stood and smiled sheepishly. "Hi."

"Hi, yourself."

"Do you have a few minutes to talk?"

She grinned. "Better than that. I haven't had breakfast yet."

The two of them sat down, Shelly took their order, and once they were alone he asked, "How was your weekend?"

"My mother wants me to come back home and help with the hotel."

"Are you going to?"

"Well not yet. I just started working here." Shelly brought her the cappuccino she'd ordered and refilled Dan's coffee cup. When she'd gone Reina said, "They pull at me. Do you know what I mean?"

He nodded. "Parents are good at it."

"The thing is I'm not sure what I want to do."

"Give yourself some time. You'll figure it out."

"You sound like my grandma; she thinks I shouldn't try so hard."

"Maybe she's right."

She took his hand from across the table. "If you're not too busy later, would you like to do something?"

"That's an offer hard to pass up." He grinned. "But today is laundry day."

"That must put a lot of pressure on you, but I think you can handle it."

He squeezed her hand gently. "What time do you get off?"

"Five."

"Should I pick you up here?"

"How about that bar where we first met?"

He hesitated a second, then shook his head. "Let's try someplace else. Some place quiet where we can talk."

She wrote down the address of the wine bar on Lincoln and Seventh where she'd met Laura and Alex. "This place is close to where I'm staying. Let's say six o'clock."

The rest of the day was uneventful and went by much slower than Reina liked. She did have a chance to speak to her grandmother and Elleanore promised she'd talk to her parents. As she was getting ready to leave Alex asked if she wanted to get a drink; her reply was rushed. "I'd like to, but I have a date. How about tomorrow?"

"Tomorrow it is. Have fun tonight."

Alex couldn't stop thinking about her. Reina was the first woman he'd been attracted to in a long time and she was out of reach. He promised Laura he'd keep his hands off. But it was irritating to him, being so close to her and not being able to touch. Dan seemed like a nice enough guy to Alex but there was something about him, something that told him Reina should be cautious.

Daniel spent the rest of Tuesday morning at the laundromat thinking way too much about what had happened the day before. Travis was curled up on the floor beside him pouting while he was folding clothes. He looked down at him. "This is the last load. Then we'll go home and get some lunch." Travis sighed and closed his eyes.

On Monday night he'd been tired after packing up the show that weekend and went for a beer at the same sports bar where he'd met Reina. The bartender, Jessica, noticed him waiting to order a beer, opened a Corona, and handed it to him across the bar saying, "If you can hang out a minute I'll save you a seat when one opens up."

She did too. He sat there and watched *Monday Night Football* while working on a plate of nachos. Dan had just promised himself he'd finish this last beer and go back to the trailer when Jess sat down beside him.

He noticed she'd changed her top; the shirt with the bar's company logo was replaced with the black camisole she'd been wearing underneath. Dan grinned as he asked, "What's going on?"

"I just got off. How about buying a girl a beer?"

Dan had no way of knowing how the night would turn out. He could have walked away, he thought afterward, but he didn't. He had two more beers with her and had a good buzz going when they left the bar. But he couldn't blame it on the beer either. She asked him for a ride home and he didn't have a problem with that. He could have said no when she asked him if he wanted to come in. But he didn't do that either.

After closing the door, she was kissing him, and he'd kissed her back. Her hand caressed the outside of his pants. "I've been thinking about this for a week," and before he could reply her tongue was inside his mouth again. His head was swimming as she pulled the camisole over her head; she didn't wear a bra. Jess took his hand and led him to her bedroom, undoing her jeans as she went.

He was hungover on Tuesday. Travis was irritated at him; he could tell that by the way the dog acted. He was irritated with himself, but Dan wasn't one to linger on feelings of guilt or remorse. And nights like the one he'd spent with Jess weren't anything new to him. Working on the road was lonely, with little time to build relationships and doing without the complexity of a relationship worked for him. At least it did before he met Reina. Now, he wasn't so sure. His opinion about sex had always been simple; it was a bodily need, no different than hunger, thirst, or sleep. Why then, he wondered, did he spend the day regretting the night before?

That night, by the time Reina got to the wine bar it was five minutes after six and Dan wasn't there yet. She got a table where it was easy to see anyone who walked in and ordered a glass of wine. It wasn't terribly busy at first but as she waited, sipping her wine, the bar began to fill up. She looked at her watch; it was a quarter after six. The waitress stopped by. "Can I get you anything else?"

Daniel was running late; after the laundromat he'd spent the afternoon playing with Travis and working on the sketches for Laura.

He got lost once looking for the address where he was supposed to meet her, found a place to park and walked in the bar looking for her.

The hostess asked, "May I help you, sir?"

"Yeah," he replied. "I'm here to meet someone… a young woman, blond, hazel eyes."

The young woman grinned. "Come this way, sir."

When Reina saw him walk in, her heart seemed to skip a little. He was handsome but still rough around the edges, she mused, as she watched him follow the hostess to her table.

Dan leaned down and kissed her cheek. "Sorry I'm late. The day got away from me."

"That's OK. I haven't been here that long."

He noticed the glass of wine she was drinking was almost empty and knew she was just being kind. The waitress came, Dan ordered a beer, and Reina asked for another glass of the Cabernet she'd been drinking. When she'd gone he said to Reina, "I missed you this weekend."

"You haven't known me long enough to miss me."

"Are you sure? Haven't you ever heard of love at first sight?"

She winked and replied, "Is that what this is?"

"Absolutely."

"And how often do you fall in love while you're on the road?"

Jess flashed through his mind as he forced a smile. "There's a first time for everything."

CHAPTER 10

Elleanore

She was lying in Adrien's arms, her legs entwined with his when she suddenly asked, "Do you love me?"

"Yes, chérie."

His admission filled her heart with joy but couldn't stop the fear. "I love you," she replied. Then gently kissing his chest, she whispered, "What are we going to do?"

They'd been seeing each other for two months and the house was almost finished. She came to St. Helena three or four times a week, meeting with the contractor, interior decorator, or landscaper. The afternoons were spent with him, in the little cottage, or winery if they could sneak away. As the weeks passed her passion for him increased to such an extent that it was impossible to think of anything but the next time she'd see him.

Being alone together became more problematic once the children were out of school. Ellie moved into the cottage with them that summer, no longer driving back and forth; she was relieved to be away from Abigail. Adrien got along very well with both her son and daughter, particularly Jane, who loved the vineyard. And, gradually, even young Roger began to loosen up as June turned to July. Adrien made a swing for them and hung it from the oak tree not far from the cottage, where the four of them would picnic. From a distance they appeared no different than any family and it was that appearance that started the spread of gossip. St. Helena was still a small town, after all.

Her husband didn't come to St. Helena every weekend but came enough to upset the tender harmony established that summer. He was irritated that she hadn't hired any servants to tend to the family's needs but had chosen to run the household herself. Finally, after a prolonged disagreement with her husband, Ellie agreed that Sofia could come and stay with them.

The three-bedroom cottage was crowded enough but after Sofia arrived it seemed that all of them were constantly bumping into one another. Ellie initially put Sofia in with Jane, which took privacy away from each of them. It was Adrien who finally came up with the solution; he gave up his room in the loft at the winery and moved temporarily into town.

As he was packing, Ellie said to him, "I wish you didn't have to do this."

"It's probably for the best, chérie."

She reached out and lightly ran her fingers across the back of his arm. "It isn't best for me."

He turned toward her, his eyes stern. "We can't hide the way we feel when we're together. People see this. Sofia will see this, what I feel for you."

Their hearts were being torn apart. Adrien knew that he couldn't support her and the children. He couldn't ask her to run away with him as he wished. Ellie was caught between the obligation to her family and her love for him. How, she asked herself time and again, could she possibly satisfy both?

Adrien's rented room was on the second floor of a boardinghouse on Church Street. He passed the cottage each day going to and from his work and would strain to get a brief glimpse of her. The days seemed to drag by for him that July; being so close yet far away from her was almost more than he could stand. The love he felt for the vines was the only thing that kept him sane.

They were moving furniture into the new house on the top of the hill and having the drapes hung when she became sick for the first time. At first, she thought it nothing more than a case of the flu but as her nausea persisted Ellie began to consider the alternative. She'd been so distracted with Adrien, the children, and Roger, Ellie couldn't remember her last cycle.

It was a Saturday. Sofia was looking after the children and Roger hadn't yet arrived from the city. But she expected him. Ellie drove into town and found the boardinghouse where Adrien was staying. She sat in her car for several minutes considering the wisdom of going in, hoping that he'd somehow see her and come out. Finally she mustered the courage to open the car door, to make her way down the walk, and up the porch steps to begin looking at the names on the small black mailboxes.

The front screen door opened, and a middle-aged, heavy-set woman asked gruffly, "May I help you?"

The woman startled Ellie and it took an uncomfortable second before she stammered, "I'm looking for Mr. Forche," and then added quickly, "he's in my employ."

She came outside with a broom and began to sweep the porch. "He's in 213, toward the back."

A moment later when he opened the door, Ellie was the last person he expected to see. He took her by the arm and quickly brought her inside before anyone could see them. "What are you doing here? It's dangerous, chérie."

He hadn't held or kissed her; she took note of this as she said weakly, "I had to talk to you."

Adrien embraced her, kissing her lips, and smiled. "And it couldn't wait?" Suddenly he knew by her expression that something was wrong. "What is it, mon ami?"

She looked up at him, frightened, with a tear in her eye. "I'm pregnant."

The two of them sat together on the edge of his bed, holding hands as he asked, "Are you sure?"

She nodded silently.

"You're sure the child is mine?"

She nodded again. "Yes… Roger has very little interest in me."

He could hear Ellie begin to cry and took her in his arms. "He's foolish, my darling." Adrien wiped the tears from her cheeks with his pressed handkerchief, kissing her lips lightly.

She kissed him back and whispered, "It's been too long."

"I've missed you, chérie," he breathed, his voice husky, as the next kiss led to another and another after that.

The distance forced upon them that summer created a sense of urgency within them as their passion increased. She pulled her skirt above her hips frantically as he undid his belt and a moment later, still clothed, he entered her. The two of them in that instant, felt whole again. Adrien came almost immediately, possessing her in the only way he could. Ellie sobbed as she felt him withdraw, lying quiet as he slowly, gently removed her clothing before removing his.

He pulled the coverlet over them, holding her in his arms, kissing her temple, neck, and lips, tenderly, as his hands caressed her body. Ellie snuggled into him, letting the calm of being together take over, until gradually she felt the desire that seemed never-ending rise again.

They made love slowly, taking the time to savor each moment. It was difficult to separate one limb from another as they moved in rhythm, interlaced, until finally there was one last gasp that escaped her lips. She trembled in release as she felt him do the same. Adrien didn't pull away this time but remained, resting in her arms, the two of them covered in sweat. He could hear her heart begin to slow as Ellie ran her fingers lightly through his hair, kissing his temple.

Her voice was barely audible as she asked once more, "What are we going to do?"

Adrien was Catholic and within the church, divorce was rarely granted. Abortion was a sin and unthinkable to him. He felt as trapped as she did, knowing that for her to leave her husband to be with him would mean giving up all she cherished. His heart ached as he replied, "Convince him the child is his."

Ellie sat up and looked at him. "You don't love me then."

"Of course, I do."

"How could you possibly want him to think your child is his?"

"I don't."

"Then why, Adrien?"

"Because he'll take the children from you."

There was only silence between them that followed. Sitting up in bed she wrapped her arms about her legs and began to rock, back and forth, trying to settle the pounding in her chest. After a moment Ellie said quietly, "You're right," and wiped fresh tears away. Then finally, she said defiantly, "I'll not give you up. Somehow we'll find a way."

He doubted that but didn't say it to her then. "Oui, chérie, we will find a way."

Sofia had arranged a picnic with the children, at noon, under the oak tree when Roger Strickland arrived. She could tell by the way her mistress and the Frenchman looked at one another that they were in love. And she suspected that Elleanore was with him. The cause of the morning sickness was clear. But Ellie had always been kind and fair to her, defending her at times.

When Roger questioned her point-blank she answered him truthfully, "She's gone to town, Senor Strickland."

"When do you expect her back?"

"I have no idea, sir."

Elleanore had just dressed and was fixing her hair when Adrien's telephone rang. He picked up the receiver, "Bonjour." A moment later he hung up and said, "Chérie, that was Sofia. She told me that your husband arrived."

Her heart was pounding in her chest as she left him to go to the grocery store before returning to the cottage. Why, she asked herself, would Sofia call Adrien unless she knew? She picked out a few things for dinner at the store, her hand shaking as she wondered whether Sofia had told her husband. What would he do if he knew? Would he take her children, as Adrien believed? It also occurred to her as she fantasized that it might be a relief if he did know. But when her thoughts shifted to her mother and father, she knew they would never understand.

Sofia was ironing clothes while keeping watch outside the front window and when the car pulled to a stop in front she went to greet her mistress. She took one of the grocery bags, looked her in the eye, and said quietly, "Your husband is at the winery, senora."

There was nothing else that passed between them as they went inside. An hour later when Roger Strickland walked into the cottage the two women were in the kitchen preparing supper. He said curtly, "Where were you this afternoon?"

Ellie was peeling potatoes in the sink, and without looking at him, replied, "I was at the grocery store. Why do you ask?"

"You belong here, with the children, not gallivanting about."

"I wasn't gallivanting about; I was buying your dinner."

His patience had grown thin, not because she went to the store but because of the disinterest and suspicion he felt. The distance between them continued to increase and his mother's observations, warning him about Elleanore's behavior, echoed in his mind.

Abigail had said, "She and the children belong here, not in the country. Whether I like it or not the girl is a Strickland now and our name brings with it responsibility."

Roger watched Ellie work for a moment. "I want you to hire a cook next week. As my wife you have an image to project that doesn't include housework."

She simply nodded. "I'll do it first thing Monday."

The ease of her agreement incensed him even more; he wanted her to challenge him. Roger mixed a Scotch and water over ice and went outside for a few moments. There was something wrong, he could sense it.

Ellie followed him. "I'm sorry I wasn't here when you arrived." When he didn't reply she continued, "There's something we need to talk about."

Now, he thought, she was going to tell him what was bothering her. He took a cigarette from his jacket pocket and lit it. "What is it?"

She was intentionally blunt. "I'm pregnant again."

Roger could feel the relief settle into him; he grinned. "Is that what it is?" He took her in his arms, his relief replaced with joy. "I was afraid it was something else. We need to get you back into the city to see the doctor."

"They have doctors here, Roger."

"But, darling, you need the best."

"I need to be in my home."

"That's what I'm saying. We'll get you home to see the doctor."

Ellie was determined to be firm. "That's your mother's home, Roger, not mine. The new house will be finished soon and I'm staying here with the children. I've already contacted the school here."

"That's absurd, Elleanore. The Stricklands have been in San Francisco for a hundred years. My business is there."

"You're gone half of the time, Roger. We're two hours from the city; it isn't as if we're moving to another planet."

He took a different tactic. "Darling, when you have time to really think about it I'm sure that you will agree, we have responsibilities there that can't be ignored. If it's living with Mother that bothers you. I'll find us someplace else to live."

"You've been saying that since we were married. But that doesn't matter now. I like living in St. Helena. I want our children to grow up here."

When they were first married, Elleanore was little more than a child. She did what others felt was expected; she did as her husband wished. But Ellie was no longer a child and didn't intend to be treated as one.

Roger knew that if he pushed her, it would most likely turn out badly. He hugged her once more to try and temporarily appease her. "We have plenty of time to talk about this."

Although she'd put up a good front, inside she'd been close to panic. It was a relief to know he didn't question the legitimacy of the life within her. He assumed the child was his. He hadn't really fought her about staying in St. Helena either. But she knew it wouldn't be as easy as it appeared. Sooner or later, the subject would come up again; he'd push her a little at a time to wear her down. And if that didn't work he'd try to bully her or have Abigail do it for him. Ellie was prepared for them.

After the children were asleep he came to her bed. She accepted his touch and the discomfort of being too dry as he entered her. It was over quickly, and he returned to his bed silently as if he was ashamed of his own humanity.

She lay there afterward, ashamed of herself for being cold to him but relieved, just the same, that it was over. Her thoughts drifted to Adrien, to thoughts of her love for him, to the gentleness of his touch, and the power he held over her.

Could she ever be, she wondered, valued for something besides her femininity? The men in her life; her husband, father, and even Adrien had built lives for themselves based on whatever abilities they possessed. Their ambition and self-worth were tied to those abilities. For Roger and her father, it had more to do with making money than anything else but with Adrien, making wine was an art. He based his success or failure on the quality of what he produced each year from the vines. She had no vocation other than that of a wife, mother, and lover. There was nothing to measure her success or failure as a person beyond that.

Abigail used those same limitations as a means to achieve power. There was a kind of control that she held over her son. His decisions were often based on her thoughts and recommendations. She exhibited the same influence over social groups in the city and on the wives of powerful men who were in those groups. She was used to getting her way. And there would be a fight when she found out that Ellie intended to stay in St. Helena.

Elleanore was tired of being bullied and treated as a child or as an adornment on the arm of a successful man. She was loved and knew now what it meant to truly love another. There was strength in that. She didn't want her children to believe they were better than others because of their social position. She wanted them to base their worth on their abilities and the care with which they treated others. If she were to stay in the city she knew that there was very little chance of that. Abigail would have her way with them. But here, in St. Helena, there was a chance for them to earn their place, to grow, and become strong.

CHAPTER 11

Laura

After her breakup with Matt Stryker, Laura put everything into the bistro. It was her way of healing the hurt. One of the things that stood between them, besides his love for someone else, was the way he made decisions without consulting her. That was something she found impossible to live with. Matt tried to get her to leave San Francisco, to move to Scottsdale; he even made arrangements to open a new restaurant there, where she would be head chef. She rejected his offer and him. The bistro wasn't much, but it was hers, it was all she had. And the thought of moving on scared her.

She agreed to a meeting with Reina's parents. Reina volunteered to drive, and Laura asked Alex to come with them. Laura sat in the back seat by herself, lost in her own thoughts, while Alex rode in front; he'd never been to the wine country and was taken in by it.

The three of them were quiet for a long time before Reina asked him, "What do you think?"

"It's beautiful," he answered while his eyes stayed fixed upon the countryside passing by. "Why would you ever want to leave?"

She shrugged her shoulders. "I grew up."

"It couldn't be as simple as that."

"No, I suppose not. I went away to school and came back. I was still living at home and one day I realized I'd never really tested my wings. I'd never let myself get too far from the nest."

He looked at her. "And now you're going back."

"No," she protested quickly, "this is for Laura and my parents. I'm not ready to come back."

Alex was thinking that she hadn't ever really left and seriously wondered if she ever would. But he didn't say it. He was falling in love with her, and he didn't tell her that either. They never did go out for that drink together; she'd been with Daniel. Nothing was said about it between them; it was understood. He just had to make up his mind to let her go but that was far more difficult than he imagined. Reina was the first person he was attracted to in a very long time, and she didn't see it.

Laura spent her early years growing up in Burbank. Her parents were from a small mountain town, Prescott, Arizona, and they moved back there when she was just starting high school. She liked Prescott, particularly being near her grandparents but after graduation she moved back to the city, first Phoenix, then Paris, and finally San Francisco. She didn't know whether she loved the pace of urban living or was simply used to it, but she did know that it felt like something was missing without the accelerated beat of it.

As the car sped farther north Laura could feel that rhythm slow. Reina glanced over her shoulder. "Are you alright back there? You're awfully quiet."

"I'm fine," Laura replied. That wasn't entirely true. She loved her work and there was a part of her that was excited at the thought of opening a new restaurant, a chance to expand her reputation. But gradually since her breakup with Matt she'd become lonely. Giving Reina a place to stay for a few days was a way for her to ease that loneliness. But there was still a piece missing in her life.

She was thirty-five years old, unmarried, and childless; her career would never fill that void. When she was younger, Laura always told herself that there was plenty of time for her to have a family. Then there was Matt and she thought he'd be the one to build a life with her. She opened the bistro instead and now she was planning something new; the decision was far from finalized but it was another step closer to the dream she'd formed as a girl. And it was another step further away from the life her mother and her grandmothers lived before her. She could feel herself becoming resigned to a life alone.

"We're here," Reina said to the two of them as she switched on her blinker for the turn into the hotel's parking lot.

Laura was impressed as she stepped out of the car; the hotel was homelike, inviting, with a sense of old-world charm. She followed as Reina led them inside; the foyer had the same feel about it, warm and welcoming. Alex seemed almost disinterested as Reina asked the girl at the front desk where she could find her parents. Laura began to explore on her own as they waited.

When Reina turned around, Alex was by himself and she asked, "Where's Laura?"

He nodded toward the interior of the hotel. "She went that way."

Laura found the restaurant within a few minutes. The dining room reminded her of some she'd seen in Europe, it was an intimate, cozy space, where one wanted to linger rather than be shuffled into and out of quickly. There were so many restaurants in hotels today, she thought, that had a cafeteria feel about them.

It was midmorning, late for breakfast and too early for lunch. Still, Laura noted, that there was no one to greet her. There were a few people still seated about the dining room and waitresses attended to them casually, almost with indifference. She began moving toward the kitchen when a voice behind her inquired, "May I help you?"

As she turned Laura was face-to-face with an attractive older woman; she smiled saying, "I was just looking around."

"Would you like a table, dear?"

"No, my friends and I are here on business."

The lady held out her hand. "I'm Elleanore Strickland. I'll take a guess and say you're Laura Patterson."

Laura took her hand; it was soft yet firm. "I am." She grinned. "And you must be Reina's grandmother."

Elleanore thought her eyes were kind but a little sad; her hands, she noticed, were used to hard work. "What happened to my granddaughter?"

"She's trying to find you and your son."

Ellie took her by the arm. "Well she'll be along directly. Would you like to see your kitchen?"

She might be a grandmother, Laura thought, but with one word she'd personalized the moment; she'd already referred to the kitchen as hers. It made her smile as she replied, "Yes… I would very much."

Fifteen minutes later, after meeting the staff and assessing the space Laura was in love. When she opened the bistro for the first time she had old, outdated equipment, trying her best to keep it functioning long enough to be replaced when she could afford it. Her office was nothing more than a closet that had been cleared out for her to use. The Stricklands had the best of everything, and the space was something out of a marvelous dream; it may not match up to what she'd used at Entretenir, but it was close enough. Just the same Reina was right. The food, Laura observed, was adequate at best.

Ellie took her arm as if to steady herself. "What did you think, dear?"

The old lady directed her outside to the patio as she replied, "It's a beautiful space, Mrs. Strickland."

"Please call me Ellie, Laura." She grinned. "Every time I hear someone call me Mrs. Strickland I look around for my mother-in-law."

Laura chuckled. "It would be a pleasure, Ellie."

Reina tried finding her father in the winery, the lab and tasting room but he wasn't in any of them. She said to Alex, "He might be in the wine cellar."

"Maybe we should try and find Laura."

She was frustrated with her father. "I suppose you're right." They began walking back through the hotel as she said, "I just don't understand him. He knew we were coming this morning."

"He might be with Laura now."

"I suppose."

"He's probably giving her a tour of the kitchen."

She'd still felt guilty about not going with him for that drink after work. Alex was too nice a guy to treat that way. Reina said apologetically, "I'm sorry about the other night."

"Sorry for what?"

"We were supposed to go out for a drink."

Alex nodded silently as they entered the restaurant and noticed Laura outside on the patio. He pointed. "There she is."

Reina breathed a sigh of relief. "She's with my grandmother."

"I guess now is as good a time as any to say I told you so."

"OK so you were right." Reina noticed that he really didn't say anything about her apology.

Laura was listening to Ellie tell her about moving to St. Helena when she was a young woman and asked, "Didn't you miss the city?"

The image of Abigail Strickland came to her, but she said simply, "I wanted the best for my children and believed we would find that here. I've never regretted my decision."

"Your son Michael runs the hotel. How about your other children? Where are they?"

The old lady forced a smile. "My oldest, Roger, runs his father's company. Jane travels quite a bit and Adriana lives in France."

"I studied cooking in Paris."

It saddened Elleanore to think how long it'd been since she'd seen her youngest child but managed not to show it. "I've heard it's beautiful there."

"Yes, it is." Laura glanced toward the door and saw Reina and Alex. "Here's your granddaughter now."

Reina gave Ellie a hug and whispered in her ear, "I'm going to kill your son."

"You'll have to find him first," Ellie replied as she hugged her back. "Laura and I have been having a wonderful talk."

"Yes we have," Laura replied, "and Ellie has already shown me the kitchen. But I would like Alex to see it."

The old lady put on a pair of glasses that hung about her neck and looked Alex over a second before saying, "So you're the one who's just friends with my granddaughter."

Reina gave her a stern look. "Yes, Grandma, we're just friends and we work together. Alex is Laura's sous-chef."

Ellie took his arm. "Well, young man, let me give you the grand tour."

Reina asked quietly as the two women followed, "What do you think?"

"I think you should be patient. We have a long way to go before I make a decision."

The truth was, Laura wanted the restaurant badly. But she just wasn't sure she wanted to leave San Francisco. And she wasn't sure whether the Stricklands wanted her to lease the space or had something else in mind.

As they walked through the restaurant once more she noticed that there were a few people being seated and asked, "Do you usually have a good turnout for lunch?"

Reina shook her head. "Not that I've ever seen. I suppose a lot of people are touring the wineries."

Alex was impressed with the kitchen but mentally critical of the staff working there and what they were serving. It seemed to him that Elleanore Strickland was just as interested in selling the positive traits of her granddaughter to him as the kitchen.

Suddenly Ellie asked, "Are you always so quiet?"

She reminded him of Reina and found her charming. "Not as a rule. But I'm a good listener."

Ellie squeezed his arm. "I bet you are." She hesitated a second before asking, "Where are your parents?"

He laughed at her abruptness. "What makes you ask?"

"I had a friend, a woman who worked with me and was deported. She was here illegally you see."

Alex became defensive. "I'm here legally if that's what you're implying."

"Oh, I'm sorry, young man. I didn't mean that… it's that we were very close and still are I think."

"Why didn't you help her get a green card?"

"My husband hired her and when we moved here from San Francisco she came with us. He hardly paid Sofia anything beyond room and board. It was like that in those days. If she had a green card, he would have had to pay her accordingly."

"I see," he replied. "I grew up in San Diego. My parents still live there."

"Do you speak Spanish?"

"Sí, Elleanore, hablo español cuando voy a casa a ver a mis padres."

She chuckled. "What did you say?"

"I speak Spanish when I go home to see my parents." He paused briefly. "What happened to your friend?"

"She's living in France the last I heard."

Laura interrupted them to ask Alex, "What do you think?"

He took a long look around the room and nodded his head slightly. "We should talk later."

Elleanore was disappointed at his reluctance to speak in front of her but understood it was out of loyalty to his employer. She said, "Reina, why don't you show your friends around the hotel. I'll be in the office if you need me."

It was Laura who spoke up. "I've got a better idea. It's almost time for lunch. Why don't you let Alex and I fix you something? I think we can stay out of your staff's way, and it'll give us a feel of what it would be like to work here."

The old lady's face brightened. "Are you sure? I can have our people prepare something."

Laura put her arm around Ellie. "You and Reina go sit down and catch up. Let us get to work."

Once they were gone Alex said, "What's going on?"

She threw him an apron and began looking for possible ingredients. "I'm hungry."

"That's not what I was getting at."

She found some bacon and chicken. "Let's call it a test drive. What do you think so far?"

"I think if you were offered the same space in the city it would be great. But moving out here is a gamble."

"And you're not a gambler I take it?"

"Not when it comes to the people I care about."

He'd never said anything personal to her before and it was moving. She placed some carrots, garlic, and mushrooms on the worktable next to him. "Are you going to help?"

"With what?"

Laura held up the chicken in one hand and the carrots in the other. "Coq au vin."

He shook his head. "It takes too long."

"That's where you're wrong. I know a shortcut."

CHAPTER 12

Elleanore

Michael was born in the second week of February the following year. Abigail wanted Roger to name him after her father, Henry Jacobs, but Ellie wouldn't have it.

They'd moved into the new house six months earlier, at the beginning of August the previous year. It was a seven-thousand-square-foot two-story structure built of stone, wood, and glass; the style influenced by Frank Lloyd Wright's organic philosophy. It seemed to blend with the surrounding landscape. The living space on the main floor was open and inviting rather than separated into several small enclosed rooms. The building's extensive expanse of windows seemed to bring more of the landscape outside the home into the interior; it felt at times like the family was living in a bubble.

Ellie was supervising two men who were delivering new bedroom furniture for the children when Sofia came upstairs to find her. She had just said to the men, "I'd like my son's bed here, I think, and the dresser over there," when she noticed her in the doorway. "Yes, Sofia, what is it?"

The maid looked at her knowingly and with some unease said, "Mrs. Strickland is downstairs, senora."

Initially there was a look of shock on Elleanore's face, her voice cracking as she replied, "Tell her I'll be down in a minute. And, Sofia put on some tea please."

"Sí, senora."

Once she was gone Elleanore took a moment to try and collect herself. She went into the master bathroom and looked at herself in the mirror, touching up her makeup and fixing her hair. She surveyed the image, saying in a whisper, "I can do this," and started downstairs.

Abigail Strickland was in the process of a critical inspection of the house when Sofia came back into the room to say, "She'll be right down, senora."

"Good," she replied bluntly.

As Ellie made her way down the stairs she was determined to be firm with her mother-in-law, knowing that even the slightest sign of weakness would work against her. The footsteps on the stone floor from her heels echoed throughout the space as she entered the living room with a smile, saying cheerfully, "This is certainly a nice surprise, Abigail. I wish I would have known you were coming; I would have prepared something special for lunch."

Abigail's look was stern as she took a seat on the edge of a cream-colored Harvey Probber sofa that was delivered the week before; her posture reminded Ellie of a predator ready to spring. "Please tell me that these rumors I'm hearing of you staying in the country are preposterous," she replied curtly.

Ellie sat opposite her in the matching upholstered chair. "On the contrary, Abigail, they are absolutely accurate."

"Then I suggest you rethink this idiotic decision. Come to your senses, young lady, before your children have to pay for your foolishness."

"I'm not a child, Abigail, and more than capable of deciding where I choose to live. If that disturbs you I'm sorry."

Sofia entered the room quietly with a tea tray and Abigail snapped, "Leave us immediately! If I want you I'll ring."

The maid stopped in the middle of the room, unsure of what to do until Ellie said quietly, "Put the tray on the table please, Sofia."

"Sí, senora."

Once she'd left the room Ellie said firmly while pouring the tea, "This is my home, Abigail. Please refrain from dictating to my servants." She felt the knot in her stomach stir as she'd said it.

Abigail Strickland was used to being obeyed and no one ever corrected her. The fact that her daughter-in-law had just done both flustered her. She hesitated briefly still bewildered before saying, "I'd like to see my grandchildren."

"They're outside playing right now. Let's have our tea... I'm sure they'll be here soon."

It wasn't until after her mother-in-law had left that Ellie realized the extent of her victory. But that was cut short when her husband returned from New York, upset by the way his mother had been treated.

"How could you," Roger lectured as he paced, "be so rude to my mother? Honestly, Elleanore, I've given you everything you want. You wanted this ridiculous house in the country; it's cost us a fortune, but I've given it to you. All I ask in return is a little peace and consideration. But what I get is this... this hostile behavior you exhibit to my mother. And she has been nothing but courteous to you."

Ellie sat patiently, listening to him for as long as she could stand it until finally the emotions that surged through her body took over. She stood from the same chair she'd been sitting in while talking to Abigail earlier in the day. "That's enough, Roger! I'll tell you what I told your mother as she was dictating to me. I am not a child. Your mother is about as courteous as a bull in a china shop. I'll not allow her to tell me where or how to live. That is my decision not hers. And I'll not be bullied by you."

She had never spoken to him this way; no one ever spoke to him this way. It was difficult enough to keep his mother pleased and now he began to feel like he was being pulled by each of them. His temper started to rise and rather than give way to it he said, "I have an early day in the city tomorrow. I'll spend the night there." And with that he picked up his briefcase and started for the door.

"Roger, don't be ridiculous... it's almost time for supper."

He turned back, glaring at her. "I'll get something in town."

It wasn't regret she felt as the door closed but relief. As she heard his car start and watched as it left the driveway, moving toward the highway she picked up her shawl, wrapping it around her shoulders, and left the house.

Ellie had convinced Adrien to move into the cottage once the family moved into the new house. They met there when they could, usually when her husband was gone on one of his trips or was staying in the city.

She found him among the vines as the late afternoon sun began to set. Her fingers cautiously entwined in his, hidden from prying eyes. "I missed you today."

He picked a single grape from the vine and put it in her mouth. "What do you think, chérie?"

She grinned. "Sweet."

Adrien nodded. "Yes, chérie. It's time for early harvest. I have workers coming to pick tomorrow."

Ellie teased him. "You'll be too busy for me then."

"Non, cher," he replied. "I am always here for you." And it was true. He'd considered going back home, to Bordeaux, to escape the trap of love and longing in which he found himself. But the thought of never seeing her again, of never being near her, was more than he could bear.

She felt a brief flutter inside and smiled. "I felt him move, just a little bit."

Without thinking he placed his hand on her belly. "I can't feel anything."

"You will, darling." She laughed. "Give it time."

Suddenly there was a voice behind them. "What are you doing, Mama?"

The lovers turned to look; Adrien knelt and smiled at Jane. "Come and see, little bird." Once she was close enough, he picked another grape and popped it in her mouth. "How does it taste?"

A smile began to gradually spread across her face. "May I have another?"

He took his pocketknife out and cut off a cluster, putting it into her small hands. "We begin making wine tomorrow, my sweet."

Ellie held out her hand. "Come, Jane. It's time for your supper… say goodnight to Adrien."

The little girl held her arms up to him instead and he swept her into his, kissing each cheek, then putting her down again. "Do what your mama says, chérie."

He watched the two of them walk away, hand in hand, and he was left alone again among the vines, more a husband than her own and more a father for her children. But that didn't help fill the empty hours with Ellie in her world and he in his.

It was time to harvest the grapes for sparkling wines, then those for the whites as September made its way toward October and the picking of what would become, one day, the Strickland's Signature Cabernet Sauvignon. Adrien's days were filled with work from early morning before the sun was up until long after it had set while Ellie remained on the hill looking out over the fields that bore her husband's name.

The life within Elleanore's body continued to grow a little each day as the weeks passed. Her husband, surprisingly, adjusted quite easily to life in the country. He found his time there peaceful, away from the city, away from his mother, and the pressure of the financial empire he'd built on the foundation laid by his father and his father before him.

Sofia became their housekeeper, in charge of an additional maid, Maria Robles, the cook, Luciana Perez, and Angel Flores, who acted as a combination gardener and handyman. A sense of equilibrium began to take shape within the family that fall, yet in spite of the calm that settled over the surface of their lives Ellie felt trapped within the confines of normalcy.

She paced the borders of her opulent cage unable to satisfy the longing that kept her up at night. The children grew strong, their cheeks filled with color, their bodies brown from hours playing in the sun. But their freedom could easily be measured in sharp contrast to their mother's lack of it.

The weather turned chilly as the rains came that November. Ellie reluctantly agreed that they would spend Thanksgiving at the Strickland home in the city, while Roger consented to Christmas in St. Helena.

Little Roger grumbled as his mother tied his tie. "I don't want to go, Mother. Why can't we stay here?" The young boy's change of heart, of his contentment away from the city and his grandmother's influence, was a surprise particularly for Eleanor.

Ellie finished, helped him put his jacket on, and straightened the collar. "Your grandmother hasn't seen you for several weeks. She'll have all your favorites for dinner. Won't you like that?"

It was Jane who replied, "It's no fun there."

"Then we'll just have to make it fun… won't we?" Ellie said as she kissed her daughter's cheek.

But it wasn't fun. The children sat up straight in the large mahogany dining room chairs, keeping one careful eye on their grandmother and the other on their father as he carved the enormous bird set before him. The boy tugged at the collar of his shirt trying unsuccessfully to loosen it without his grandmother seeing. Ellie tried to keep the conversation light, but her attempts were cut short by the stern gaze and critical replies of her mother-in-law. Abigail Strickland sat regally before them, her repressive nature dictating the mood of the time spent together. Even Roger found the afternoon with his mother tedious.

After dessert was served and the children waited restlessly at the table for the adults to finish their coffee Roger said, "I'm sorry, Mother, that we have to leave so soon but I promised Elleanore's parents that we would stop by before we return home."

As Abigail watched them go, a feeling of sadness settled over her. She'd become a matriarch without a following, left alone by those who should have been closest to her. With some effort she left the window, her balance aided by a silver-handled cane, and pushing the sorrow into one of the forgotten corners of her soul, she replaced it quickly with that false sense of superiority she'd relied on for a lifetime.

Roger felt guilty leaving her; his mother had directed the course of his life for as long as he could remember, sometimes physically but always emotionally. There was still a small scar, just above his upper lip, that served as a reminder of the power she held over him. Despite his mother's abusiveness he'd never really separated himself from her and honestly didn't know if he could. Moving to St. Helena was the farthest he'd been away from her since college and Stanford was thirty minutes away.

If feelings of thankfulness were absent within the walls of Strickland House, the opposite was true in the home of Edward and Rosemary Thomas. Both grandparents doted on their grandchildren as they did their daughter. The softening of Roger's stiff, reserved posture hadn't escaped either of them any more than their daughter's distance.

They'd been in her parents' home for less than an hour when Ellie found herself alone with her mother. Rosemary opened the conversation lightly. "The country seems to be good for the children."

Elleanore had been thinking of Adrien off and on throughout the day, wondering what he was doing, where he was spending the holiday. That concern and the afternoon spent with her mother-in-law had exhausted her. She answered her mother simply, "I think so."

"The country seems to agree with your husband as well. I don't think I've ever seen Roger so relaxed."

"Yes," she replied. How could she possibly explain the resentment she felt toward him for staying at home more? And more importantly how his presence kept her from her lover.

Rosemary took her hand. "I don't know what's bothering you, Ellie, but I'd like to help if I can."

She squeezed her mother's hand. "It's been a long day, Mother. I'm tired is all."

"I'm always here if you want to talk, sweetheart."

"I know, Mama."

Sofia had found Adrien earlier that morning in the winery. With the family gone to the city and the rest of the staff at home for the holiday they were the only two on the property and she didn't see any reason why they should spend the day alone.

He sensed her approach and said, "The vines will be dormant soon." She stopped a few feet from him as he continued, "We wait now, for new life to begin."

She wasn't quite sure whether he meant the vines or the child Ellie was carrying. "Would you like to have dinner with me? There's just the two of us."

The offer surprised him; he turned to look at her. "Oui, Sofia, I'd like to very much."

"Is two o'clock this afternoon alright with you?"

"I'll be there."

Adrien had, until that afternoon, avoided Ellie's new home; he'd always met her elsewhere. It felt odd to him going there as he walked up the stairs to the veranda and knocked on the large oak door. A moment later Sofia opened it, wiping her hands on an apron as she greeted him, "Buenas tardes, Adrien. Come in please." She sensed his hesitation. "There is no one here but us."

Stepping through the threshold he marveled at the beauty of the interior as Sofia led him past the great room toward the back of the house to the kitchen. "We didn't celebrate Thanksgiving where I grew up," she said. "If you were hoping to have turkey I'm sorry to disappoint you."

"Non, non, c'est bon. We didn't in my country either." It was hard for him to imagine Ellie living here or accept that she was accustomed to it. She'd grown up in a world of wealth and privilege and he was poor by that standard.

Adrien and Sofia ate together in the kitchen. He'd brought a nice bottle of red wine that he knew was perfect, ready to be opened. She served him shrimp stuffed avocado as an appetizer, squash soup, and baked chicken with guajillo cranberry sauce.

He had tucked the large linen napkin into his collar to avoid spills on his good shirt and the only tie he owned. "C'est magnifique," he said as he carefully dipped his spoon away, filling it with the rich mélange of vegetables and herbs. "Where did you learn to cook?"

He was handsome, she thought, despite his manners that appeared strained in her company. "My mama taught me, before I came here."

"Where are your parents?"

"My mother lives in Ensenada. I haven't seen my father since I was a little girl."

"I'm sorry. It must be difficult for her."

"Sí." She paused for a second. "I send her money when I can."

They were quiet for some time when she said, "Senora Strickland is unhappy I think."

Her wine glass was almost empty; he refilled it and replied, "That's not something that has to do with us."

Sofia was young, passionate about life and came to Ellie's defense. "She loves you. It hurts her not being with you."

"She has the life she's chosen."

"Maybe she would like a different choice."

"Look around you, Sofia. I could never give her anything like this."

"Things don't bring happiness."

Adrien pushed his plate aside, and replied impatiently, "Don't you think I've thought of that? It's not just all of this"—he waved his arm through the air— "it is more, far more. She could lose the children and that would kill her."

Sofia stood and took their plates to the countertop by the sink. "He will find out sooner or later."

CHAPTER 13

The offer was too good for her to pass on and she knew it. The Stricklands were committed to aesthetic and physical improvements of the restaurant as part of a long-term lease. And Laura agreed to open in six months.

She called Alex into her office at the bistro the day after the documents were signed. "I'll want you to manage everything here while I'm gone. Once we open I'll want you with me in St. Helena."

"Who will run this place?"

"You'll train Shelly to take over as manager; she's been working here since I opened. And you'll need to find a new cook to train."

"What about Isabella?"

Laura thought about that for a second. "She's a good choice… but you'll need a new prep cook."

"I'll get it done."

As he started to leave she said, "Alex, I'm counting on you."

He was standing in the doorway and looked back at her. "I know, Chef."

The truth was that this was his big chance too, he knew it, and it scared him a little. Laura's decision to open the new restaurant was a step closer to a dream that he'd had most of his life.

During the next six months Laura was in St. Helena more than she was in San Francisco. At first, she drove back and forth, and the hours were killing her. After the first week she'd just put in a ten-hour day and was packing up the car when Elleanore approached her in the parking lot. "Excuse me, dear," the old lady said quietly. "Would you like to spend the night here rather than drive back to the city?"

Laura had meetings the next day, back to back, with the contractor, an interior decorator, and a food distributor. She'd considered getting a room for the night but didn't want the expense. Relieved, she smiled back. "I wouldn't want to be a bother."

Elleanore took her arm. "Nonsense, dear." She chuckled. "We might lack a lot of things, but we have plenty of rooms."

Once the decision to open the new restaurant was made events began to unfold of their own accord, pushing her toward a new life and away from what she'd become accustomed to. The plans for the remodel called for the formal dining room to be separated physically from the space to be used for breakfast and lunch. New carpet, lighting, drapery, and tile were installed during the first few weeks. The furnishings, tables, chairs, and linens began to arrive during the fourth month.

Laura developed a routine of spending the first four days of the week in St. Helena and the weekends in San Francisco. Time went by much faster than Laura anticipated in the beginning, but she made her six-month deadline.

It was late the night before her grand opening as she sat by herself, nursing a glass of wine at one of the empty tables, looking at what she'd created, thinking and rethinking everything, afraid that somehow, something was forgotten.

Alex made one last evaluation of the kitchen before turning out the lights to leave. He noticed Laura sitting by herself, stopped for a wine glass at the bar and sat down to join her. Pouring a glass of wine for himself he said, "Are you ready?"

Her fingernail tapped the side of her glass. "Are you?"

"I asked you first."

She forced a grin. "I'm scared."

He shrugged and took a sip of wine. "What's the worst that can happen?"

"I fail."

"You won't, Chef."

"And you know this because?"

"Because I have faith in you."

She finished the last bit of wine and squeezed his hand gently as she stood up. "Thank you for everything, for taking this leap with me."

"It's a big chance for both of us."

Laura turned to leave. "I think I'll take a nice long walk before bed and try to calm down."

"Buena noche, Cocinero."

"Buenas noches, Alex."

As she walked outside the landscape was bathed in moonlight. Laura walked to the limits of the property toward the vineyard. It was peaceful among the vines as she strolled along, lost in thought, thinking about what the next day would bring.

She'd stopped for just a moment looking up at the cloudless sky when a voice behind her said quietly, "Good evening."

Laura turned quickly in the direction of the sound and saw the backlit figure of a well-dressed man standing a few feet away. "You startled me!"

He approached slowly. "I didn't mean to. But it's not every day I find a beautiful woman walking among the vines."

Her eyes glanced toward the large house on the hill. "You bought the Strickland's house?"

"Quite some time ago, yes." His hand extended toward her. "David Steele."

She recognized him now from the tabloids. He was older and not as tall as he looked in the movies; his hair had started to recede and there was gray at the temples, but he was still handsome. She took his hand and replied, "Laura Patterson."

"Are you staying in Michael's hotel?"

"You know Mr. Strickland?"

"Yes, we're quite good friends actually."

"That seems odd to me," she replied, "that the two of you would be friends after purchasing his family home."

They started to walk back toward the hotel through a row of vines. "Not really. Michael isn't all that interested in things. It's the vines and the wine that he cares about."

When Laura actually observed Michael Strickland working in the hotel it seemed to be nothing more than a job for him. It was his wife and mother who carried the majority of responsibility. She actually hadn't seen that much of him the entire time she'd been in St. Helena. "That's what I've heard," she said noticing a slight limp when he walked. "And what are you interested in, Mr. Steele?"

His answer was blunt yet honest. "Privacy."

They walked in silence for several minutes before she said, "There's something I'm dying to ask but I'm afraid it will come out all wrong."

He chuckled. "Why am I no longer acting; is that it?"

"I didn't want it to sound rude, but yes, that's it. I've never had much time to go to the movies, but I've always enjoyed yours."

David had gone over this dozens of times in his mind and almost as often with the media. He still didn't have a concrete answer. "The truth is… I don't know really. There was the accident; I broke my leg in several places. But I knew the studio could work around that." They had almost reached the hotel when he stopped to look into her eyes. "I think I just got tired of it all. I'd had my run and it was a good life for a long time."

She gazed back at him with the lights of the hotel accenting his features, thinking the lines of age in his face made him better-looking not less. Laura smiled at him. "This is my stop."

He extended his hand again. "It was a pleasure meeting you. I hope you enjoy your stay."

"I actually work here now… in the restaurant, I'm the new chef."

David usually avoided public events but reconsidered. "Yes… I received an invitation. Maybe I'll see you tomorrow."

"I hope so. Thank you for walking me back."

"It was my pleasure."

The last thirty minutes had seemed surreal to her as she made her way to the room the Stricklands had given her temporarily. She was tired of living out of a suitcase and knew it was time to find something permanent. But during the remodel there had just been too much to do.

Laura had just put on a nightgown and taken off her makeup when there was a soft knock at the door. The safety chain was still in place as she opened it to peek out; she shut it once more to take the chain off and opened it again. "It's late, Reina."

"I know," the young woman said sheepishly. "I couldn't sleep."

"Come in then. But only for a minute."

Reina sat on the edge of her bed. "I've been looking everywhere for you."

"I met your neighbor tonight."

She kicked off her shoes, fluffed the pillows, and put her feet up. "You talked to David… really?"

Laura got under the covers and lay down on her side. "Really."

"He doesn't talk to many people… except maybe my father. They're both kind of strange but lovable."

"I didn't think he was strange at all… maybe a little sad though."

Reina rolled onto her side facing her. "You've done a beautiful job with the restaurant. And we have a ton of RSVPs for tomorrow." Her voice trailed off as she started to close her eyes. "Everybody who is anybody in Napa will be here."

"Reina, don't go to sleep."

She yawned. "I won't."

"Reina?" But it was too late. Laura got back out of bed, covered her with a blanket, and turned out the light.

Laura named the restaurant Mélange, the French word for "blend." And that's exactly what she wanted to present, a menu that combined the best cuisine from around the world, presented with her own personal twist. She prepared a limited menu for the evening; a selection of three entrées—one meat, one fish, and one vegetarian—to choose from. Each dish was paired with a specific wine selection.

Pork chops were refrigerated overnight in a honey brine, browned in a skillet the night of the event then put in the oven until the desired interior temperature was reached. Each chop was accented with snap peas, tomatoes, shallots, onion, parsley, and chives. The dish was served with a 1995 Russian River Valley Pinot Noir. Wild marinated salmon was broiled, served with a sour cream, mustard sauce and accompanied with the same Pinot Noir or Pinot Gris, depending on the preference of the guest. The vegetarian selection was a Parisian gnocchi, browned, and sprinkled with shaved cheese, parsley, and chives, then served with a butter sauce. The dish was paired with a Cabernet Sauvignon that had once been one of the Strickland Signature wines.

The guest list included a variety of people from the valley, the Russian River area, Sonoma, and San Francisco. Each guest was given time before being seated to enjoy a cocktail or glass of wine as they took in the ambiance of Mélange and had a moment to meet the new chef. Laura worked the room with Elleanore or Reina at her side, meeting some of the most influential, notorious, and famous members of Northern California society.

David Steele watched her from a distance; he could see that even though it may not have been comfortable for her Laura greeted people with grace and charm. He admired that. It was something that when he began his career in Hollywood he found difficult to learn.

His thoughts were interrupted by a middle-aged woman who insisted on talking to him about his movies, an affair he was supposedly having with a young starlit that she'd read about in the gossip columns, and of course when his next film was coming out. This was exactly why he avoided public gatherings; he was always trapped by those who couldn't differentiate between the hype related to life as an actor and the person. He longed to be, at times, just a person.

Before the studio changed his name, he was David Allan Kline. He grew up in a small Kansas farming community not far from the Missouri River. Acting came as natural to him as breathing, stories from books and movies filled his head, and he loved bringing the characters to life, even as a young boy behind his grandfather's barn. And yet David could barely remember that boy from so long ago.

Michael Strickland watched as his friend was becoming steadily unnerved by the woman badgering him and felt it his duty to interrupt. He cleared his throat. "Excuse me, Mrs. Wilkerson, but I believe my wife is looking for you."

"Oh, Michael," she cackled, "thank you so much. I must tell her what a marvelous party this is." And she was off, across the room, searching for her next victim.

David held up his wine glass as if to toast him. "Bless you, Michael."

"I would expect nothing less from you. What are friends for after all."

The actor's eyes were still fixed on Laura. "I met your new chef last night. She seems nice."

"Laura doesn't work for us, David. This place is hers I'm just the landlord."

"Is that right?"

"She worked for Moreau at Entretenir for several years and opened a small bistro in the city after that. My daughter works for her."

"Is she any good?"

A devilish grin spread across Michael's face. "Good at what exactly, David?"

Steele ignored the remark and changed the subject. "The vines should flower soon."

"It's supposed to get colder the next few days," he replied. "If it looks like it's going to freeze I'll take care of it."

"You're a good friend, Michael. How are your vines coming along?"

"It's been a good start this year. And I think I've found that blend I've been looking for. I'd like you to try a sample."

David was watching Laura make her way around the room; she began to approach them as he replied, "Anytime... anytime at all."

Laura smiled and held out her hand. "Good evening, Mr. Steele. I'm so happy you decided to come."

He took her hand. "I wouldn't miss it."

Michael interrupted. "Now, David, you know it takes something short of a miracle to get you to mix with the rest of us."

Their eyes fixed upon one another. As she pulled away from David's grip, the touch of him lingered; Laura became flustered for a moment. "I hope you enjoy your dinner."

He asked casually, "Will you have a drink with me later… after all of this is over?"

"I'd like that. But it might be a late night for me."

He smiled. "I can wait."

CHAPTER 14

Alex

His day started at four in the morning, driving into the city to shop at the fresh fish and vegetable markets while it was still early. He bought for both stores, dropping off some of what he'd purchased at the bistro before returning to St. Helena.

Alex balanced a large box of fresh halibut in his hands while making his way from the back door of the bistro toward the kitchen. Isabella was working the grill and nodded to him as he set the box on the prep table. He addressed Federico Baez the new prep cook quietly but with authority. "Tengo dos cajas más de verduras en la camioneta."

"Sí, Chef," Federico replied and left to get the rest of the order.

He made his way toward the La Marzocco machine to make himself an espresso. Shelly was in the process of correcting a new waitress over a mistake she'd made and glanced at him from the corner of her eye. When she finished Alex was sitting at one of the tables looking at the painting that Daniel Whitman had done. He knew that Reina was still trying to get over him. The artist had stayed, as he did each year for the month of November, and then was gone. Dan talked briefly about staying in the Bay Area, but it was nothing more than that. She hadn't heard from him since.

Shelly put a breakfast burrito in front of him and sat down. "Isabella made it for you. How was your weekend?"

The restaurant in St. Helena was still going through growing pains. The grand opening was a success and many of those invited that night had returned during the first month for dinner. But all of the tables were rarely full, the staff was still trying to come together, and they hadn't been reviewed by any of the major food critics in the Bay Area. The lack of publicity was a problem that Laura hadn't anticipated. She'd never needed it before.

When she opened the bistro, it was already an established business with a customer base that remained loyal. The location was in a major tourist sector of San Francisco. In St. Helena, the reputation of the prior restaurant was a negative one and it was in the country, outside of a small town. It's true that Napa Valley was one of the great destination spots in the world, but it was still a farming community. There was little if any walk-in business and Laura had no advertising budget; they were relying on word of mouth alone to build clientele. She was worried, he could tell, and even though neither of them shared their fears, he was worried too.

Alex grinned at Shelly. "We're getting there. How was yours?"

She handed him an envelope filled with receipts from the weekend. "I think she'll be pleased." As he took a bite of the burrito Shelly said, "She has a crush on you."

Immediately the image of Reina passed through his mind before he asked, "What do you mean?"

"Izzy, you know, Isabella, she does everything but jump through hoops when you're here."

He chuckled. "You're loco. I'm too old for her. The jóvenes are probably lined up outside her papa's door."

She grinned. "What is jóvenes?"

"You know," he said, "the young men."

Shelly shook her head. "You guys are so dumb sometimes. Izzy doesn't have any family, at least here in the United States. I don't even think she's legal."

Alex put down his knife and fork and looked at her. "That's not our problem and I don't want it to become one." He pushed away from the table and stood up. "And I don't want you to bother Laura with this. She has enough to be worried about."

Shelly stood facing him, his macho posture didn't faze her. "All I said was she has a thing for you. I have no intention of telling Laura anything I shouldn't." She began to get angry. "I thought you knew me better than that."

He grumbled an apology before leaving and glanced at Isabella on the way out; her eyes caught his and Alex quickly turned his head to avoid the contact. All the way back to St. Helena he thought about what Shelly had said and it bothered him. Alex felt a responsibility toward Izzy; he began to worry that she might be undocumented, and he worried about who she was living with if not with her parents. "I should have asked her these things," he scolded himself in the car. "No," he replied, "these things are none of my business." Even after he said it he knew that he'd always known there was a chance she was illegal. Laura must have known it was a possibility when she hired her. He tried telling himself that it wasn't his business, but then whose business was it if not his. She worked for him as much as Laura.

When he reached the hotel, Alex had a prep cook and one of the busboys help him unload the van. The kitchen was beginning to get busy with an early lunch crowd. A conflict was beginning to take root between Laura and the chef who was responsible for preparing breakfast and lunch. Mélange operated almost as a separate business entirely. They shared the same kitchen with separate dining areas and the two crews weren't getting along.

Laura had just finished an argument with him about the shabby way the kitchen was left by the time her staff arrived. They were forced to finish cleaning before they could begin work. When Alex walked into her office she was still furious, and he overheard her say, "That man is impossible."

She looked at him sternly. "Do you know it took us fifty minutes yesterday to get that kitchen in good enough shape to start dinner. And he knows exactly what he's doing!"

"Too many chiefs," Alex replied as he sat across from her.

"What's that supposed to mean?"

"It means that all of us might be better off if you managed the kitchen, if we had one staff that answered only to you."

Laura rested her elbows on the desk and put her face in her hands. "We set it up this way so we could concentrate on a dinner menu. My time would be divided because of the additional responsibility."

"You're here most of the time anyway. Managing the additional staff shouldn't be a problem. It would probably be easier." He'd been working on what he wanted to say on the drive back from the city. After a brief pause Alex said, "We'd want a cook that we know could do it. Someone we trust."

"And do you know someone?"

Alex set the envelope of receipts on her desk. "Shelly had a good weekend."

"Good," she pushed the envelope aside. "Answer my question."

He hesitated briefly before taking a deep breath. "We could bring Izzy up from the city. She's doing a good job there."

"And who would replace her?"

"I'll find someone."

"We could find someone and train them right here." She sat back in her chair. "What's really going on?"

They never lied to one another and he wasn't going to start. "She's a young girl. Shelly told me this morning Izzy has no family in the city. I think she would be better off here. And you could continue to train her; she's a fast learner."

Laura shook her head and smiled. "I didn't realize that you're such a softy."

"It's not that," he replied indignantly. "I think it would work out for everyone. We have a problem and I thought it might work. If you don't like the idea that's fine with me."

She grinned. "You don't have to get yourself in such a snit. It is a good idea. And I think you're right. Isabella is too young to be on her own. I've been concerned about that myself." Laura opened the envelope with the receipts. "I'll talk to Shelly and see what we can do."

The daytime chef was fired; Laura kept most of his staff with the understanding that their continued employment would be based on the quality of their work. She had to fire two others by the end of the first month.

Izzy agreed to come to St. Helena and a month later, Alex helped her move. He'd rented a small two-bedroom cottage for himself in town. And unable to find any place for her to stay, he offered her a room temporarily; she agreed.

Once they arrived and were unloading her things he said to her, "It's not much, but it should do until you find something else." She nodded silently and followed him into the house; Izzy hadn't said more than two words the entire time they were on the road. And it was making him nervous. He left her bags in her bedroom and said faintly, "I'll let you get settled here. I need to go check on the restaurant." He didn't really, it was his day off, but Alex had no idea what else to do; her silence was unnerving. He'd noticed the same thing at the bistro when they worked together but she'd always been a quick learner and there were plenty of other things to do that acted as a distraction.

It was late Monday afternoon, Mélange was closed for the evening, which offered Laura the one day of the week to catch up on her paperwork. Alex came into her office and sat down opposite her. Without looking up from the stack of bills that she was deciding which to pay and which ones could wait she murmured, "It's your day off and the restaurant is closed."

Without knowing what else to say Alex asked, "Do you need some help?"

She put down her pen and looked up at him. "No, I need more money to pay these bills." Laura could tell by his body language that something was bothering him. A bottle of Michael Strickland's Cabernet Sauvignon was sitting on her desk; she poured each of them a glass.

"Isn't it a little early?" he said.

"We're closed and it's after five. Why aren't you with Isabella?"

"She makes me nervous… she never says anything."

Laura grinned. "She's your project. If that's the worst thing you have to deal with you'll be lucky."

"What do you mean she's my project? We decided she'd be better off here."

She shrugged. "It was your idea. And speaking of your ideas, how's the new cook working out for Shelly?"

"He isn't as good as Izzy, but I think he'll be alright once he gets the hang of things."

"Did you tell Isabella she's opening tomorrow with you?"

"Sí."

Laura asked, "What do you think of the wine?"

Alex held the glass to his nostril briefly to breathe in the bouquet before taking a sip. "It's good." He took another sip. "Very good."

"I'm thinking of using it as our house Cabernet. What do you think?"

He smiled for the first time since he'd sat down. "I think Senor Strickland is a bit loco, but he knows his wine."

She chuckled. "Me too. But he's harmless."

"You're sure of that?"

"I'm not sure of anything." She arched her back and stretched. "I've got a date and need to get ready."

"With the actor?"

Laura nodded. "Mmm… he finally wore me down."

Alex finished his wine as she started to stand. "I was hoping you'd come over to my place for dinner and help me with Izzy."

She put on a jacket and picked up her purse. "Like I said, she's your project. Besides, with any luck we'll find her another place to stay soon." After locking her office, the two of them were walking toward the front entrance when Laura reminded him, "Be careful with your project."

"What do you mean?"

"I mean she's a pretty girl."

He immediately took offense. "I'm almost old enough to be her father."

"You're not her father; you're a man and she's a woman." They continued to walk in silence and once she'd unlocked the door to her car she said, "When I was young, working as an apprentice in Paris, I had this mad crush on the chef I worked for. Well… you know how long the hours are and we worked together a lot. One thing led to another…"

"I see," he interrupted her. "You don't need to draw me a picture."

She slid behind the wheel and looked up at him. "He was married. I didn't know, and it hurt. Be careful, Alex."

Fifteen minutes later he sat in the van looking at the house; he could see Izzy moving about inside. Finally, Alex got out mumbling to himself, "I'll find a place for her soon."

The aroma of supper cooking hit his nostrils immediately as Alex came in and shut the door. All his life he'd lived alone; he'd always come into an empty house and the thought that someone was waiting for him to come home was foreign. He couldn't see her and called out, "Isabella, I'm back." There was no immediate answer as he went into the kitchen to take a beer from the refrigerator and twist the top off. She wasn't in her bedroom; he knocked lightly on the bathroom door. "Izzy, are you in there?"

"Sí," she replied softly. "I'll be out in a minute."

He made his way back into the living room and turned on the television, to surf for a minute until he found a baseball game and sat down to watch, putting his feet on the coffee table. The Giants were playing the Dodgers at home. He'd almost forgotten about her when he heard the bathroom door open and her voice saying quietly, "I'm finished."

Alex turned his head in the direction of her voice and glimpsed her briefly, a towel wrapped around her body shutting the door to the spare room where she was staying. He groaned and got up to get another beer.

The Giants were ahead five to three in the top of the eighth; the Dodgers had two on and one out when he heard her door open. A moment later she startled him by saying, "The enchiladas should be ready. I'll set the table and we can eat."

He was still in awe; her hair had always been pulled up on top of her head or in a ponytail at work and he'd never seen her in anything but work clothes or jeans. She was beautiful; he'd always known she was pretty, but he really had no idea just how attractive she was.

The shock on his face amused her and she smiled down at him. "You'll scratch the coffee table with your shoes."

Alex immediately sat up. "Can I help?"

She shook her head and left him there just as the Dodger first baseman, Jeff Kent, knocked in two runs to tie the score. He turned off the television and went into the kitchen. Izzy was getting their food out of the oven as he opened the refrigerator for another beer. She said softly, "Get one for me, por favor."

He grabbed two and twisted the cap off both before handing her one. Isabella took it, their fingers touching briefly before she raised the bottle. "Gracias, mi amigo. Salute."

Her eyes, gazing into his, were dark brown, almost black, and as dark as the long thick hair that fell over her shoulders. He smiled. "It is my pleasure, Isabella."

Later as he lay in his bed Alex was kept up thinking of Isabella. There was a subtle charm he'd missed before and a quiet sense of humor that began to unfold as they shared their supper. Afterward he helped her clean the kitchen, both working quietly but each self-consciously aware of the other. And when it was time to say goodnight he found himself disappointed that the evening was over. Before going to her room, she kissed him on the cheek and said, "Dormir apretado, Alex." He didn't sleep well and neither did she.

CHAPTER 15

Laura

When Elleanore had first shown her the cottage Laura fell in love with it. The small house was on the edge of the vineyard hidden behind a stand of oaks, maple, and black walnut trees. It was the same cottage built by Ellie's parents and the one she'd lived in as a young woman. She shared her love with Adrien there and Michael's life began within its walls.

Ellie never considered renting it until Laura. She'd kept it just as it was then. Michael encouraged her to find tenants, but she refused. For reasons impossible to pin down she felt fate pulling her. And she finally gave way to that voice inside that told her this young woman belonged there.

It was within walking distance to the hotel, through the oaks, on a path almost hidden from the eye. That's the route Laura took after leaving Alex that first night when he brought Isabella to St. Helena. She was still touching up her makeup in the bathroom when there was a knock on the door. He was early, she thought, as she opened it to see Elleanore standing there.

"I was out for a short walk and hoped you'd be here," the old lady said.

Laura smiled. "Come in, Elleanore." She glanced at her watch.

"I hope I'm not a bother, dear."

"You're never a bother. But I am afraid I'm going out in a few minutes."

Ellie was familiar with every corner within these walls; the memories were everywhere. This is where she'd last seen Adrien, the day she believed Adriana was conceived. "With David I expect," she said as her eyes wandered about the room. Elleanore rented the house to Laura furnished. Most of the upholstered furniture had been replaced over the years along with the bed they'd used while making love. There were a few things left, after he'd gone, things he couldn't take with him. And things she couldn't part with.

Laura said to her, "Do you mind if I continue to get ready?"

"Not at all, dear."

"Is there something I can help you with, Elleanore?"

The elderly lady sighed. "I was just out for a short walk but now that you mention it, dear, you could start calling me Ellie."

"I think I can manage that."

She'd just excused herself and gone into the bedroom to change into the only dress she'd brought with her to St. Helena. The rest of her clothes were still at her home in the city.

Elleanore raised her voice as much as she could to be heard. "How long have you been seeing David Steele?"

Laura walked back into the living room. "Would you zip me up, Ellie?"

There was something about Laura that reminded Elleanore of Adriana. Her daughter was older but the two of them had that same independence and drive to achieve what they wanted in life. Her hands shook a little as she reached for the zipper to pull it up, the swelling of her joints making it more difficult. She gave the younger woman a gentle pat on the back when she'd finished. "You look very nice, dear."

"Thank you so much. But if you want me to continue to call you Ellie, you must start calling me Laura. Is that a deal?"

She chuckled. "It's a deal. But you still haven't told me how long this has been going on with David."

"May I get you something, Ellie, a glass of wine or water?"

"Water would be fine, Laura."

She poured herself some Chardonnay, took a bottle of Evian from the refrigerator and brought them into the living room, giving Elleanore the water. The two of them sat down on the sofa in the living room and Laura said, "He's asked several times, but this is our first official date."

Ellie twisted the cap off the bottle and took a drink. "What do you mean it's officially a date?"

"He waits for me sometimes until I finish work and we talk."

"That's the way it was with Adrien and me in the beginning," she replied without thinking. Elleanore hadn't meant to say anything; it just came out.

Laura was a little confused and taken aback. "Who is Adrien, Ellie?"

Just the mention of his name and this place, where they'd been together so many times, had her mind drifting back to the past again, to the love she'd lost. She heard Laura's voice saying faintly, "Ellie… Ellie! Are you alright?"

She came back to the present suddenly, doing her best to disguise the way her mind had been drifting lately. "Yes, dear, I'm fine. I was just wool gathering for a minute."

"You gave me a scare."

The old lady patted her hand gently. "I'm fine, Laura. The memories just get all jumbled together at times."

There was a knock at the door and Laura called out, "Just a minute."

As she opened it David was smiling back at her saying, "You look lovely."

Laura was still concerned about Elleanore but forced a smile in return. "Come in, David. We were just having a drink. May I get you something?"

He noticed Ellie sitting on the sofa and said as he walked in, "I'll have whatever you're having." And then he leaned over to kiss the old lady's cheek. "How's my favorite girl?"

Elleanore replied with a devilish grin, "Apparently I've been replaced." She nodded toward Laura. "It looks like she's your girl now."

"What can I say? You know I have a weakness for beautiful women."

Laura handed him a glass of wine. "I didn't know the two of you were an item. I suppose I should have asked around about you, David, before I agreed to go tonight."

"Caught red-handed," he replied. "I'll have to find a way to make it up to both of you. Would you like to join us for supper, Elleanore?"

"I'd love to but unfortunately it's past my bedtime." She started to stand, and he stood to help her. "Thank you, David," she said as she squeezed his hand. "I better be getting back to the hotel."

"We'll take you," Laura said as she began to rise. "I don't want you walking back by yourself in the dark."

Ellie chuckled. "Nonsense, dear. I've been walking that path since I was a youngster." She took one more look around the cottage. "You two young people have fun and I'll see you tomorrow, Laura."

The three of them went outside together and as they watched Elleanore make her way toward the path, disappearing into the darkness, Laura said with concern in her voice, "I'm worried about her, David. She was acting a little strange a while ago."

He opened the car door for her, went to the driver's side and slid in behind the wheel. "I'll call Michael from my cell phone to make sure she gets home alright."

"Thank you. Where are we going by the way?"

"If you don't mind I thought we'd go into the city. I have reservations at Entretenir."

"You know I used to work there."

"Yes, I thought it might be fun for you to see some of your old friends."

"Armand might be less than appreciative."

"I talked to him," he replied, "when I made the reservations. He's looking forward to seeing you."

The next hour went by quickly as he drove through the dark countryside, the lights of the distant city becoming increasingly close. She watched him, as his eyes stayed fixed on the road ahead, the lights from the dashboard highlighting his features. "Tell me something about yourself," she said. "Not about Hollywood but before."

He smiled. "What would you like to know?"

"Tell me anything that pops into your head."

David thought for a moment, then said, "When I was a boy," he began, "we lived in Kansas City. I couldn't have been more than five or six. I remember my folks had gone out, to the country club I think. My father was a charming man, everyone loved him, but he drank too much. They were in an accident; my mother was crippled, and he was killed."

"That's horrible, David. I'm so sorry."

"It's OK. I've come to terms with it." He chuckled nervously. "I think I paid for my shrink's yacht coming to terms with what happened." The past began to unfold again for him. "We moved in with my mother's parents on a farm in Kansas not far from the river. They raised me... my grandparents."

"What about your mother?"

His jaw tightened. "She never got over it, his death I mean. It was close to Halloween, I remember that because the corn was drying in the fields. I went to school that day in this cowboy outfit for a costume. I came home from school and knew something was wrong when I went into the house." There was a moment of hesitation before he continued. "They'd found her that afternoon; it was an overdose of pain medication and alcohol."

Laura didn't know what to say; her life as a child was filled with love and family. There'd been tragedy but not to her parents or siblings. Her childhood had been boringly normal. Suddenly he took her hand to reassure her. "It's really OK. After we moved to the farm was the first time I remember beginning to live in stories. I would act them out, playing different characters, dressing up. For years I was more comfortable playing someone else than being myself."

"And now?" she replied.

They were in the city and he stopped the car in front of the restaurant's valet stand. "And now I work on just being me." He grinned. "Let's go. I'm starved."

A young man opened her door and Laura got out pulling her jacket close to hold out the chill. She took David's arm as they went inside and Thomas, the maître d', immediately greeted her with a kiss on each cheek. "Bonsoir, chérie, it has been too long."

"It's good to see you, Thomas. Is Henri working tonight?"

"Oui, Chef," he replied.

"We'll be in the bar for a few moments before we're seated."

Thomas bowed with a nod of his head. "As you wish."

She took David's arm again as he said, "Old home week."

"I tried to warn you." She leaned into him. "This was my home away from home for a long time. It was hard to leave."

He was just about to ask her why when the bartender came around the bar and took her in his arms saying, "Where have you been? I go to the bistro and you are never there."

Laura replied proudly, "I've opened a new restaurant, Henri, in the wine country."

David Steele was used to being the center of attention when he walked into a room and wasn't accustomed to sharing that attention. Still she intrigued him; the people here obviously loved her.

Laura began to introduce the two men when Henri said, "Yes, I've been a big fan, Monsieur Steele. It's good to have you with us. And you've brought such a wonderful surprise. Please"—he gestured with his hand— "join us here at the bar. I've something special for you, Laura."

Henri went back behind the bar taking a bottle of Chardonnay to present to them; "A '95 Domaine d'Auvenay," he said with a grin. "I've been saving it, chérie."

Laura tried the sample he'd poured for her. "It's delicious, Henri. Thank you so much."

Armand Moreau, the owner and head chef of Entretenir, came out of the kitchen making his rounds about the restaurant drifting a little at a time toward them. "Bonsoir, ma douce," he said at last as he kissed each of Laura's cheeks. "The wine is to your liking?"

"Yes, Armand, it's very nice," Laura replied.

His attention shifted to David. "Monsieur Steele, it is a pleasure to have you with us once more."

"The pleasure is all mine, Chef."

"You are too kind, monsieur. But if you could only help me convince this lovely creature to come back to me I would be forever in your debt."

"If you're talking about Laura she has her hands full right now."

Armand put his arm around her. "But you belong with us, chérie. You are the daughter I've always longed for. My best pupil."

She grinned at him. "You are full of shit, Armand. You like me around, so you can spend more time with your mistress."

"That's unfair, chérie, besides Nicole has left me for a bigger fish. He promises her they'll be married." His shoulders shrugged. "How can I possibly compete? My wife would never understand."

"You will never change, Armand. Marie is too good for you."

"Au contraire, chérie, Marie lives as she wishes. I am nothing but a slave to her needs."

Laura took a sip of wine. "You told me once that we're married to what we do. That there wasn't enough room for anyone or anything else in our lives."

"I… know and it is true. Marie is perfect for me n'est-ce pas? She lives as she wishes and I do the same."

"She certainly sounds patient," David said.

Armand raised Laura's hand to his lips and kissed it softly. "This one will break your heart, Monsieur Steele, if you let her. Mine, I'm afraid, will never heal until she comes back to us." Before they could reply he said, "Au revoir. I'll make you something special," and he was off to another table greeting other customers.

"He's a piece of work," David said as he left.

Laura smiled. "Maybe so. But he's a genius in the kitchen."

CHAPTER 16

Elleanore

It was Michael's third birthday and the guests for his party were beginning to arrive. Adrien was in the laboratory testing the sugar content of various wines with a refractometer, keeping his mind busy. Ellie had brought their son to him earlier that morning to wish him well. But, because her husband was at home, the time spent together was short. It felt to him as if he was being torn apart. He'd watched from a distance as Michael grew, wanting to tuck him in at night, to play with him during the day, yet none of that would ever be. He knew it and the pain was becoming unbearable.

Elleanore was dressing Michael in the new outfit she'd bought specially for the day. The three-year-old asked innocently as she helped him into his pants, "Is Adrien coming to my party, Mama?"

A twinge of guilt struck home. "No, sweetheart, he has to work today."

"But I want him to, Mama. Adrien's my friend."

"I know, dear, but he has to work." She tucked in his shirt carefully and fastened the belt. "Maybe we can take a piece of your birthday cake to him later."

"When, Mama?"

Her husband knocked on the door lightly. "The guests are beginning to arrive."

Michael pulled away from his mother and shouted, "Daddy!" running to him with his arms out.

Roger picked him up and held him over his head for a second before kissing him on the cheek. "How's my birthday boy!"

The youngster squirmed out of his arms, held on to his hand, and began to tug him from the room. "Let's go, Daddy… let's go see."

"Slow down, little man," he said as he was pulled along. "We should wait for your mother."

Ellie forced a smile. "I'll be right down. You go ahead." When they were gone she went to the window, looked out toward the winery and the fields beyond. The hurt she felt was seated deep within her; she could feel her lover slipping away and was too big a coward to do anything about it. There was no sign of him among the vines and she couldn't help but wonder where he was, what he was doing now.

Sofia knocked lightly on the door. "Senor Strickland ask for you."

"I'll be down in a minute." As the housekeeper was about to leave Ellie stopped her. "Sofia."

"Sí, senora."

"Would you see if he's alright? As soon as you can get away."

"I will, senora."

Adrien had given up trying to work; he opened a nice bottle of Cabernet instead and had already drunk most of it. He was in the winery on the second floor, where he'd lived once when he first began working at the vineyard. And where he'd made love to Elleanore for the first time. He could hear Sofia below calling his name and went to the top of the stairs holding on to the railing for support. "I'm up here!"

Sofia climbed the stairs slightly out of breath. "It's been a long time since I come here."

"That's right," he said, his words slurred. "I forgot they put you up here once as well." He stumbled his way back toward the table and the bottle that was upon it. "I'm celebrating the birth of my son. Would you care to join me?" He held up the bottle that was nearly empty, grinned, and waved his arms about the room. "We have more."

She tried taking it from him, but he turned away, pouring the remainder into his glass. Sofia pleaded with him, "Por favor, Adrien. This is not the way."

He had trouble maintaining his balance and sat on the edge of the table. "And what way is there for me, Sofia?"

"I don't know, mi amigo, but this is not it."

He put his arm about her waist and pulled her close. "Maybe this is a better way," and his lips met hers.

Sofia pulled away from him. "Senora Strickland ask me come here."

Adrien snickered. "And we all do as Senora Strickland wishes."

"Sí, Adrien… we do. Until we choose differently."

He slumped down into a chair, covering his face with his hands. "I can't leave or stay?"

It didn't seem appropriate for her to point out that one or the other was not the only option for him. Sofia's loyalty to her mistress and to him prevented it. She was caught in the middle and continued to walk that delicate balance between. Neither Elleanore nor Adrien knew that she was in love with him. In the beginning Sofia thought her feelings were nothing more than sympathetic attachment but one day the reality of her attraction grabbed hold of her. And its grip held fast to her heart.

She watched as he nodded off in the chair. It was too far to the cottage for her to help him get there. But there was still the bed in the other room. Sofia shook him awake and put his arm around her neck. "Help me, Adrien." With her assistance he struggled to his feet while she guided him into the other room and sat him down upon the bed.

"Tu es une merveilleuse, Sofia," he mumbled. "You should get out of here, get married, have babies." When she turned to leave he grabbed her hand. "Merci, mon ami." His eyes closed again, and his hand fell away from hers. "Kiss my little boy for me."

Tears started to form as she made her way down the stairs and began walking back to the house. Sofia wiped them away quickly as she went in the back door, hearing the family and guests singing "Happy Birthday" to Michael. She watched from a distance as the boy blew the candles out and his mother sliced the first piece of cake.

She cared for Elleanore, feelings that ran deeper than employer and employee; they'd become close friends. Sofia helped serve dessert and coffee to the guests and when she'd finished she stood off again to the side, catching sight of Abigail Strickland staring back at her. What, she wondered, was the old lady thinking?

Ellie brought Sofia a slice of cake and whispered, "Did you find him? Michael wants to see him."

Lies didn't come easily to her. "I look but no, senora."

An expression of sadness came over her mistress as she replied, "Thank you for trying."

Sleep didn't come easily to Ellie that night; thoughts of him nagged at her conscience. She was too weak to let him go, but life without him was unimaginable to her. Roger's breathing as he lay next to her was heavy. She left their bed quietly, put on her robe, and checked on the children before going downstairs. Sofia was in the kitchen having a cup of tea. Ellie said quietly, "I couldn't sleep."

Sofia nodded. "Yo tambien, senora. Would you like some tea?"

"That would be nice," she replied.

Quietly the young woman stood and turned on the burner under the kettle. "I lie to you today," Sofia confessed.

"About what?"

"I find Adrien like you ask me to. He had much wine and I think it will upset you if I say."

Elleanore suspected it was something like that; Sofia lacked the necessary talent for lying. Her sense of integrity didn't allow for it. "I'm sorry," she said, "that you were put in that position. It wasn't fair of me."

Sofia was leaning against the stove waiting for the water to boil as Ellie took a seat at the table. "He is"—she fought to find the right word— "destruyendo a sí mismo senora. He ruins himself for you I think."

The truth of her words hurt but there was no anger or blame she felt because of it. Sofia was her friend, perhaps her only one, and if she couldn't accept the truth from her, how could she deal with it from anyone else? "I don't know what to do, Sofia. Life without him would be empty for me."

She put the boiling water into a cup with the tea bag and set it on the table beside Elleanore. "It is not, senora you have your babies. But he is alone."

Ellie could see the wisdom within her friend's words but didn't really believe it. She knew that her children would grow, they would leave, and she would be left alone with a man she didn't love. It was an outcome that to her seemed unavoidable. She felt trapped. Elleanore gazed into her friend's eyes. "You care for him a great deal, don't you?"

"Sí, senora, as I do for you."

The tea continued to steep as they sat next to one another silently. Ellie picked up her spoon, put the draining tea bag into it, and wrapped the string holding it about the spoon to drain the last drops into her cup. She set the spoon with the bag aside. "What should I do?"

"I don't know, senora. He must choose." She hesitated briefly before saying quietly, "I think maybe he has senora and that is why he drinks too much wine."

The thought took Ellie by surprise. "You think he's going to leave."

Sofia lowered her head and whispered, "Sí, senora."

It was a Sunday the following day; Ellie slept late. Roger was reading the paper and having breakfast when she came downstairs. She kissed him on the cheek. "I'm not feeling well. Would you mind terribly taking the children to church without me?"

He set down his paper, looking at her over the top of his glasses. "Are you alright?"

"Yes, just tired. It's probably nothing more than a virus; I'm sure I'll feel better by tomorrow."

"What about Michael?" He grinned. "I'm not sure I can handle him without you."

She hadn't thought of that; the three-year-old could be unmanageable in church. "You'll have to leave him with me I suppose," she said.

He looked at her curiously. "You're acting very strange this morning. Maybe you should see someone."

"I'm just tired, Roger," she replied emphatically. Ellie felt her eyes begin to fill with tears and not wanting to let him see her cry she left. Panic was beginning to take hold; she wanted to see Adrien, to be reassured, to ease the fear that was beginning to take control of her. She went to the kitchen and asked the cook, "Have you seen Sofia this morning?"

"No, senora. I think maybe she go to mass."

After Roger and the two older children had gone she took Michael by the hand and went to find Adrien. They walked down the hill past the vines, through the stand of oaks, to the cottage where he stayed.

Adrien had slept in the winery until past midnight, waking up with a splitting headache. He made his way back to the cottage but couldn't get back to sleep until almost dawn. Remembering bits of what he'd said and done with Sofia the previous afternoon made him feel foolish and ashamed. His entire life had been spent with one purpose in mind until meeting Elleanore; everything changed after that. He was, he believed, off course, adrift, and needed to right himself before it was too late.

This was the pattern of his thoughts when he answered the door to see Elleanore and Michael standing there. He gazed into her eyes and then said to Michael with a smile, "This is a wonderful surprise."

"May we come in," Ellie said softly.

"Oui, Elleanore, please. How was your birthday, Michael?"

The little boy began to quickly rattle off all the high points of the day before, what he'd received as gifts, and ended by saying, "I wanted you to come but Mama said you were working."

"I'm sorry I wasn't there. Your birthday is a special day."

The small space seemed confining to her. "Could we take a walk?"

"Oui, Elleanore." He grabbed his coat and battered fedora from the rack by the door and taking Michael's hand said, "Let's go see what we can see."

There couldn't be any sign of intimacy between them now that Michael was old enough to repeat or misread something he'd seen. Consequently, they walked together, avoiding contact, Michael walking between them holding each of their hands.

When they were in the trees, safe from prying eyes, she let go of her son saying, "Michael, go and play for a few minutes." Once she couldn't be overheard Ellie came right to the point. "Sofia told me she thinks you might leave. Is that true?"

He hadn't confided his thoughts to anyone and was surprised that Sofia was able to read him that well. "I have to think about it, chérie. This is half a life we live."

She knew she'd sound desperate but said the words anyway. "Better half a life, my love, than none at all."

"I am outside looking in, chérie, and you are inside looking out. The distance between grows with time. You must see that."

"Any part of you, any time with you, is better than nothing at all. You know that, Adrien." The silence from him that followed was enough for her to know that Sofia had been right.

As they followed him, Michael had made his way to the old oak where the swing that Adrien had put up for the children, hung. The boy turned and shouted back to them, "Push me, Adrien. Please push me."

Adrien lifted his son into the wooden seat. "Hold on tight to the rope, Michael," he cautioned as he gave the boy a gentle push. "That's a good boy."

Michael was giggling and shouted, "Higher, higher!"

He pushed a little harder, his eyes fixed on the boy, ready to act if need be, yet calling out to him, "You're a brave boy, Michael."

Jane started to feel ill in church and Roger left with the children before the sermon began. He wanted to return home as quickly as possible believing that his daughter had the same virus that her mother had. But once he'd turned off the highway toward the house he saw them from a distance. It was a vision anyone would mistake as a family outing, two parents playing with their child. He stopped the car and watched briefly until their son said, "Look there's Mama. She must be feeling better."

"Yes," Roger said, "she must be."

Later that night after the children were asleep and she'd checked on Jane for the last time Ellie came into the bedroom where her husband was in bed going over his company's financial report for the last quarter. As his wife began to undress he asked, "Is Jane alright?"

"She's sleeping soundly. I think it was too much cake yesterday more than anything else." Ellie started to brush out her hair. "But I'll keep an eye on her tomorrow."

"I saw you today with Adrien," he said.

"Jane told me," she replied. "I was taking Michael for a walk and we ran into him."

"How is he?"

"Fine I think." She went into the bathroom and began taking off her makeup while Roger went back to the reports he'd been reading earlier.

A few moments later when she came to bed, he took off his glasses, set his paperwork on the nightstand, and turned the bedside lamp off. She quickly gave him a kiss goodnight and rolled onto her side away from him. He lay there a moment in the silence of the dark before saying quietly, "I love you."

Her eyes opened suddenly, only to feel the pain from the lies between them. There was nothing left for her but the effort it took to be silent.

CHAPTER 17

Alex

"I like living with her," Alex said to Reina as the two of them sat in the bar after closing to have a drink.

She chuckled. "I bet you do."

"It's not like that. We're just friends." He changed the subject abruptly before she could respond. "Have you heard from Daniel?"

"No." She took the last swallow of the margarita Alex had made for her and held up her glass saying, "More please."

He went back behind the bar and began making her drink. "I'm sorry about that."

"Me too. But he told me what he was about from the beginning. I just didn't listen."

"He's a prick," Alex replied while shaking the contents before pouring it into her glass. "But I liked him."

Reina sighed. "Me too."

"You know what they say about falling off a horse."

She looked him in the eye and replied softly, "You get back on."

His face was inches away from hers. "That's right."

"Do you have anyone in mind?" she whispered. He leaned toward her; his kiss was sweet, the taste of tequila, salt, and a trace of lime lingering on her lips. "That was nice."

Alex came back around to where she was sitting, slipped his arms through hers, pulling her close. "I don't want nice." And he kissed her again, intensely this time. He heard her moan as his tongue entered her mouth, his hands exploring her body. Each kiss building to the next, his leg was between hers rubbing softly, their breathing increasingly labored as the moments passed. "I want you."

"My parents are upstairs," Reina replied with a husky whisper.

"We'll go to my place," he said kissing her again.

"Isabella."

Alex groaned. "This is a hotel, there has to be an empty room somewhere."

The moment was lost; she pulled herself away from him. "It's probably not a great idea anyway. We're friends and I don't want to lose that for a night both of us might regret."

He gently brushed a lock of hair from her eyes. "Speak for yourself."

Reina stood and kissed him once more quickly. "I'm going to bed, my bed… alone." She kissed him again. "I like you a lot, Alex."

He watched as she walked away thinking how close they'd come, how close he'd been to being with her. It was worth it, to gamble on their friendship for the chance of something more. That's what he told himself as he slipped on his jacket, took the keys from his pocket and headed toward the parking lot.

Isabella was asleep on the sofa with the television on when he walked in the front door. He turned off the set and gently shook her. "Heh, it's time to go to bed."

She opened her eyes sleepily and smiled at him. "I left some supper for you."

"Gracias, Izzy." Alex was tired and frustrated from his experience with Reina. He stripped his jacket off, dropped it over the back of a chair, and went to the kitchen to see what she'd left for him. There was a covered plate of chicken enchiladas in the oven. "I'm starved," he said as he grabbed a fork from the drawer and dug into the plate of food, still standing by the countertop.

She stretched sleepily, stood, and picked up his jacket to hang it in the closet. "How was your shift tonight?"

"We had a good crowd. It gets better all the time." He took another bite and studied her thinking that without makeup and her hair pulled back Isabella looked like the little girl that she'd been a few years before. "These are good. You should ask Laura about putting them on the menu."

"It's my Aunt Rosa's recipe."

He set his plate in the sink and ran water over the top. "I'm going to bed. It's late and you should too."

"You are not my father, Alex," she replied suddenly impatient. "I'm tired of you treating me like a child."

The sudden burst of emotion from her surprised him. Izzy was quiet and reserved as a rule, a person who showed very little of what she felt or thought. He asked innocently, "What is it?"

She shook her head. "You are such a fool. Me voy a la cama." And with that Izzy walked away to go to her bedroom leaving him by himself wondering what on earth got into her.

Isabella had watched him for months flirting with Reina, first at the bistro and now, every time she came to St. Helena. It hurt and disappointed Izzy. At first when he asked her to come here she thought that there might be a chance for her, that he might see how much she loved him. But Alex was blind to anyone but Reina. She knew that tonight, when he came home late, knowing that he'd been with her; Izzy could smell her on him.

The next morning, Laura went to the markets before going to the bistro for a meeting with Shelly. Alex slept in and by the time he was awake Izzy had already gone to work. Her harsh words still bothered him, and he couldn't stop thinking about them. What did she mean when she said he was a fool?

After his shower, he dressed and left the house to have breakfast at the hotel where he could get a decent coffee and some of Isabella's chilaquiles. She made them with green sauce and put a fried egg on top with asiago cheese.

It was almost eleven by the time he walked into the kitchen and the staff was busy with a late breakfast crowd in the dining room. Izzy didn't look at him when he came in.

One of the equipment additions Laura insisted on during the remodel was a new espresso machine. Alex was addicted to decent coffee in the morning and preferred making his own. He noticed that the staff started picking up the pace once he arrived. They knew that Laura was gone, but Alex was her assistant and their level of concern increased. He took his coffee and sat in a corner booth, out of the way to watch.

The waitress in his section was a new girl named Angie; she was a pleasant enough local girl who still lived in Napa with her parents. As soon as he sat down she was in front of him asking nervously, "Would you like something to eat, sir?"

"I'd like Izzy to make me her chilaquiles, over medium on the eggs and, Angie, you can call me Alex."

"Yes, sir, I mean Alex, yes sir," she replied. "I'll be right back." And with that she scurried off into the kitchen.

She wasn't kidding. A moment later she was back saying, "Isabella says they aren't on the menu."

"I know they're not on the menu, Angie," he said impatiently. "She makes them for me all the time."

The girl was trembling now. "I'm sorry, sir."

He slid out of the booth and stomped toward the kitchen walking directly up to Isabella. "In the office now, por favor."

As he started to walk away Izzy said without emotion. "I'm busy now."

"Carlos," he said emphatically to the prep cook, "relieve Isabella for a moment."

"Sí, Chef," he replied.

She followed him to the office, getting madder by the minute, saying rapidly as she went, "Sí el piensa que voy a saltar en cuaiquier momento que dice saltar el hombre es una locura!" When she entered the office, he was already sitting as she slammed the door. "If this is about not cooking the breakfast you want I don't have time this morning. It's busy. Laura's not here."

He was frustrated. What could he say? She was right, they were busy, and neither manager had been there. But he sensed it was something more than that. He pointed to the chair opposite him. "Please sit."

"I would rather stand."

"OK then, why am I a fool?"

Izzy's emotions shifted from anger to the sadness she felt because he preferred Reina over her. She wiped a tear away quickly. "You chase a woman who cares nothing for you."

He didn't know exactly what he expected her to say but this took him by surprise. "My life and what I choose to do outside of work is my business, Isabella. You are acting like a jealous woman."

She looked down at him defiantly. "Sí, sí, I am a woman. But you treat me like a child or your little pet. I make my own way here from Merida. It is long way. But I know I can do this thing. You and Laura help me, and I say to you gracias, but I don't need you. I can take care of myself." When he didn't reply she said, "I go back to work now."

With his elbows on the table, Alex ran his fingers through his hair and sighed. "Go on then." She turned and left; when he was alone he realized that unknowingly he'd broken one of Laura's basic rules. He'd become emotionally involved with someone he worked with and it had become a problem. Alex knew he was walking the line with Reina, but she wasn't the problem. It was Izzy. And somehow, he had to make it right again.

Laura had driven into the city the night before and slept at home for the first time in weeks. Reina, she noticed, had been taking good care of the place. Early the next morning she went to the fish and vegetable markets to shop for both restaurants. Afterward she arrived at the bistro just as Shelly was opening; the two of them had a meeting scheduled that morning. It was after one by the time she was finished and on her way back to St. Helena.

The kitchen was busy preparing for the evening menu. She greeted everyone pleasantly before heading to the office to put away her things. Alex followed her and shut the door. When she heard it click, she thought, she'd been away less than twenty-four hours and something had already gone wrong. Laura sat down behind her desk. "What is it?"

He didn't know where to start and said instead, "How did everything go?"

"Fine," Laura replied, "but you're avoiding my question."

Alex nodded, leaning back against the door with his hands in his pockets. "I think I've screwed up."

It had been a long day; she'd been up since four and was still tired from the drive. "Tell me what's going on."

"Isabella is mad at me."

"Why?"

"When I gave her a place to stay I thought I was being nice. Shelly told me weeks ago that Izzy was attracted to me and I didn't listen. I thought at the very most it was a crush. But I think it's more than that."

"What are you going to do?"

He'd begun to pace. "I don't know. I like Izzy a lot and the last thing I'd do is hurt her intentionally."

Laura was impatiently blunt. "Fix it. Talk to her and work it out. I don't want to lose her. And Alex, find somewhere else for her to stay." She stood up and started putting on her chef's jacket. "Let's get to work."

It was a little after eleven when Alex returned to the house; it was dark and silent inside. Izzy's door was shut, her light was off, and there was no supper waiting for him in the oven. There was a newspaper open on the table they used for meals. It was the classified section with three different apartments for rent circled in pen. She was right, he thought, he was a fool.

During the next two days he tried talking to her privately but there was no time in the morning because of his trips into the city. He worked in the restaurant's kitchen at night and she was always in her room by the time he returned home. Finally, he wrote her a note and left it on the bathroom mirror where she would be sure to see it.

Dear Isabella,

I'm sorry I've disappointed you. I've been inconsiderate and would like to talk this out with you. Please give me a chance.

Sincerely, Alex

The following day he was scheduled to be off. Isabella usually was home by three in the afternoon; Alex waited for her. When she walked in the door he was watching a soccer match on television, he sat up, and immediately turned it off. Before she could speak he asked, "Can we talk?"

She put down her purse and hung up her coat. "Sí." Izzy sat down on the edge of the couch beside him, waiting to hear what he wanted to say. Now that he had the opportunity, Alex wasn't sure how to start and she became impatient. "You want to talk so talk. I listen."

"You're right I have been foolish."

She interrupted him. "Sí!"

He took a deep breath. "I like you very much and I haven't done a very good job considering your feelings. When you first moved up here I planned to help you find your own place. But we were getting along so well together I didn't see the harm in you staying here. That was wrong of me. I'm your boss and it's something I shouldn't have done."

"Laura is my boss," she replied stubbornly.

That was a point he didn't want to argue. "Yes, that's true." He paused. "I hope that you will forgive me, and we can be friends again."

"Is that all you say?"

"Yes, except I can't imagine how hard it was for you to come here to the United States. I was born here but my folks immigrated, and they've told me stories. You've never told me about your family or why you came here alone. But I'm sure you have your reasons. I think you are very brave."

She became flustered and started to blush, saying quickly, "I go now to take a bath." Izzy stood and turned the television back on. "Brazil will win this match I think." And in the next moment she'd left the room.

A few minutes later he heard the water begin to run in the bathroom, Brazil scored, and time ran out. He turned off the set, grabbed a beer from the refrigerator, and went out the back door to sit and think. He thought of Reina and of Isabella. Izzy was younger by several years but more mature in many ways; Alex guessed that she had to be.

Reina had been protected her entire life, by those she loved and by the society in which she lived. She was in her late twenties and living on her own for the first time. He was attracted to her, he wanted her, but Alex seriously wondered if there ever could be any more than that between them.

Izzy was so much different; she'd probably been born an old soul. She wasn't the kind of woman you played games with, she was the type you married or left alone.

The bathroom window was no more than twenty feet away from where he was sitting; Alex could hear her singing something quietly in Spanish that he remembered from his childhood. For a brief moment his mind imagined her there in the tub, her long dark hair up off her shoulders and tiny frame slick with moisture.

CHAPTER 18

Laura

She lay in her bed next to him, content, with his arms about her. David was a patient and thoughtful lover. When she'd come back to the cottage after her trip to the city he was waiting for her on the porch with flowers. It was late, the day had been unbearably long and all she wanted was to climb into bed and sleep; that's when she saw him sitting there on the porch in the moonlight. Laura reached out her hand to take his and led him inside. He started to speak, and she held a finger to his lips. "Shh."

It was first light when she awoke to feel the warmth of him next to her. She was already late for work but in spite of it Laura stayed in bed listening to the soft rhythm of his breath. She gently stroked him until he began to respond then took him in her mouth for a few moments before mounting him. She rode him slowly at first, languishing in the feel of him inside but soon the pace quickened until both of them shook with release. Laura smiled down at him. "Good morning."

His hands still cupped her buttocks. "That was a pleasant surprise."

"For me too." She swung her leg off of him and got out of bed. "But I'm late for work."

"So you're kicking me out."

She called back as she turned on the shower. "You can join me in here."

The tension between Isabella and Alex had lingered for several days; the young woman's mood made it much more difficult. But Laura refused to intervene. She believed it was important for both of them to work it out on their own. If she became involved it could make matters worse. Then later that week Izzy came to work smiling and the kitchen became peaceful once more.

Seeing David became a daily occurrence. He never bothered Laura at work but came for supper occasionally. They spent most of their nights together but always at the cottage. It was close to her work, within walking distance and she was comfortable there. On her days off they would go out together, to dinner, a wine tasting, and sometimes a movie.

She asked him once if he missed it, being in motion pictures, and he said, "Sometimes. But films are changing and it's hard to find a decent script."

"Do you still get offers?"

"Occasionally but not as often as I used to." He hesitated a moment. "There was a film in the '30s, a black-and-white called *Sullivan's Travels* with Joel McCrea. It was about this film director who wanted to make a serious movie about the downtrodden during the Depression. His journey led to the realization that laughter and joy can do more for people than describing problems they're already aware of." He snickered as he said, "I think that sometimes Hollywood takes itself too seriously and tends to forget that."

"What kind of movies would you make if you could?"

"That's simple—comedy, romantic comedy. But critics, God help them, are unmercifully cruel to comedies."

She chuckled. "I came very close to asking if critics and awards really matter. And yet I get so frustrated because we're never reviewed by the San Francisco papers. They don't know we exist."

"Maybe you should think about a decent PR person."

"Maybe," she replied.

The first time he invited her to his home for dinner she was amazed. The glass, wood, and stone structure had aged well over the years. There was an element of an era gone by that remained but like a beautiful painting or sculpture, the beauty was timeless. The only structural change he'd made since the Stricklands left was a walled-in patio and gardens in the back of the house.

It was his retreat, a refuge from the outside world. "This is beautiful," she said to him and meant it. But she thought it was a little sad as well, for him to live here in this big house by himself. There was no life to it; it was like living in a museum.

They had dinner on the patio by candlelight. A small, middle-aged Asian man served each of them a glass of Chardonnay. And as the wine was being poured David said, "Laura, this is Tuan."

The servant bowed slightly. "Enjoy please, miss."

"We've been together a long time haven't we, Tuan?"

"Yes, boss, long time together."

Laura smiled and held her hand out to him. "It's very nice to meet you, Tuan."

He took her hand and smiled back. "Yes, miss… you are first guest in long time." With that said, he bowed to her once more, set the wine in a bucket of ice and left as quietly as he'd come.

"We are both refugees," David said. "Tuan is from Vietnam and came here right after the war."

She took a sip of wine, then asked, "And you?"

David ran his index finger along the rim of his glass. "I've fled from the past… Hollywood and my wife." Before Laura had time to ask he added, "She left me for my best friend at the time; that was fifteen years ago. I was shooting a film on location in South America. When I got back she was gone."

"Were you married long?"

He shook his head. "A couple of years. She was an extra on a picture I was working on and we got to know one another. I wanted a family and Alice, that was her name, wanted a career."

"Did she get what she wanted?"

David laughed. "She had no talent. There were a few bit parts but that was all."

Tuan brought each of them a salad, quietly, efficiently, and was gone. Laura changed the subject. "My cousin was married to a woman from Vietnam. They met while he was stationed there."

"Did it work out?"

"He was killed but she came to the United States with their son and lived with my grandparents for several years. Her son and I were very close to the same age."

David asked suddenly, "Haven't you ever wanted to consider marriage?"

She finished a bite, wiped her mouth with a linen napkin, and placed it carefully back into her lap. "I almost took the leap a few years ago."

"What happened?"

She smiled. "A difference of opinion."

"How about children?"

"I'm not sure it would be such a good idea. My hours are long. It can be tough on a family."

"But you'd consider it," he replied and took a bite.

"It would have to be the right situation with the right man."

He nodded and grinned. "So that's a yes?"

"That's a maybe. My parents met in high school and are still happily married after thirty-some years. If I ever take the leap, that's the way I'd want it to be. But it just doesn't seem like it works out that way anymore."

The plates were cleared, and the main course served; Tuan refreshed their wine and asked, "Anything else, boss."

"No, Tuan, thank you."

"I be in kitchen if you want me."

Laura picked up the chopsticks next to her fork, carefully took a bite of what appeared to be whitefish cut into small pieces and seared to a crisp crust on the outside. The taste took her by surprise and she quickly reached for the glass of water next to her. "It's hot!"

He chuckled. "That's the jalapeno peppers and cilantro. Tuan is an exceptional cook, but he does have a tendency to get carried away. You might try it with some rice."

When they were finished, and while Tuan was clearing the table, they moved inside for an after-dinner drink in the living room. There was a slight chill in the air and Tuan had thoughtfully started a fire in the fireplace. David was standing next to it while she sat not far away on the sofa; he turned to her and said, "I'd like you to stay tonight."

"I have to work tomorrow."

"We can get up early."

She stood and walked up to him, putting her arms around his waist. "I know it sounds silly. But spending the night here, with you, seems like a big step for me. I'm not sure whether or not I'm ready for where that might lead."

David didn't really understand the difference but understood that for her there was one. He nodded. "The offer is always open."

Laura kissed him. "Thank you."

"Come on, I'll give you a ride home."

"It's a nice night; we could walk."

He smiled. "I'll get your coat."

They didn't say much on the way to the cottage. David seemed thoughtful as they strolled along, and Laura finally said, "A penny for your thoughts."

He was holding her hand, brought it to his lips and kissed it gently. "I was thinking about how difficult relationships are. It's been a long time since I've dated anyone more than once or twice and the only thing I know is it doesn't seem to get any easier. If anything, it gets harder the older you get."

"I suppose you're right," she replied. "But don't you think it's worth the journey? All the getting to know one another, the learning how to trust and open up to another human being again."

David nodded silently, then after a moment said, "I like you very much, Laura. But I don't think that you want to get serious with anyone right now."

"Are you saying that you're serious about me?"

"I'm not sure I can be any other way." He shrugged and put his arm around her. "I think what I'm trying to say is that until you're ready it might be best for us to have some time away from one another to think."

She stopped and turned to look at him. "You're saying it's all or nothing."

"I'm saying that casual relationships aren't what I'm looking for. I've had my fill of that lifestyle and know that in the end it's not worth it."

"I don't think of you as something casual, David."

"But you don't think of me as something more than that either."

Laura was getting frustrated. "I'm not saying that. Are you intentionally trying to be a pain in the ass tonight?"

"I'm trying to let you know how I feel. Your problem is you want to control every situation and that's an impossibility. That's why you're more comfortable in that cottage or at work. It's your territory. You refuse to move beyond your comfort zone."

She could feel the anger begin to rise, tried her best to control it but suddenly exploded. "You're a great one to talk to me about comfort zones, hiding away here, separating yourself from the outside world. At least I get out there and try. Sure, I might be cautious about relationships, about learning to trust again but you weren't dumped by a fiancé the day before your wedding and I was. And," Laura began as she started to stomp away, "and what's wrong with being able to control something you're good at? I am disciplined enough to control my situation because that's what it takes to be great at what I do." She began to walk away again, stopped, and turned back. "I'll find the rest of the way home. I can do that by myself as well."

She left him there by himself standing in the moonlight wondering just when he lost control of the conversation. David shook his head and smiled, whispering to himself among the vines, "Wow."

Her mind was agitated to such an extent that sleep became impossible. She tossed and turned, justifying in her mind all that she'd said to him, then doubting herself, wondering if there was truth to what he'd said. Maybe she was a control freak, maybe she wasn't any good at relationships because relationships were uncontrollable. She pounded her fist into the pillow twice, then fluffed it, before laying her head down again. A thought came to her suddenly. Maybe, this wasn't about her at all; maybe this was just his way of breaking it off and shifting the blame to her. Laura finally fell asleep just before three; her alarm went off at five.

When her boss came to work the next day, Izzy could tell something was wrong. But it was a busy morning and she quickly forgot about it until later when Laura snapped at her. Izzy was concerned enough that when Alex came to work later that day she mentioned it to him. "I don't know what it is," she told him, "she yell at me for no reason."

It wasn't like Laura. Izzy might just be oversensitive, Alex thought, but still he felt it was important enough to find out. He went to her office and knocked. "Hola, Chef."

She asked abruptly, "Did you get everything we need for the menu tonight?"

"They had some nice black cod that I picked up."

The last thing in the world she wanted to discuss was whitefish. Laura looked up at him from her desk and said impatiently, "Well, is there anything else? If not, get to work."

He came in and shut the door quietly. "Izzy says that you yelled at her."

"I didn't yell at her for heaven's sake!"

Alex tried his best to remain calm. "That was her impression."

Her focus returned to the computer as she replied irritably, "We both know she gets overemotional."

Alex sat down across from her. "What's going on?"

"Nothing," she said with a sigh, exasperated. "Can't I simply be in a bad mood once every couple of years without the rest of you feeling injured?"

"We've worked together a long time, Laura. You're my friend and I'm just concerned."

"Well stop being so concerned and get to work. We have a lot to do before tonight."

He stood up. "Yes, Chef."

When he'd gone she shut the door and wiped a tear away. "I can do this," she said to herself. But thoughts of David, of what he'd said to her, and how she responded simply wouldn't clear her mind. And she was too exhausted to fight it.

Later that night when everyone had gone home, she turned off the lights and began her walk back to the cottage, through the stand of oaks. But he wasn't there waiting for her, the house was dark, and she knew that once again she'd pushed away someone she cared for.

CHAPTER 19

Elleanore

She made her way slowly down the path, through the stand of trees, with the memory book clutched tightly to her breast. Elleanore knew that Laura took Mondays off and in the last few weeks she'd been going into the city to spend the night there. She suspected it was because of David; he hadn't been around in weeks either. But she knew that Laura was at the cottage today. She was sure of it because she asked Alex.

During the last month Laura had put off cleaning the house in St. Helena so many times that there wasn't any other choice but to dig in and get the job done. She was working on her second load of laundry and scrubbing the kitchen floor when she heard a knock. It was Elleanore.

The old lady smiled cheerily. "Good morning, Laura." She began moving through the door saying, "Do you mind if I come in?"

Laura simply took a deep breath and replied, "No… that's quite alright. I'm just catching up on housework."

"My, my," Ellie replied as she looked about the living room, "you certainly have your hands full."

"I'm afraid I've put it off too long."

"It's understandable, dear. You're very busy. I could have one of the girls who work in housekeeping come over if you'd like."

Laura wasn't in any mood for idle chitchat, but she liked Elleanore. "Is there something I can do for you?"

Ellie went into the living room and sat on the sofa, holding the book in her lap. "A cup of coffee or possibly some tea would be nice if you have it. But don't go to any trouble."

"It's no trouble." And yet it did trouble her. All she wanted to do was finish an unpleasant task and the last thing she wanted to do was entertain. "I'll put on some coffee," she said with a muffled sigh and strained smile.

A few moments later she came back and sat next to Ellie. "It'll only take a few more minutes."

She smiled. "I'm in no hurry, dear."

Laura pointed to the book. "What's that you're holding?"

The old lady chuckled. "I almost forgot. That's the reason I came." She opened it slowly and said quietly, "Come a little closer. I want you to see. This is my memory book"—she chuckled again— "but not all of them I hope."

Most of the photographs in the front were old black-and-white snapshots. Ellie pointed out pictures of herself at various ages, some of her parents, all taken at some time during the '30s and '40s. "I was very happy then," she said smiling, "but spoiled I'm afraid."

There were ticket stubs from a Gene Krupa and Anita O'Day concert she'd gone to on her sixteenth birthday, a program from her high school graduation, and a newspaper announcement of her marriage to Roger Strickland. She ran her fingers across her wedding picture. "It's hard to believe I was that young and silly once." She gazed into Laura's eyes. "I thought he was my Prince Charming, you see. But he wasn't. Roger was just a man."

"You were a beautiful bride." There was a photo of a rather stern older woman dressed all in black. "Who's that?" Laura asked as she pointed.

Ellie frowned. "Roger's mother, Abigail, Sonny and Jane's grandmother."

"And Michael's."

"Oh no, Laura," she replied amused at the thought of it. "not Michael."

Laura was taken aback for a second. "Why not Michael, Elleanore?"

The question was ignored. "It smells like the coffee's done, dear."

"Do you like anything in it?"

"A little cream and sugar, dear, but not with any of those phony sugars with all the chemicals. They're bitter."

She fixed each of them a cup and put two of Tony Morello's day-old croissants into the microwave. Laura carried everything on a tray, setting it on the coffee table. "Here we are."

"You shouldn't have gone to all this trouble," Elleanore said graciously.

Laura wasn't quite sure what choice she had but she took a sip of the coffee and a bite of croissant, suddenly realizing this was the first thing she'd had to eat all day.

Most of the photographs changed from black and white to color Polaroid snapshots of Ellie's first two children taken in the city before the move to St. Helena. Everyone in the family looked stiff, always formal, in those images, including the children. Ellie turned the page and there was a photo of the cottage. She smiled. "That was the day we moved here. I never went back to the city afterward."

"Who's that?" Laura asked while taking another bite.

"Sofia," she said, and her eyes began to well up. "She worked for us"—her fingertips traced the edges of the photo— "but she was much more than that to me. We were very close friends."

"And the man standing next to her. Who is he?"

The old lady wiped a silent tear away. "Adrien… he was the vintner."

There were several more photos of the family and several of Adrien Forche, some with the two oldest children and one where he was sitting on the steps of the cottage next to Elleanore. They seemed very happy, and Laura noticed that it looked like their hands were touching. The dried remains of a wildflower lay pressed beside the photo.

She turned the page and there was a picture of Elleanore holding a baby, standing next to her husband with Sonny and Jane in front of them. Laura said, "That's David's house on the hill and you must be holding Michael."

She nodded. "We moved in a few months before he was born. Everything changed after that. Not right away of course. Roger began spending more time at home with the family and less time in the city.

The simpler times, here, were over." She turned her head to look at Laura. "The happiest days of my life were spent right here, in this cottage. I've never told that to another soul. But it's true."

The rest of the book showed Elleanore pregnant with their youngest child, Adriana, next to various shots of her brothers and sister. The photographs eventually showed Adriana as a beautiful little girl, with dark hair, almost black, with milk-white skin and dark eyes. She looked nothing like her brothers and sister. There were several more photos of the children as they grew but few of Elleanore or Roger and none of them together.

Laura felt compelled to ask, "Why did you come here today, Ellie?"

The old lady appeared surprised and shut the book. "I didn't want you to make the same mistake I did."

"What mistake is that?"

Elleanore reached out and took Laura's hand. "Love… true love, is hard to find, dear. When we do find it, it's important to have the courage to hang on with all our strength. I didn't have that kind of strength, the faith and trust to believe in it enough." She was beginning to cry. "And then it's over and there is nothing in the world that will help you get it back."

The easiest thing for Laura to believe was that Ellie was simply an elderly lady who was reliving the past, reliving her regrets whatever they might be. But instead she asked, "Why are you telling me this?"

Her reply was simple and to the point. "David loves you, dear. And I think that you love him." She squeezed her hand. "Don't push love from your heart, Laura… hold on to it!"

"Whatever would make you think that David Steele loves me?"

"I'm old, Laura, not blind. It's the way he looks at you and the way you look at him when he talks to you."

Laura hadn't realized that the time she'd spent with David was so carefully observed. She'd intentionally kept their moments spent together private. But apparently not private enough. She pulled her hand away from Ellie. "How many other people are talking about this, about David and me?"

Elleanore shrugged and chuckled a little. "How would I know that? Most folks are so busy paying attention to themselves, they don't have the time to pay attention to what's going on right under their nose."

"And you do have the time."

"Well, dear, yes I do. There's not any real trick to it. I'm not a busybody or anything like that; I don't gossip. It's simply a matter of paying attention to those you care about."

It was impossible for Laura to be mad at Ellie, she liked her too much. Besides she knew that her intentions were sincere. "Listen, Ellie, I don't have the time to be in love. I'm certainly not sure how I feel about David or how he feels about me. Maybe we can be friends again but that's up to him. I can't be something more to him than I'm ready for."

Elleanore laughed. "You make love sound like a bus schedule, dear. It's not, believe me. I was like you once, thinking that there were so many things more important than the love I felt. There isn't. And all that remains afterward are the memories and the thoughts of what life might have been like if you'd done it differently." She reached out and squeezed Laura's hand again. "A life of regret is a hard pill to swallow."

"What do you possibly have to regret? You have a wonderful family. Everyone I know loves you."

Eleanor's expression became serious and a little sad. "I gave up the one person who made my life worthwhile."

The picture was becoming clearer to Laura. "Ellie, what happened to Adrien and Sofia?"

Images of the day he'd left came to the surface again, a day in which she felt as if her heart was being torn from her body watching him go. She wiped a tear away. "He went back to France, to a small town close to Bordeaux called Libourne."

"And Sofia, what about her?"

Elleanore stared into space thinking about the day Sofia came to her, to tell her how she felt about Adrien. She remembered how shocked and hurt she felt. The old lady hung her head, one hand gripping the other nervously. "She went to join him there. They wrote each other for a while and one day she told me how she felt about him; she said she planned to join him in France. That was the last time I saw or spoke to her. But we write to one another." Suddenly Ellie began to weep.

Laura took the woman's tiny body in her arms to comfort her. "What is it?"

When she was calm enough Elleanore confessed. "I miss him so. Every day, at least once a day I think of him."

It was suddenly clear to Laura why she'd said that Abigail Strickland wasn't Michael's grandmother. "Is Adrien Forche Michael's father, Elleanore?"

She gazed at her through the tears. "Of course, dear, and Adriana's."

"Do they know about their father?"

"Adriana does," she said as she composed herself. "I'm not sure about Michael. She may have told her brother."

"Why would Adriana know about him but not Michael?"

Ellie was tired suddenly and a little agitated. "I'm feeling a little peaked dear. Would you happen to have a little whiskey?"

"No. But I think I have some brandy."

"That'll be fine."

The liquor seemed to help; she finished it quickly. And as if she felt the need to explain Ellie said, "I know I shouldn't drink this early, but I usually take a little bit during the day." She took a sip of coffee. "Adriana was always a headstrong girl. But she never really felt as if she belonged. And Abigail treated her differently; I think she knew that she was Adrien's child. The likeness between him and her is truly remarkable; I saw it, but Roger never did, at least in the beginning. I loved her the more for it, seeing so much of Adrien in her."

"When did Adriana find out for sure?"

"Michael was in college when she found the letters. Sofia wrote them to me. We both loved the same man and each other; she would let me know how they were doing. It helped me stay close to them. I had the letters hidden away with some photographs they'd sent. I think Adriana knew right away when she saw the pictures of him; the letters only confirmed it." Elleanore stood and walked to the window looking out. "There was a terrible fight between us, and Roger overheard it. He came in and she told him."

"What happened?"

"Adriana went away to school." She snickered. "Roger and I remained the same." She turned back to look at Laura. "He already knew you see. The Strickland name had to be protected from his point of view. He stayed in the city most of the time after that and I remained here. We would get together on holidays when the children came home. Roger our oldest was married shortly after that and he began working for his father. Jane married, then Michael, and we became grandparents."

"What happened to Adriana?"

A tone of sadness returned to her voice. "She went to France to attend university and never came back. I haven't heard from her in years. Sofia sends me photos and always lets me know how she's doing. Adriana had a child, Marie, but never married; she settled with her father and Sofia in Libourne."

"Why don't you go see them?"

"My daughter has no interest in seeing me. I might as well be dead to her."

"But it doesn't have to be that way, Ellie. You just told me to do everything I could to hold on to love. Shouldn't you be doing the same?"

"It's too late for me."

Laura stood and went to her. "But it's not. You owe it to yourself, Elleanore. And to them."

After she'd gone, thoughts of Elleanore—what she'd said, and the pain that she hid so well—kept running through Laura's mind. Particularly those last words, *It's too late for me,* repeated themselves. Laura thought to herself, it can't be too late for me, I'm still young, there are more fish in the sea than David Steele. But she knew her arguments were weak. She had put everything into her work for over ten years, doubling that effort after her wedding to Matt Stryker was canceled. It was all she had, all that she could rely on.

She opened a bottle of Pinot Grigio, poured herself a glass, and looked about her clean kitchen before going to take a bath. Afterward she spent the time to fix her hair and makeup carefully, applying perfume behind both ears, in between her breasts, and to each leg.

Two hours later Laura started up the hill toward his house, not even sure that he was there.

It was twilight at harvest time, and there was a chill in the air with the scent of the vines, the trees, and soil filling her nostrils. Little by little over the last several months being closer to the earth, to a simpler way of life began to take hold; she no longer felt the same joy being a part of urban life. San Francisco no longer held that sense of magic that it once had when she was younger. During the last few times Laura had gone there, her time was spent either in the bistro or at home; the busy streets, filled with people, left her with feelings of restlessness.

Tuan answered the door and said with a slight bow. "Good evening, miss."

"It's good to see you, Tuan. Is Mr. Steele at home?"

He smiled. "Mr. Steele say he always here for you, miss. Please come in."

She waited in the foyer as Tuan left her a moment to tell David that she was here. As her eyes looked about the large room with its elegant furnishings it was difficult for her to imagine a family living here, to imagine Elleanore here, or Michael, with his brother and sisters. The design inside and out was sculpturally asymmetrical, relying on the natural landscape as motivation for form and shape. But to Laura it was discomforting, cold, something that stimulated visual sensitivity but lacked a feeling of being lived in.

She heard Tuan returning before seeing him, his footsteps echoing across the stone floor. He bowed slightly. "Please come, miss. Boss in library."

He was sitting by the fire reading when she came in; he put down his book and stood, smiling at her from across the room. David nodded toward a dish she was holding in her hands and said, "Greeks bearing gifts."

Laura held it out to him and grinned. "An apology of sorts for being such a bitch… a lemon soufflé."

He took it from her, opened the lid to take in the aroma, and handed it to his butler. "We'll have it in here, Tuan, with some brandy and coffee."

"Yes, boss," he said and left quietly.

"It's one of my favorites. I've ordered it several times at Mélange."

She smiled. "I know." There was a short pause. "I wasn't sure you'd let me in."

"I told you the door was always open."

There was a devilish glint in her eye as she replied, "You said the offer was always open. And you meant sex."

"That true, but it's never just been about sex."

Laura put her arms around him, looking up into his eyes. "I know… that's why I put the brakes on. I was scared. I think I still am… a little anyway."

"And now."

"And now I just want to see where this takes us."

He cupped her face in his hands, kissing her deeply. "That's enough for the present. We'll work on the rest."

CHAPTER 20

Reina

He came back in November the same as he did every year. But it was Reina who weighed on his mind not the shows he'd scheduled. Daniel gave Travis a scratch behind the ears as he said to him, "She's probably not around anymore. And even if she is she's probably hooked up with someone, so don't get your hopes up." Travis kept his eyes on the road.

Reina spent the weekend in St. Helena and had a meeting with Laura on Tuesday morning to go over wine and beer purchases for both restaurants. But her mind was occupied with other things. She'd seen ads for the art show at Fort Mason and wondered if he was coming back this year.

Laura had lost patience with her. "Are you feeling alright this morning?"

"Huh," Reina replied. "I'm sorry, my mind's been somewhere else today."

"Well get it together and come back to us."

"Yes, Chef."

She'd received one postcard and one letter from Daniel in a year, and it wasn't much of a letter. He didn't own a computer or cell phone, which meant email was out of the question. And the last time they spoke on the phone was six months ago. She did the only thing she could think of; she called Alex and invited herself over for supper, so she could talk to him about it.

Alex missed Isabella. He was grateful in the beginning after she'd moved out; they'd patched up the fight between them, but he hadn't considered how much being near her every day meant to him. He did now but had no idea what to do about it. When Reina called and asked to come over, he thought it was a perfect opportunity to get her take on it.

He'd just poured the sauce he'd prepared over the fish fillets, sprinkled cilantro over the top and closed the oven when there was a knock on the door. Reina opened it, knocked a second time, and walked in. "Alex, you decent?"

"I'm in the kitchen," he called back. "You want a beer."

"Please," she replied. "Something certainly smells delicious."

He popped the top off two Coronas and handed her one. "I'm baking tilapia. It'll be done in about twenty minutes. Let's go out back."

She hadn't been to the house since Isabella left and Reina could see that the place lacked her touch. It wasn't messy but the little things, like a vase of fresh flowers, a scent of candles, and the artistic way Izzy arranged things, were missing. Reina could see the undercurrent of masculine disorder and chuckled. "You miss your housekeeper?"

"What are you talking about?"

As they walked outside she noticed a new table and chairs on the patio. "Izzy took good care of you."

It was as if Reina had read his mind. "Sí, sí, I miss her. She's a pain in the ass sometimes but yes I liked it when she lived with me."

Reina sat down. "You like her."

"Of course, I like her."

She grinned. "I mean you like… like her."

"She's a child."

"She's a young woman and very pretty."

How could he possibly argue with the truth? She was, he knew it, but he felt ancient compared to her. "I'm too old for her anyway."

"You didn't think you were too old for me."

"That's different."

"How so?"

"You're older."

"Thanks a lot."

He took a drink of his beer. "You know what I mean."

"I think you're making excuses." She hesitated as she watched his expression and then the realization came to her. "You're scared."

"You're full of shit."

Reina laughed; she could see the discomfort on his face, the same longing and doubt she felt for Daniel. She leaned in closer to him and knocked her bottle against his. "I know how you feel… but she cares for you. Everybody knows it. Why don't you just ask her out?"

"You know why I won't."

She shook her head impatiently as she said, "Break the rules for once. Ask her out."

"Laura has given me the chance of being a chef, a real chef. I won't betray her."

"Then talk to her about it. Tell Laura how you feel. She'll understand."

Alex took another long drink of his beer and looked at his watch to keep track of the time. "Sí, she might understand but it won't make a difference. There are reasons for her rules."

"You won't know unless you ask."

He was tired of talking about Izzy and changed the subject. "Why did you call me today?"

It was her turn, she thought, to confess. "Dan might be coming this weekend to the show at Fort Mason. I'm afraid to go and afraid not to. If I go and he's with someone else, it would hurt a lot. And then again, he might not even be there this year."

"He knows where you live… right?"

"Right."

"And he has your cell number."

"Yes he does but—"

"But nothing, if he wants to be with you, let him get in touch." Alex stood and said, "I have to take the fish out of the oven. I'll be right back."

"Is there something I can do to help?"

He nodded. "You can set the table out here."

After they finished fixing their plates and took them outside Reina was thinking about what Alex had said. And as she sat down again she said to him, "You're right. It's up to him." She carefully took a forkful of salad. "But what if he tries and can't find me? What if he comes to the bistro and I'm not there?"

Alex finished a bite of food. "You change your cell number?"

"No."

He smiled. "Eat your fish."

A moment later they heard the doorbell; Alex put his napkin on the table and started to get up. "I'll be right back."

When he opened the door, Isabella was standing there smiling. "Hola," she said enthusiastically. "We were going out. Do you want to come?"

He saw Angie behind the wheel of her car and Carlos sitting in the back seat. This was the first time she'd asked him anywhere and he couldn't go. "I'm sorry," he began.

Reina was curious and had just stepped inside the house when Isabella saw her. The two women stared at each other for a second and he tried to explain as she turned to walk back to the car. "Izzy wait," he called after her. "It's not what you think. We were just having supper and talking." She opened the car door and before he even thought about what might happen as a result he said with panic in his voice, "We were talking about how I feel about you." That stopped her.

She closed the door again softly, then turned and leaned back against it as she said, "And what did you say?"

He approached her cautiously one step at a time. "I told her how much I missed you being here with me."

"This is something you should say to me, not another woman." She shook her head. "Puedes ser tan estúpida a veces."

"I know… I do stupid things when I'm around you. I can't help it."

Reina was standing in the doorway smiling and called out to her. "I told him to just ask you out."

He was a foot away from her now; Izzy looked up and gazed into his eyes. "You should listen to her."

Alex was at a loss for words to explain what seemed evident to him. His shoulders slumped. "It's not as easy as that."

She gazed at him for a second, irritated, and said no louder than a whisper, "Eres un estúpida y un cobarde," then turned to open the car door once again.

His arm reached out to hold the door, to stop her from going, their bodies touching, the scent of her filling his nostrils. "Por favor espere, Izzy."

She did wait, turning into him, her breasts brushing lightly against his chest. "I'm sorry for saying you are a coward; you are not. But if you want me, you must want me enough to say so to anyone who asks."

He gently brushed a lock of hair out of her eyes and spoke to her softly so no one else would hear. "What am I going to do with you? You drive me crazy."

She lowered her eyes. "Sí, I know."

Alex lifted her chin lightly with his finger and kissed her lips softly, a gentle kiss. "I am too old for you, you know."

Izzy grinned as she stared him down. "You need me."

He whispered in her ear, "Only because I love you."

"Laura will not understand," she replied. "But you must tell her these things." Isabella opened the car door. "Tell her I love you too." She kissed him once more and quickly slid into the passenger seat. "Buenas noches, mi amor."

Alex watched them drive away as Reina walked up beside him saying, "I guess that settles that."

"I'll probably get fired."

She chuckled. "Probably." Reina put her arm through his. "The things we do for love never seem to make sense."

"Or it's the only thing that does," he replied with a sigh.

Reina thought about his last comment off and on that night and all the way back to the city the next day. She had meetings with salespeople the rest of the week. If they represented wineries in the Napa area, she usually met with them at the restaurant in St. Helena. But for anyone else, mostly liquor and beer reps, it was easier for both to meet in San Francisco.

It was a quarter past eleven by the time she parked and entered the bistro; Shelly was talking to a customer and waved at her. Reina's responsibilities had increased at the small café now that Laura and Alex were spending most of their time in St. Helena. She was unofficially Shelly's assistant manager, covering for her on her days off and doing everything from seating people to taking their money. She'd even become a decent barista. But her primary duty was still the purchase and inventory control of wine, beer, and liquor.

She stashed her belongings in the small office in the back, made herself a cappuccino, and sat down in one of the booths to go over the list of supplies she needed to order. There was a lull in the restaurant before the lunch crowd started to come in. When Shelly had time she wandered over, smiled, and said, "A friend of yours was in here this morning asking about you."

It felt like butterflies dive-bombing inside of her as she looked up expectantly to ask, "Was it Dan?"

"In the flesh. I told him you'd be in today."

"Did he say anything else, where he's staying or how to get a hold of him?"

Shelly nodded with a grin, pulled a piece of paper out of her apron and handed it to her. It was a small drawing of her with the city skyline in the background; underneath was a note that read, *I've missed you. Can we meet later for a drink? Call me.*" He included his new cell phone number.

"Call him, girl," Shelly said with a grin. "What are you waiting for?"

Dan was staying at the San Francisco RV Resort, just south of Daly City a little more than fifteen minutes from Fort Mason, next to the ocean. He was walking with Travis, heard his phone, and threw the dog's ball down the beach. "Hello."

"Is that you, Daniel?"

Just hearing her voice made him feel weak in the knees; Travis returned the ball and Dan threw it again. "Yes," he replied. He felt like he was so far out on thin ice, there didn't seem like any hope of getting back. "I'm glad you called."

Reina promised herself that she wouldn't make any big deal out of his silence while he was away. She also promised herself that she wasn't going to be that girl he called up every time he came to the city. "It's been a long time."

He cringed, knowing he should have been better about keeping in contact with her. "Would you have a drink with me? So, we can catch up."

She sensed his discomfort and wanted to make him suffer, just not too much. "Gosh, Dan, I wish I would have known you were coming into town. I would have taken some time off. Let me look at my calendar." Reina let him stew for a minute before saying, "I've got a meeting later today… let's see, I could get away about nine."

The disappointment hit him harder than he expected but a few minutes with her was better than none. "Nine it is. We can go anywhere you say."

Reina didn't want to go to any of the places they'd been together before; it would be too much like picking up where they left off. She wanted to pick a place where she would be comfortable, and he would be off balance. "How about Entretenir? The bar shouldn't be crowded by then and my meeting is close by." There was no meeting; she was lying but felt justified.

Dan had no idea where it was or what kind of place but didn't care; the point was she agreed to meet him, the rest he'd have to work out as they went along. "I'll see you there at nine."

She smiled as she said, "Tonight then."

Before she could hang up, he said quickly, "Reina… I missed you."

"It's good to hear from you, Daniel," she said quietly. But after hanging up a part of her felt guilty for giving him a hard time. The thing was, he never seemed to sound like someone who would play with her emotions, but he did, knowingly or not.

He arrived at the restaurant fifteen minutes early and immediately felt underdressed in jeans, T-shirt, and an old brown leather jacket he'd bought years ago after his first big sale as an artist. He felt uncomfortable but there wasn't enough time to change what he was wearing.

The maître d looked him up and down judgmentally, then asked with a questioning smile, "Excusez-moi, may I help you, sir?"

"I'm meeting someone in the bar."

The small Frenchman motioned with his hand. "This way, sir."

He settled himself on one of the stools at the far end, and at that moment, desperately regretted that he'd quit smoking.

Henri, the bartender, was pouring Grand Marnier into a snifter while chatting with a customer. He excused himself and asked, "May I get you something, sir?"

"A beer," Dan replied. "I'm waiting for a friend."

"What kind of beer, sir?"

"You have Coors?"

He nodded. "Yes, sir." Henri noticed Reina walk in wearing an elegant black suit, the skirt slit to mid-thigh with a white blouse that accented her cleavage, high heels, and a simple strand of pearls around her neck. He nodded to her and smiled. It surprised him when she sat next to the gentleman in jeans. But over the years at Entretenir he'd seen many stranger things.

Dan stood as he saw her walk toward him, not sure whether to kiss her. But she turned her head while giving him a slight hug, kissing him lightly on the cheek. She looked beautiful he thought, and he felt awkward. "I didn't have time to change," he said in a feeble attempt to excuse the way he was dressed.

"You look just fine, Daniel," she replied while taking a seat, and crossing her legs to give him the maximum effect she hoped to achieve.

The bartender set the beer in front of him and a glass of Cabernet for her saying, "It's good to see you, Reina. Would you like a bottled water tonight?"

"Yes please, Henri." Once he'd gone, she turned back to Daniel. "Tell me, how have you been?"

The cool, sophisticated air she presented wasn't something he remembered or appreciated. When he thought of her it was always about how much fun they had being together. She looked great, certainly sexy, he thought, but this wasn't the girl who kept him up at night, wondering what she was doing and who she was with. This wasn't the girl he longed to hold in his arms again. This was someone else entirely. He took a long drink of his beer and said, "I'm sorry but maybe this isn't such a good idea." He stood, putting a twenty-dollar bill on the bar. "It was great to see you again." And before she had time to react he started to walk out.

A sick feeling hit the pit of her stomach as she watched him go, knowing that she'd taken her act too far. Reina picked up her purse to hurry after him and had just gone outside when she saw him get on a motorcycle down the block putting on his helmet. She took off her heels and covered the twenty feet between them quickly, grabbing his arm to turn him around toward her. Her voice raised gradually as she said, "That was just rude in there. How dare you come back here after not communicating with me for months and just expect me to drop everything and dance to your tune! I'm not just someone you can bang every time you're in town and feel the urge!"

His eyes stared intently into hers. "I thought you knew me better than that." He closed the visor to his helmet and popped the clutch to peel out down the street.

She stood on the curb watching him leave as it started to rain. "Well, Lorraine," she whispered to herself with a sigh, "that didn't go the way you wanted it to."

CHAPTER 21

Alex

It was his day off, a day to sleep in; he reached for her, but she was gone. Alex opened his eyes, looking around the room until he saw a glimpse of Izzy in the bathroom putting on her makeup. He stayed where he was, watching her for several minutes until she turned off the light, came back into his bedroom, and picked up her purse. "Come back to bed," he pleaded, patting the disheveled covers next to him.

Isabelle looked down at him thinking that he looked like a little boy, lying there with his hair all a mess. "I've got to go." She leaned over and kissed him quickly. "Think of me today."

As she started to walk out he asked, "Will you come over later? We can have supper together."

She gazed at him from across the room. "Are you going to tell her today?"

He groaned, covering his head with a pillow for a second before throwing the covers off him to get out of bed. "I just need to have some time to figure out the best way."

Izzy's eyes scanned his body admiringly, then smiled. "You better do it soon or somebody will do it for you. Ten un buen dia, mi amor. I'll call you." And she was gone.

He slid into a pair of jeans before shuffling his way into the kitchen. There was coffee already made and a note letting him know she'd left an omelet in the oven and some fruit she'd cut up in the refrigerator. Alex poured his coffee and took a sip while wondering just how he was going to tell Laura. She'd probably fire them both, he thought. There was always the taco truck; he considered this with a grin for a moment, thinking of working there with Izzy side by side.

A knock on the front door interrupted the thought and after opening it, Reina walked past him saying as she came in, "I've really screwed up this time. You have to help." She continued toward the kitchen, took a cup down, and poured herself some coffee. "I was just going to let him squirm a little for treating me like shit." She began to pace. "But he turns things around and makes it sound like I'm the one who's out of line. And I'm not... am I?"

"Slow down. I just got up," he said while closing the door. Alex poured himself a little more coffee. "Why don't you start from the beginning, so I can catch up?" While listening to her he got out a plate, the omelet, and the fruit from the refrigerator.

He was putting a slice of bread in the toaster when Reina stopped her story long enough to say, "Are you going to eat all that? The omelet looks really good."

Alex got out another slice of bread, put it in the toaster and pushed the handle down before reaching for another plate. She started to pace again. "So he just leaves me sitting there in the restaurant! Can you believe that?"

Rather than answer, he waited for her to continue. "Well I was really pissed by then, anybody would be, and I followed him outside. He's sitting on this cool-looking motorcycle, and I really let him have it."

The toast popped up, he buttered it, put it on her plate with half the omelet and some fruit, then handed it to her. "What'd he say?"

She popped a grape in her mouth and shrugged. "He just rode away!"

Alex sat down at the table in the breakfast nook. "Come on, Reina, what did he say?"

"OK, OK," she replied while stuffing another piece of fruit in her mouth. "He said he thought I knew him better than that." She took a big bite of her omelet. "What does that even mean anyway?"

"You went out of your way to put him down."

"I just wanted to let him know I'm not easy. That I don't go out and sleep with just anybody every time they snap their fingers."

"Why didn't you talk to him about it? You know, two adults having a conversation, clearing the air. Respect goes two ways, Reina."

She pushed her plate aside and holding her toast in one hand, took another drink of coffee with the other. "I'm a mess," she replied with a sigh. "You're right… I shouldn't have played games with him. But I liked him, and he made me feel cheap."

"The other day you said he was up front with you from the beginning."

"He was," she insisted with a sigh. "And now he doesn't want to have anything to do with me."

"How do you know? Talk to him, apologize and see what he has to say."

"Do you think it'll work?"

He shook his head while cutting another bite of his omelet. "I have no idea. But, the way I see it, you have nothing to lose."

She glanced at her watch. "Oh shit!" Reina finished off the rest of her coffee in one gulp. "I've got a meeting with Laura in thirty minutes."

Once she'd grabbed her purse and left he felt relieved that some sense of sanity had returned. But soon thoughts of Izzy and their predicament replaced Reina's tirade. Alex knew from the moment he first kissed her that he was in love and probably had been for quite a while. He'd simply shoved romantic thoughts of her aside and didn't know why entirely. Maybe, he thought, it was because he knew from the beginning that she wasn't someone you played with; she was a woman you married or left alone.

Laura knew that something was going on with Isabelle; she just didn't know what yet. The girl was absolutely glowing. Then she thought of David and wondered if other people thought the same of her. If she wasn't glowing she knew she was close to it. Her mind shifted back to him regularly during the day and every time she saw Ellie, the woman gave her these knowing smiles as if she knew exactly what she was thinking.

She was smiling to herself thinking of him again when Reina knocked on her office door and rushed inside. "Good morning, Chef," she said. "You look… well I don't know how you look, beautiful, I guess. It must be something in the water; Izzy's on cloud nine."

Laura let that pass and intentionally put on her game face. "It's nice to see people in a good mood around here." She motioned for her to sit. "How about you? You find Mr. Right yet?"

"I found him and lost him. I don't know quite where to go from here."

"Follow your heart," Laura heard herself say then abruptly changed the subject. "Did Shelly give you the financials for the bistro?"

Reina handed the file to her. "Business is steady. Wine and beer sales are OK, not great, but stable. They'd be better if Shelly stayed open at night."

"You argued against that before we opened this place."

"I know, and I still think that was probably the best decision. But we should keep our options open."

"I'm not going to increase staff costs there, particularly while we're still trying to increase business at Mélange." Laura didn't say anything, but they were just breaking even at the restaurant in St. Helena. It was the bistro that helped make ends meet. She'd put all her savings into the restaurant and didn't believe she had any other choice but to keep struggling. The business they received from locals and guests at the hotel was decent. But they weren't a destination restaurant yet, a place where the public went out of their way to patronize. They needed some coverage by the San Francisco papers and local magazines for that; they needed positive reviews from some critics. Her marketing budget was exhausted and David's idea about hiring someone to do public relations was a good one, but she didn't have the money. The mounting pressure she felt was one of the reasons she'd fought with David and pushed him away. But now that they were back together she'd realized that he made what she was going through worthwhile.

When Laura worked as sous-chef de cuisine at Entretenir she longed to have creative control of her own restaurant. She had that now but there were moments when she longed for that simpler time when the only thing she had to worry about was preparing food.

At one o'clock that afternoon she was just about to take a break before she had to return in a couple of hours to start getting ready for the dinner crowd. There was always more for her to do on Alex's day off; she was put in a situation of doing his job and hers for the evening. Laura had just left the hotel when she had to dig for the ringing cell phone in her purse. It was Alex. "Hi," she said, "you tired of lying around and want to come back to work?"

"We need to talk," he replied, "and I think it would be good to do it out of the restaurant."

"I was just walking over to the cottage to take a break. Do you want to come over? We can talk there."

"When?"

"Right now is fine with me." She was about to hang up but stopped. "Alex… are you alright?"

"Yes," he said quietly. "I'll be there in thirty minutes."

She felt sick inside after hanging up; she was sure that he was going to tell her he was quitting to go to work somewhere else. He was good, too good for what she paid him. She'd known it was only a matter of time till someone approached him. When she worked at Entretenir, there were other restaurants that offered her employment several times, but Laura always remained loyal, never leaving to work for the competition. But Armand Moreau, the owner and head chef of Entretenir, always treated her very well.

Earlier that morning she'd set a large jar outside the cottage to make sun tea the way her grandmother Lizzie Hanson had shown her. She'd just brought it into the house and was in the process of fixing two glasses when there was a knock on the door. Her heart sank as she opened it; she could tell by his expression that whatever he had to say, it wasn't going to be anything she'd appreciate.

Laura forced a smile. "Come in, Alex… I was just fixing some tea. Would you like a glass?"

"Sure," he said as he closed the door to follow her to the kitchen.

She handed him a glass and picked up hers. "Let's sit outside."

There was a patio in the backyard; it was small with a nice flower garden that Laura had brought back to life with a little hard work. There was an old wrought iron table and chairs that looked like they had been there as long as the cottage. She took a seat and motioned for him to do the same. It was clear that this meeting was terribly difficult for him. "Please… tell me what's on your mind."

The last thing in the world he'd ever want to do was intentionally disappoint her, to have her think less of him. But he was backed into a corner and felt there was nothing else for him to do. "I've learned so much from you. And I really appreciate it… I do."

She could feel it coming; he was going to quit. When he hesitated she urged him to continue. "Just say it."

"I'm in love with Izzy." He gazed into her eyes a moment and then hung his head. "I know it's something that shouldn't have happened." He looked at her and said hurriedly, "I'm sorry. Whatever you want to do I'll understand, just don't fire her, it's my fault. I can go."

This was the last thing she'd expected to hear but now that it had been said, it made sense. There were rules about members of her staff dating one another, rules that she learned while working for Armand and they were in place for a reason. On the other hand, she could tell he wasn't going to give her up and if Laura fired him, she believed Izzy would leave as well. She decided the best thing she could do was stall for a while, to give herself time to think and consider the options. "Does she love you?"

Alex nodded slowly. "I think so. I'm going to ask her to marry me."

"You couldn't have been dating her long. What if she says no?"

"I'll wait for her. I know we belong together."

She tapped her nails on the table and took a drink of her tea. Finally she said, "I have to have some time to think about this. Then we'll see."

He sensed that she was giving him a way out. If he married Izzy it might be a way for both of them to stay at Mélange. "Alright, Chef," he said with a sigh of relief.

Laura stood up. "Do you have a ring picked out yet?"

Alex shook his head. "Not yet."

"Get it done," she said with a slight grin.

"I will, Chef."

After he'd gone Laura's tension began to ease; a few moments before she was sure she was going to lose him. But now there was a chance, maybe even a good chance that she could keep Alex and Isabelle. All she had to do was take her time before deciding and if she waited long enough, the problem just might solve itself.

Reina received a call from Alex a few minutes later. "Hi."

"I need some help," he replied.

It was a long day, but the restaurant wasn't particularly busy, and Laura got off earlier than expected. David was waiting for her in the bar. He gave her a hug and quick kiss on the lips. "How'd it go today?"

Carl, the bartender, was doing his best to finish closing the bar when he saw his boss come in. He poured her a glass of the imported Pinot Grigio she preferred and placed it in front of her.

She recognized his attentiveness with a nod of her head and a smile. "Thank you, Carl." Then she focused her attention on David saying, "I'll tell you about it later. Right now, I just want to enjoy this glass of wine and talk aabout anything but work."

He told her of the frustrations he was having with the company he'd partnered with that took care of the fields and produced the wine from his grapes. They put his name on the bottle but the product they manufactured was average at best. "My contract," he said, "is up this year and they want to renegotiate. Their marketing department claims that the name Steele doesn't have the influential identification it once had." He snickered. "But I don't think my name on the bottle means as much as the swill they put inside."

"If you're unhappy find another vintner."

David shrugged. "I don't know anything about producing wine. That's why I signed with these people in the first place. I wouldn't know where to start."

Laura got up to go behind the bar, found the bottle she was looking for and keeping her hand over the label, poured David a sample of the red wine it contained. "Take a sip and tell me what you think."

He inhaled the aroma briefly before tasting it. A moment later he smiled. "That's wonderful."

She set the bottle down and turned it so he could see the label. He read, "Mélange Signature Reserve Cabernet Sauvignon. Huh, where did you find it?"

Laura leaned over the bar and said quietly, "It's Michael's. Right now, we sell this for three hundred dollars a bottle and people are collecting it."

"He's never said anything to me. But now that I think about it … Michael gave me a bottle for my birthday about a year ago. I've never opened it." David took another drink. "How did you find out about it?"

She smiled. "Elleanore gave me a bottle to try and Michael agreed to let us offer it here, at the restaurant. Apparently, the basic formula was originally created years ago. Michael has all the original records from the family's winery, he found several formulas and has been experimenting with them."

David shook his head. "I've always thought of him as likable but kind of an odd duck." He took another drink. "I'll be damned!"

"If you're looking for someone to produce wine for you, Michael just might be your guy. It certainly wouldn't hurt to ask."

CHAPTER 22

Ellie packed the memory book on top of her clothes and struggled to shut the suitcase. Michael was watching her and finally said, "This is ridiculous, Mother. You can't go running off halfway round the world."

She chuckled. "Nonsense, people do it all the time."

"Not when you're eighty years old."

Her look was stern as she replied, "I'm not eighty yet. Now are you going to help me with this suitcase or do I call one of the bellboys?"

Ever since the night she talked with Laura, Elleanore had been thinking about this. But it was the dream that convinced her. Adrien was still young, looking the same as he did the last time she saw him but there seemed to be a sense of urgency as he beckoned her to come to him. The discomfort she felt after waking troubled her. She had to go.

Michael, with effort, zipped the suitcase shut. "Then I'll go with you."

"Someone has to manage the hotel."

Erica, Ellie's daughter-in-law, walked into the bedroom. "I've talked to Reina on the phone; she's agreed to accompany you."

Ellie felt badgered and with a sigh she sat on the edge of the bed. "Reina has a job to do. So do you, Erica. I am perfectly able to take a trip by myself without the entire household coming apart."

Laura was sitting behind her desk listening to Reina requesting time off to go to France with her grandmother. "None of us have any idea what's gotten into her. She just came down from breakfast and made the announcement yesterday. My folks can't go and it's too dangerous for her to do this alone."

What Reina didn't know that Laura did was that she was the one who suggested that Elleanore should go. She felt that most of the responsibility rested on her shoulders. "Go then," she heard herself say. "You have the vacation time and it would be a great opportunity for you to meet your aunt."

Reina looked at her curiously. "How did you know about my aunt? Nobody talks about her."

"Your grandmother told me."

"Daddy says she's always been the black sheep of the family… going off to Europe the way she did, never communicating with any of us."

The only thing that Laura felt she could do was listen; she couldn't talk to Reina about what she'd found out from Elleanore. It would betray her trust. But on the other hand, if Reina went with her grandmother to France, the chances were that she would find out sooner rather than later. Laura asked, "When do you have to leave?"

"At the end of the week."

"Make sure all your loose ends are tied up before you go." She came around her desk and gave Reina a hug. "And have a good time. Be patient with Ellie; I expect seeing her daughter again will be difficult for her emotionally. She'll need your support."

As Reina left Laura's office she began thinking about Daniel; she'd waited a year to see him again and when she finally did it was a disaster. Now that she was leaving she was concerned that she wouldn't have the chance to make up for what she'd done. Late that same afternoon she made up her mind to go back into the city, find him, and apologize. The thing was, she had no idea where he was staying and the only person who might would be Shelly. By the time she got to the bistro, it was closed, and she was gone. Reina didn't know her home number.

She drove to Fort Mason, but the show hadn't started to set up for the weekend yet. Frustrated, Reina decided to go to Laura's place near

Golden Gate Park, where she was staying, and start packing for her trip. On the way she stopped at the sports bar where she'd met Dan for the first time, hoping he might be there. He wasn't, and the place was almost empty.

The young bartender, Jessica, was working and recognized her. She smiled, thinking about her one-night stand with Daniel while wiping off the surface of the bar. "What'll you have?"

"A glass of white wine please."

Jess poured her a glass and set it in front of her saying, "You're Bambi."

"Huh," Reina replied, then realized what she was referring to as Jess pointed to the game being played on the television. She nodded. "Yes."

"You haven't been in for a while."

Lost in her own thoughts she replied, "No I haven't." Reina suddenly realized that it was odd for the bartender to know the code name she used for the game. She asked, "How did you know that… about Bambi I mean?"

Jess was washing glasses to keep busy. "Your guy was in here the other night." She chuckled. "He got really wasted, kept raving about you, about Bambi. I had to phone for a cab."

Reina didn't have anything to lose as she asked hopefully. "He didn't say where he was staying did he?"

"I helped haul him out to a cab. He told the driver the San Francisco RV Resort. If you find him, tell him Jess says hi."

"Thanks a lot," Reina said as she put a twenty on the bar and hurried out.

Thirty minutes later she convinced the manager of the resort to give her Daniel's space number. His truck and bike were parked there but he wasn't around. Reina could see the coastline from the front door of his trailer and began walking toward the ocean, hoping to find him. It was twilight with the light from the remaining rays of the sun shining on the surface of the water. She saw him on the beach with Travis throwing a ball out into the surf with the dog bounding after it.

Travis caught her scent before seeing her, dropped the ball on the beach, and ran to Reina, soaking wet. He knocked her to the sand and began licking her, she was laughing as Dan turned to see them together. It was hard for him to still be mad at her while watching them play.

"Come, Travis," he commanded, his voice firm. The retriever stopped what he was doing, gave Reina one final lick, then went to him. Dan gave him a pat. "Good boy!"

Reina got to her feet, brushing the sand and wet from her dress. She said, loud enough for him to hear over the sound of the waves, "I've been looking for you all afternoon."

He said to Travis. "Go get your ball, boy." And the dog was off again. Dan approached her, not sure what she wanted. His reply was blunt. "Why?"

She brushed the hair out of her eyes. "I wanted to apologize for the other night. It was wrong of me and I'm sorry."

Dan nodded his head slightly. "How did you find me?"

"The bartender Jessica. She says hi."

"I was pretty loaded the last time I was there. I don't remember much after the first couple of drinks."

It was almost dark and the two of them began walking back toward the resort with Travis beside them. Reina had been rehearsing what she wanted to say all afternoon but now that she'd found him she was at a loss for words. "I was hurt," she began, "when you didn't call or write." He listened but didn't respond. Reina continued. "I like you a lot and didn't want you to think I'd just sleep with anyone. It's not like that with me."

"I know that," he answered. "I'm sorry too."

"And you made me feel cheap. I thought we had something, something worthwhile maybe."

He gazed into her eyes. "If I made you feel that way I'm sorry… I would never do that intentionally. It's just… I don't trust it. The farther I was away from you the easier it was to think that it was just a good time between us and nothing else. I thought I could just go back to my life and it would be alright. But this year, the closer it got to doing the show again, the more I looked forward to seeing you. I thought maybe we could"—he hesitated— "but then I saw you the other night and you weren't the same."

"Wait a minute," she replied defensively. "Have I ever given you any reason not to trust me?"

"Well yes, sort of, the other night making me go to that place knowing I would look foolish!"

"But that was a few nights ago. You said you didn't trust me last year."

He turned away, running his hands through his hair, then looked back at her. "I didn't say I didn't trust you." Dan sighed. "I don't trust the whole idea of two people being together, loving each other till death do they part and all that. People let you down."

"When have I ever let you down? And don't say the other night. I was just punishing you a little; it was dumb and wrong of me. I admit that."

It was getting dark, there was a chill in the air and Reina had on a light blouse and short skirt. Seeing her shiver slightly, he said, "We should go in. You're cold." He started walking back toward the trailer.

She grabbed his arm. "No damn it! You're not just going to walk away again. I want an answer."

The light breeze that an hour before felt good in the sun began to pick up as dark clouds started to roll in across the ocean from the west. "It's not you! Everything always seems fine at first but pretty soon it falls apart and you don't even have the good memories. You just have regret."

Reina stepped closer to him, close enough that she could almost feel the heat from his body. "Who was it that hurt you?"

The passion, love and disappointment he felt for her were all mixed together with the past, a past that had kept him imprisoned for much too long. He couldn't stand being this close to her, inches away, without touching her. His arms suddenly reached out, pulling her into him, kissing her deeply.

She pulled away. "No. Not till we finish talking about this." He started to turn away again; Reina pulled him back toward her. "If I walk away from here now I at least want to know why. And if I stay it can't be ignored. So just say it, whatever it was that made it so difficult for you to trust me."

"OK, but let's go somewhere where we can talk and not freeze to death at the same time."

Reina shrugged her shoulders. "OK."

They left Travis in the trailer and Daniel handed her a spare helmet as he mounted his bike. "It's not far," he said as she gripped him around the waist; the vintage Indian Motorcycle roared to life. They sped down the highway for five minutes before he turned off at an exit and came to a stop at a junction. Across the street there was a sign that read, "Winters," with a large green neon martini glass shining above it. He turned left and parked on the street in front of a bait shop. She swung her leg over the back of the bike and began to straighten her skirt saying sarcastically. "Nice neighborhood."

Daniel held her hand as they crossed the street. "It grows on you."

Another sign was advertising live music on Friday and Saturday nights. "This is so you," she said as they walked through the front door. It was the middle of the week but crowded.

Luckily two people at the bar were leaving, Daniel quickly took their stools and ordered beers on tap from a pretty brunette who was clearing the space. "I guess this isn't the best place to talk," he said loud enough for her to hear over the music and people.

"It's good enough," she replied as the bartender brought their drinks and stuffed the check into a rocks glass. Reina took a sip of her beer, watching his expression, noticing the uneasiness. "We can sit here all night if that's what it takes but I want this out in the open. Talk to me."

He shrugged, took a drink, and shook his head. "It's not you, it's me. I live the way I do because there's no commitment. There's always a new town, a new show, new people." His hand waved briefly around the room. "I found this spot because I have the time. I sit here, in places like this, a shadow on the wall and watch. It's like I'm always outside looking in and wondering what it would be like to be one of them instead of me, what their lives are like. Then I'm gone again to another place in another town. But the people aren't that much different. I'm left wondering what it is about me that makes me feel so separate?"

The two of them had known each other briefly the year before but they never seemed to journey beyond their initial attraction. As he took a drink of his beer she asked, "What does this have to do with my question?"

"Give me a break," he replied as he set his glass back on the bar. "I'm getting to it." Dan had never talked to anyone about his past and doing so now was difficult for him. "I told you I was from Montrose. But that was only half true. That's where I graduated from high school. My dad worked in the oilfields. When I was a kid we traveled all over, mostly Wyoming and Colorado. But my family came from Texas originally, that's where I was born. We lived in this dingy thirty-foot trailer," he said while taking another drink of beer. "I was about six, first grade I think. The bus dropped me off after school and my mom was gone. Poof"—he snickered— "like magic. One day she's there and the next she's gone."

She took his hand, but he pulled it away. "I'm sorry, Daniel."

"I don't blame her," he continued, "my pop was a drunk and not a nice one. She was his punching bag."

"Did he hurt you?"

He shook his head. "Not physically." For a moment his mind drifted back there as he stared into space. "Anyway, when I was eight he brought this woman back to the trailer and he tells me she's my new mother." There was contempt in his voice. "Her name was Gladys. He met her in a bar… they were drinking buddies. A few years later he bought some land in Montrose and parked the trailer there. He'd take off for months at a time to one job or another and left me with her." His voice trailed off as he finished his beer in one long gulp before saying quietly, "Just the two of us."

Reina had no idea what she expected him to say before he began but this wasn't even close. The details that he'd intentionally omitted were left to her imagination. She had no idea how to respond or how to make some feeble attempt of saying she was sorry.

Daniel saw the discomfort and took her hand. "It's in the past. Don't worry about it."

"How can you say that?"

He made a gesture to the bartender with his hand for another round. "It's not a matter of trusting you. I believe people do whatever it is they want and to hell with the outcome. It's just easier not to get involved."

"You sound so cynical. And believe me I get that you have a reason. But it's not a good enough reason for you to stick yourself out on an island away from everyone else. It's not fair to you or me… or anyone who cares for you."

She watched him nod silently and said, "If you want anything to work between us, you're going to have to come halfway."

"I thought I was doing that," he replied impatiently.

"You're beginning to, and I appreciate it but you have to be able to take a certain amount of risk."

"About what?"

There was a wall within him that she couldn't seem to get beyond. She reached out and turned his head toward her saying, "Getting hurt. There's never a guarantee that you won't be. I might disappoint you in the end, but you'll never know, I'll never know where this might go unless you're willing to give it a decent shot." Her voice softened. "It's a gamble, Daniel." She kissed him softly. "I'll take that gamble if you will."

He ran his fingers through his hair. "We come from two different worlds. I'm not a good bet."

"Maybe not but we can try." And when he didn't respond she said, "There's something else. I have to leave town for a few days, a week, ten days at the most. I know the timing is bad but it's not something I can help."

"Where to?"

"France, with my grandmother. I have an aunt who lives there. She needs someone to go with her and I said I would."

"Lucky you."

"I want to be here… with you."

"When's your flight?"

"Day after tomorrow."

Dan gazed into her eyes. "Stay with me till then."

"There's a lot for me to do to get ready."

He shifted his body toward her and put his arms around her waist. "We'll do it together."

"OK," she replied, then kissed him deeply. "How long are you staying?"

"A month." He gently caressed the contour of her face. "Like last year."

"And you'll still be here when I get back."

"I'll be here," he said. But even while saying it Daniel knew that his plans were never fixed. He stayed as long as the money came in but never long enough to take root in one place.

CHAPTER 23

Elleanore

She dreamt of him again, of that last day as he finished packing, of the harsh words that she'd never been able to take back. Then there was the feeling of being lost, searching through a fog of nothingness, but never really being able to get her bearings.

The turbulence woke her, followed by the sound of the captain's voice letting the passengers know that they were descending into Charles de Gaulle International Airport. Reina was packing her things away as Ellie put her seat back in the upright position, confused briefly before remembering where they were and why.

The anxiousness returned; Ellie began to second-guess her decision to come, to see them one last time. For a few short years, their lives had been intertwined but that was a long time ago. What were they like now, she wondered repeatedly, after spending a lifetime together?

She'd written Sofia, who encouraged her to come. There was no word from her daughter. The thought of it made her hands shake as she struggled out of her seat, waiting to disembark. The passengers in front and behind her seemed insufferably close; Elleanore was afraid she might faint as the doors opened and the line of bodies began to move slowly forward.

The flight took ten hours and another two by the time they were processed through customs and arrived at the Hotel de Crillon not far from the Place de la Concorde. It was originally a palace built in 1758, commissioned by King Louis XV, and was turned into a luxury hotel in 1909.

Their room was on the sixth floor overlooking a relatively quiet pedestrian street. The furnishings were all done in white and gold with a dark red maroon for variety in the rug and drapes. It was late afternoon in Paris; Reina pulled the curtains shut and helped her grandmother lie down on the king-size bed to take a nap.

She pulled back the coverlet to cover Ellie, saying, "Rest now, Grandma."

Reina was concerned, the trip had been difficult on her grandmother. And she was still thinking of that last day with Daniel. There was something wild and sad about him, a vulnerability that didn't make him any less attractive.

She left the room quietly to let her grandmother rest, went back down to the lobby and outside to explore. The city seemed overwhelming from this vantage point, marked with an extravagant opulence from days gone by mixed with the frantic pace of modern civilization. Reina took a deep breath and began to walk, to try and sort out the emotions that fought within her.

The room was dark when Ellie opened her eyes. "Reina," she said softly. "Are you there?" Without an answer she started to get up, to make her way carefully to the window and open the curtains. The lights of Paris lit up the night. She looked to her left and saw the Eiffel Tower, the landmark rising gracefully above the city. But she fixed her gaze farther beyond into the black thinking of her youngest child, Adriana, of Adrien, and Sofia.

Elleanore turned with the sound of the lock as Reina walked in, turning on the lights. "Grandma, what are you doing standing in the dark?"

"I just woke up and you weren't here. I was worried… where have you been?"

Reina started taking off her coat, scarf, and gloves. "I've been walking along the Seine," she replied gleefully. "I had a café au lait and croissant in a little sidewalk bistro on the Champs-Élysées." She kicked off her shoes and took Ellie's hands. "It's just as magical as Laura told me it was. We must hurry though… it's getting late and our reservations are in an hour."

"I don't know, dear. Maybe we should just call room service. We have to leave early in the morning."

"Absolutely not, Grandma." Normally it took months to get into Lasserre, but the chef was a friend of Laura's. "I can't tell her we stayed in and ordered off the hotel menu."

Their reservations were at nine and it was well past midnight by the time they returned to the hotel. The restaurant was an unforgettable experience; Ellie loved watching Reina's childlike enthusiasm, but her mind was elsewhere. It was almost three in the morning before she fell asleep and after ten the next morning when she awoke.

They ordered coffee and breakfast brought to their room as they prepared for the day. Reina had her coffee, a plate of fruit, cheese, and a croissant in the bathroom as she put on her makeup. Elleanore was ready, waiting patiently for her granddaughter who was saying, "The drive should take us about five hours."

Ellie was fretting as she replied, "We should have taken a train or bus. I wanted to be there sooner."

"It's alright. It'll be easier to have a car."

There was a knock on the door; Elleanore stood saying, "I'll get it… it's probably housekeeping." As she opened the door, her mind was unprepared for what she saw.

A beautiful middle-aged woman with long dark hair streaked with bits of gray said, "Hello, Mother."

Ellie's eyes began to tear, as she said astonished, "Adriana."

"Are you going to invite me in?"

It was difficult for Elleanore to know what to do; instinctively she stepped forward to embrace her daughter. But Adriana walked past her outstretched arms into the room.

Reina called out, "Who is it, Grandma?"

Adriana's feelings were mixed; she was still angry with her mother but unprepared for the elderly woman before her. "That must be Lorraine," she said. "Michael told me she was coming with you."

Reina came into the room but stopped suddenly. She'd seen pictures of her father's sister when she was much younger; Adriana as a young girl was pretty but the woman before her was beautiful. "Aunt Adriana… is that you?"

Adriana embraced her, kissing each cheek delicately in turn. "You look so much like your grandfather."

Ellie said quietly, "The resemblance is remarkable isn't it."

"Except for the color of her hair," Adriana replied to her mother. "It's beautiful, the way I remember yours." The memory hurt, even as she said it, and she quickly changed the subject. "I came down yesterday to spend the night with friends. I'll drive and we'll have time to talk."

"I'll call and cancel the rental," Reina replied.

The bellman and valet helped load their bags into an early'90s Peugeot sedan. Adriana noticed the excessive tip her mother gave each man and slid behind the wheel. She was silent as she pulled the vehicle out into the city traffic, traveling south, past the Eiffel Tower, and across the Seine.

The tension between her grandmother and aunt was thick enough to cut with a knife. Reina sat in the back seat nervously and finally said, "I'm anxious to meet your daughter. How old is she now?"

A slight guffaw escaped Adriana's lips. "Marie is twelve and a pain in the ass most of the time."

"It's a difficult age," Ellie observed. "You were no different."

"The situation is completely different," Adriana countered.

"I just meant she'll grow out of it… you did."

Reina didn't miss the strain of the conversation and decided to shift to something else. "What made you decide to live here… in France?"

Adriana glanced at her mother. "You didn't tell her."

Ellie looked out the window as Reina asked innocently, "Tell me what?"

"That is so like you, Mother," Adriana said contemptuously. She took a cigarette from her purse and lit it, rolling the window down a few inches.

"You shouldn't smoke," Ellie admonished her gently.

"I'm an adult, Mother. If I want to smoke I will."

The patience that Ellie promised she would exercise was quickly running out. "Do it then if it pleases you. It's your health."

"I don't smoke that much."

"The amount is also up to you," Ellie cautioned.

Adriana stamped out the cigarette. "Is that better now?" She paused briefly before voicing a demand. "Why are you here?"

"I want to meet my granddaughter, and to see you. Is that a crime?"

Reina had closed her eyes, listening to the two of them but staying quiet when her aunt asked, "How are your parents?"

She sat up. "They're fine. Daddy wanted me to ask you to come home for a visit. They would like to see you and meet Marie."

"My brother is a nice man."

There was a but coming, Reina sensed it, yet it never came. "Daddy's been making some wonderful wines, she told her. His Cabernet is exceptional."

"He comes by it naturally," Adriana replied. "And your mother. Is she still at the hospital?"

"Yes."

Two hours later they stopped at a small café in Tours for something to eat. When Reina excused herself to go to the restroom, Adriana said to Ellie immediately, "I don't want you to hurt them."

"Why would I possibly do that? I love them."

"You don't even know them anymore. My father is no longer strong, and Sofia's heart is too generous for her own good."

"You have such tender feelings for him but not for your mother. I'm not as strong as I once was either." Ellie wiped away a tear. "You haven't so much as touched me once, let alone give me a kiss. After so much time I would have thought you'd have learned to forgive. But I see now that it's beyond you."

The anger that Adriana carried over the years had become a part of her. It was something she'd learned to live with, but the negativity tainted her. She loved her mother but couldn't get beyond the lie that stood between them. The distance created as a result was passed onto Marie, her daughter. The horrible thing was that Adriana was aware of the effect and that in turn angered her.

As they continued to travel south, the cloud cover that hung over Paris gradually gave way to sunshine. Reina had switched from the back seat to the front to allow Ellie the chance to nap in the back. She said to her aunt as she drove, "It's beautiful here. I can see why you stayed."

"It had nothing to do with the countryside," Adriana replied curtly.

The trip that Elleanore envisioned was turning out much differently than the one she imagined. Sofia warned her, but she had no idea the extent of Adriana's bitterness. Why, she wondered, did her daughter choose to carry such a burden? It had been such a long time ago and Ellie truly believed that the decision she'd made then was the best for her children. Why, she asked herself, didn't Adriana understand that? These were the thoughts running through her mind as she kept silent with her eyes closed and listened.

"Why did you stay then?" Reina asked innocently.

Adriana sighed. "It's a long story… and the things we do, Reina, are not always just about one thing. We make decisions not realizing what will happen as a result." When the words were voiced the image that came into Adriana's mind was that of her mother. And then she thought of her father, then Charles, Charlie Winthrop, Marie's father.

"What do you do," Reina asked, "for a living I mean? Do you work in the wine industry?"

"Heavens no," she replied. "I'll leave the making of wine to my father and brother." The words were out of her mouth before she considered the result. "I do freelance ads for the fashion industry."

Ellie opened her eyes when she heard the reference to Adrien, Adriana's father, and said, "She studied art at the Sorbonne. Your aunt was a skilled painter, Reina."

"Really. Would you show me something you've done?"

The life that Adriana wanted for herself when she was a young girl living in Paris was long gone, lost in the reality of single parenting. The thought of it was painful. "I don't do it anymore," she replied bitterly, "there's not the time."

"That's too bad," Reina observed regretfully. "I didn't think Grandfather cared much about making wine. He always seemed disinterested to me. Daddy's the one who's always had the passion for it."

Adriana glanced in the rearview mirror and glared at her mother. "I'm tired of this. Are you going to tell her, or am I?"

Ellie was backed into a corner and just as tired of the lie as Adriana. But she believed that it was important to protect her other children. She asked quietly, "Does Michael know?"

Adriana replied impatiently, "Of course he does, Mother! So do Jane and Sonny. They simply avoid the subject for your benefit."

"Avoid what subject?" Reina asked innocently.

"Go ahead and tell her," Ellie replied. "You've been trying to get around to it all day."

Adriana's response was blunt. "Adrien is my father and Michael's."

Reina was momentarily taken aback. "Adrien Forche is my grandfather?" She turned around and looked at her grandmother for confirmation. There was no need for an answer, she could see it in Elleanore's eyes. "Grandma, why didn't you ever tell me this?"

How, she wondered, could she ever explain to someone who'd grown up in an entirely different era what it was like then, when she was young? It was a different time with different values. And the options for women were much different now than then.

Despite the feelings that were seated deep within her Adriana felt sorry for her mother. She said to Reina, "Mother thought it was best. I'm sure you've figured out by now that the Stricklands are a difficult brood."

Reina continued to look at Elleanore. "Did Grandfather know?"

Ellie nodded. "Yes."

"And that's why he was so hard on Daddy."

"He absolutely couldn't stand me," Adriana replied, "and Abigail punished me for it as long as I can remember."

"Roger loved you and Michael," Ellie insisted. She'd had her fill of the blame and taking the brunt of it. "He had a difficult time showing it. How could it be any different for him growing up with a mother like Abigail Strickland? And by the way, Adriana, she punished anyone who crossed her! She certainly didn't single you out."

Reina turned back around and looked out the passenger window at the landscape going by. There was too much for her to absorb in such a short amount of time, too much to fit into the life she thought she'd understood. She became quiet and quickly wiped a tear away before it had the chance to fall.

Now that the time had come to clear the air Elleanore wasn't finished. "I was afraid Roger and Abigail would take Sonny and Jane from me. I wanted to be with your father, Adriana, but I couldn't give up my children. You know they would have taken them."

Adriana kept silent but she knew that her mother was right. The Stricklands wouldn't have let Ellie leave him with all the children, and they had the power to stop her. It was a different time, she thought, and a woman's place was at the mercy of a society dominated by males. The Abigail Stricklands of the world were an exception; they knew how to use the male to gain power and wealth. And giving up that position was something they fought to keep. Adriana detested those within her own gender who were a part of it; they were just as responsible.

It was getting dark as they arrived at Saint-André-de-Cubzac; Adriana continued to weave her way through the streets until she reached the Route de Libourne and continued to head southeast. "It's another thirty minutes away," she informed them.

Reina asked, "Will we go through Bordeaux?"

Adriana shook her head. "No. This road takes us straight into Libourne. They're probably saving supper for us."

The anxiety that Ellie felt earlier that morning turned to anticipation as her attention fixed itself on the road ahead.

CHAPTER 24

Laura

The test stick read positive; it was the second one. Laura threw it in the trash thinking to herself that it was impossible; she'd been on birth control for years. She wound her hair on top of her head before fastening it with a clip, applied lipstick, and shut off the bathroom light. There had to be a mistake, she concluded, and decided to call her doctor in the city for an appointment.

The morning was chilly; she grabbed a black leather jacket from the closet just inside the front door, put it on, and wrapped a multicolored scarf about her neck before leaving the cottage. The hues of fall were vibrant as she walked through the woods toward the hotel. She hardly noticed the beauty of the day as her mind struggled with the potential problem at hand. The test was wrong, she was sure of it. If she was pregnant, and that was a big if, the only lover she'd had since Matt was David. And that would mean she'd conceived early in their relationship. If it hadn't been their first time together, then it would have been close to it. She remembered it was late that first time, she'd been walking back to the cottage and David was sitting outside, waiting with flowers. Laura began to rack her brain trying to remember if she'd used protection; she'd forgotten before, in the past, but there was such a long time between lovers her occasional forgetfulness had never been a problem.

She saw Michael working among the vines, waved back to him, and thought of Reina. She'd been gone for two days and Laura could already feel the pressure of dealing with the extra work. She felt a certain amount of pride knowing that Reina volunteered to accompany her grandmother and she was proud of Ellie for going. The woman had loved one man for decades, raised his children, lost him and her daughter. She hoped that Ellie could find closure.

Laura took off her scarf as she made her way across the lobby of the hotel toward the restaurant. She glanced at her watch; it was after eleven. Matt, her ex-fiancé, had given her a Rolex; she'd sold it to help finance the opening of the bistro. Mélange was a dream she'd worked hard to create, just like the bistro before it. There wasn't time for a child.

As she passed by, Angie said to her, "Good morning, Chef."

Laura smiled at the waitress as she asked, "How are you this morning?"

"Fine, Chef," she replied and then added excitedly, "Did you hear about Alex and Izzy? They're getting married."

Everything seemed to be unraveling all at once, she thought, and replied with a smile, "I know. They're a perfect couple." As she was about to turn and walk away she stopped and asked, "Angie, would you bring me an Americano please, in my office."

"Yes, Chef."

She hung her coat and scarf on the rack just inside her office and picked up the phone to dial the long-distance number for her doctor; she was a friend she'd known for several years. Laura was still on hold when the young woman brought her coffee. "Thank you, Angie."

"Is there anything else, Chef?"

"Yes. Has Alex come in yet?"

Before she could answer the receptionist's voice came over the speakerphone, "This is Doctor Holland's office. May I help you?"

Laura picked up the phone and took it off speaker. "I'd like to make an appointment please."

Angie waited while her boss finished the call and wrote down the appointment time on her calendar before saying, "No, ma'am, he isn't here yet."

"Let him know I want to see him when he gets in."

"Yes, Chef."

Laura turned on her computer and took a sip of coffee, waiting while it booted up. Her idea the year before at the bistro was to have a traditional Thanksgiving supper for people who either wanted or needed to go out, to be with others on the holiday. It hadn't worked out, but it was still a good idea and she was determined to do it this year at Mélange. They were already taking reservations.

For the next hour she was on the computer tweaking the menu for the following week and the one she'd planned for Thanksgiving Day. She knew that she should be going over the bills but didn't want to face them. Once Laura turned off the machine and fastened her chef's coat she went into the kitchen to observe. Isabelle had her staff working efficiently. She tested a sauce simmering on the stove, nodded her approval, and walked on. The staff had really come together and despite the day's pressure she felt a momentary sense of pride.

Laura was talking to the baker, Tony Morello, when Alex walked in. When they first opened Mélange, Tony continued to work at the bistro until the business at the new restaurant grew to the point where he was needed full-time in St. Helena. He had a wife and small child; the move out of the city wasn't a problem for them.

Isabelle had just finished the lunch rush when she saw Alex; she made her way toward the back of the kitchen by the office and freezer. This was their meeting place when they wanted a moment alone. He noticed Izzy leave and met her there, laughing as he twirled her in his arms, kissing her. "I missed you today."

She cupped his face in her hands, kissing him back. "Yo también, mi amour."

Laura stopped outside her office and said loud enough for them to hear, "Alex, I need to see you for a minute."

He kissed Izzy quickly and whispered, "I'll see you later."

"I love you," Izzy said and kissed him once more.

Alex grabbed his charcoal black chef coat with the red pinstripe, buttoning it up when he walked into her office. "Yes, Chef."

They were a good-looking couple, Laura thought, as she looked up at him from behind her desk. She handed him the menu she'd laid out for the next week. "We have five more days before Thanksgiving. I don't want to be short of any inventory. There are a lot of reservations already and the hotel will be full. We don't want to disappoint our clientele. It's too important."

"Yes, Chef."

"With Reina gone, you and I have to take up the slack. I'll be meeting with her vendors. This will give me less time in the kitchen, and you'll have to cover." She paused briefly. "And, Alex, I have a doctor's appointment next Tuesday. You'll be in charge."

There was an element of concern in his voice as he asked, "Is everything alright, Chef?"

Her stomach felt queasy. "Yes, it's just a checkup. I've been putting it off way too long."

His dark eyes were fixed intently into hers sensing there was something she wasn't telling him. "I want you to know how much you mean to me. Not just for the job but teaching me what you know. And about Izzy. You know I'd do anything for you."

The sincere expression on his face mixed with his admission moved her and she felt her eyes begin to water. She lowered her head. "I know. Now get to work. I'm busy."

Alex nodded. "I'll make sure we have everything for the holiday." He left quietly, shutting the door as he went.

Laura put her elbows on her desk, resting her face in her hands, asking herself with a whisper, "Why are you so emotional?" She wiped away the tears. "The best thing is to keep busy." And with that in mind she left her office and went into the kitchen.

The weekend was one of the busiest Mélange experienced since they opened. For the first time in a long time, Laura began to see some light at the end of the financial tunnel. On Sunday after work, she spent the night with David. They were lying next to one another; she was cuddled into his arms after making love as he said, "You're certainly in a good mood."

She kissed the palm of his hand and replied smiling, "Everything is coming together. I can feel it. We'll still have some rough patches, but I really think we're finally over the hump."

"You've been open less than a year… that's good."

"We might be in the black this month."

He kissed her temple. "Are you taking the day off tomorrow?"

"No, I'm too busy and I have to go to the city on Tuesday."

"I'll go with you."

"That's alright. It's business and I have to check on the house now that Reina's gone."

"Michael's been worried about her."

"About Reina, why?"

David got out of bed and started toward the bathroom saying as he went, "He wouldn't tell me. I do know he didn't want his mother to go to France. They argued about it, but you know Elleanore. When she gets something in her head there's no convincing her otherwise."

Laura threw the covers back and put on a chemise that her cousin Lia had given her for her birthday two years before. "Elleanore has people she cares about there. It's important for her. Michael should understand that."

He shifted the conversation suddenly. "Why don't you want me to go with you on Tuesday?"

She was looking in the mirror over the dresser while brushing her hair. "It's not that I don't want you to go."

"Then what is it?"

It was an opportune time to tell him, but she wasn't sure of the pregnancy yet. She knew if she told him they'd have to deal with a whole different conversation. And she didn't want that, at least for now. "I have to see my doctor."

"What's the matter?"

"It's just a checkup. I've been putting it off and need to get it done." She looked at him as he came back into the room; he didn't seem to doubt her. Laura kissed him. "I'm fine, don't worry." She smiled. "Come back to bed. It's getting late and I'm a working girl."

She was sitting on the exam table waiting for Margaret Holland, her gynecologist, to come back into the room. The door opened suddenly, and the doctor came in smiling. "You are definitely pregnant, Laura." She handed her a business card. "This is an associate of mine, an obstetrician, Dr. Singh, she has an office downstairs. You should make an appointment today."

"Are you sure, Margaret?"

"Yes. Because of your age Dr. Singh should give you some genetic counseling but if she doesn't, ask her." She noticed some concern in Laura's face. "You're a very healthy woman, Laura... I wouldn't worry."

"I'm not ancient, Margaret."

Dr. Holland chuckled. "No, but you are thirty-five and it doesn't hurt to be careful." She started to open the door. "I'll let you get dressed. And don't look so serious. Go out and celebrate... but no liquor." She smiled warmly. "I'm happy for you."

"Margaret," she asked quickly, "do you have children?"

"Three," she replied. "Two still at home and one in college. Why do you ask?"

"My work, the hours are so difficult. It could be hard on a child."

The physician shut the door again. "My husband and I did it. And there were difficult times." Margaret sat on the exam table and took her hand. "I wouldn't give my children up for the world. And I know you, Laura. You'll be a wonderful parent."

Laura nodded. "Thank you."

On the way out of the building she stopped by Karen Singh's office and scheduled an appointment for later that month. Afterward she stopped at the bistro briefly and met with Shelly before going to her home by Golden Gate Park to check on it. The entire time Laura thought of David and struggled with the best way to tell him.

Two of Reina's vendors were scheduled to meet with Laura the next day in San Francisco. She spent the night in the city and the next morning she was sick for the first time. The meeting was to be held at the bistro and as Laura arrived she noticed Daniel Whitman sitting outside having breakfast; Travis, his golden retriever, was lying quietly next to him.

She stopped. "Good morning, Dan."

He looked up and smiled back. "Laura, it's good to see you." Daniel stood and held out his hand. "Shelly said you might come in today."

"How have you been?"

"I've been gettin' by." He knew it was too soon, but he asked anyway, "Have you heard from Reina?"

"No, not yet," she replied. "I think she called her parents when they arrived." Travis was looking up at her, wagging his tail expectantly. Laura knelt and scratched him gently behind the ears saying, "You are such a pretty boy… yes you are."

Daniel grinned. "He'll never let you be if ya keep that up."

Travis was given one final stroke before she stood again. "People ask all the time who did the painting in the bistro and where you're showing your work. Are there any galleries we can refer them to?"

"No, still freelance."

"You're not getting any younger, Dan. Maybe it's time for you to settle down. I know Reina would like it if you did."

He asked hesitantly, "Do you really think she would?"

"I'm sure of it." An idea came to her suddenly. "Dan, how would you like to do another painting for me?"

Nodding toward the bistro he replied, "I don't think you're short on space in there."

"I don't mean here. I have another place in St. Helena, north of Napa. If you have the time I'd like you to come up and talk to me about it." She held out a business card for Mélange. "The restaurant is in a hotel owned by Reina's family."

"Reina talked to me about your new place. I'd like to see it." He looked at the card. "I'll be pretty busy over the holiday weekend. But I should have some time next week."

She held out her hand. "I'll look forward to hearing from you." As they shook hands she said, "I'm late. It was really good to see you, Dan."

There was a slight nod of recognition from him. "You too, Laura." When she started to walk away he said, "You're real pretty this mornin'. You sorta glow."

She was taken aback by the compliment and wasn't quite sure how to take it. "Thank you, Dan."

It occurred to him then that she might have misinterpreted what he'd said. "I wasn't makin' a pass or anything. Sometimes the words just come out before I have time to think about it." He paused. "If you talk to Reina, tell her hi from me. I miss her."

"I will. See you next week."

Laura was exhausted by the time she arrived back at the cottage late that afternoon. She knew that she should check in at the restaurant but was aware that if she did she wouldn't leave. She took a nap instead and it was dark by the time she opened her eyes. Her first thought was of David.

There was a knock on her door, and she got up to answer it. David was standing there and said, "I expected you back earlier and got worried. Alex told me he hadn't seen you yet."

She didn't reply but wrapped her arms about him instead and said in a whisper, "Come in. We have to talk."

CHAPTER 25

Elleanore

Adrien and Sofia lived in a four-bedroom two-story stone house built in the late 1850s modernized at the turn of the twentieth century and in serious need of repair when he purchased it as their home seventy-five years later. Toward the back of the property there was a second small two-bedroom house built several years later that he'd used as a rental. When Adriana came to live with them with Marie, he remodeled the rental for her.

Their home was within walking distance of Libourne's city center and on market days Sofia would walk with Marie to the square to buy fresh fruits and vegetables. On the day of Elleanore's arrival they were coming back from such a walk but not to buy produce; it was late November and they'd gone to the pharmacy for Adrien's heart medicine.

Despite her age Sofia still drove but it was a nice day and she enjoyed the time with Marie. The two of them were extremely close and the twelve-year-old spent as much or more of her time with her grandparents than she did with her mother. Marie was irritated because her mother hadn't taken her to Paris to meet her grandmother. "She never lets me do anything I want, Grand-mere."

"Your mother needs to talk to Elleanore first. They haven't seen each other for a very long time. N'est-ce pas?"

"What should I call her?"

"Let's see, you could call her Grand-mere, the same as me."

Marie giggled. "That's silly. If I call both of you Grandmother, both of you will be turning around going oui, oui, oui. It's confusing."

"How about Mamie then?"

The little girl let go of her hand and skipped ahead. "I like that. I'll call her Granny." She twirled twice and began walking backward. "Will I like her?"

"Oui, mom cher... you will. I like Elleanore very much. We have been friends for a long time."

There was a question Marie had been dying to ask. "Why did Grand-pere marry you and not Elleanore?"

Sofia knew that sooner or later the time would come when curiosity would get the best of Marie. "Ce n'etait pas cense etre."

"I know but why wasn't it meant to be?"

"You are full of too many questions, Marie." It didn't matter how many years they shared together; these thoughts haunted her married life. Adrien had been in love with Ellie and Sofia was in love with him. She felt she'd always been a second choice for him. She'd always hoped that their own children would bring them closer together but that was not to be. It seemed the two of them over time settled into an existence that might have lacked great passion, but they were comfortable and enjoyed one another. It wasn't until Adriana and Marie entered their lives that they finally became a family. And true happiness followed.

Twilight descended; the electric lights in the house were old and the image in the ancient mirror hanging on the stone wall didn't help him knot his tie. Adrien had been struggling with it for fifteen minutes when he heard Marie and Sofia come in. He gave up, put on his suit coat, grabbed his cane, and hobbled down the stairs to meet them.

Marie was in the kitchen with Sofia, who had just hung up her coat and was putting on her apron. She'd prepared her version of coq au vin earlier that afternoon, so it could easily be reheated when their guests arrived. The scent from the chicken stew still hung in the air mixed with the fresh bread she'd baked that morning.

The twelve-year-old heard her grandfather coming down the stairs and into the hallway. She ran to meet him, wrapping her young arms around his waist saying, "Nous avons tes médicaments, Grand-père."

He kissed the top of her head lightly. "Merci, mon coeur."

"Your pills are on the table, Adrien," Sofia told him. She gazed at him in his suit, the one he wore to mass on Sundays and thought how good he looked. "It's getting late," she said. "I thought Adriana would be here by now."

Adrien sat down at the table in the middle of the kitchen. "It's a long trip. They'll be here soon."

Marie noticed his tie was undone and knelt in front of him and began to carefully wrap one end around the other, slid the completed knot up to his neck and straightened the collar of his shirt. "There, Grand-pere. You look beautiful."

"You are the beautiful one, chérie"—he smiled at her— "my beautiful papillon."

Sofia watched the two of them a moment, thinking to herself how lucky they both were to have Marie in their lives. She leaned over and kissed her husband on the mouth softly. "You are still a very handsome man."

"Merci, chérie," he said, looking up into her eyes. They were kind eyes he thought, filled with love. Adrien believed himself to be a very lucky man. When he finally came to the truth that Elleanore would never be his, he believed he'd lost the love of his life. But for years his feelings for Sofia simmered, the love within him growing with each passing year until it filled his being. Then Adriana arrived from America and he thought that nothing could make him happier. But that was before Marie was born and the two of them came to live in Libourne.

When Sofia encouraged Elleanore to come for a visit he was afraid. Not because he was still in love with Ellie but because he knew that this might once again raise the doubts he knew his precious wife harbored. He smiled at her and said lovingly, "Je t'aime, mon amour."

He started taking his pipe from his pocket to clean and fill it when Marie called out from the front parlor, "Maman is here!"

Adriana stopped the sedan in front of an old stone building that even in the dark Reina could see was decrepit. Elleanore was in the back seat straining to see the family she missed so desperately. Suddenly the front door opened and a beautiful young girl with long dark hair emerged, running to meet them. "Maman, Maman," the girl cried.

Elleanore started to get out when she saw Adrien and Sofia standing backlit in the doorway. Time seemed to stop for her in that second; she felt as if she was coming home again after a half century away. They were the two people in this world who completed her.

She'd just taken a step toward them when Marie stood before her saying excitedly, "Etes-vous ma grand-mere?"

Adriana said quickly, "Use your English, Marie."

"Oui, Maman," and looked at Ellie expectantly. "Are you my granny?"

Ellie smiled and spontaneously hugged her granddaughter with tears in her eyes. "Yes, I suppose I am."

Marie took her hand and began lightly pulling Ellie toward the house saying, "We've been waiting for you for the longest time."

It was Sofia who made the first move toward Ellie, crying now, as she crossed the distance between them. When she was close enough Sofia reached out to caress Ellie's face briefly with shaking hands before taking her in her arms saying, "It has been too long."

"I've missed you so," Ellie replied as she held Sofia tight against her.

The two women were crying and laughing as they walked arm in arm to the house. The person who Elleanore had come halfway around the world to see was not the old man keeping his balance with a cane for support but the man she loved. Once they reached him Ellie kissed each of his cheeks before saying with a quiver in her voice, "It took a lifetime but I'm here."

These were the two women Adrien had loved in his life. He put his cane aside, balancing it on the doorjamb, put one arm around Ellie and the other around his wife saying quietly, "The Lord has blessed us today."

Marie watched the three of them and though she might not have completely understood she sensed the intense love between them.

It was one of those small turning points in life that help build who we are. Adrien saw her, took the arm that held Ellie and pulled his granddaughter into the circle of their embrace.

Reina hadn't understood the depth of her grandmother's feelings until that moment. Adriana was just as surprised and said to her, "Come, let's get the bags and take them in."

"I thought we'd probably stay in a hotel," Reina replied.

"Nonsense, you are family. You will stay with us."

Adriana picked up two pieces of luggage, one large the other small, and started carrying them to the house. The walkway was made of several large pieces of flagstone leading to the front door, each one surrounded by bits of grass from the small front yard. Reina struggled with her suitcase, pulling it across the uneven ground, her six-inch heels making the effort more difficult. She whispered to herself, "That's OK. Don't worry about me."

"Are you my cousin?" Marie asked.

Reina stopped and said as she took a deep breath, "Yes I am."

"We have the same grand-pere."

"Yes, we do," Reina replied as she began struggling with the suitcase once again.

"I'll help… if you want. We could carry it together." Without waiting for an answer Marie went to her and took hold of the handle on the side of the suitcase. The two of them continued to make their way inside the house with the case, setting it down in the entryway.

Marie led the way into a small parlor with a large round oak table in the middle of the room covered in a crocheted white tablecloth that had begun to yellow with age. The extra chairs were lined against one wall. The wallpaper was old and faded. Reina could hear laughter coming from another room. "Ils sont dans la cuisine," Marie began then quickly corrected herself. "In the kitchen… come, I'll show you."

Elleanore was sitting at the rectangular kitchen table watching while Adrien opened a bottle of red wine and Sofia began to heat up their supper, the three of them talking and laughing among themselves. It was then that Ellie noticed Reina with Marie standing in the doorway.

She stood suddenly, realizing she hadn't introduced their granddaughter. "Adrien," she said, "this is Michael's daughter, Lorraine… Reina."

The old man set the bottle down and smiled at her. "I've waited a very long time for this day." He picked up his cane and walked across the few paces that separated them and took her in his arms. "Merci," he said to Reina, "for bringing our Ellie to us."

Reina was overwhelmed by him, by this strange place, and the relationships that a short time ago were unknown to her. She felt out of place, as if she didn't belong, and that discomfort was felt by Adrien as he held her briefly. When they broke their embrace and she gazed into this old man's eyes she saw her father there, looking back at her.

Michael had made it very clear, to his mother, that he didn't want anything to do with Adrien. Roger Strickland had never treated him the same way after finding out about Elleanore's lover. The Strickland business was eventually turned over to his two older children, Sonny and Jane. Michael never stopped trying to regain his love. He blamed his mother and Adrien for the distance created between them. That is why he fought with his mother when she told him she was going to France. And it was why he refused to go with her. He failed to consider that his daughter would go in his place.

During supper and afterward Reina watched them, thinking that she'd rarely seen her grandmother as animated and at ease. While Reina was paying attention to Sofia, Adrien, and Elleanore, Adriana was studying her. She sympathized with Michael's daughter but was convinced that like the rest of the Stricklands she was spoiled.

After the dishes were done Adriana finished her brandy and took one last sip of coffee before saying to Marie, "It's time for you to be in bed."

"Maman," Marie protested, "let me stay a little longer."

"Your grandmother and aunt will be here when you get home from school tomorrow."

Reina asked Marie with a smile, "Would you show me your room?"

The girl jumped up overjoyed. "Puis-je aimer, Maman?"

Adriana nodded. "Yes you may… but make it quick. I'll be home soon."

Marie led her through the kitchen to the back of the house and out a side door. The night was dark, and Reina asked, "Where are we going?"

"Maman and I live next door." She held on to her cousin's hand as they made their way across the side yard to a small stone dwelling with one single light shining in the window. The door was unlocked as they went inside. What would have been a parlor or living room had been turned into a workspace for Adriana. The light was from a lamp sitting on a battered flat-topped desk next to a Mac computer and printer that had fax and scanning capability. There was a drawing table next to the desk with several preliminary sketches for ads Adriana was working on.

Marie turned on another lamp next to a large, overstuffed chair that had seen better days. "My room is this way," she said, waiting for her. They went up a steep flight of stairs to a narrow hallway.

The girl's room was tiny with a single bed along one wall, a small desk, and chair. The stone walls were painted a dark red, filled with posters of all sorts next to drawings and paintings that Marie had done. There were two dolls resting beside a stuffed bear leaning against her bed pillows looking back at them.

There was a sharp contrast between Reina's black Armani suit and this meager décor. Marie was suddenly disheartened and for the first time in her life she felt unworthy. Tears began to well up in her eyes when her cousin said suddenly, "Did you do these paintings?"

"Oui," she replied quietly.

Reina was amazed. "They're wonderful, Marie." Suddenly a black and white cat with one blue eye and one brown rubbed itself against Reina's leg. She picked it up and said with a grin, "Is this a friend of yours?"

Marie took the cat from Reina's arms possessively. "Her name is Amaline."

The sound of Adriana coming through the front door downstairs broke the spell between them. The young girl was relieved as she heard her mother's voice say loud enough for them to hear, "Marie, c'est l'heure du lit."

She held Amaline close as she said to Reina, "It is time for bed."

Seeing the distressed look in her young cousin's face Reina asked, "Would you show me around after school tomorrow?"

Marie considered the request briefly and felt it would be rude to refuse. "Yes," she replied hesitantly, "if you would like."

On impulse she cupped Marie's face in her hands, kissing her quickly. "Sleep tight. I'll see you tomorrow."

As she came downstairs she could see Adriana pouring brandy from a decanter into two glasses. "I should be going," Reina said.

Adriana forced a smile, handed her a glass, and pointed to the chair. "Please sit. This is the first chance we've had to be alone."

Reina did as she asked and watched while her aunt lit a fire in the fireplace that had been prepared earlier. When Adriana was satisfied that the flame had taken hold she stood and said, "You've had a big day."

"Yes. It's been a lot to take in." She hesitated a moment before saying, "Marie is a wonderful girl. And her paintings are beautiful."

Adriana reached for a pack of cigarettes on the mantle she kept hidden behind a framed photo of Adrien and Sofia. She lit one and said apologetically, "Mother's right. I should quit." When there was no response she said, "Michael's unhappy that you came here with her. He doesn't think Mother would have come without you."

"Do you think that's true?"

"No," she snickered. "Mother's always done as she pleases. I doubt that's changed. I told him so."

"You don't like her very much do you?"

"Non, au contraire." She seemed to switch easily without pretense from one language to the other. "My mother is very likable. But I love my father very much, and Sofia. I would hate to see them hurt."

"You can't control that, and neither can I." Reina paused a moment. "And what about your mother's love? For you and for them."

She threw her cigarette in the fire. "We'll see." Adriana looked fixedly into her eyes as if she was trying to decide whether to say more, then replied, "It's late. You're tired and so am I."

Reina finished her brandy and began making her way to the door. "I'll see you tomorrow then."

Adriana crossed the room and hugged her. "Sleep well." And then as an afterthought she said, "I'm glad you came."

As she heard the door click shut Marie got up from the top step where she'd been listening and went to her bed. A moment later her mother came in, tucked the covers about her and said in a whisper, "Bonn nuit, mon amour… mon enfant."

Laura

"Are you sure?"

She nodded. "Pretty sure. And wipe that ridiculous grin off your face. This is serious."

He was sitting across from her on a chair next to the fireplace; the faint sound of crackling wood could be heard between them. "I can't help it," David said softly as he crossed the few feet between them. His hand reached out tentatively to touch her belly. "I'm going to be a father!"

"We could be parents is more to the point."

"What do you mean could?"

His expression became serious, she stood and walked away a few paces. "If we go ahead with the pregnancy we have to decide how it's going to work. If… we don't… we have to know that too." With her back turned she quickly wiped away a tear, then facing him once more she said, "I don't think I can be a single parent. And I won't give up my work."

David was still on the floor looking up at her. "Of course not. I wouldn't want you to."

He stood slowly and came to her as she turned her head away crying now, saying softly, "I love you."

His hand reached out and gently turned her face toward him. "I want to marry you, to have this child, and another and another, if we can."

Laura chuckled lightly as she wiped her eyes once more. "I think we better take this one child at a time." The look she gave him was sincere. "I'm not trying to pressure you into something… into marriage. It's not like that."

His arms wrapped around her, bringing her close against him. "I know that." He grinned. "Look at it this way. We can throw all caution aside; the damage is already done."

As she started to look away from him again David held her head still, kissing her lips. Laura sighed, kissing him back, then said softly, "This is what got us into this mess."

"I know," he replied kissing her again. "Isn't it wonderful?"

She whispered into his ear as she held him, "I do love you."

"I know," he replied again, kissing her harder, his hands moving down her back to cup her bottom, then back again, across her breasts this time.

She felt his erection pressing against her, the fingers of her hand reaching down to stroke him lightly, unzipping the trousers to search inside, to grasp him. He moaned softly as she brought him to the edge of desire quickly, then stopped, and began pulling him gently toward the bedroom saying, "Come… please."

Moments later, their clothes thrown carelessly to the floor, he entered her forcefully, seeking that crest that would satisfy the growing need between them. Their movements rising and falling in a rhythmic dance not so much different than the waves of the sea. She peaked rapidly then crashed to the other side finding a brief release before letting the tide of passion bring her to the edge once more. Again and again she came before feeling him fill her as she surged to greater heights screaming, "Yes!"

The doubts she'd harbored seemed to fade as he held her in his arms. Sleep came easily, peacefully, beside him. She was for those few precious moments between them content.

Laura's menu that Thanksgiving was traditional, but each guest was given a variety of items to choose from. They offered roast turkey, and hickory smoked ham with pineapple glaze and garnished with maraschino cherries. Sides included sweet potato casserole with pralines, brown sugar and butter; mashed potatoes; green beans with bacon; Waldorf salad; and Brussels sprouts with red pepper and avocado. For dessert there was pumpkin pie with walnut crust or warm cinnamon apples served with vanilla gelato.

Laura worked in a comfortable rhythm beside her staff, her thoughts wandering back to those years long ago when she worked beside her grandmother, learning, creating for the Hanson family gatherings. And she was in love, particularly thankful that David Steele came into her life unforeseen, planting the seed of life within her.

Mélange ordinarily didn't open its doors until five in the afternoon. But on Thanksgiving their first seating was at eleven that morning, the next at two, then five, and finally eight in the evening. The hotel was busy for the weekend, which meant that the restaurant used for daytime guests was kept open for breakfast and lunch. The two different spaces shared the same kitchen, which wasn't a problem normally; they were open at different times. The kitchen was divided between Isabelle's staff and Laura's. During Mélange's first seating at eleven Izzy was in the middle of a lunch rush; despite all the preparation they'd gone through days before, chaos began taking over and tempers started to flair.

A serious quarrel broke out between Angie and one of Mélange's prep cooks. Laura intervened immediately as several people began to argue. She had to shout to be heard, "Stop this now!" In less than a minute it was quiet. "I don't care what shift you normally work. I don't care if you've never met the person working next to you. We are still a team. Act like it or leave." Silence followed as she continued, "OK, that's better. We've all worked in kitchens smaller than this. Respect one another. Alex, I want you to help coordinate my staff and Izzy's." Her eyes surveyed each person in the room as her voice became calm yet firm. "Come on, people, this is a holiday. Let's make it special for our guests!"

The rest of the day went by without incident and when it came time for Izzy and her staff to get off work for the day several of them stayed to help. Laura made sure to tour the dining room during each seating, greeting people, and thanking them for coming. When the last guest was gone for the evening they all sat down together, most of them for the first time in fourteen hours. They ate, drank, and celebrated together until after midnight.

Laura was the last to leave; she wrapped her scarf about her neck, put on her leather jacket, turned out the lights, and locked the doors. On her way back to the cottage she glimpsed Michael sitting on a bench by an old oak tree. She walked over to him. "What are you doing out here this time of night?"

"I couldn't sleep," he replied. "This is the first Thanksgiving I can remember without my mother. Or without Reina for that matter. If it wasn't for you I'm not sure that Erica and I would have bothered."

"I'm glad you had dinner with us. Where is your wife?"

"She took a shift at the hospital. They were shorthanded tonight." He could tell Laura was about to leave but before she had a chance he said, "This tree has been here my entire life."

"Has it really?"

He nodded. "We used to picnic and play here when I was a child. Adrien made a swing for us. I can remember him so well sometimes, the strength of his arms as he pushed me."

"It sounds wonderful."

"I remember once as a boy wishing that my father was more like him. That was before I knew Adrien was my father." As Laura started to say something he stopped her. "That's OK… I know you know. Mother told me."

"You didn't want her to go to see him."

There were tears in his eyes as he said, "I knew I was always different than Sonny and Jane. Adriana did too but she had the courage to do something about it. I just wanted to belong, to be a Strickland… to be loved. The Stricklands never gave me that. I can still remember the day when he looked at me differently… the disappointment in his eyes. It was never the same after that."

Laura sat down next to him, taking his hand. "Love can be a messy business."

He took a drink of Cabernet from the bottle and offered her some, which she declined. "This wine, the one you like so much. I made it by using his notes, Adrien's notes. I found them in the winery years ago. I made a few changes but it's his for the most part." He paused briefly before saying, "I've always wanted to be very good at this, at making wine." Michael gazed into her eyes. "Adrien was more than good… he was great. There's not a school in the world that can teach what he can do."

"It sounds like you admire him very much."

He sighed. "Admiration and jealousy are two sides of the same coin."

She squeezed his hand gently. "Why don't you go and see him, talk to him? It might make a big difference to both of you."

He shook his head. "I'm afraid it's too late for that."

"Is it?" Before he could answer she changed the subject. "Do you want to know a secret?"

"I would love to know your secret."

A grin spread across her face. "I'm pregnant."

Michael smiled. "David?"

"I love him very much."

"You're both lucky."

She stood up. "Yes we are." Laura turned to walk away then stopped and said to him, "Think about what I said before, about going to see him. You might not have much time left."

"I know."

With so much to do, the rest of the weekend seemed to fly by. On Saturday reservations piled up and customers waited as much as an hour for a table. Laura hadn't the time to go over her accounts or pay bills until the following Monday, her day off. Rather than go to her office she stayed at the cottage, spread the paperwork, checkbook, and calculator on the kitchen table and after a late breakfast sat down to work.

By two o'clock that afternoon there was one thing that clearly brightened her day. After the immediate expenses were paid and the checks were written for her employees there was still a comfortable amount of money left in her account. Her first thought was to tell David. She smiled as she stood to stretch her back, grabbed a jean jacket from the closet and began the walk through the woods, past the old oak, and uphill past the vineyards.

It was a beautiful late November day; the air was crisp but the sun without a cloud in the sky warmed her. The leaves on the vines were a brilliant array of yellows, orange, and reds, the scent of fall intoxicating. The harvest was complete, the grapes fermenting into wine.

Her mind was occupied with silly, frivolous thoughts as she walked along; she dreamed of how it would be with them, the nursery they could plan together, how the restaurant would receive one, maybe two Michelin stars, and the joy she knew there would be when the baby was born. A vision of her mother and father, holding their grandchild in their arms, made her smile.

Laura stopped suddenly, fifty yards from the house; she saw a black Aston Martin DB9 convertible pulled up in front. A woman with dark hair got out dressed in a short yellow dress with a coat to match. She grabbed a yellow bag trimmed in black and began walking toward the door. A moment later Tuan opened it; they smiled at one another briefly before she kissed each of his cheeks and went inside.

Her mood darkened instantly as she stood there. Laura considered confronting him now, with her there, and ran the drama briefly in her mind before disregarding the idea. The woman, whoever she was, was dressed to the nines and Laura was in jeans and an old T-shirt she'd bought at one of her cousin's concerts in San Francisco. Whatever she decided to do, there was one thing that was perfectly clear. She'd been through a similar situation with Matt Stryker and didn't find out until days before her wedding that he'd been in love and had a child with another woman. That, she reminded herself, wasn't going to happen again.

She fought off tears as she made her way slowly back to the cottage. A day that had started with so much promise had turned; Laura tried convincing herself that she was jumping to conclusions but simply couldn't get past her fear. Suddenly she noticed a faded red pickup truck parked in her driveway and as she cleared the trees she saw Daniel playing ball with Travis. She took a deep breath, and smiled as she called to him, "Hello there."

He turned around and waved. "I hope you don't mind… Alex told me you might be here."

"It's fine. I was just out for a walk."

Daniel nodded toward her car. "I figured it was something like that. Do you have some time?"

She shook the hand he held out. "Come on in."

He followed her up the porch steps and said firmly to Travis, "Stay."

"It's alright, he can come in," she replied as she opened the door. "Can I get you something to drink?"

Travis curled up on the rug by the fireplace as Daniel looked around the cottage. "Anything's fine."

She opened a bottle of Aqua Panna for herself and a bottle of Coors for him. "I'm sorry but I completely forgot you were coming."

Dan sensed a strain in her voice, an uneasiness as she handed him the bottle. "If this isn't a good time I can come back."

Laura sat down on the sofa in the living room and motioned him to do the same. "As a matter of fact your timing is perfect. I need the distraction."

He took a drink. "If you're still interested I'd like to do another painting for you."

The last thing in the world she wanted to do was discuss business, but it was better than being alone with her thoughts. "I have a place behind the hostess station at the restaurant. We've hung a framed print there, but I'd like something nicer, something that depicts the romance of the area." Once the word *romance* came out of her mouth her stomach turned and she thought she might be sick.

"Are you alright?"

She stood quickly and hurried to the bathroom, kneeling in front of the toilet. Laura hadn't closed the door; Dan was worried and went to check on her. He grabbed a washcloth from a rack beside the sink and soaked it in cool water before holding it to her forehead. She took it from him and held it to her face. "Thank you," she said, forcing a smile as she began to stand.

"I can give you a ride to a doctor."

Laura shook her head saying, "I've seen one." She walked into the living room and took a big drink of water. "I'm pregnant."

"I thought you were only supposed to get sick in the morning."

"It's a lie, an old wives' tale, believe me."

"Is there anything I can do?"

"Yes, you can paint me a painting. And while you're working you can stay here. I have an extra room and you won't have to commute."

"Are you sure?"

Rather than answer him right away, she went into the kitchen and wrote him a check for a down payment. A moment later she handed it to him and asked, "When can you start?"

CHAPTER 27

Elleanore

"No one will tell me, Grand-pere."

"No one will tell you what, Marie?"

She looked up at him as they walked slowly toward the tobacco shop; afterward they would stop at Café Pascal where her grandfather would have his café au lait while Marie had a pastry and hot chocolate. It was a ritual the two of them shared after Adrien picked her up from school on Fridays.

"Why you married Grand-mere and not Mamie."

Adrien mulled that over for several moments after entering the shop while ordering tobacco for his pipe and selecting some cleaners. He paid, then said as they were leaving, "Is love a small thing, Marie?"

The question confused her, and she hesitated before saying, "I don't understand."

"Is it tiny like a speck of dust or immense like the ocean?"

She giggled and said, "You can't measure love, Grand-pere."

"I didn't ask if it could be measured, Marie. Both of us know it cannot."

She held on to his hand tightly, aware that his balance wasn't what it once was. "I love you, Grand-pere, and Grand-mere, and Maman."

He chuckled. "And you love chocolate cake."

Marie giggled again. "Oui very much, and Christmastime. Christmas is coming soon, Grand-pere."

"Oui, c'est, mon petit papillon." They reached the café and even though it was chilly they sat outside to enjoy the last remnants of fall.

An elderly waiter with thinning white hair came out to greet them, wiping the table quickly. "Bonjour, Adrien. How are you, Marie?"

She replied excitedly in French, "My grandmother is visiting from the United States, Monsieur Moreau."

"Is that so, Marie? You'll have to bring her to supper one night."

"Could we, Grand-pere?"

Adrien smiled at her knowing it was difficult for him to deny her anything. "We'll see."

They ordered and a few moments later the waiter brought Adrien's coffee with her pastry and chocolate, smiling as he set it before her. "Bon appetite, Marie."

"Merci," she said quickly while picking up her fork as her grandfather fixed his pipe. A moment later she took a careful sip of her drink and said, "I think that love is so big it's impossible to imagine how big."

He nodded as he lit his pipe. "I think so too. I love you, Marie, more than it's possible for me to describe. I love your mother, and Sofia. I love my son Michael, in America, and his daughter. And I love Elleanore; she is special to me. But in this life, Marie, we marry once, and my choice was and always will be your grand-mere. The love I feel for her is as bright as the summer sun."

Marie picked up the napkin that still lay folded next to her plate and wiped her mouth. "Oui. I do too."

Adrien watched her for a few moments as he enjoyed his coffee and pipe. When she finished he chuckled. "Come," he said, "she'll be worried."

Reina found it difficult to sleep that first night and was tired and irritable the next day. The bed was small, her body cramped, her legs unable to stretch out because of the footboard. She began to resent the time away from home when she could be spending it with Daniel. Being separated from her parents on Thanksgiving didn't help. But on that Thursday Sofia, knowing that it was an American holiday, baked chicken with a traditional breadcrumb stuffing, potato dauphinoise, grilled asparagus, and apple clafouti for dessert.

The next day Reina went for a long walk and happened to see Adrien and Marie sitting at Café Pascal and was just about to call out to them when they got up to leave. She was wearing jeans tucked into tall black boots with four-inch heels, a white blouse, silk scarf, and a dark red leather jacket. Her outfit made it difficult for her to catch up to them, but Marie heard her shout and pulled on his sleeve saying, "It's Reina, Grand-pere."

The old man stopped and waved to his older granddaughter with a smile. "Bonjour, Reina."

She was out of breath by the time she caught up to them. "Bonjour," she repeated. "I was just out for a walk and saw you leaving the café."

"It's too bad," he replied, "that you didn't see us sooner. We just had our coffee and chocolate."

Reina looked at the twelve-year-old with a twinkle in her eye. "Let me guess… Marie had the coffee."

This amused Marie despite the fact she'd become distrustful of her cousin. It wasn't entirely the things she wore that made her feel unworthy and a little jealous or the way she treated her family. Reina was always courteous and friendly. But there was something, an air of superiority she sensed, that angered Marie at times. She'd felt the same a few times around other tourists, particularly Germans and Americans, not in Libourne so much but during those times she'd been with her mother in Bordeaux or Paris.

The old man asked Reina as they continued toward home, "What do you think of our little town?"

"It's charming." There was a moment of hesitation before she continued, "But I was wondering… why here? Why this town?"

The old man thought it only natural that she should ask. "My mother and I lived here when I was not much older than Marie is now." The images of that time, the occupation had never left him. "We lived with my aunt and uncle in the same house we live in now."

"And your father?"

"I was born in Paris. We evacuated the city when the Nazis came and went to live in Toulouse. My father was active in the resistance, arrested, and we never saw him again." He shrugged his burly shoulders. "We had nowhere else to go." They walked several more paces before he said, "My uncle was a vintner and so am I." The old man stopped and looked at his oldest grandchild. "It was fate you see."

"Why do you say that?"

He chuckled. "Fate brought me to Libourne where I learned a trade that eventually led to a job in America. I met your grandmother there and here you are."

"But it wasn't predetermined," Reina argued. "You had choices, so did my grandmother."

"Oui." He nodded. Adrien tried again to help her see what he sensed to be true. "Do you remember the old song about the hip bone being connected to the thigh bone?"

"Yes."

"The Germans swept down upon us from the north. My world was turned upside down the same as thousands of others. There was no choice in that, only the need to survive. My father was a school teacher but what he wished to teach was no longer acceptable. That choice was taken from him. After he was taken we had nowhere to go but to my uncle, no money." Adrien began once more to hobble along between his two granddaughters. "I worked in the fields, learning a trade, and never finished school. That was something my father would have hated. But life forces decisions upon us. They might not be the ones we'd choose but we do what we must."

Now that the discussion had come up Reina didn't want to let it go. She wanted to know what it was that brought her grandparents to the point of betraying Elleanore's husband, the man she always thought of as her grandfather. It wasn't that she was particularly close to Roger Strickland, she wasn't. He lived in San Francisco when she was young, and they rarely saw him. When she did visit him with her parents the man seemed cold and distant. Her father was always upset afterward; she did remember that. But with Marie close by and not knowing how much her young cousin knew of her grandfather's prior life she chose to be silent.

It was Marie who asked, "Mais Granny etait mariee, n'est-ce pas?"

He was aware that she spoke in French knowing Reina wouldn't understand. "Oui she was married. And loving one another was wrong in the eyes of many. But the question I have for both of you girls is, do we have a choice of those we love?" He let that sink in briefly. "Or is love another wind that is forced upon us? A force that is without choice despite law or convention." He shook his head and chuckled. "The heart, my darling girls, is open and needs love to fill it."

In that instant, the image of Daniel flashed into Reina's mind. She hadn't talked to her parents or her grandmother about him. She'd confided some of her feelings to Laura but most of what she'd shared was with Alex. "I have a friend," she began, speaking to Adrien.

Marie giggled. "A boyfriend I imagine, Grand-pere."

"Let Reina finish, Marie," he said, gently scolding, but with a soft squeeze to her hand.

Reina looked at her and smiled. "Yes, a boyfriend, Marie. He's an artist, a good one I think." Adrien and her young cousin were very quiet with only the echo of their footsteps and his cane on the walkway. "He doesn't live in California; he travels around showing his work. I went out with him for about a month a year ago. And I saw him again right before I came here. I like him very much, but it doesn't seem like it can work out between us."

When it seemed to him that she'd finished Adrien asked, "Do you love him?"

She nodded silently, then said, "Yes, I'm afraid I do."

"Love is nothing to fear," he replied. "It comes to us in the most unexpected of times, without reason." Adrien took Marie's hand again. "Talk to your grandmother. She will know better than anyone what to tell you."

She was comforted by his advice, but Reina didn't speak to her grandmother about what she'd told him, at least right away. And Marie didn't share what she'd heard that afternoon. But Marie's original skepticism of Reina began to slowly shift. She wondered if there might be a reason her cousin acted the way she did.

Elleanore and Sofia spent most of their time during those first days with each other as if the decades they'd been apart didn't exist. They were the best of friends and closer than most sisters. Loving the same man didn't stand between them but was simply a fact they shared. There was very little jealousy or envy between them. They were of an age now when love in all its forms and mystery was too precious to handle carelessly.

The two of them were preparing supper while everyone else was out of the house when Ellie asked, "How bad is it?"

Sofia was peeling potatoes. "His heart you mean?"

"Yes."

She set one peeled potato aside and picked another. "I've never known anyone with a heart as big as his. But it is fragile; it beats with an irregular rhythm."

"Are you worried?"

She set down the peeler, wiping her eyes with the back of her hand. "It is what it is. We are old, and our time is running out."

Ellie quickly took her in her arms. "It will be alright."

"I'm glad that you are here," she replied. And then as they heard the front door opening, Sofia quickly kissed her cheek.

Marie came running into the kitchen saying, "Bonjour," as she hugged Sofia. She turned to Elleanore then, still unsure of her.

Ellie smiled and kissed the top of Marie's head, letting her fingers run softly down her cheek. "How was school today?"

"Bien, Mamie."

Adrien slowly hung up his coat and hat as Reina did the same. She said to him quietly, "Thank you."

"What for, child?"

She blushed. "For the advice I guess."

"Trust in your heart, chérie. It will not let you down."

Adriana had a deadline coming up from a major account and had been trying unsuccessfully most of the day to come up with an idea for an ad campaign to be launched the following spring. She was sitting at her drawing table, frustrated, and tore up the sketch she'd been working on. She looked at her watch; it was time for Marie to be home.

She'd become hardened over the years, raising her child, without a man to hold her at night. There were times when she'd go to Paris, like she did a few nights before, and spend it with a special friend, a man she'd known for years who was married, unhappily. It wasn't love alone that she found in his embrace, but brief physical relief. Afterward she felt empty. Marie was growing up and Adriana knew her daughter would be gone soon.

Most men her age looked at younger girls, girls like Reina. Adriana knew that she felt some resentment toward her niece. Reina was young with a future that wasn't fixed ahead of her.

She'd just looked at her watch again when she spotted Marie running across the yard toward the house. The front door quickly opened a moment later. "Bonjour, Maman!"

"You're late," Adriana heard herself say. "I was getting worried."

"It's Friday, Maman. We stopped at the café."

"Your grand-pere spoils you."

She ignored the bait that she knew would precipitate an argument between them. "We saw Reina," she replied instead. "She walked home with us." Marie picked up the wadded-up paper on the floor and looked at the drawing. "This is good, Maman."

"It's trash, Marie," she said with disgust. "The concept is weak."

Sensing the blackness of her mother's mood, the twelve-year-old began to go upstairs with her book bag. "Grand-mere says supper will be in an hour, Maman." She ran up the last few steps before her mother could reply.

Adriana watched her go, knowing that Marie was in flight from the bitterness that grew steadily within her mother. She had dreams when she was Marie's age that were lost somewhere as maturity came upon her. It didn't happen all at once; the loss was gradual. But she still carried the remnants of those teenage dreams after finding the letters when she was sixteen. There were still some dreams left after going to Paris. And a few remained after the man she loved left her with a baby to support.

There were times, in the beginning, when her daughter was a newborn that she considered going back to her family in California. But in her heart, she believed there was no place for her there. She went to her father instead and with his help she built a life for herself and for Marie. It took years, but she survived. And now as her father and Sofia grew older each day she was able in many small ways to pay them back for what they'd done for her.

The bitterness took root because in her heart she knew that one day soon her daughter would be gone and so would her parents. She would be alone. And the fear that sprang from these thoughts fed her sullen state. More than anything else Adriana wanted to tear the fear from her breast as easily as she had the failed drawing from her sketch pad.

CHAPTER 28

Laura

Mélange was busy for a Monday night and most of the staff were still recovering from the holiday weekend. Allan Walters, one of the waiters, came in with an order and said to Alex, "David Steele just came in with someone."

Alex was putting the finishing touches on a grilled Dungeness crab entrée prepared with white wine, garlic, and butter. He called out, "Order up," and as the plate was taken away he merely gave Allan a stern look before walking away. A half hour went by before he glanced through the windows in the kitchen doors to survey the dining room. He didn't see them. It was Laura's day off and he considered giving her a call, then rejected the idea.

It was after eleven before he was finished for the night and stopped by the bar for a glass of red wine. The bartender, Loren Mitchell, finished her pour and continued to restock the area before closing for the night. Alex asked, "Did you see David Steele tonight?" She nodded but kept her silence. A smart move Alex thought but she pushed the subject. "Was he with someone?"

Loren didn't appreciate gossip, in fact, it irritated her. She was pretty, with shoulder-length dark brown hair and a full face. Most of her life she'd been self-conscious about her weight, and she felt more so now because she'd found out that her girlfriend was having an affair with someone else. When David Steele came into the restaurant with the brunette, they sat at the bar for a few minutes until their table was ready. The woman with him was beautiful.

"Well," Alex asked again, "was he?"

She was systematically cleaning and checking the liquor level of each bottle on the back bar. Loren stopped, then said quietly, "Yes," and returned to what she was doing. She liked Alex, but her loyalty was to Laura. And as if she knew that his glass was almost empty she turned and refilled it saying, "Laura's been good to me. Whatever is going on is her business not mine."

He gave a slight nod and said, "Good point."

After checking the kitchen and dining room once more, Alex locked the doors to Mélange and walked outside into the parking lot. As he started his car he thought of stopping to see if Laura was still up then changed his mind. But as he drove by her house he noticed a faded red pickup parked in front. "What," he whispered to himself, "is going on?"

The person he wanted to talk to most was Izzy and she was asleep by the time he arrived home. He'd sensed for several days that something was going on with Laura; he just didn't know what it was. Alex knew how much she seemed to care for David Steele and that they'd slept together. It didn't make any sense that she would suddenly be with someone else and so would Steele. But apparently that was the case.

When he got home Alex went into the kitchen, poured himself a glass of port, and began fixing himself a sandwich. Izzy stood in the doorway to their bedroom. "How was your night?"

Alex turned to face her and smiled. "You should be asleep."

"I heard you come in," she replied. "When are you coming to bed?"

"In a minute. I just wanted to get a bite to eat."

Without her makeup and wearing her cotton nightgown she looked much younger than she was, he thought, as Izzy shuffled over to him in her slippers. She kissed him and said sleepily, "Hurry, I miss you."

"Five minutes," he promised. Alex didn't want to bring up the subject of Laura. Izzy had to get up for work in a few hours and he didn't want her to worry or be upset. He knew how much Isabella cared for her. By the time he'd finished his sandwich he'd convinced himself that there was a logical conclusion for the whole thing. Then while cleaning the kitchen he suddenly remembered where he'd seen the truck before. It belonged to Daniel Whitman. "No," he said with a sigh and thought of Reina.

Alex undressed quietly and slid into bed next to Izzy. She reached out with her back to him, snuggling her buttocks into him as she took his hand and held it to her breast. "I love you," she whispered drowsily.

He held her to him. "I love you too."

The next morning Laura was in the shower letting the hot water run from the top of her head, down her neck, to her back and breasts. She was trying her best to get her head on straight. If David was seeing someone else, she thought, he'd been hiding it well. Instinctively she'd felt that he loved her. It wasn't possible for him to lie about that; she would have sensed it. But Matt had loved her and chose someone else. And it was difficult for her to trust again, to commit herself to something so easily that could be brushed aside.

Dan was in Laura's spare room still lying in bed, listening to the shower, and thinking of Reina. Travis came in and pulled at the sheet with his teeth. "OK, boy." Dan smiled and tossed the covers aside. He pulled on his jeans and went into the kitchen without his shirt or shoes. There was coffee in the pot. He looked in several cupboards and found a cup. Travis nudged him. "I'm coming... give me a second."

He filled a cup and headed for the front door to let Travis out. Dan followed him onto the front porch and took a sip of coffee while the golden retriever checked out the perimeter of Laura's yard. It was a beautiful day. Daniel sat down on the porch steps thinking to himself that it was no wonder Reina loved it here so much. Travis came back and sat next to him, the two of them looking out toward the east. "I could get used to it here," he said to Travis. "Maybe it's time to settle down, boy." He scratched behind the retriever's ears. "Would you like that?"

The weekend had been busy, and David hadn't seen much of Laura. He'd been planning to stop by to see her on Monday but that afternoon Monica Reed, his agent, showed up on his doorstep with a script she wanted him to read. Early Tuesday morning he said to Tuan, "When

Ms. Reed comes down, tell her I'll be right back. I want to check on Laura."

"I will," Tuan replied and watched as David drove away.

As he pulled into Laura's driveway the first thing he saw was Daniel's truck. The next thing he noticed as he got out was the half-naked man sitting next to the golden retriever on her front porch. He sighed, thinking to himself, just when you begin to be sure of something life throws you a curve.

Dan watched as the car pulled to a stop and a good-looking older man got out. He called out loud enough for him to hear, "Hi. Can I help you?"

Anger was beginning to simmer as David asked, "Is Laura inside?"

"She's in the shower."

David wanted more than anything to deck this arrogant young man, go in the house and confront her, but instead he said with all the restraint he could muster, "Would you tell her I'm here please." He couldn't resist adding, "And you might put some clothes on while you're at it."

Dan took a sip of his coffee. "I would if I knew who you were."

Laura was in her bathrobe with a towel wrapped about her head getting a cup of coffee when she heard voices outside. She saw Daniel talking to David through the screen door and stepped outside saying curtly. "Good morning."

"It was a few minutes ago," he snapped.

She took a sip of coffee and folded her arms across her chest. "Is your friend still here?"

"What friend?"

"The woman with the sports car."

The tone of their voices was tense; Travis whined looking from Laura to the man who'd just arrived.

"You mean Monica?"

"If that's her name."

"It was the last time I checked." He nodded toward Daniel. "Do you want to introduce me to your guest?"

Dan started to stand saying, "I better give you two some space."

"I'd rather you stay," Laura replied, then added, "Daniel Whitman this is David Steele."

Dan held out his hand, but David ignored the gesture.

David was so angry he was about to explode and rather than say something he knew he'd regret he replied, "I can see you're busy."

He opened the car door and was about to get in when she said, "Have fun with Monica."

Losing whatever control he had left, David yelled back, "We work together!"

She turned, opened the screen door, and shouted back, "Don't work too hard!" Laura heard his car door slam, the engine start, and the sound of his wheels spinning in the gravel drive as he drove away. She wiped a tear away and went to dry her hair.

Dan sat there in the aftermath of their confrontation assuming that he'd just met the father of Laura's child. He put his arm around Travis saying quietly, "Maybe we should stay single." Travis licked him across the face.

When Alex opened his eyes she'd already gone; the bed seemed empty. He couldn't even imagine what it would be like now being without her. Izzy completed him in ways he couldn't define. Then he thought of Laura, of David and the woman who was with him at Mélange. And he thought of Dan's truck parked outside Laura's house in the middle of the night. How could something so precious as one person's feelings for another be treated so carelessly, he wondered? He knew that Laura loved David; he was sure of it. Then why? he asked himself again. Alex liked David and Dan well enough, but Laura and Reina were his friends and that's where his loyalty lay. He looked at his watch; it was after nine and Laura would be going to work soon.

Laura was fixing breakfast for the two of them as Daniel pulled on his boots. "Are you sure," he asked again, "that it's alright for me to stay?"

Laura was still trying to get over her mad. "Yes, it's fine."

"I'll get the things I need at the trailer and be back this afternoon. My next show isn't for another ten days. I should be able to be finished by then."

"That's perfect," she said as she put his omelet on a plate and set it in front of him.

Dan was silent while he ate until finally he said, "You like that guy, David, a lot." When she didn't respond he asked, "Is he the father?"

She brought her breakfast to the table and sat down next to him. "I don't want to talk about it."

"He was really mad seeing me here. Before you came out I thought he was gonna clip me one."

That thought brought a smile to her face. "Are you in love with Reina?"

It was as if she was reading his mind; all morning he'd been thinking about her, wondering where she was and what she was doing. He replied, "I'm not even sure what that means." Dan stood and took his plate to the sink. "People say the words, and I really believe they mean them at the time but then things change, they change, and it's not the same anymore. How many people do you know," he asked, "who aren't divorced or haven't experienced a serious breakup?"

"My parents and both sets of grandparents," she replied and finished her last bite.

"Really?"

"Really," she replied as she finished her coffee.

He picked up her plate still thinking about her answer and said, "You finish getting ready for work. I'll do the dishes."

Later as the two of them were leaving she handed him a key to the cottage. "I probably won't be back till very late. Make yourself at home."

"I'd like you to show me the space where you want the painting. It'll help me get an idea of how large a canvas I'll need."

Alex wasn't scheduled to work until one, but he wanted to talk to Izzy and knew she usually took her break between ten and eleven. When he pulled into the parking lot he saw Laura and Daniel walk into the hotel together. By the time he'd gone through the hotel to the restaurant he saw Laura pointing to a place on the wall behind the Mélange hostess station. As he approached, Alex said cautiously, "Good morning."

The two of them turned and Laura smiled, saying, "I'm thinking of another painting right here. What do you think?"

The painting Daniel had done for the bistro had changed the quality of the look within the whole room; Alex was aware of that. And he knew that this was a perfect place for another. "It's alright with me if that's what you want."

She looked at him curiously, then snapped, "I wasn't asking your permission. I wanted your opinion."

Dan sensed the tension in Laura's voice and held out his hand. "It's good to see you."

Alex shook it and said to her, "Dan does great work. I'm sure it will look great."

"I think so too," she replied, then turned to Daniel. "I'll see you later. Don't wait up for me tonight." And she was gone leaving the two men alone.

After seconds of uncomfortable silence Dan finally asked, "Have you heard from Reina?"

Alex shook his head and answered him curtly while walking away, "No."

The one thing that Dan had avoided since those teenage years, living with his stepmother, was emotional entanglements. And somehow, he'd become immersed in one. By the time he got back to his truck where Travis was waiting he said to the retriever while sliding behind the steering wheel, "We'll finish this job and be on our way." Travis looked back at him. "There's no sense in getting involved in other people's troubles." Travis stayed silent, looking toward the open road as Dan pulled out of the parking lot onto the highway. "We'll go get our stuff, do her painting, and get back to some kinda normal." But Dan didn't totally believe what he was saying. Reina had somehow planted a seed within him; he cared for her, more than he thought possible. And these people were a part of her life, good or bad.

Alex and Izzy were sitting on one of the tables toward a secluded spot in the kitchen where they could talk without being disturbed. She stared at him. "Are you sure of this?"

He nodded. "I heard her tell him not to wait up for her."

"You have to talk to her."

"It's none of my business."

Izzy finished her lunch. "I don't believe it. Laura would never do something that would intentionally hurt Reina." She slid off the table and began to pace, thinking about what she suspected and whether she should tell Alex. Suddenly she blurted it out, "I think she's pregnant."

This was a curve Alex wasn't expecting. "What makes you think so?"

"She's been sick, you know, I've heard her in the bathroom. I thought it might just be the flu at first but it's not. And she's been really emotional lately, not like herself."

He thought of what she'd said a moment before replying, "If this is true we have to be there for her. When she's ready to tell us, she will. Until then, we do what we can for her."

"Sí, mi amour," Isabella replied as she took him in her arms to kiss him. "Will you be home early tonight?"

He nodded. "I'll try."

CHAPTER 29

Reina

Elleanore and Reina had been in France for a week. The three elderly friends were in the main house, Adriana was working in hers, and Marie was still in school. But Libourne was a small town with little to do and Reina was restless. It wasn't as romantic or exciting as she thought the wine country of France would be. She missed her friends, she missed Daniel, and she missed her job.

Adrien watched his oldest grandchild from the kitchen window; she was sitting by herself outside. He put on his hat and coat, put his pipe and tobacco into his pocket, and opened the door. "It's chilly this morning," he said to her.

She nodded with a weak smile. "It is, yes. I needed some fresh air."

"I thought," he began, "that you might like to visit some of the wineries here." Adrien grinned. "You might find something, for your business."

"I'd like that," she replied smiling back at him. Reina wasn't ready to accept Adrien as her grandfather emotionally, but he was gradually endearing himself to her. The old Frenchman seemed to have a genuine interest and affection for her.

He borrowed the keys to Adriana's sedan and they were off together by late morning. Their first stop was the Chateau Coutet, a vineyard that had been family owned for four hundred years. The estate was gorgeous, even during the first days of December, and the wine superb. As they were leaving he said to his granddaughter, "That is where I went to work when I was a boy. Where my uncle taught me about the vines."

Their next stop was a smaller vineyard than the first. The winery was a beautiful neoclassical stone structure built along the river with a restaurant attached where they had lunch. Adrien embraced the waitress, wishing her good day, and ordered two glasses of Cabernet to go with their meal. When Reina took that first sip, the wine seemed almost familiar to her, as if she'd tried it someplace before. "What do you think?" he asked with a smile.

"It's very nice, familiar somehow."

"I worked here," he replied, "for almost thirty years." Adrien studied the palms of his hands. "I know the vines here as well as I know these. It was my life… here." He tapped the side of his glass. "This wine is my legacy. Paul Fournier, the owner and vintner, worked with me from the time he was a boy, no bigger than Marie. All that I know of making wine I've shown him."

"You must be very proud."

"I am, and here he is now."

She followed his eyes to see a good-looking man of about forty approaching their table. Adrien stood and embraced him, kissing each of his cheeks, saying, "Je t'ai manqué, mon ami." He held on to the younger man as he looked at Reina. "Paul this is my granddaughter from California."

He took her hand, kissing it lightly. "C'est un plasir de recontrer quelqu'un sí adorable."

"English, my friend," Adrien insisted lightly. "Please sit with us a moment."

Reina grinned. "I have no idea what he said, Grand-pere, but it sounded wonderful."

Adrien was touched; it was the first time she'd referred to him as a grandparent. "You must watch this devil," he said quickly, to cover the emotion that welled up within him. "He is a scoundrel at heart. But such a talent," he said laughing.

"And where would I be without you to guide me, Adrien?" Paul smiled and winked at Reina turning his attention to her. "How long are you staying with us?"

"Not long," she replied. "Another week."

"That's too bad," he said with a sigh. "There is so much to see and to do."

The look in his eyes was exciting; she crossed, then uncrossed her legs restlessly. "I have to get back to work."

"And what is it you do in California?"

Adrien answered him. "She buys wine and liquor for a restaurant in St. Helena."

Paul's attention shifted as he smiled at her. "In that case we must talk business. You must buy from us. The wine of Bordeaux is among the best in the world, n'est-ce pas, Adrien?"

"It is, my friend," the old man replied.

Paul stood. "Excusez-moi un moment s'il vous plait." He gazed into Reina's eyes. "I'll be right back."

She watched as Paul spoke briefly to the woman who had waited on them and a moment later returned with three bottles of red wine, opening each with a corkscrew. "We'll let them breathe a moment."

A few minutes later the waitress brought each of them their salads, a sliced loaf of baguette, a cheese plate and large bottle of spring water. Paul poured each of them a small taste of one of the reds he'd brought to the table earlier and said with a smile, "Bon appetit."

Reina raised the glass to her nose, taking in a floral scent accented with raspberry, and took a sip, to cherish the flavor before swallowing; the taste was smooth, juicy, and sweet with a hint of spice. She was impressed.

"Adrien's genius," Paul said, "is in the blend. This is what makes Chateau Fournier special. Our vineyard may be small, but the satisfaction is in the quality not the quantity." He poured each of them some water to cleanse their palates and another sample.

Reina noticed that this sampling was more intense with an aroma of roasted coffee and blackberries that lingered on the tongue. "These are very nice garage wines," she said. It wasn't meant to be a derogatory comment but one of respect. It was a term used to describe the commitment of the vintner to excellence despite the size of the winery or vineyard.

"Oui," he replied, "if you like."

By the time their lunch was finished Paul had agreed to ship three cases of each blend to Mélange and Reina couldn't wait to call Laura and tell her what she'd discovered. As Paul escorted them to their car his hand gently rested on her back. "Merci, Reina," he said, "I know we'll work well together." He opened the car door for her. "I hope to see you again soon." He embraced Adrien saying to him, "I've missed you. Come see me again soon."

The old man's eyes began to water. "Au revoir, mon ami," he replied and sat behind the wheel.

"Give Sofia and Adriana a kiss from me," Paul said as he closed the door of the sedan.

While they were driving away Adrien said to Reina, "His wife left him some time ago. She lives in Paris now. Their children are in university."

"Are they divorced?"

"Non ma douce. Gabrielle, his wife, is a strict Catholic. But changes come sooner or later n'est-ce pas?"

"Oui," she said, "they do." She thought of Dan again and then the image of Paul followed. She could still feel the warmth of his hand on her back and his kiss on her cheek while saying goodbye.

"It's time to pick up Marie from school. She'll be jealous if she knows I took you to Chateau Fournier without her."

Reina grinned. "Mum's the word."

"What is this you say… mum's?"

"It means I won't say anything." She watched his profile as he drove and thought to herself that her grandfather must have been a very handsome man when he was young. It was no wonder her grandmother fell in love with him. "Does Marie," she asked, "have an interest in making wine?"

He chuckled. "Non, she has an interest in Paul Fournier. The man spoils her."

"Thank you for taking me today."

"I was proud of you… the way you negotiated with him." He chuckled. "And your knowledge of the wine was magnifique. Paul should not have expected anything less from the granddaughter of Adrien Forche!"

The pride this old man felt toward her brought a tear to Reina's eye. No one in her family, her mother, grandmother, or even her father, who thought of very little else but making wine, seemed to recognize her knowledge. Despite that she said, "I've learned a great deal from my father. He studied enology and viticulture at the university."

"Chérie," he said excitedly, "you learn about the vines in the field not in books. The making of wine begins here"—Adrien pointed toward his heart— "and the finish ends on the tongue. If you have no sense of it, all the books in the world will not help you. Paul's father, Marcel, knew that. That's why he apprenticed his son to me."

Adrien suddenly became quiet; a darkness seemed to come over him and finally she asked, "What's wrong?"

He said to himself as much as to her, "The past haunts us, chérie. I should have shared what I know with my son."

"We can only do the best we can, Grand-pere. All of us have regrets, n'est-ce pas?"

He took her hand across the seat. "Your French is coming along, and it has only been a week. Give us time, chérie, and you will become a true French woman."

They could see Marie talking to one of her girlfriends in front of the middle school as the sedan came to a stop. The twelve-year-old noticed Reina in the passenger seat next to her grandfather and frowned while getting in the back seat saying, "Why did you bring the car today, Grand-pere?"

"We went for a ride, Marie. How was school today?"

"Comme ci comme ca."

He set the bait for her. "I was just telling Reina that we don't learn everything from books."

"Like making wine, Grand-pere," Marie replied with a grin.

"Oui," he said emphatically.

"It comes from the heart," Marie replied, her tone mimicking him. She giggled. "We know, Grand-pere, but books will do until something better comes along."

"Nothing is better than hard work and experience," he insisted.

Reina interjected, "My father has shown me one of your journals, Adrien. Daddy learned a great deal from what you've written."

He'd forgotten about his journals that were left behind when he returned to France. "I never imagined," he said, "that Michael might find my research and use it." For the last half century Adrien wanted more than anything to be able to make a difference in the life of his son. But he'd always assumed it was something that would never come to pass. Apparently, he'd been wrong.

Reina turned in her seat to look at her cousin. "It wasn't just what your grandfather wrote, Marie. There were illustrations he used in the margins that were beautiful."

"You see, Grand-pere," Marie countered, "we do learn from books. You should do this again. Write down what you know and share it."

"I have, Marie. They remained at Chateau Fournier when I left."

"But why, Grand-pere? They are yours."

"Marcel Fournier paid me to work for him. My notes were done while I was there. They belong to their family now."

Reina interrupted, "That's why you left your journal in St. Helen?"

"I suppose," he replied. "Monsieur Strickland paid me for the work. I left it there."

"But he didn't care about what you'd written," Reina remarked. "Nobody used that information until Daddy found it in the winery."

Marie slumped down into the back seat. "That's not fair," she said just loud enough to be heard.

"It might not be fair, petit fille," he replied to Marie, "but it was the right thing to do."

This was something neither of the girls could argue. But just the same Reina thought it was unfair that her grandfather's work couldn't be shared with more people. "Could you write down more of what you know for my father?"

"Oui, I could," he conceded, "but it has been too long and I'm not the man I was once."

Marie leaned forward, resting her elbows on the front seat. "I could do the illustrations for you, Grand-pere."

"We'll see, Marie."

"I would help you too," Reina offered.

Adrien gradually began to consider what the girls were saying. He couldn't do the physical labor anymore, but his mind still held fast to all that he'd learned throughout the years. This could be something, he thought, to pass on to them, the part of him, that he believed was worthwhile. "We'll see," he conceded in a whisper, "we'll see."

Adriana had just finished the ad proposals she'd designed and emailed them to the agency in Paris. Marie came in, put down her book bag, and kissed her mother on the cheek. "Bon apres midi, Maman."

"How was school today?"

"OK." Marie went into the kitchen, put three madeleines on a small plate, and poured herself a glass of milk. "Did you know that Grand-pere wrote books about making wine?" She took a bite of a madeleine and plopped down in the overstuffed chair in the living room across from where Adriana worked.

"He didn't write books," Adriana corrected. "They were notes he kept in journals. I haven't seen him work on them since you were a baby."

Marie took a drink of milk. "Paul Fournier has them."

"How would you know that?"

"Grand-pere told me so. He said it was the right thing to do, to leave them. I don't think it was fair of Paul to keep them."

"I don't either, Marie," she replied. "I'm meeting someone for dinner. You're going to spend the night with your grandparents until I get back."

"I'm not a child, Maman. I can stay by myself."

"They look forward to the times you stay with them."

It was after six by the time Adriana had taken a bath, put on her makeup, and dressed for the evening. Her appointment was at eight in Bordeaux at Le Capon Fin. The restaurant had a long history, created in 1925 and awarded three Michelin stars in 1933. Times had changed, certainly, but quality never went out of fashion.

She walked downstairs and saw Marie watching television. "Have you done your homework?"

The young girl sighed. "Yes, Maman."

"I'm leaving now. It's time for you to go next door." When Marie didn't respond but continued to stare at the program she was watching, Adriana turned it off. "Get your coat. It's chilly outside."

While the sedan was merging onto N89 toward Bordeaux, she glanced at her watch and noticed it was past seven; the restaurant was still an hour away. By the time she crossed the river into the city and turned right onto Rue Condillac, Adriana was already thirty minutes late.

As she hurried inside the restaurant there were several people waiting to be seated. The maître d' made eye contact and smiled. A moment later he approached. "Bonsoir, madame. Monsieur Fournier attend, de cette facon, s'il vous plait."

"Merci, Louis," she said, a little out of breath, as she followed him to a quiet corner of the dining room.

Paul stood as she approached, kissing each of her cheeks. "Bonsoir."

"Bonsoir," she replied while kissing him back. The maître d' held her chair for her as she sat down. A glass of red wine was already poured for her. She took a sip and said in English, "I'm sorry I'm late. I had a deadline to meet. It couldn't be helped."

They'd been seeing each other for eight years, most of the time in Paris until his wife left him and then some of the time, like tonight, in Bordeaux. Adriana met him shortly after coming to Libourne; it was a flirtation at first. Marie was a baby then and her father worked for him. The flirtation turned to something more when her daughter turned four; she was lonely and so was he. Unknowingly she'd become the person she'd run from, a mistress, no different than her mother.

CHAPTER 30

Daniel

It was dark by the time Daniel returned from the city and turned into the driveway beside the cottage. He unloaded the materials he'd needed beside an old detached single-car garage. It took several moments for him to open the old wooden roll-up door. He used a flashlight to find an electric light hanging from the ceiling that was turned on and off with a pull string. It was burned out. He went inside the house to find where Laura put her light bulbs.

Still standing on the stepladder he pulled the string again, the light suddenly accenting the immense amount of junk stored and forgotten there. Travis was looking up at him expectantly as Dan said, "I know it's a mess but it's doable." Travis cocked his head first one way then the other then whined as if he had his doubts. Dan grinned as he stepped down. "You're such a pessimist."

He left his easel, the canvas, stretchers, paint, and toolbox outside next to the garage and went into the house looking for a beer. Laura drank wine. He turned to Travis. "I can't do this without beer. And pizza, we need pizza."

The highway that ran past the hotel turned into the Main Street and downtown area of St. Helena. Daniel found a small market that sold beer and asked the clerk for a pizza place close by. A few minutes later he left Travis in the truck while he ordered a build-your-own regular dish with smoked mozzarella, spinach, arugula, tomatoes, and Italian sausage. It was after seven by the time they got back to the cottage.

He worked on cleaning the garage for the next two hours, separating things to be thrown away, decades of old newspapers and dried-up paint cans, from those he'd planned to ask Laura about. There was a rusted girl's Schwinn bike that looked like it was at least fifty years old and a wooden ping-pong table propped up against a wall next to a couple of sawhorses. He set the sawhorses in the middle of the room, parallel from one another about five feet apart and set the ping-pong table on top releasing a fog of dust. Daniel coughed and stepped back. He looked over at Travis who was standing far enough away from any harm. Dan said, "Don't give me that look. I'll use it as a worktable."

The hardest part was getting rid of the buildup of dust, dirt, and cobwebs. But when he finished, standing just outside the door, looking at the job he'd done, he said to Travis, "It's a good start." Dan gave him a pat as he turned out the light. "But right now it's time for a bath." Travis whined again as they walked toward the house. "Not for you, for me."

His life had become composed of casual, temporary relationships. He was aware of it and trusted rather than feared the lack of involvement. The love he felt for Travis was his single emotional commitment. The animal trusted him and for a long time that was enough. But Reina, somehow, changed what for so long he'd relied on, his solitude. Now, there was Laura. He was concerned for her. She had this defensive shield that made her seem tough on the surface, but Daniel was beginning to believe it merely acted to disguise a deeper vulnerability. She'd been hurt, he suspected. And the wounds were still raw, not like his. His had scarred over long ago. But they weren't forgotten.

He'd been lying in the old claw-foot bathtub; water that moments before had been hot was now lukewarm. Travis was curled up on the floor. "If I owned this place," he said to him, "the first thing I'd do is put in a shower… not a small one either, but one of those where you can sit down if you want." Travis didn't move. Daniel pulled the plug and stood with the water dripping from his body as he grabbed a towel to begin drying himself.

A moment later after stepping out of the tub he heard a sound from the other room, the front door. Travis pricked up his ears and immediately went to investigate. Daniel closed the door, took his jeans down from the hook on the back of it and put them on just as the bathroom door opened.

Laura was embarrassed and immediately began backing away saying, "I'm sorry… I thought you'd gone to bed."

His watch was on the countertop next to the sink; he picked it up, glancing at the time and saw that it was just past nine. "It's still early. I didn't expect you for a while yet."

She found it difficult to focus, the two of them so close together in that small room, his body fresh from the bath, still moist in places. Laura backed away. "I'll let you finish up."

He dried his hair with a towel and combed it back, out of his eyes, pulled on a clean T-shirt and went into the other room to look for her. She was sitting next to the fireplace with a cup of tea, the wood was just beginning to ignite. Daniel asked, "Are you alright?"

"Yes, just tired. It was slow tonight."

"Did your guy get in touch today?"

Laura shook her head. "No. I really thought we had something going but I guess not." She felt her belly. "He didn't ask for this. I can't blame him."

Daniel sat down opposite her. "Listen, I don't know a thing about this guy."

"David," she replied.

He nodded. "David. But I've got a pretty good idea that he cares for you. He wouldn't have acted the way he did if that wasn't the case."

"Do you think so?"

"Yes," he said, "I do."

The hardest thing about the pregnancy so far was not being able to have a glass of wine, particularly tonight. The morning sickness and lack of energy only added to her discomfort. She said irritably, "He's used to having anything he wants at his fingertips. Why would he want to be tied down with me?"

"Has he asked you to marry him?"

The ring finger of her left hand was bare; she caught herself rubbing it lightly. "We talked about it, but he hasn't proposed." Laura added quickly, "I just told him a few days ago… and we've been busy." She snickered. "Apparently he's been very busy."

"He said something about it being about work," Dan replied. "Maybe all of this is just some misunderstanding." He said it out of kindness, but he didn't entirely believe it. Daniel tended to look at people as easily from the dark side as the light. People were just people from his point of view, saints at times, sinners most of the time, all of them cast in tints of gray.

Travis got to his feet, stretched, came to Daniel, and gave him a nudge. He scratched him behind his ears and said, "I've got to take him out."

Laura was exhausted; it didn't feel like she had the same amount of stamina she was used to. And she hated that. She was used to being on top of things, all the time, in control of the world she'd created. Alex had the night off and it was difficult for her to muster up enough endurance to manage without him. Then he came in unexpectedly; she didn't have to ask, he just took over. After another thirty minutes she'd made her excuses and left.

The night was turning colder as Daniel stood on the front porch with his hands in his pockets and waited for Travis. His heart had gone out to Laura, and he'd felt the bonds of their relationship tighten. He felt his breathing quicken, the feeling of being trapped taking hold and the urge to flee rising from the pit of his stomach. Travis came out of the darkness, up to the porch next to him, waiting. Daniel knelt down and wrapped his arms about the large dog and said, "We can't just take off this time, boy, not yet. She needs us."

Daniel brought three more logs inside for the fire to replace the ones she'd used. He stacked them neatly into a brass basket designed to hold them, picked up the poker and began to stoke the fire while she watched him from the sofa. "Do you love this guy?" he asked.

"Yes," she replied without hesitation, "I think I do."

The fire flared up; Daniel put the poker back into its stand and stood beside the fireplace. "You've got to be able to trust him or it's not going to be any good. This woman you saw, you don't really know anything about her. She could be anybody, a sister, coworker, whatever… you didn't give him a chance to explain. Why is that?"

Her mind immediately went back to Matt Stryker, the memory still uncomfortably fresh. "I was supposed to be married a few years ago," she began. Laura locked eyes with him. "Before I opened the bistro I was still the sous-chef at Entretenir. Matt, that was his name, swept me off my feet in a matter of days; he asked me to marry him after a few months." Her eyes began to water, and she quickly wiped the tears away. "He proposed to me on our first Christmas Eve together. I remember thinking then that it was too good to be true." She snickered. "But we're girls right? We're all taught to want the whole Prince Charming thing."

Daniel had a pretty good idea but asked anyway, "What happened?"

The tears were coming again as she answered him, "I wasn't Cinderella or Snow White. I was the rebound girl, his second choice. And she came back into his life a few days before the wedding." Laura wiped her eyes and blew her nose. "That's it. Now it feels like it's happening all over again."

"Have you talked to David about this?"

She shook her head and replied in a whisper, "No."

"If you're going to make it with this guy—with David—he has to know who you are. Not just the good stuff either but all of it." There was a moment of silence between them with only the sound of the fire crackling in the fireplace. "I'm probably the last person who should be giving advice about love. I avoid getting too involved like it's the plague. But if you love him, it seems to me you have to give it a shot. Even if it's risky."

Laura stood abruptly and before he realized what was happening she hugged him saying quietly, "Thank you. Reina's a lucky girl."

"I don't know about that."

She smiled. "I do." Laura picked up her cup and saucer. "I'm going to bed. I'll see you in the morning."

The next morning as Daniel was getting dressed, the sun had just begun to highlight the vines on the western hills behind the cottage. He made coffee and took Travis out while it was brewing. It was beautiful in the early moments of the day; he could feel the inspiration within him begin to take seed. Travis came back, the two of them went back inside and the retriever watched as he poured the pot of coffee into his thermos and brewed another one for Laura when she awoke. He put his sketchbook, pencils, and watercolors in his backpack. The two of them walked back outside again, trying carefully not to wake her. He looked down at Travis. "Let's go to work."

The last painting he'd done for Laura was meant to emphasize the beauty and grandeur of the Bay Area. He'd done that successfully. His intent was to do the same, here, in wine country. The problem was that it was the tail end of fall, and the beginning of winter would soon be upon them. There was very little color left on the oaks, elms, and on the vines. And yet the moodiness created from bare limbs in contrast to the evergreens fascinated him. He began snapping pictures for reference with his Nikon, as the two of them walked along. Beyond the vineyard Daniel saw Mount Saint Helena in the distance among a mist of clouds floating through the valleys between the hills. He sat down to sketch. One drawing led to another and then another as the morning passed. The chill he'd felt earlier gave way to enough warmth that Daniel removed his jacket by ten. Travis lay content in the sun.

David had seen the young man with his dog pass by while he was having breakfast on the veranda. Curiosity finally got the best of him as he said to Tuan, "I'm going out for a walk. Let me know if she calls."

"Yes, sir," he said with a short bow. Tuan was worried about his employer; he'd rarely seen him this upset. The last time had been a disaster.

It took David the better part of an hour to find him. He was unsure what the young intruder was doing at first until he was close enough to see the sketchbook. As he approached, the golden retriever suddenly rose to his feet and barked.

Daniel turned to see David about thirty feet away. He hated being interrupted while he was working but forced a smile. "Good morning."

"Good morning," David replied as he took a few steps closer. Not really knowing how to break the ice between them he said clumsily, "You like to draw."

"Yes," he answered while rising to his feet to get the kinks out. Daniel held out his hand. "We got off to a bad start yesterday. I'm sorry about that."

David shook his hand. "I suppose we did."

"I've worked for Laura before. I did a painting for her place in the city."

"She hired you to paint a picture," he replied incredulously.

"A girl I go out with, Reina, got me the gig."

A smile began to slowly spread across his face. "And Laura gave you a place to stay while you're doing the painting."

"That's about it."

David put his hands in his pockets and shook his head. "I feel foolish. You must have thought I'd lost my senses."

Daniel started putting his things into his backpack. "Not really. Anyone might have made the same mistake." He picked up the backpack and put it over one shoulder. "She's been pretty upset though. About whoever it is that's staying with you."

The two of them began walking along together. "Monica is my agent," he explained. "She has a script she wants me to read."

"Why did she come clear out here? Why not just send it in the mail?"

He chuckled. "When Monica wants something she's like a dog with a bone. I'm afraid I haven't been very good at returning her calls. She thinks there's a part for me in this screenplay that could spark my career again."

"So, you're an actor?"

David was taken aback. There was a time, not very many years ago, when he was on the cover of every gossip magazine in the country. "Yes," he replied. "I'm an actor... at least I was once."

"Why'd you quit?"

The half-truth came out easily. "I got tired of the Hollywood thing and never having a moment's peace."

"So, you came here to get away."

"That's about the size of it."

"And how's that working out?"

David stuck his hands in his pockets and smiled. "It's peaceful, at least most of the time. I'm afraid the last couple of days have been an exception."

"It's funny," Daniel replied. "The only time I really feel at peace is when I'm working."

"Don't misunderstand me. I like acting and making films; it's all the hype that goes with it I don't like."

"You mean like signing autographs and going to awards shows on television, that kind of thing." Dan chuckled. "It must be a tough life."

They'd reached David's house and the two of them stopped. "Taking privacy for granted is easy to do. I know because I did. And then one day when you don't have it anymore you begin to see how precious it is." David held out his hand again. "I'm sorry about yesterday."

Daniel shook hands with him. "Why don't you come down to the cottage with me and say hello?"

"Do you think she's still mad at me... about Monica?"

He slapped David on the back and chuckled. "You won't know if you stay here. Come on," he urged, "let's go find out."

Laura hadn't been nauseous at all that morning. She'd slept in for the first time in months, took a long bath, and was enjoying a cup of tea on the front porch when the two men walked through the woods toward the cottage. Travis ran ahead of them and came bounding up the porch steps toward her. She set her cup down just in time to keep it from being knocked out of her hands and embraced the large dog, saying as she scratched him behind the ears, "Hey, big boy! What have you been up to huh?" Still petting the retriever, she glared at David as he approached.

It was Daniel who spoke first. "I was doing some sketches this morning and ran into a friend of yours."

"I see that," she replied.

There was an uncomfortable moment of silence until Daniel said, "Well I'm starved. I think I'll go in and get something to eat." He opened the screen door saying, "Let's go, Travis, and give these people some space."

She was beautiful, David thought, sitting in the morning sun. "I'm sorry about yesterday. I was out of line."

"Me too," she said quietly.

"The woman you saw was my agent. I didn't know she was coming; she just showed up."

It felt to Laura as if a huge weight had been lifted. She smiled. "Dan told me it might be something like that. I guess I jumped to conclusions."

"We both did," he replied gently. "I love you."

Laura's eyes began to water as she stood to go to him, to wrap her arms around his neck, kissing him gently. "I love you too." There was a second of hesitation before she admitted to him. "I've been burned before. It's not an excuse but it's something I have to learn to work through."

He kissed her back, more intense this time, letting the intimacy linger. "Do you want to talk about it?"

"Not now," she said softly as she nestled into him. Laura took his hand to lead him into the house. "We'll get to it later."

CHAPTER 31

Reina

"What do you mean you're not going back?"

Elleanore was at a loss for words. She'd come to her granddaughter's room early that morning to try and explain why she couldn't return to California. To explain to her that here, in Libourne, is where she wanted to spend the remainder of her life. She'd put off telling her for as long as she could, but their flight was scheduled to leave in two days.

Ellie rose from Reina's bed and walked over to the window, looking out, at the street below. "I've lived my life," she explained, "for my family. My parents when I was younger, a husband, then my children"—she turned and stared at Reina— "and you. It's time for me to be with the other half of my family. I hoped after meeting them you'd be happy for me."

"I do care for them, Grandma; they're nice people. But you have a home and people who love you in St. Helena, people who count on you."

"I've been thinking this over for a long time. It's not something I decided on the spur of the moment."

Reina crossed the room to her grandmother incredulous. "You planned this from the beginning. Didn't you?"

Ellie nodded slowly. "I knew if I told anyone, particularly Michael, the children would find some way to stop me." She paused. "I lied… and I'm sorry for that but not for what I'm choosing to do."

"Do they know?" she asked quietly, pointing downstairs. "Are they a part of your little deceit?"

"I did talk to Sofia and Adrien about it before we came. But I made them promise to let me tell you."

"How about Adriana and Marie?"

"I haven't told anyone but you yet."

"Well you need to start rethinking this right now!" Reina started to pace. "You're in a foreign country, Grandma. You can't just decide to stay."

"Yes, I can, Lorraine."

"But what if something happens?"

"It's not as if I'm moving to some wasteland, Lorraine. There will be problems, there always are, but they'll work out. I can come back to St. Helena any time I want."

Marie could hear their raised voices as she came up the stairs; she listened outside the door for a minute before knocking lightly. A second later Reina opened the door to her bedroom. "Yes, what is it?"

"It's time for breakfast."

Reina gave her a stern look. "Why aren't you in school?"

"It's Saturday. There isn't any school today."

"Is that so." She ran her fingers gently through Marie's hair. "Tell your grandmother we'll be right down." Reina started to close the door as the young girl began making her way back down the hall, then stopped her saying, "Marie."

"Oui," she said while turning around to look at her cousin.

"Were you listening at the door?"

Marie smiled. "Non, but I heard you talking just for a second."

Reina didn't entirely believe her, but she nodded just the same. "We'll be there in a moment."

Adrien was drinking his coffee at the table in the kitchen while reading the paper. Sofia had spent the morning making fresh croissants that were cooling on the countertop. She placed a platter of fruit, butter, jam, and goat cheese on the table, saying to her husband, "They've been up there a long time."

He turned the page. "I know."

Marie walked into the kitchen. "I told them."

Sofia kissed the top of her head. "Gracias. Please sit down." She walked back to the stove. "Your hot chocolate is almost ready."

Adriana came through the back door into the kitchen. "Bonjour," she said with a smile. "I hope Marie was no trouble last night."

Her father noticed earlier that morning that Adriana hadn't come home the night before. Marie had spent the night with them. Adrien wasn't critical of his daughter. He knew she had needs the same as anyone, but he'd always hoped that one day she would find someone to share her life with. He also knew that Paul was her lover; a lover who could give her no future. It hurt him knowing that two of the people he loved the most felt they had to hide their relationship from him. "It was a pleasure to have her with us," he replied as he turned another page of the paper.

Sofia took the newspaper from his hands. "It's time for family."

"Non, Sofia," he protested.

Marie took a sip of her hot chocolate. "Is Mamie going to stay with us?"

Her grandparents exchanged a look as Sofia said, "Are you listening at doors again?"

"They were arguing, Grand-mere. It was hard not to hear them."

The sound of footsteps could be heard coming down the stairs. Sofia poured a cup of coffee for Ellie and Reina, then took her seat at the opposite end of the table.

Reina said quietly as she came into the kitchen, "Bonjour," before sitting down next to Marie.

Ellie passed by Sofia and gently squeezed her arm, then sat next to Adriana. She took a sip of coffee. "I'm sorry we're late coming down."

Adrien's attention was fixed on the two of them. "Bon appetite."

The food was passed silently from one person to the next until Marie, after applying jam liberally to her croissant, finally asked, "Are you going to stay with us, Mamie?"

Adrien smiled at his granddaughter's lack of tact as Ellie admitted, "Yes, dear."

Sofia took Adriana's hand and smiled at Ellie as she said, "We are blessed that Elleanore has agreed to stay with us."

Pulling her hand away Adriana looked at her mother as she asked sternly, "Why wasn't I consulted about this decision?"

It was Adrien who answered her. "The choice is Elleanore's to make; she is family and always welcome here."

Adriana began to respond angrily but the expression on her father's face stopped her. She wiped her mouth. "Excusez-moi."

His reply was firm. "Vous n'etes pas excuse! We are a family and we'll conduct ourselves as one." He looked across the table at his wife. "This is a happy day for us." Adrien's gaze shifted to Adriana, then Reina. "I expect both of you to be happy for us as well."

Adriana nodded begrudgingly. "Oui, Papa."

Reina was silent until she looked into his eyes. "Oui, Grand-pere."

"Bon," he replied and began to butter his croissant.

After breakfast Adriana, Reina, and Marie remained in the kitchen to do the dishes. Adrien, as a rule, spent his Saturdays playing chess with Philippe Dubois, a longtime friend he'd worked with at Chateau Fournier. Sofia and Elleanore used shopping as an excuse to spend time alone together.

Adriana was helping clean the kitchen with Marie and Reina; she addressed her daughter, her voice firm. "It's time for you to clean your room."

"Yes, Maman."

The young girl did as she was told and once Adriana saw her running across the yard to their home she asked Reina, "Did you know my mother was going to do this?"

"No, I certainly did not. Grandma told me this morning." She finished drying a plate and stood on her tiptoes to put it in the cupboard. "My father is going to have a fit when he finds out."

Adriana had finished washing the dishes and began cleaning off the table, the stove, and countertops. "This is so much like her; she has something she wants, and it doesn't matter how it might affect others."

Reina finished drying the last dish. "I think she might want to be near you and Marie for a while."

"She wants to be near my father is more like it. Elleanore lost that right a long time ago. Has anyone considered how Sofia might feel about this?"

To try and lighten the conversation Reina smiled and said, "Maybe they have some sort of geriatric ménage a trois going on."

Adriana frowned. "It's not a laughing matter."

"Maybe not, but it's none of our business either."

"That may be the case for you; you'll go back to your life and forget all about what's happening here. I'll be left to clean up the mess." She shook her head and sighed saying, "I need a cigarette. Let's go outside."

"That's not the only way to look at this… it might give you a chance to know Grandma. She's really a nice person."

Adriana took a cigarette out of the box she'd kept in the back pocket of her jeans and lit it, blowing smoke away from them. "Elleanore really has you wrapped around her finger. Believe me she was spoiled as a child and still is."

"People change, Adriana. The person you think you know might not even exist anymore. Give her a chance. That's something you haven't done the whole time we've been here. You're either working or you're not around."

"My life is not going to come to a screeching halt because my mother decides she wants to be a part of this family. The world, believe me, doesn't revolve around her."

"What's happened to make you so bitter? I know it's not just your mother."

Adriana flicked her ash into the grass and inhaled once more before saying, "Life is not the box of chocolates you might think it is. We don't all get the things we want." She sighed. "I am over forty, unmarried, with no prospects. The career I wanted once will never happen. The one I have is nothing more than a job that pays the bills. Very soon Marie will leave for university, my parents will die, and I will be an old maid, alone." She wiped a tear away quickly and inhaled her cigarette once more before putting it out.

"That is really looking at things half empty. It doesn't have to be that way. There are other possibilities."

"Such as," Adriana replied as she began to rub her arms for warmth.

"You're still very attractive and talented. Once Marie goes away to school you could go back to Paris and make a new life for yourself." Reina hesitated a moment before saying, "Have you ever thought that maybe you're using your father and Sofia as an excuse to stay tucked away here in Libourne?"

Adriana said indignantly, "That's ridiculous. You've been here long enough to see that they need me."

"What I see is that you need them as much or more than they need you. They take care of Marie, Sofia fixes most of the meals, your father takes Marie to school and picks her up."

Adriana knew that she was right. When she first moved to Libourne it was out of necessity. But since that time, it had become more of a crutch, a convenience for her. It was safe; Paul was safe. He couldn't marry, which meant that their relationship was limited to an occasional supper and a night of sex; it would never go any further and her heart felt a certain amount of safety because of it. Falling in love again was not a risk she was willing to take.

The silence that followed led Reina to apologize. "I'm sorry, Adriana. You're right, this is your business not mine."

"No, you're right. I have been hiding here, using my parents as an excuse." Reina shivered in the cold and folded her arms across her chest. Adriana noticed and suggested, "Why don't you come over to my place? I'll make some coffee and we can talk some more. We haven't had much of a chance to get to know one another."

Reina's teeth were chattering, and she was rubbing herself to keep the chill off. "I'd like that."

As they walked across the yard Adriana said, "It's not an excuse. But I did have a big job to finish. It was just bad timing."

"That's OK. Adrien and Paul Fournier have been showing me around." She chuckled. "Unfortunately, Paul only wants me to buy wine from them. He hasn't introduced me to his competitors." She grinned. "But Grand-pere has."

This news about Paul startled her. He hadn't mentioned that he'd been meeting with Reina; she had to wonder how many things he hadn't seen fit to mention. She asked cautiously as she opened the door to her home, "Do you like Paul?"

Reina shrugged. "He's charming. But I kind of feel sorry for him."

"Why is that?" As she waited for an answer, Adriana went to the kitchen to heat water for coffee.

"He can't go on with his life. His wife's religion keeps him tied to her."

She shook her head and smiled. "It's also a convenience for him. A mistress would know that there is no future with him. And Paul likes it that way."

"How would you know that?"

Adriana gave her a knowing look, then let her eyes gaze up toward the upstairs where her daughter was supposed to be cleaning her room. "We are friends with Paul. I've known him a long time and so has Marie."

It was clear to Reina by her aunt's expression that the relationship with Paul Fournier was deeper than friendship. "I see," she replied. "Is that OK with you?"

She took coffee beans from the refrigerator and began to grind them. "We have an understanding," she admitted. "It works for both of us."

Marie heard them come into the house and go to the kitchen. She sat quietly at the top of the stairs, listening.

The downtown area of Libourne was bustling with activity as Elleanore and Sofia were window shopping. Sofia asked, "How did it go with Reina?"

"As well as can be expected; I think she thought I'd lost all my marbles at first. But Reina is fair. She'll do what she can to ease her father's anger."

"I'm glad you're staying. We have been apart too long."

"Do you think Adriana will ever forgive me?"

"She blames you for everything. It is convenient for her. But one day Adriana will have to face the fact that the way her life has turned out is not about you. She has made her own choices. Now that you're staying it might help her figure that out."

"Why is it so necessary for people to find blame? Life is hard enough."

"I don't know, mi amor. There was a time Ellie when I worked for you in St. Helena that I hated you. You had the man I loved, everything I wanted and couldn't have. I blamed you because he wouldn't look at me. But because I loved you as well my anger and jealousy ate at me. It was like a cancer."

Ellie took her hand. "I'm sorry."

Sofia squeezed back gently. "That was a long time ago."

"Why didn't you ever tell me?"

She sighed. "One day I realize loving another is something we choose to do. It can't hinge on what we expect. It must be given freely."

CHAPTER 32

Daniel

During those first early days of December, Christmas fever was rapidly beginning to spread. Reservations at Mélange through the New Year were close to being filled. Michael was overseeing the decoration of a fifteen-foot tree in the lobby of the hotel when Laura came to work. He stopped her as she was passing by and said excitedly with a grin, "Reina and my mother are coming back today. Their plane should land in forty-five minutes."

"I know. She called me yesterday. We're so happy she'll be back." Laura knew but promised she wouldn't say anything about Elleanore. Reina wanted to tell her parents in person and had sworn her to silence. She looked at her watch. "I've really got to go." Laura wasn't a very good liar and she felt that soon he'd see the guilt written all over her.

"Go on," he replied with a grin. "Merry Christmas."

"Merry Christmas, Michael," she said and quickly went on her way toward the restaurant. He was an odd duck she thought as she walked along. By all appearances he was a gentle, thoughtful man, who loved his family deeply. He managed the hotel because there was no other choice. But his passion was directed toward the vines he grew that adjoined the hotel and the wine he made from them. That and his family, his wife, child, and mother were the most important parts of his life. The rest of his family he rarely mentioned. Laura had never met his older brother and sister. He never mentioned Adriana or his niece.

It was hard for her to understand the Strickland family. They were totally different than her own. Even as busy as she was, Laura was very close to her siblings; they spoke on the phone regularly and the same was true of her parents. Her mother's family was the same way. But Michael's family appeared so severely splintered that there seemed to be no hope for them to reunite. The thought saddened her.

Daniel had fastened one-by-two-inch strips of pine together into a large rectangle; cotton duck was then stretched across the surface and held in place with staples. The large canvas was lying on the old wooden ping-pong table as he applied an acrylic gesso primer to the fabric.

The garage did have electric outlets that provided power for two four-foot fluorescent light fixtures he'd hung from the rafters above the makeshift table. Daniel had just applied the last strokes of gesso onto the four-by-five-foot canvas when he sensed someone behind him. The double doors had been left open to provide extra light and ventilation; Daniel turned to see David Steele in the doorway. He motioned him inside. "Good morning."

David came forward slowly and said with a smile, "I like what you've done with the place."

"It'll do for a few days."

The sketches he'd done the previous week were tacked up on a wall and a small acrylic painting was on an easel next to the worktable. David looked at the drawings carefully, going from one to the other. Some of them were in pencil, others in dry pastel, and some a mixture of watercolor and marker. "These are very good."

Dan had just put his paint roller in a bucket of water to soak for a moment and was cleaning off his hands. "Thanks."

"I'd like to talk to you about doing something for me."

"Sounds good," he replied. Daniel felt the bonds tighten again, the sense that he was being tied down. But work was work and he couldn't look a gift horse in the mouth.

David asked, "Have you met Reina's parents yet?"

"Can't say as I have."

"I hear she's coming back today."

Daniel nodded. "That's the rumor."

The actor grinned. "You're not particularly talkative, are you?"

"Not unless I have something to say." He paused briefly and said apologetically, "I spend a lot of time alone… it's hard for me to switch gears sometimes."

"There's no need to apologize. I understand much better than you might think." He picked up the small painting on the easel, holding it into the light for a better look. "The reason I'm here is to invite you to lunch. It'll give me a chance to show you the spot I have in mind for a painting."

Dan's clothes, hands and forearms were spotted with paint. "I'll need to get cleaned up."

"Take your time," David replied as he looked at his watch. "Tuan should have lunch ready in an hour."

Alex and Izzy often ate together in the morning during her break before the lunch rush. But today he'd promised Reina that he would pick her up at the airport. He'd been standing outside of the security gates for several minutes when he saw her waving to him. She closed the distance between them quickly, embraced him, kissing his cheek and he felt tears as she whispered, "I missed you."

He kissed her back. "Sí Reina, me too."

She held on to him as they started walking toward baggage claim. "How is everything?"

"I am in love and getting married," he replied with a grin. "Laura is pregnant, and Daniel is living with her. Mélange is doing great." He squeezed her tight and kissed her temple again. "That about covers it."

"I understand you thought Laura and Daniel were having an affair. Is that right?"

"Sí, but I recovered quickly. I was a fool to think that Laura would do that to you. It was a silly misunderstanding."

"I know you were just worried about me."

He chuckled. "Maybe a little."

They'd reached the baggage carousel, but the luggage hadn't arrived. She looked tired, he thought. And as the first few bags began coming down the ramp Alex asked, "Are you sure you want to face your parents today? Maybe you should stay in town for the night."

Her smile was strained as she replied, "I'm fine." But once the bags were loaded into the car and they were leaving the parking garage her eyes were already becoming heavy. By the time he was crossing the bridge on Interstate 80 she was asleep. She dreamt of Adrien and her father; two men she loved, separated by distance and time, each carrying the sorrow of separation.

The day was beautiful, in the low seventies; it was warm in the sun with the lingering scent of fall still in the air. Daniel and David ate lunch on the veranda with a view of Sugar Loaf Ridge to the west and Mount Saint Helena to the north. David said quietly as he was about to take a bite of the salmon Tuan had prepared, "Reina's father is a friend of mine." Dan nodded, as if he understood, but didn't reply. He continued, "I'd like to think that you and I are becoming friends."

Dan finished a bite and looked him in the eyes. "Why don't you just cut to the chase and tell me what's on your mind?"

David met his stare. "Alright. Reina is a nice girl, I like her. We've known each other since she was in pigtails. She's not the kind of woman who is looking for a one-night stand." He took another bite of fish. "And I suspect that you are looking for nothing more than that."

"You're right." He wiped his mouth with the linen napkin. "I am that guy and you're probably right about Reina." Daniel looked out into the distance at the hills beyond, then turned back to David. "But what we do or don't do together is our business. It's still a free country... or at least as free as it's gonna get."

He could see the anger in the younger man's eyes. "I'm sorry if you think I'm interfering in your life. That's not my intention."

Dan leaned back in his chair and took a drink of water from the crystal goblet next to him. "Of course that was your intention. Let's put the shoe on the other foot for a minute. How do you think Laura's family would feel if they knew you'd knocked her up?"

"She knows I love her."

"I'm sure she does but that's not what I'm saying. What goes on between you and Laura, whether you end up getting married or not, is up to the two of you. It's none of my business and it's none of her parents'. Both of you are over twenty-one and you make your own decisions. I'll make mine and Reina will certainly make hers."

There was an uncomfortable edge between them until finally David chuckled. "I see your point. I'm sorry. And if it makes you feel any better Laura and I are going into the city to shop for rings. She has a doctor's appointment tomorrow and we'll take care of that afterward."

Daniel smiled. "Congratulations… I didn't think you had the balls."

"Why is that?"

"I figure the longer a guy stays single the harder it is to give that up. Let's face it, both of us have reasons for being unmarried. I don't know about you, but I haven't even come close." He gave him a half-hearted smile. "Until recently at least."

David took a sip of the Chardonnay Tuan selected for lunch. "So you're saying you have feelings for Reina."

Tuan came quietly out onto the veranda with a tray of coffee with two cups and saucers. He poured one cup for Daniel and another for David before clearing their plates. "Is there anything else, Mr. Steele?" he asked quietly.

"No, Tuan, thank you." David continued to stare at Daniel for a few seconds and when he didn't respond he said, "You're right. It is easy to become fixed into the lifestyles we create for ourselves. Change is always difficult. But when I took the risk to leave Hollywood and come here, the change was good for me. It brought peace into my life. And because I had the courage to leave I met Laura. I'd almost given up finding someone until her." He added cream and two teaspoons of sugar to his coffee, then stirred. "Life is full of little miracles, but we have to pay attention or they're lost."

Daniel drank his coffee black; he took a sip and nodded. "I admire you for that… I do. But maybe the old saying is right on… it's hard for a leopard to change its spots."

"I'm not saying it's easy. It wasn't for me, I assure you. But it was necessary… at least for me. If you're not serious about Reina, the best thing would be for you to move on." Tuan had left a humidor on the table earlier; David opened the lid, took out an imported cigar from Cuba, inhaled the scent and asked, "Would you like one?"

"No thank you." Dan paused briefly while David lit his cigar before saying, "I'm not sure how I feel about Reina. That's what I hoped to find out when I came back but she had to leave. Maybe it's fate. Maybe, we're not supposed to be together."

"Maybe," David replied as he exhaled. "You'll really never know unless you give it a chance. It seems to me," he said, "and you can correct me if I'm wrong, but when the going gets tough you have a habit of leaving."

He was embarrassed by the accuracy of David's perception. Daniel nodded. "That's pretty close. But I usually don't get involved enough for it to get tough."

"So, you're saying that Reina is an exception to the rule."

Daniel finished his coffee and stood. "Listen, as much as I've enjoyed the lunch and our little talk, I've got to get back to work."

David stood as well. "Do you mind if I give you one last piece of advice?"

He shook his head and snickered. "You might as well. There's not much that's been holding you back so far."

As the two men walked inside and through the house to the front door David said, "Commit to something. It really doesn't matter whether it's your painting, Reina, or whatever… just follow through with something you care about."

"You're assuming I haven't committed myself to my work."

"No. I'm not saying that. You do what it takes to get by; you sell just enough to keep doing what you're doing. I've seen enough of your work to know how talented you are. But you don't stay in one place long enough to build an audience. You're not in any galleries and I would bet you don't have an agent."

Travis had been lying in the sun. The retriever got up and stretched lazily before walking up to them while they were talking, waiting for Daniel to finish. He sensed a hint of anger in his tone.

Daniel was trying his best to suppress the resentment that was building within him. He held out his hand. "Thanks for lunch."

David shook his hand. "I'm serious about that painting. I'd really like you to think about doing one for me."

"I don't know," he replied, shrugging his shoulders. "I have a show in San Jose next week and then I'm supposed to go south."

"It's up to you, but I wish you'd think about staying."

He stared into David's eyes for a minute. "I have commitments. It might not mean much but they pay the bills." Before there was a chance of a reply he gave Travis a pat and said, "Let's go, boy."

All the way back to the cottage Travis listened to him rant. "I don't know where the hell that guy gets off lecturing me about what I do and how I do it. And I do commit to things." He looked down at Travis. "I take good care of you, don't I?" Travis grinned back at him. "You don't need to be in some gallery to be committed to the work. I work hard. What the hell does he know anyway? He sits up there in that house and probably hasn't done a lick of work in years. The truth is he's probably washed up and nobody wants his sorry ass."

Reina opened her eyes briefly as she sensed the car pulling into the parking lot of the hotel and coming to a stop. Alex shook her gently. "We're here."

She moved the seat upright and smiled half-heartedly. "Home sweet home. I guess I better go and face the music."

"It wasn't your decision," Alex reminded her. "It was Elleanore's. Your father will understand that."

"He expected me to watch out for her."

"And you did just that… but it doesn't mean you could force her to do something she doesn't want to do."

She nodded and opened the door. "I know, you're right."

Michael and two of the hotel staff had spent the morning decorating the Christmas tree in front of a window in the lobby. He kept glancing outside periodically as they worked, waiting expectantly for Elleanore and Reina to return. When Alex hadn't arrived by noon he went to the hotel restaurant and ordered some of Izzy's enchiladas. It was after one by the time he saw the car pull into the parking lot and stop. He'd just gone outside to meet them when he saw his daughter and Alex get out; Elenore wasn't with them.

CHAPTER 33

Michael

He met her halfway across the parking lot with the sound of worry in his voice. "Where's your grandmother?"

Alex excused himself. "I'll take your bags and put them in the lobby."

Reina nodded. "Thanks." She turned to her father and gave him a hug, kissing his cheek. "Grandma wouldn't come back with me."

Michael sighed. "I knew she was up to something." He glanced at his daughter and saw the discomfort in her face. "It's not your fault, sweetheart. I should have gone with her."

"It wouldn't have done any good, Daddy. Grandma knew she was going to stay from the beginning."

He nodded as his arm wrapped around her waist. "Of course she did." Michael kissed her temple. "You must be exhausted. Let's get you settled."

Telling him wasn't as bad as Reina thought but she still felt as if she'd failed him and that hurt. "I'm sorry, Daddy."

He gave her a gentle squeeze. "So am I, sweetheart, but you have nothing to be sorry about."

By the time Daniel returned to the cottage the canvas he'd stretched and primed was dry enough to sand. When he finished he applied another coat of gesso to the surface. The work kept him busy and dulled the anger enough that he began to replay the conversation with David Steele in his mind. The actor was friends with Reina's father; it made sense that he would be concerned. In fact, Steele had only said what Dan had said to himself hundreds of times. That was what angered him; someone else knew a part of the truth.

Dan could still hear the echo of his father's words and the smell of whiskey on his breath. "Ya ain't worth a shit drawin' them pictures all day. It's time ya got a job." He remembered his father swaying over him, grabbing the sketchbook from his hands, then tearing the drawing from the pad, wadding it up and throwing it to the floor. It was only one of many confrontations between them, but it was the final one. Daniel remembered grabbing for the work and the pain when his father's fist backhanded him. That was the last time; he packed and was gone as the sun came up the next morning. He'd been traveling ever since from one town to the next. But, he wondered now, was he going somewhere then or just running away? And if he was running, then what was he running from?

He cared for Reina; he cared for her a great deal. It was wrong, he thought, to be involved with her. Steele was probably right about that. In the end he'd probably let her down, he'd leave when things got difficult. And things always became difficult sooner or later. Dan rarely smoked anymore but he kept a pack in his toolbox just in case he got the urge. He took one out to light it but when he turned he saw her silhouette in the doorway.

She smiled at him. "Miss me?"

The doubts and anger within him in that moment evaporated as he saw her. Daniel crossed the distance between them and took her in his arms, kissing her intensely. "How did you know I was here?"

Reina kissed him back, letting her tongue slide into his mouth, content at last in his arms. "Alex told me."

He was so excited to see her he'd forgotten about his paint-splattered clothes. Daniel chuckled as he stepped back. "I'm a mess."

"No, you're not," she replied as she took his hand and began walking toward the cottage.

"Where are we going?"

She led him into the house then the bathroom and stripped the T-shirt from his body. "Let's get you cleaned up," Reina said as she turned on the water in the tub.

Dan looked down at her as she tested the water and said aloud what he'd been thinking. "I missed you more than I thought possible."

Reina looked back at him and smiled. "Me too." She reached for the buckle to his belt, loosened it, and gently pulled his pants down. He was semi-erect as she stroked him, once, then twice. She shut the water off. "Get in."

He did as she directed and watched while she lit several candles before removing her own clothes, then folded them neatly before stepping into the tub behind him. Her legs straddled each side of his body as she soaped her hands and began scrubbing him gently, first each arm, his hands, and fingers. Dan leaned back into her as she caressed him, lost in the pleasure of her touch, the pain and anger of his past drifting away temporarily.

She kissed his neck. "Feel good?"

"Un huh," he replied as he felt her hands move from his chest, lower, into the water to touch him, then just as he began to respond Reina took her hand away. He groaned. "You're a tease you know."

"I want to save you for later," she replied while nibbling on his neck.

"How much later?"

She whispered into his ear. "Not long."

"How was your trip?"

"We'll talk about it later. I just want to be with you now." She pushed him forward gently resting her hands on the sides of the tub; she stood up and stepped out to grab a bath sheet.

He watched her, thinking to himself how wonderfully feminine, how graceful she was with each movement as she dried the excess moisture from her skin. Reina wrapped the towel around her body, took another off the rack and held it out to him. As Daniel stood she began to carefully wipe him dry. He reached out suddenly and gripped her hands.

Reina looked up at him. "What is it?"

Rather than answer he stepped from the tub and took her in his arms, kissing her intently, his voice husky. "I want you." And with that he picked her up in his arms and carried her to his bed.

It was Daniel who took command this time, teasing her just as she'd teased him, kissing her mouth, taking a nipple between his lips, sucking one then the other. There was a moan that came from deep inside of her as she reached for him, wanting to feel him, to urge him on. But Daniel moved his body just out of reach as his kisses began the descent lower until they reached that inner core longing for release. She came the first time as he drew that tiny bud of flesh into his mouth, her body arching upward as the wave of release washed over her. He moved up once more to kiss her mouth, but she was far from finished; Reina's hips moved against him, involuntarily seeking contact until her fingers finally guided his manhood inside. They were unprotected; he gazed into her eyes questioning as she reassured him with a whisper, "It's OK."

Michael spent the afternoon where he always did when he wanted to think—the winery. He'd gone there for as long as he could remember, even as a boy. The journals were in the old vintner's quarters on the second story above the oak barrels and vats of fermenting grapes; he remembered playing here, he remembered Adrien and how he wished that his father was more like him. That was before he finally had to accept that Adrien was indeed the man who'd given him life. Adriana never had the opportunity to know their father as a child, but he did. He'd felt guilty then for feelings beyond his control and tried unsuccessfully for years to make up for this small emotional betrayal. But the more he tried with Roger Strickland the greater the chasm between them seemed to grow until one day Michael finally stopped. It was shortly after that when Adriana discovered the letters and told him the truth, a truth he'd always sensed but never voiced. He was then hopelessly caught between a father who'd left him and a stepfather who rejected him.

He mounted the stairs to the floor above, picked up one of Adrien's journals and sat down with it in a large, overstuffed chair. It was carefully written in English rather than his father's native tongue. The books were beautiful, full of illustrations alongside the text; Michael never tired of looking at them. They were for the most part more of a record than a diary. He included recipes, critical evaluations, and observations as well as ideas he intended to try. There was a small sketch in the back of Elleanore. He turned to it and thought of the man who had drawn it.

His emotions were mixed about many things; his father, mother, and siblings certainly were on that list. But not the vines he cared for lovingly and the wine he made from them. He was passionately committed to each. They were his purpose, the anchor that kept him secure. Why then, couldn't he just let his mother be, let her do whatever she chose to do? He wasn't her guardian after all. This was the argument he struggled with now, an argument he was losing. Elleanore's hold on him ran deep.

Laura observed Alex at one of the tables in the dining room as he took a lean cut of filet mignon medallions and began sautéing them in olive oil rather than butter. He added shallots and garlic to the skillet then stirred briefly before putting in the mushrooms. The customers looked on spellbound as he removed the skillet from the heat, added the cognac and lit it with a match. As the flames died down he added the demi-glace, simmered it for another minute then transferred the meat to their plates, spooning the sauce on top.

She smiled with pride while watching him, then continued her rounds, speaking briefly with several of the regular customers. From the corner of her eye she caught sight of her mentor, Armand Moreau, sitting quietly in a corner table with a middle-aged couple. Laura couldn't help but wonder what he was up to? Without hurrying she made her way from table to table until she made eye contact with him. "Bonsoir, Armand."

"Bonsoir, chérie," he replied as he stood kissing each of her cheeks in turn.

"This is a pleasant surprise."

"Chérie," he replied, "I'd like to introduce Madame Rene Lawrence of the *Chronicle* and her associate Frederick Meyers. Monsieur Meyers writes for *Cuisine Today*."

Laura could feel the butterflies swarming within her as she held out her hand and smiled. "It's a pleasure to meet both of you."

Rene shook her hand and smiled. "Armand has told us some wonderful things about you, Chef." She winked. "I think he wants you to come back to Entretenir."

"Non, non, non," Armand protested. "Laura has matured into a beautiful butterfly who needs to spread her wings, to fly, n'est-ce pas?" He stood and pulled out a chair. "Please, chérie, sit with us a moment."

Laura had no idea what he was up to, but she knew Armand and he never did anything without a purpose. She smiled cordially and took a seat, aware that her mentor was able to maneuver the situation to his benefit, to make himself appear as the superior, the artist bestowing a gift on his pupil. But that didn't matter. The two people sitting across from her could, with the words they wrote, increase their business tenfold overnight. That did matter.

She noticed immediately that someone had taken their food order and they were just finishing a bottle of an Opus One red wine blend. With a slight gesture of her hand she attracted the attention of their waiter, and he immediately came to her side. Laura said quietly, "Would you bring a bottle of the '99 Oak Swing to the table please."

It wasn't a question and the young waiter nodded quickly saying, "Right away, Chef."

Laura turned to Armand smiling. "Oak Swing is made right here in St. Helena by the owner of the hotel, Michael Strickland."

It wasn't necessary to explain who he was; Armand had known the Stricklands for years and Michael's older brother was one of his better customers. There were, of course, rumors about the family, but Armand didn't pay attention to them. He did remember that years before the Stricklands made wine, but he had no idea that Michael continued the tradition. Why he wondered would Laura order a bottle of garage wine for two such important guests?

Frederick Meyers spoke up. "I'm sure you don't remember me, but I was impressed with your work years ago when you were Armand's sous-chef. He's very fond of you."

"Of course, I remember you, Mr. Meyers." Laura grinned. "We always knew when you came into Entretenir. Armand made sure everything was perfect."

Armand raised Laura's hand to his lips and kissed it briefly. "You are the perfect one, chérie. My greatest pupil. Nothing has been the same since you left."

Rene said, "Tell us a little about yourself, Chef. My readers would enjoy all the gory details."

It was Armand who replied, "She is an artist. That's all anyone really needs to know."

The waiter brought the bottle of wine, opened it to let it breathe, and poured a small sample for Rene Lawrence. As she tasted it, the expression on her face changed very little, then with a slight nod of her head she said, "Very nice."

Laura glanced up at the young waiter. "Thank you, Paul."

As the young man began to pour each of them a glass he quietly mentioned to Laura, "The appetizers are coming right up, Chef."

She held a hand over her glass to let him know she wasn't drinking. "Tell Alex I'll be there in a moment."

"Yes, Chef."

Once he'd gone Laura turned her attention back to the two journalists. "There's really not much to tell. I grew up in Burbank; my father is an aeronautical engineer. When he retired we moved back to Prescott, Arizona, where I graduated from high school. My grandmother began teaching me how to cook and I knew right away that this is what I wanted to do. I went to school in Paris, started my apprenticeship and that's where Armand found me." She grinned. "And here I am."

Rene asked, "Have you ever wanted a more traditional life, a husband, and family?"

Laura laughed. "When I worked for Armand I was much too busy to even think about it."

"And now," Meyers inquired.

"I am seeing someone." Laura was saved for the moment as the appetizers arrived. She stood, held out her hand to Rene first then Meyers. "It was a pleasure to meet both of you. I have to check on your entrées, but I'll make sure and come back before you leave."

As she started toward the kitchen Laura noticed Michael Strickland sitting by himself at the bar. She stopped beside him and with his back

to her, put a hand on his shoulder. "Good evening, Michael. Are you and your family joining us for supper this evening?"

He shook his head. "Erica is working, and I haven't seen my daughter all afternoon."

Laura had a pretty good idea why he hadn't seen Reina. "Let me fix you something to eat? It's on the house."

Michael shook his head again, dejected. "No, that's OK. I might get something later." His eyes looked into hers. "Did you hear about my mother?"

"Yes, I did, Michael. I'm sorry it's upset you."

Armand had seen her stop in the bar, excused himself from the two journalists and went to find her. He saw Laura talking to a guest at the bar and interrupted them as he approached. "Chérie, we need to talk."

She turned to her mentor. "Armand, I was just speaking to Michael Strickland. I was about to tell him how much you enjoy his wine."

He hadn't taken the time to notice who she was talking to and realizing he'd been rude, apologized, "Excusez-moi s'il vous plait." Armand held out his hand. "Michael, it has been such a long time, I'm afraid I didn't recognize you. Votre vin est magnifique!"

The last thing in the world Michael wanted to deal with was a Frenchman. He was tired and fed up with the whole country. And Armand Moreau had been in America for more than thirty years, long enough that the periodic French phrases came across as pretentious. "I'm happy that you enjoyed the wine."

Armand kept his hand on Michael's shoulder. "I must order some for Entretenir. You will select for me, oui?"

"Certainly, I would be happy to."

"C'est merveilleux. I will phone you tomorrow. But tonight, if you will excuse us, I must talk to this lovely woman." He glanced at Laura as he said it. And once he'd taken her far enough away from the bar Armand said emphatically, "Chérie, it was difficult for me to convince those two critics to come with me tonight. I did this for you. They want a story. And, chérie, this is something you don't want to neglect."

"I'm not going to neglect them, Armand. I was just about to go back to the kitchen to work on their order." She kissed his cheek. "Thank you for bringing them. Now, go back to your guests while I check on your food."

"Oui, chérie." As she turned to walk away he suddenly stopped her. "I love you, Laura. You are the daughter I wish I might have had."

She could see his eyes begin to water as he said it. He had taught her more than Laura could ever repay. There were times while she worked for Armand when she hated him; he was egotistical and demanding. But he made her a better chef. He never let her settle for just being good at what she did; he demanded excellence and once when she complained about it he said quietly, "If the kitchen is too hot for you, chérie, you are always free to leave." Now, as she looked back at him she could see the love and concern for her that somehow over the years she'd either missed or taken for granted. Laura walked back the few paces between them to hold him tight. "I love you too."

CHAPTER 34

Laura

Rene Lawrence's article came out in the *Chronicle* the following Friday. Alex was reading it aloud during Izzy's midmorning break. He was thrilled while reading the last line to her. *"Mélange is truly nouvelle cuisine with an American twist at its finest,"* he said emphatically and set the paper aside.

Izzy smiled and took a bite of quiche. "Has Laura seen it yet?"

Alex shook his head. "I don't know but here she comes now. We'll ask."

Knowing that Reina and Daniel were making up for lost time Laura had spent the last few nights at David's. It felt good and she was on top of the world as she walked into the kitchen toward her office in the back, waving to Alex and Izzy. "Good morning, you two."

Alex held up the paper. "Have you seen this yet?"

"Read it this morning," Laura called out as she went into her office to hang up her coat and put her things away. A moment later she walked back out while putting on her chef's jacket. She smiled at the two of them. "This just might be a big break for all of us."

Reina had agreed to meet her father for breakfast. She hadn't spent a lot of time with either of her parents since she'd been back, partly because her father was so upset about Elleanore and partly because she knew her time with Daniel was limited. He was waiting for her in the hotel restaurant when she walked in; Michael was in a booth by himself staring down a cup of coffee. She slid in next to him. "Good morning, Daddy."

"Good morning, sweetheart," he replied.

Angie had been waiting on Michael and when she saw Reina walk in she ordered a café au lait for her and took it to the table. They ordered breakfast and when the young waitress had gone Reina asked, "What did you want to talk to me about?"

He looked like he hadn't slept. "I want you to tell me about them."

She was a little confused. "Do you mean Adrien and Sofia?"

He nodded. "Yes, and my sister. And Marie, my niece."

During the time that she'd been home, her parents were so upset about Elleanore not coming back with her, neither of them had asked much about the trip until now. She told him most of what she remembered, describing Libourne and the wine country there. And toward the end she said, "I like Adrien. He's nice and so is Sofia." There was a slight hesitation before Reina added, "Nobody said anything… but I don't think he's well, Daddy."

Michael suddenly seemed alarmed. "What makes you think that?"

She shrugged. "The medication he takes, and I don't know… the way he acts some of the time. It's like he's really tired."

"That's not unusual, sweetheart. Adrien must be almost eighty by now and elderly people get tired."

"It's not like that, Daddy. And he doesn't act like an old person anyway. I felt like I could talk to Grand-pere about anything. He just seems to know so much… and he's written other books, Daddy. Like the ones he left here. He left them with the Fournier winery when he retired."

"Why would he do that?"

"Grand-pere says that he wrote them while working for Paul Fournier, so they rightfully belong to him."

Michael gazed into his daughter's eyes. "You just called him Grand-pere. Is that the way you think of him?"

Reina lowered her head, then nodded briefly. "Yes." She turned her head toward her father. "I know he loves me. And I know it saddens him not knowing you." She took her father's hand. "You should see the way he talks about you. He's proud of you, Daddy."

"He doesn't know me."

"Yes, Daddy, he does. Grandma has written to him about you; she sent him pictures, lots of pictures of you when you were little, when you graduated from high school and wedding pictures of you and Mom."

Angie brought their breakfast and asked, "Is there anything else I can get you?"

Michael shook his head. "No, thank you," he replied and suddenly reached out to squeeze Reina's hand gently. "We're just fine."

Mélange was busier than usual for a Friday night and their reservations for Saturday were filled. By early afternoon on Saturday, their seating for Sunday brunch reached maximum capacity and the hotel was packed with tourists, most of them from San Francisco. Laura began to be concerned about having enough food to make it through the weekend.

First thing Monday morning Laura was still exhausted; she raised her sleeping mask and glanced at the alarm clock on the nightstand. It was after nine. This was the first time in several days that she hadn't spent the night with David and the void in the bed beside her felt uncomfortable. She was the one who told him that she needed a night in her own bed to catch up on sleep. And it was true, she did. The two of them had a habit of staying up late every night talking and making love.

The floor was cold as Laura got out of bed; she put on a robe and slippers before making her way toward the kitchen for coffee. Normally she didn't bother with a robe but since Daniel had been sharing the house with her she had little choice. Reina was sitting at the kitchen table drinking coffee, dressed in one of Daniel's long-sleeve work shirts and nothing else. Laura was hoping for a few moments alone but smiled nonetheless. "Good morning."

Reina smiled back. "Good morning to you."

Laura poured a cup of coffee, then added a little cream and sugar. "It was quite a weekend. Thanks for helping out."

She chuckled. "I'm not sure how helpful I really was."

"You helped out where you could and that's important." She sat down at the table next to her. "Dan working already?"

Reina nodded. "He was gone when I woke up." She grinned as she said, "I understand that congratulations are in order."

She rubbed her belly. "I'm not real sure how I feel about it yet."

"Nice ring anyway," she replied while glancing toward Laura's left hand. "When's the big day?"

"We haven't set a date yet."

"Do your folks know?"

"Yes, I called them last week." She took a sip of coffee. "They're both thrilled with the thought of another grandchild." Laura noticed the curious look on Reina's face and laughed. "Not from me. My brother and sister have children."

Reina smiled. "And how about David? Do they know about him?"

There were a few seconds of hesitation before Laura replied, "They're happy for me but… I was going to be married once before and it got called off at the last minute. I can't ask them to go through that expense again. David and I have decided to have a small wedding, here, in St. Helena."

"At the hotel?"

She shook her head. "Heavens no, at David's house on the hill. We're thinking late May or early June, after Alex and Izzy get back from their honeymoon."

Reina couldn't hold back and giggled briefly. "I leave for two weeks and everybody starts getting engaged. It's like the flu."

"I know, right." She chuckled. "I thought it might be something in the water. By the way, how are you and Dan doing?"

"Mmm, wonderfully satisfying… and noncommittal," she replied as she stood and refilled both of their cups.

"Are you OK with that?"

"For right now, sure." There was a long pause as she looked through the kitchen window toward the garage where he was working. "But I'm not going to wait around for him to show up once a year." She sat back down. "My feelings for him are already a little too intense."

"Do you love him?"

Reina shook her head. "I don't even want to go there. If I even think it, things could get sticky between us."

"It seems to me that you either love him or you don't. How does he feel about you?"

"Can't tell," she replied. "There are moments when I think he does but then he puts up his wall again. It's like he's always testing me just a little at a time to see what I'll do. I know I can't live like that. If it's going to work between us he must believe it will. And I'm afraid that Daniel won't be able to do that. There will always be a certain amount of doubt, a lack of trust standing between us."

Laura felt sad for her; there was a time when she believed she could count on Matt, the man she'd planned to marry. But it turned out that her faith in him was unjustified. "Trust can be deceptive," she replied. "The things we believe to be true, aren't always. And it's hard to work beyond that. It's like once you're burned you stay away from fire." It was still hard for her to talk about how hurt she'd been after breaking up with Matt. "I was afraid of getting involved again for a long time. And once David came along it seemed to me to be too good to be true. I tested him and almost lost him because of it. Daniel helped us work through that."

Reina was surprised. "Really?"

"Yes really. It's like Dan knows more than he lets on; there's this quiet depth to him that he hides."

She nodded. "You got that one right; he's a great one for hiding out."

"All I'm saying, Reina, is that if you give him enough rope he just might figure it out. And that could be good for both of you."

The back door opened, and Daniel walked in, his shirt and pants splattered with paint. "Good morning, you two." He leaned over and kissed Reina. "I hope I didn't wake you this morning."

She felt her heart flutter as she replied, "You didn't." Reina knew she was getting in too deep and, as much as she knew it might end badly for her, she couldn't just walk away and save herself.

He poured the last of the coffee into a cup and began making more. "I have to get back to the city in a couple of days and thought it best to start early. I'm almost finished with your painting," he said to Laura, "but bringing it all together at the end can be tricky."

"We'll miss you," Laura replied.

Daniel leaned against the counter and took a drink of coffee. "David says he wants me to do a painting for him."

"You can always stay with me again. There's plenty of room and I don't think Reina will mind. Will you, Reina?"

She smiled. "No, I kind of like having him around."

He stared into Reina's eyes. "That's great. I'll tell him I'll do it." Daniel sipped his coffee and then said, "The show next weekend is in San Jose. If it's OK, I'll be back about this time next week."

"It's OK with me," Laura replied. "Is it OK with you, Reina?"

The coffee finished its drip, Reina stood, refilled her cup, and kissed him quickly. "I can live with that."

The next few days went by quickly and the reservation list for Mélange was filled by Thursday. Reina continued to stay in the extra room in the cottage after Daniel and Travis left for San Jose. Laura spent most of her nights at David's, which allowed Reina some privacy. But the privacy turned to melancholy. Late Friday afternoon she'd just finished work when there was a knock on the cottage door. When she opened it, her father was standing there. "Hi, Daddy."

"May I come in?"

"Sure," she said. "What's going on?"

He came in and she shut the door. "I was hoping you would tell me what's going on. You haven't seemed the same the last few days at work. And your mother and I have been worried." He hesitated briefly. "When you told us you were moving over here with Laura, your mother and I understood you needed some space. But when you didn't introduce us to the painter we wondered why."

"He's just a friend, Daddy."

"Are you saying you're not serious about him?"

Reina wasn't a very good liar in the best of circumstances and certainly not when it came to her father. She lowered her eyes and sighed. "I don't know. I like him a lot but even if I was serious I don't think he's ready."

"I see," he said. "I'm sorry."

"I am too." She poured each of them a glass of the red wine he'd made and handed one to him. "It makes me a little sad, but I'll get over it."

He nodded. "I have a favor to ask."

"What is it?"

"I need to be gone for a few days and would like you to help take care of the hotel. I've talked to Laura and she's OK with it."

"That's fine with me, Daddy. You know I would do anything for you and Mom. Is she going with you?"

He shook his head. "No. She has to work, and this is something I need to take care of personally."

"It sounds mysterious."

Michael smiled. "It's not." He picked up the bottle of the wine she'd just poured and looked at the label. "You know why I call my wine Oak Swing?"

She shook her head. "No."

He put the bottle back on the table. "When I was a little boy we used to have a swing on that old oak tree by the hotel. The swing's been gone for years but we used to picnic there when we were children before Adriana was born. When I think of the good times as a child, I think of that."

There was a sadness to his tone that moved her and as he stood to leave she wrapped her arms about him. "I love you, Daddy."

"I love you too, sweetheart." He started for the door then paused. "I'd appreciate it if you'd fill any orders for the wine if they come in."

"Sure… no problem."

Michael kissed her cheek. "If that painter had any sense he'd grab on to you while he has the chance."

She grinned. "His name's Daniel."

"Well bring Daniel to the hotel the next time he's in town and introduce us."

Reina kissed him again. "I will, Daddy."

CHAPTER 35

Adrien

Christmas was ten days away. Marie was waiting for her grandfather on the street outside of school; he was late and her grand-pere was never late. She began to worry. A few more moments went by when she saw Elleanore come around the corner, walking toward her. Marie ran to her grandmother saying, "Where's Grand-pere? He always picks me up."

Ellie was a little out of breath from the walk but smiled. "He wasn't feeling well." She saw the anxiousness on the little girl's face and added, "It's just a cold, nothing to worry about."

"Oh," she replied with an air of disappointment difficult for her to hide. It was Friday and on Fridays Adrien always took her to the café for a pastry and hot chocolate.

"He said to tell you to take me to Café Pascal for hot chocolate."

Marie smiled now knowing that he hadn't forgotten what day it was. "Come with me, Mamie," she replied, "I'll show you the way."

Adrien had been in bed most of the day, sleeping off and on. He'd just started reading when Sofia walked in smiling. "I made you some chicken soup."

"Bon, I'm hungry."

She set the bowl on the nightstand, straightened the pillows to help him sit up, ladled a spoonful of soup and held it out to him. He gave her a stern look. "I'm not an invalid… yet."

"I like taking care of you." Reluctantly he opened his mouth to let her feed him. "That wasn't so bad was it." He grumbled as she filled the spoon once more. "Elleanore and Marie should be back soon."

"It is our day together," he replied as she fed him another spoonful. The soup felt good and his mood began to lighten. "I miss being with her."

"I know you do but there will be other Fridays. You need to work on getting better so this cold doesn't get any worse or you'll have to see the doctor." He grumbled something she couldn't make out. "What did you say?"

"I said I'll be fine." There were the sounds on the stairway. "Maybe that's Marie now."

But it was Adriana who came into their bedroom to ask, "How are you feeling, Papa?"

"Beaucoup mieux, chérie," he replied.

Sofia stood up and handed the bowl of soup to Adriana. "See if you can get him to finish this. I have to start supper." She glanced back at her husband. "And don't let him talk you into giving him his pipe."

The two women exchanged knowing looks as Adriana took the bowl and sat down. "He'll be a good boy. Won't you, Papa?"

Adrien gave his daughter a sour look. "Don't talk to me as if I was a child. I'm your father. Treat me with some respect."

"Oui, Papa," she replied as she held out another spoonful of soup.

"How are you getting along with your mother?"

She dipped the spoon into the bowl once more and smiled. "Better than I would have thought. She comes over to the house sometimes at night to visit. It's nice."

"I'm glad. It's time the two of you forgave one another."

That put Adriana on the defensive. "What have I ever done to her that needs to be forgiven?"

He reached out with his hand to take hers. "You have taken all the anger you've built up and blamed all the bad that has happened in your life on her. It hasn't been fair, and you know that."

Her eyes began to tear; she wiped them away quickly and replied, "Maybe you're right." He grinned, and she added, "I said maybe." Adriana smiled back and held out the spoon again. "Here take this last bite."

"You are beautiful when you smile."

She set the bowl on the table and dabbed his mouth with a napkin. "And you are a devil."

"One of my best days was when you and Marie came to live with us."

"And you have so many days to choose from I suppose," she replied with a wink.

"Oui, the day I met your mother, the day Michael was born and the day you were born." There was a long pause before he said quietly, "When I left Elleanore and Michael to come back here before you were born my heart was broken. It was as if someone had cut the love from me and thrown it away. Sofia saved me. The day we married was a special day, one of the best."

Adriana kissed his temple. "I love you, Papa."

"Je t'aime comme bien, ma douce."

They heard the front door downstairs slam shut and footsteps running up the stairs. A second later Marie burst through the door and was hugging her grandfather, holding him tight. "I missed you, Grandpere. I was worried when you didn't come to school for me."

"I missed you too, mon petit papillon." He kissed the top of her head as she lay nestled in his arms. "Did you take your Mamie to Café Pascal?"

"Oui, Grand-pere."

Marie's mother looked down at the two of them thinking how she'd been robbed of moments like this when she was a young girl. And thankful that her daughter had what she had missed. She picked up the empty bowl leaving them time to spend alone. When Adriana turned she saw Elleanore standing in the doorway.

She gazed into Ellie's eyes, then suddenly, kissed her mother quickly on the cheek. "I'm glad we're together now, Mama." As Adriana began walking down the stairs there was a knock on the door; she called out, "I'll see who it is."

As she opened the door a man stood on their doorstep with his back to her. "Oui, je peux vous aider?" When he turned she was confused at first. "Michael, is that you?"

The last time he'd seen his younger sister she was eighteen. The years had been kind, but it was still a shock to see his sister now at middle age. He smiled. "It's been too long, Adriana."

She set the dirty bowl aside on the entry table in the foyer and hugged him saying, "Come in please."

He apologized. "I'm sorry I didn't call first. I guess I thought that if I did I'd lose my nerve."

Adriana continued to hold on to him as she led him into the house toward the kitchen. Sofia was taking bread out of the oven as they walked in and for Michael the years seemed to melt away as he saw her. She was an old woman now but still beautiful; he said softly, "Buenas tardes, Sofia."

"Buenas tardes," she said automatically before turning to look at him. She hadn't seen Michael since he was a little boy, but she recognized the eyes, and the features that were so much like Adrien's. The tears started to fall as she approached him, wrapping her arms around him, kissing each cheek, then his lips. "I have prayed for this day."

The scent of her, the smell of fresh bread, spice, and a subtle fragrance of fresh flowers filled his nostrils as she held him close. The memories of a past he'd thought were long forgotten began flooding the surface of his mind, taking him back to a time when he was truly happy. He whispered in her ear, "I've missed you."

Sofia took a step back to get a good look at him. "You have turned into a very handsome man, so much like your father." She'd said the words honestly and openly, forgetting the pretense Michael had lived with most of his life.

There was a moment of silence until Michael asked, "Is Adrien here?"

The old woman nodded. "Sí. He's upstairs."

"Papa has a cold," Adriana said still gripping his arm affectionately. "It's not serious. Come, I'll show you to his room."

Michael followed her up the stairs, the butterflies swirling about inside of him. Adriana entered the room first saying, "Papa, there is someone here to see you."

Adrien had been listening to Marie tell him about her day and the trip to Café Pascal and how the waiter, Marcel Bouvier, flirted with Elleanore. Ellie was sitting on one side of him, still chuckling at the story and Marie was on the other as Adriana came into the bedroom with her brother. The two men gazed into each other's eyes as Adriana said, "Marie, this is your Uncle Michael."

The little girl certainly knew of him, the stories anyway, and Reina had told her a great deal more. But she was still unprepared for how much he looked like her grandfather. She held out her hand hesitantly saying, "Bon après-midi, monsieur."

He took the hand gently in his. "And it's a pleasure to meet you, Marie."

Ellie was sitting on the edge of Adrien's bed; she stood, crossing the room to her son, and put a hand softly on her granddaughter's shoulder. "Let's give your grand-pere and uncle a moment, Marie," she said quietly and kissed her son's cheek. "We'll be downstairs."

Adrien's gaze was fixed on his son as the two women and Marie left the room. Silence filled the space between them until the old man finally said, "You've grown into a fine-looking man."

Michael had flown halfway around the world to see him and was at a loss for words. The man who lay in bed next to him was not the one he remembered as a boy. He remembered someone larger than life. And he could still feel the strength of Adrien's arms holding him, the way he'd knelt beside him once to show him how to tell when the grapes were ripe for picking. Suddenly the old man began to cough and that was enough to bring Michael back to the moment. He picked up a glass of water on the nightstand and handed it to him. Not knowing exactly what else to say he replied weakly, "It's been a long time."

The old man took a drink and handed the glass back with a chuckle. "A lifetime," then added, "I'm sorry I'm not feeling better. It seems the older I get the harder it is to put up with illness. I've never had the patience to be sick."

"You'll be well soon."

Suddenly Adrien reached out and took his hand. "Tell me, Michael, why are you here… why now?"

He shrugged. "I don't know exactly. I just felt like I needed to see you."

"It's not about your mother?"

"Not really. She's always had a mind of her own." Michael hesitated a moment, then began to tell the truth he'd carried for a lifetime. "Before you left I used to wish that you were my father. I loved you so much and then you were gone."

"I didn't want to leave. It was impossible for me to stay any longer."

Michael's head was lowered, feeling the heat from Adrien's hand gripping his. The question was difficult, but he had to ask, "Did you love me?"

"Bien sur les fils," he replied quickly, then added in English, "yes very much." His eyes began to water. "You were my son, but I had no right to you. The hardest thing I've ever had to do was leave."

There was a slight nod to Michael's head as his thumb gently caressed his father's hand. "I'd like us to get to know one another, to spend time together."

"Oui, I would like that."

The two of them began that afternoon and into the evening; they talked not so much as father and son but as two people discovering one another for the first time. Michael told him of his family, stories of Reina when she was young and of his wife, Erica. They spoke for the longest time about the craft that each of them shared, sometimes disagreeing and at other times discovering exactly how much they were in tune. Adrien spoke to him of Sofia, of his love for her and Ellie, about the bond that was forged between them. And when he spoke of Marie his eyes began to well up with pride. He said to Michael, "When your sister had the courage to come here, to live with us, her baby was the first child I've been able to help raise, to see grow. It's been a blessing having her with us. And it has helped heal the anger I felt not being a part of your life."

This was the first time in Michael's life that he began to see the past through Adrien's eyes. He sensed his pain and admired him for the struggle it took to move beyond it. But once darkness began to descend upon the countryside of Bordeaux there was a brief knock on the door; Adriana opened it to say, "Papa, I've brought you your supper."

Adrien started to struggle to get out of bed replying, "I'll not eat here like an invalid. Tell Sofia I'm feeling much better and will sit with the rest of our family." And it was true, he was much improved.

The days went by quickly after that first meeting and the time Michael planned to stay was coming to an end. But he didn't want to leave. Adrien's cold was all but gone and the two of them, father and son, took long walks with one another each day. They visited the wineries in the area, particularly Chateau Fournier, and spent the afternoons at Café Pascal playing chess. When one of Adrien's cronies would come in he'd introduce Michael saying jovially, "This is my son. He came to visit me all the way from America." And there was a sense of pride in his voice that filled the room. Neither of them dared mention the day when he would have to leave.

Michael slept in the same bedroom at his sister's home where Reina had stayed when she'd visited. Adriana had just kissed Marie goodnight and came downstairs; her brother was drinking a glass of brandy. She said to him, "It's been nice having you here. Papa hasn't been this happy since Reina left."

He was staring into the fire. "Reina cares for him a great deal."

She poured herself a glass of wine and came to sit next to him. "You did a good job with her, with Reina. I like her."

His gaze shifted toward her. "You were right coming here, to come and find him years ago. I've wasted so many years not knowing him."

"We make choices, Michael, but it's not always easy to see what the result will be. There are always bumps in the road no matter which one we choose."

A sigh escaped him as he took another drink. "Erica and I are just going through the motions for Reina's sake. We haven't been... together for several years." This was the first time he'd admitted this vocally and Michael was surprised at the relief once it was done. He snickered. "I tried so hard to have the perfect marriage, to have everything we didn't have as children. But it's all been false. Both of us know it."

Adriana could see the pain in his face. "I'm sorry, Michael. You've been together for a long time."

"Almost thirty years. We're really nothing more than two wounded souls finding refuge with one another."

"What does Erica say about this?"

He shrugged. "Nothing. She has her life and I have mine. We've never talked about it."

"What will you do?"

"I have no idea."

"You have to talk about it, Michael, to her. If there's any hope at all you won't know unless you do."

He finished his drink. "That's a can of worms best left unopened."

"You're wrong, Michael. If there's hope for the two of you, you must try and find it. And if there isn't it's best that you know."

"I'm afraid of what she'll say if I do."

"Anything is better than living a lie, Michael."

CHAPTER 36

Daniel

The show in San Jose was slow for the first two days; Daniel was beginning to be concerned that he wouldn't be able to make enough money to cover the expense of the trip. And his mind kept returning to Reina. He wanted nothing more than to be with her once more, to hold her in his arms. But a cold, deep fear nagged at him, the fear that it would never work out. He believed there would always be something that he or she would do or say, an impasse, that gradually would grow into a chasm between them.

It was Sunday morning the last day of the show; he was having his coffee and reading the paper to Travis who was lying patiently at his feet. Daniel closed the paper and said, "What's the worst thing that could happen?" Travis didn't answer but glanced up at him. "It'll either work out between us or it won't. I think we should at least give it a shot with Reina." With the mention of her name the golden retriever wagged his tail and began to look around expectantly. Daniel gave him a pat. "She's not here, boy." Suddenly Travis got to his feet anyway, went to the opening of the canopy booth and began to sprint away.

Daniel almost spilled his coffee as he quickly got to his feet to find his dog; he saw him fifty feet away licking Reina on the face as she knelt beside him. She looked up and called to him, "Hi there!"

He walked toward her slowly. "We were just talking about you."

She hugged the big retriever once more, gave him a pat, and stood smiling. "Something good I hope?"

"What are you doing here?"

"Checking up on you," she replied as her lips met his.

"We've missed you," he whispered as his arms wrapped around her. "I never thought I could miss someone so much."

Reina chuckled. "There's a first time for everything." She took his arm in hers and nodded toward his booth. "It looks like you have customers."

Two women were looking at his paintings, talking with one another quietly as they made their way toward them. The taller of the two women looked to be in her forties, the woman with her maybe ten years younger; they were clearly a couple. Daniel said casually, "If there's anything I can help you with let me know." Reina noticed that they were looking at one of the paintings Daniel had done from the sketches he'd made while working on Laura's first commission. It was a large piece, the center point of his display and priced at five thousand dollars.

Travis was the one who broke the ice by walking up to them wagging his tail. The younger woman knelt down and said to him, "Aren't you a pretty boy!"

"His name's Travis," Reina replied. "It looks like you've made a friend."

"My folks had a retriever when I was growing up. I've always wanted one." She gave the dog another long soft stroke across his back, then stood, holding out her hand. "I'm Marlene."

The handshake was firm. "Reina Strickland. It's nice to meet you."

Marlene put her arm around the woman with her. "This is Casey. We really love your work."

"It's my boyfriend's actually."

Casey asked, "That's a view of the city from Vista Point isn't it?"

Daniel had taken his seat again just inside the booth and replied, "Yes."

Reina chuckled. "He's a man of few words."

Marlene laughed. "I can see that."

He got up from his seat and held out his hand. "Daniel Whitman. I completed this piece last year while I was working on a commission for the owner of a small café in the city."

"That's where I've seen your work," Casey acknowledged, "in the Bistro at the Bay."

"That's right, Case," Marlene replied, "we love that place."

Reina said, "That's where Daniel and I met. I work for the owner, Laura Patterson. She has a new restaurant in St. Helena called Mélange." She took a card from her purse and handed it to Marlene. "Check it out if you're ever in the area."

Daniel wanted to shift the conversation back to his work. They might not buy the larger piece but there were several smaller works he'd done of San Francisco that he thought he might be able to steer them toward. He was just about to guide them gently toward some of those paintings when Casey handed him a card saying, "Are you showing anywhere in the city right now?"

"No," he said quietly, "I'm not."

Casey put her arm around Marlene. "Give me a call. I'd like to see some more of your work."

After exchanging a pleasant goodbye, the two women strolled away hand in hand but not before Marlene gave Travis one more hug. Reina sounded disappointed as she said, "I was sure they were going to buy that painting." He handed her the card, which read Ashcraft/Flannery Gallery of Fine Art. There was an element of surprise in her voice. "This is a big deal, Daniel. I've been to this gallery; it's not far from Union Square."

"Casey Ashcraft," he said to himself quietly. "Do you think she's the owner?"

She smiled and nudged him with her hip. "Well yeah, Daniel, I do."

This could be the chance for him, he thought, to get off the road, to settle down. But just as fast as the possibilities came to him the doubts he felt cast a shadow over them. He'd have to give up the freedom the road provided.

Reina noticed him become serious. "What are you thinking?"

He put his arm around her instead. "I'm thinking I'm glad you're here. Maybe you've brought me some luck." Daniel kissed her just as another couple stopped in front of the booth. "It's time for me to go to work."

It turned out that Reina did more than provide a piece of luck; she sold two small paintings that afternoon. And it was clear to him that she had a knack for engaging people, a talent he didn't possess. When he asked her about it she said simply, "I like people. Making a deal with someone whether you're selling wine or art is just about people communicating. You already know they're interested, or they wouldn't be here."

"I've never been that good at selling my work."

They were in the process of packing up the show and loading his truck. He didn't have to ask, she just pitched in. "Talk to Casey," Reina encouraged him. "Let her sell your work. That way both of you will do what you do best."

That made sense to him. He'd never admit it to anyone, but the shows were tedious for him. The only reason he did it was to keep painting. He loved the process, the skill and thought it took while working with his hands, creating something on paper or canvas; it made him feel worthwhile. And it was that sense of doing something valuable that kept the darkness at bay.

Reina followed him to his trailer and helped him unload. Afterward they went to the bar where they first met, had something to eat, and he watched while she played trivia. When she was five hundred points behind the person closest to her Daniel chuckled. "You've lost your touch."

"I haven't," she replied frustrated. "It's the categories tonight."

The laugh that followed was more of a guffaw. "Categories my ass! Who doesn't know that Gary Cooper played Lou Gehrig in *The Pride of the Yankees*."

She punched him playfully in the arm. "Me, apparently." Reina pushed the console aside and took a drink of her beer. " 'Take me home or leave me forever.' I bet you don't know that one."

"Meg Ryan… *Top Gun*."

"Well, Maverick," she said as she stood, "take me back to your place. I'm exhausted and have to get up early."

As they were walking out together Daniel realized how comfortable he'd become with her. They were like two pieces of a puzzle that fit perfectly; their differences weren't a sign of something missing between them but were a necessary balance that added rather than detracted from the whole. He thought as they drove back to his trailer that if he was unable to make this work with her he would probably remain alone the rest of his life.

Reina made love with the same ease, the same sense of knowing what he wanted and needed as she did everything else. As they lay together in each other's arms afterward he whispered in her ear, "You've bewitched me."

She chuckled. "Is that a good thing or bad?"

"I'm spoiled for anyone else now."

"Good," she said with a yawn while rolling over with her back to him. Her buttocks spooning into him.

"So you're done with me now. You've had your way and that's it?"

Her eyes closed as she said quietly, "I've got an early start."

Daniel lay there next to her, listening to her breathe softly and whispered, "I think I love you."

Reina was lingering pleasantly between wakefulness and sleep as she replied with a contented sigh, "I love you too."

The weight of the words once they were said made it difficult for him to sleep; it was unclear which admission bothered him more, his or hers. Daniel tossed and turned fitfully until five when he finally gave up and got out of bed quietly to avoid waking her. He slipped into a pair of jeans not bothering with a shirt, closed the bedroom door, and stepped the five feet into the cramped trailer's kitchen to make coffee. Travis had made a bed for himself on the cushioned bench that wrapped around the table at the far end of the vehicle. The dog jumped down and stretched before coming to say hello to him.

Fifteen minutes later the two of them went outside for a walk along the beach. The fog was thick, hanging over the coastline like a blanket; the early morning chill felt good. He took a sip of his coffee while watching the waves wash the shore, his mind still haunted by their last words the night before. She'd said them with such ease. And it was suddenly clear to him that he could run from her but not from the way he felt.

Travis nudged his leg, looking up at him then toward the trailer. Daniel smiled and gave him a pat. "You hungry? Let's go back then." He could tell when he went inside that she still wasn't awake. The retriever went right to the bedroom door, gave it a push to open it and jumped onto the bed next to her. Reina felt the mattress shift and she began to stir, rolling over to see the big brown eyes looking back at her. She grinned and said sleepily, "You're not the same guy I went to bed with last night." The dog seemed to smile as he crawled closer to give her a lick. She kissed the top of his head, then gave him a light push, just enough to give her the room to crawl over the top of his body and get out of bed. With nothing on but one of Daniel's T-shirts Reina immediately started for the bathroom. Daniel was pouring a cup of coffee for himself and another for her as she said in passing, "I'm freezing."

He chuckled. "Put some pants on." While she relieved herself, he handed her the cup of coffee. "I think I got it right but if you need more cream or sugar it's on the counter."

She took a sip and said drowsily, "It's perfect. What time is it?"

"A quarter past six."

He heard the toilet flush and the shower being turned on as she said loudly, "I've got to get going."

Reina closed the bathroom door, then a moment later, yelled, "I'd invite you to join me but there's not enough room to turn around!"

While she was getting cleaned up he fed Travis and began to fix breakfast for the two of them. He made an omelet with plenty of vegetables because she liked it that way and had just flipped it in the skillet when she came out with a towel wrapped about her body. She gave him a quick kiss. "I used your toothbrush. I hope you don't mind."

Before she could turn to go back to the bedroom to dress he took her in his arms, kissing her deeply before saying, "Thank you for yesterday."

She grinned. "That's a two-way street."

He stammered, "I mean for helping me with the show... for being there. It was nice working together."

Reina felt his hands roam down her back to her buttocks, caressing them. "None of that. I've got to get back to St. Helena." She made her way toward the bedroom. "My dad went to France to see my grandmother. I told him I'd take care of the hotel." She put on the same jeans and blouse from the day before. "I shouldn't have left yesterday but I really wanted to see your show."

"You've seen it plenty of times."

A chuckle escaped her. "OK you caught me. I missed you."

"I missed you too. I've been thinking a lot about that this morning." Dan took the toast out of the toaster and began to butter it. "Breakfast is ready when you are."

She piled her hair on top of her head and held it there with a clip. "Good, I'm starved. Hard work and sex do that to me."

He smiled, cut the omelet in half, putting each half on two plates, and set them on the table before refilling their coffee cups. She sat down on the bench. "This looks great."

Daniel sat across from her and for a moment watched her eat before asking spontaneously, "Do you think we can make it work?"

Reina took a bite of omelet, aware that it was a loaded question, and knowing he was weighing the words from the night before. She took a sip of coffee. "I don't believe that we choose who we love. My grandfather and grandmother have taught me that. We can't control it any more than we can control the next breath. The only choice we have is to decide what we want to do about it. I love you and that works for me. It's free, there's no obligation. You have to decide what works for you."

There was a slight nod of his head as he picked up his fork and took a huge bite of his breakfast saying, "I can deal with that."

There was an empty feeling inside of him thirty minutes later as he watched her go; it felt like a part of him was being cut away. Travis stood beside him and when the car was out of sight Daniel said, "Come on, boy. We have a phone call to make."

CHAPTER 37

Reina

Reina stopped at Laura's house in the city for a quick change of clothes and to put on some fresh makeup before going to the bistro to have a quick meeting with Shelly. The small restaurant was slammed with people by the time she arrived, and the manager didn't have the time to talk. The article about Laura and Mélange had boosted their business as well.

She wanted to give them a hand but was already late and drove straight to the hotel in St. Helena instead. It was after eleven when she arrived, and her mother was working the front desk, obviously perturbed. Erica glared at her saying, "Where have you been?"

Before Reina could answer they were interrupted by a couple checking out. And after they were gone her mother said, "We need to talk."

"If it's about yesterday I'm sorry. I was with a friend."

Erica shook her head knowing that her daughter was talking about the artist she still hadn't been introduced to. And she didn't believe that their relationship would last long enough for that introduction to take place. Rather than get into a debate about her daughter's choice of sexual partners she stayed on point. "Your father wants us to spend

Christmas in France with those people over there. This is all your grandmother's fault!"

"It's no one's fault, Mother."

"That may be, Lorraine, but I for one have no intention of gallivanting halfway across the world to spend the holidays with people I don't know and don't wish to. I have a job. And since your father has decided to leave and you feel you can just take off whenever you get the urge it's obvious that I'm left once again taking up the slack. Neither of you are being fair!"

Reina knew there was no point in arguing with her mother when she was this upset and said instead, "I told you I was sorry. I'll call Daddy and talk to him but right now I have to talk to Laura. Is she here?"

"Yes, she came in about an hour ago."

She kissed her mother. "It'll work itself out, Mama. Don't get yourself so upset… it's not good for you."

There were tears in her mother's eyes that were quickly wiped away as she turned and walked into the hotel's office. Reina followed her saying, "What is it, Mama?"

Erica sat down, wiped her eyes once more, and blew her nose. "It's not working out between your father and me."

This admission was a shock, but Reina collected herself enough to ask, "What do you mean? The both of you seem happy together." Even as she said the words Reina knew that it wasn't true. She knew they'd just been going through the motions for a long time. And it saddened her.

The tears were flowing freely now as Erica said, "I'm scared." She stood and started to pace. "I'm scared of staying and too frightened to leave."

Reina crossed the space between them and took her mother in her arms. "There's nothing to be frightened about. Whatever you decide to do I'll be there to support your decision." The words sounded hollow and even as she held her mother a sadness for both her parents began to set in. She honestly believed that the decision to make a life with another person was a leap of faith. And she knew she was still willing to make that leap with Daniel despite the failure that her mother had just confessed.

Erica suddenly collected herself enough to say abruptly, "My shift starts at the hospital in an hour. I have to get ready."

And that was how they left it.

Laura was in her office going over the menu for the following week when Reina knocked lightly on the door. She looked up over her reading glasses and motioned for her to come in saying, "You certainly look down in the dumps for someone who's just had a day off with her lover."

Reina sat down across from her. "My parents are having relationship problems. I don't know what to say to either of them."

This wasn't something that was entirely a surprise to Laura; she'd noticed the emotional distance that seemed to exist between the two of them. But it was none of her business. "Is there anything I can do?"

"No, I think it's been coming for a while now. It's just sad."

"They've been together a long time."

There was a debate going on within her that Reina needed to air. "Do you think it can ever work out with Daniel?"

Laura took off her glasses and got up to close the door, so they wouldn't be interrupted. "Yes, I do," she admitted as she sat back down. "He does have issues, but I suspect if he ever finds someone"—she smiled while saying it— "he loves enough, well then he'll be in it for the long haul. The thing is, Daniel wants to believe it's possible to find that kind of love, but he's afraid to trust it. Trust is something that should be learned when we're young; it was for me. But unfortunately, that's not the case with everyone. If you want him to believe in you, you have to believe in him."

Reina replied defensively, "I do believe in him… but it's hard… you know. I feel like everything is a test to see what I'll do. When he hears about my parents I'm afraid it will be like saying see… this is what happens, people leave, they hurt you in the end. And I'm not sure how to fight that?"

"Don't fight it. That's his battle not yours. Just love him while he's going through it."

"My mother says that Daddy wants us to spend Christmas in Libourne with my grandparents."

There was a sigh as Laura ran her fingers through her hair. "That's one of our busiest times of the year, here, and at the bistro. I count on you, Reina."

"I know, Chef." Reina began to feel that she was being pulled from all sides. "I told my mother that I'd call him. She's adamant about not going."

It had been so long since Laura had spent Christmas with her parents she couldn't remember the last time. And she felt guilty asking Reina to do the same. She hesitated a second then said, "Give me some time to think about it. Maybe we can work something out."

Reina shook her head. "Even if I wanted to go I couldn't; Mother would assume I was picking sides."

Alex knocked on the door lightly and opened it a crack saying, "David's here. He said if you don't get a move on you'll be late for your appointment."

"Tell him I'm coming," she said while gathering her things together. As they both left her office she said to Reina, "Your mother is responsible for her own choices. It's unfair for you to have to choose between them."

"Thank you, Chef," Reina replied, then suddenly gave Laura a hug.

Laura was quiet for a long time as David drove them into the city. Finally, he asked, "What's the matter?"

She'd been thinking about Reina's parents, about how they'd lived together for more than a quarter century and appeared outwardly to have a good marriage. But beneath the surface it was a different matter.

When she didn't respond he said, "Laura… did you hear me?"

"I heard you," she replied as her emotions began to surge. "My whole life I've wanted a relationship like my parents and my grandparents. It's like I've built up this romantic illusion. But what if none of it's true? What if it just doesn't work that way anymore? I mean we assume that it should; two people meet, fall in love, have children, and live happily ever after. Maybe monogamy just doesn't work anymore and the whole soulmate thing is nonsense." Tears began to well up in her eyes that she quickly wiped away. "You and I are about to bring a child into a world where nothing seems to last. Marriage is becoming as antiquated as eight-tracks and cassettes."

David was a patient man and learned during the last few weeks to ride out the emotional waves that took hold of her. He asked quietly, "Is your parents' marriage nothing more than an illusion?"

"No," she replied, "but in today's world it seems passé."

"I'm old-fashioned and happen to see value in that. I want to spend a lifetime loving you. If that's passé then so be it."

That was exactly what she wanted to hear. Laura didn't want to doubt; she wanted reassurance. She smiled and in a whisper replied, "I love you too."

Reina's responsibilities at Mélange and at the Bistro on the Bay had increased gradually over the last year. Laura relied on her much more than she did in the beginning. Just as Alex was her assistant in the kitchen, Reina acted as an assistant to help her manage the dining areas at both restaurants and at the bar in St. Helena. The staff in both locations liked and respected her. And now she was responsible for managing the hotel while her father was away. She'd taken one day for herself and her mother was angry.

When she first went to work for Laura in San Francisco it was done for the sole purpose of living on her own in a larger city. Somehow that goal had been set aside and she'd ended up right back where she'd started. Reina had no one to blame but herself; she'd been the one who made the choice to recommend her parents' hotel to Laura. But during moments like today when she was feeling sorry for herself, it seemed to her that the harder she tried to get away from the town where she'd grown up the more she was sucked back in. Maybe, she thought, that was why Daniel avoided being tied down to any place or anyone. He was free of those constraints.

The day before, when she was helping him in the booth, and selling his art, it was fun. For one day no one was pulling at her; she felt free. And he'd told her he loved her. He probably thought she was asleep when he'd said it but still the words had passed his lips. If he asked, she wondered, would she leave her parents, the hotel, the restaurants,

Laura, and all her friends for him? Yes, Reina thought, maybe she'd do just that.

It was after nine that night before Reina felt she was caught up enough to quit for the day. Her mother had come back to the hotel exhausted after her shift and went directly to their apartment. Reina had stopped by the bar to have a glass of wine. The restaurant had been busy for a Monday and the dining room was still half full. She was passing the time of day with the bartender when suddenly she sensed someone approach and turned her head to see Daniel.

He grinned. "Miss me?" She didn't say a word but slid off the barstool and wrapped her arms around his neck, pulling him close. "I'll take that as a yes," he said as she continued to hold him tight.

She kissed him and whispered, "I thought you'd be leaving. San Jose was your last show here wasn't it?"

There were tears in her eyes that he brushed away gently with his fingertips. "I still need to pick up Laura's painting from the framer and hang it. David Steele wants me to paint one for him and I have an appointment with Casey Ashcroft at the end of the week." He kissed her again. "I guess I'll just have to stick around for a while."

"But where will you stay?"

"I told Laura I'd be back. I'm still staying at the cottage with her. She says she's not there very much anyway. And it gives me a place to paint."

"Where's Travis?"

"He's at the cottage."

"With Laura?"

"No, she's at David's. We have the place to ourselves."

"Did you walk over?"

He shook his head. "I brought my bike."

She grinned. "Well what are we waiting for? I'll get my jacket."

Laura was lying beside David, her body nestled into him, content. "It was amazing wasn't it," she said softly, "to see such a little thing and hear the heartbeat."

David chuckled. "It was all pretty abstract for me until today. I'm still getting used to the idea of being a father."

"I know," she replied with a giggle. "It's like a before and after. One minute life is just about you and the next there's this tiny life that you have to think about, to take care of and be responsible for."

He kissed her temple. "You'll be a great mom."

"I hope so." There was a moment of quiet between them before she asked, "Do you care whether it's a boy or girl?"

"I haven't thought about it... but it doesn't matter to me really. How about you?"

"I don't care. But if it's a girl I'd like to name her after my grandmother. If that's OK with you."

"I suppose so." And after a moment he said, "You don't talk about your family very much."

"After my grandparents died it wasn't the same. How about you? You haven't told me much about your folks."

"Well, with my grandparents raising me from such a young age, I didn't get to know my parents well. I was only five or six when they died, so I don't have many memories of them."

"Are your grandparents still living?"

David didn't respond right away. "No," he said finally.

"I'm sorry."

"It was a long time ago."

Laura started to get up, pushing the covers aside and went to the bathroom. A few moments later when she walked back into the room she said, "I want my parents to come... to the wedding. You promised it wouldn't be a large wedding."

He motioned for her to come to him. "And I meant it, but these things tend to get out of control. You have a large family. I don't."

What he'd said was true.

The next morning David was having coffee on the back patio while Laura was upstairs in the master bath getting ready for the day. He was reading the *Los Angeles Times*, a habit he'd acquired very early in his career as an actor. Tuan quietly interrupted him. "Excuse please, Mr. Steele... Mr. Whitman here to see you."

"Show him out here, Tuan."

"Yes, sir."

A few moments later as he heard footsteps approaching David set the paper aside and stood smiling. "Good morning, Daniel. I wasn't sure I was ever going to see you again after our little talk the other day."

Dan chuckled. "I was pretty pissed."

David grinned and motioned for him to take a seat. "Would you like some coffee?"

"That'd be great."

As he poured a cup for his guest and refilled his own, David asked, "What can I do for you this morning?"

"I thought maybe we could do something for each other. That is if you're still interested in a painting."

"I am. Does this mean you're going to stay with us for a while?"

"Yes," he said as he took a sip of coffee.

"I'm glad."

"It's not much of a commitment but it's what I can manage right now."

David tapped the paper. "I haven't lived in Los Angeles for ten years, but I still read the reviews. I think about going back sometimes, to act again… to see if I still can. But my roots run deep here now. I'd miss it too much."

"It is beautiful here."

"I suppose you've told Reina you're staying."

Dan nodded. "I did and I am trying."

"That's all any of us can do."

His expression turned serious. "I don't want her to get hurt."

"Life is a tough nut. It's not always fair and there're a hundred ways for her to be hurt. The only thing you can do is control what you can control and be there when she needs you to be." But as he said it David wasn't thinking of Reina at all; he was thinking of Laura.

CHAPTER 38

Daniel

Daniel knew she was torn between the demands of her mother, her father's request, and the sense of responsibility she felt for her work. Christmas was a week away. David had given him a sizeable advance and Laura paid him the balance for the painting he'd finished and hung for her. He left the travel agency and got into his truck where Travis was waiting patiently with his head hanging out the window. He turned on the ignition saying, "If we go you're going to have to be good." Travis turned to look at him and barked. Dan smiled and scratched him behind the ears. "OK… OK, so you're always good."

Daniel looked at his watch; it was a quarter past eleven. His appointment with Casey Ashcroft was at one that afternoon, which gave him just enough time for lunch at the bistro. Shelly Andrews saw him waiting for a table outside and said quietly to the hostess, "You see the guy outside with his dog. See that he gets seated at one of the tables out front as soon as you can."

The young painter had been coming to the Bistro at the Bay for three years and had never seen it so busy. He kept glancing at his watch afraid that there wouldn't be enough time to get something before his appointment when a pretty young girl smiled and said, "Your table's ready, sir." Thirty minutes later he was just about to pay the bill and leave when Shelly came outside to say, "I wanted to say hi before you took off. I haven't seen you for a while."

Passing the time of day wasn't one of Dan's strong suits but he liked Shelly and told her he'd just finished a show in San Jose and was working in St. Helena.

She asked, "When are you going back to LA?"

He was at a loss for words. For him to say openly that his intent was to remain in Northern California was the kind of verbal commitment he wasn't ready for, at least yet. The answer he gave was the truth or as much of the truth as he was willing to admit. "I'm not sure." Dan reached for the wallet in his back pocket and took out a twenty to hand to her.

Shelly wouldn't take it. "It's on the house. Tell Reina I missed seeing her the other day. We've been real busy lately." She gave Travis a quick pat.

The ties that were beginning to confine him were becoming more evident to others while his mind was still doing battle with whether to stay and be a part of Reina's life or leave again. But the love he felt for her tipped the scales. "I will," he replied, "and thanks for lunch."

There was still fifteen minutes to spare before his meeting with Casey. When he called to set up the appointment she told him to bring three paintings that best represented his work. He brought two landscapes and a portrait he'd done of Reina from memory the previous winter.

It was Marlene who greeted him as he walked in with the work. She smiled and held out her hand, which he shook. "It's good to see you again. Casey is talking to a client, but she should be off the phone before long. May I get you something while you wait? We have bottled water, or tea."

He shook his head. "No, I'm good. But would it be alright if I bring my dog inside, he's in the truck?"

She smiled. "I think it would be alright."

"Good, I don't like leaving him alone out there. I'll be right back."

It took the better part of three hours before his meeting was finished and he was able to fight through rush hour traffic on the way back to St. Helena. He could feel the anxiety within him ease as the miles passed by, the truck moving farther and farther away from the city. As he pulled into the driveway to park in front of the garage at the side of the cottage, a sense of relief came over him. And when he opened the door Travis bolted from the vehicle. Daniel grinned with a sigh as he watched him go. "It feels good to be home doesn't it, boy?" And it did. The two of them were just beginning to establish roots; the feelings were new, they were fragile, untried, but they were there and getting stronger every day.

When Reina walked into the cottage two hours later the first thing she smelled was supper cooking and wondered if Laura had decided to spend the night with them rather than with David. The table, she noticed, was set for two. And as she walked into the kitchen Daniel was working there.

He was chopping vegetables for a salad with his back to her, listening to music on an iPod. When she slipped her arms through his he jumped, surprised at the touch. And as he turned to look at her she chuckled. "I didn't mean to startle you."

Dan took one of the earbuds away from his ears, his heart beating fast. "I guess I'm not totally used to living with someone yet."

She put the earbud he'd removed up to her ear. "What are you listening to?" Before he could respond she smiled. "I'd never suspect you were a Martina McBride kinda guy."

"What can I say? I'm a born romantic, a real junkie for Nora Roberts by the way so don't dis my woman."

"I thought I was your woman," she replied, followed by a kiss that was long and lingered. "And how did your meeting go today?"

His face broke out into a broad grin. "She wants me to do a show in June! And she's gonna hang the three paintings I took down for her to see."

"That's great, darling," she replied kissing him again.

No one had ever said that to him before; he'd never been with anyone long enough for casual words of affection to ever be used by him or about him. It was new, but it felt good hearing it. "I made dinner, so we could celebrate."

"Smells delicious."

"I've got skills."

She gave him a playful pat on the rear. "You certainly do."

"Would you open the wine? It's in the fridge," he replied as he went back to work. And as she opened the bottle and poured each of them a glass Daniel said, "Casey asked me where I went to school to learn how to paint."

"What did you tell her?"

There was a pause before he replied, "I never went... I just sort of saw what I liked and started doin' my own thing. I don't know one art movement from another."

Reina put a glass of wine beside him. "You don't talk about your past, about how you got started or what it was like for you growing up."

"I try not to dwell on it."

"Well how did you get started?"

He finished preparing the salad, set it aside, and picked up his wine. "I was always drawing as a kid. My pop was either at work or in a bar and I spent plenty of time alone. Pop thought I was weak, spending my time doin' art and he wasn't a spare the rod kinda guy. He thought he could beat it out of me." Just saying the words brought the moments of fear and insecurity he'd felt as a child to the surface. It was an admission he'd never told another soul. "When Pop remarried it didn't get any better... if anything it was worse. Finally, when I was fifteen I took off thinking I could make a living as an artist in LA." He took a drink of wine and snickered. "I got as far as Vegas when the money ran out and I started living on the streets." There was a distant look in his eyes as he relived that time.

"You don't have to do this," she said, watching the pain within him rise to the surface.

He forced a smile. "It's OK. You should know what you're getting into." Dan turned off the oven. "I got picked up by the cops and sent to juvie. They had an art program and sent us to school. It wasn't that bad. But that's where I spent my sixteenth birthday. A month later I was placed in a foster home... that's when I took off and made it to LA. I got a job painting houses. There was this old man who took me under his wing and trained me. I still use some of the techniques he showed me when I'm working."

"When did you start painting pictures?"

"By using house paint on Masonite. The materials were leftovers I picked up from work. One weekend I went to an outdoor show in Culver City and knew I could do a better job than some of the things I saw there. A year later I'd saved up enough to enter a show and I've been doin' it ever since."

Her curiosity was piqued now as she asked. "Has there ever been anyone close to you besides me?"

He shook his head. "I've never trusted it. Never wanted to until now."

"Do you trust me?"

"I want to… but it's hard for me. I think it's there, then the past creeps in and it's hard gettin' past it."

She crossed the few feet between them, wrapping her arms through his, nestling into him. "Give it time. I'm scared; this is new for me too, loving you." Her breathing quickened as she kissed his neck, his lips, and slid her tongue into his mouth. "I don't ever want to let you go," she whispered. Her hands moved down his chest, letting her fingers caress the front of his jeans, kneading him until she could feel him respond, kissing him with more intensity. She felt her moisture begin to flow, the need inside building.

Dan cupped her face in his hands and chuckled. "Our supper will get cold."

"I don't care," she replied, her voice deep and husky.

They fit together perfectly, each intuitively aware of the other's needs and desires that quite naturally established a rhythm between them. There was nothing forced or with any sense of awkwardness; it had been that way from the beginning. Their movements seemed to rise and fall like waves washed upon a shore until after one final thrust he emptied himself within her as she came, their bodies slick with sweat.

Reina's heart was beating intensely in her chest as she felt him begin to withdraw. "Don't leave," she pleaded softly while gripping his buttocks, keeping him in place, "please."

He looked down at her, lying under him, feeling her hips begin to gradually rotate once more, saying to her softly, "I love you."

She leaned up enough to kiss his lips, her tongue intertwined with his. "I love you too," she whispered as her hips continued to rock gently until he began to answer her movements with his own.

They ate in bed by candlelight while Travis slept on the floor beside them. Reina covered herself with the denim work shirt he'd been wearing that day, sitting cross-legged on the mattress next to him. She took a bite of the meal he'd prepared saying, "Have you thought about what you're going to paint for the show?"

"No," he replied, "not really." He reached back to the nightstand to grab an envelope and set it down upon the sheets between them.

"What's this?"

"Open it and see."

She wiped her hands and picked it up noticing the logo of a travel agency on the front of the envelope. There were two plane tickets to Paris inside. Reina looked at him expectantly. "Does this mean you'd go with me?"

He grinned. "I already cleared it with Laura. And she said she'd look after Travis while we're gone."

"But you can't afford this," she replied as she set her plate aside to hold him in her arms. "I can't let you do it. It's too much."

"It's done," he said as he kissed her once more quickly before rising from the bed to take their dishes into the kitchen. "I've always wanted to go to France, and this is a perfect opportunity." His hands were full and as he was about to leave he turned to say, "Unless you don't want me to go?"

"That's not it and you know it," she said as she started to follow him. "I want you to meet my family."

"That settles it then," he countered while setting the dishes next to the sink. "Do you want to wash or dry?"

"I'll wash," she said as she grinned at him. "That's the least I can do."

David was sitting next to the Christmas tree by the fireplace having a glass of brandy when Laura walked in the front door. Tuan helped take her coat off. "Good evening, Miss Patterson," he said while waiting for her to hand him her scarf and gloves.

"Good evening, Tuan. Where's David?"

"Mr. Steele is in the living room, miss."

"Tuan, I would like you to try and call me Laura."

He gave her a slight bow. "Yes, miss, I will. May I get you anything?"

"A cup of green tea would be nice."

"Yes, miss."

She crossed the expansive foyer toward the living room where he was sitting quietly looking thoughtfully into the fire. Laura kissed him gently on the lips and sat down on the arm of the large overstuffed chair he was sitting in. He took her hand and kissed it. "How was work today?"

"Busy," she replied with a sigh. "Better busy than the other way around." There was a book sitting on the table beside him that looked to be about half finished. "What are you reading?"

He picked up the book and handed it to her. "It's by your great-grandfather. Have you read it?"

She read the title aloud, "*Mary*," and shook her head. "No, I haven't read any of his books."

"You should. He's interesting."

Tuan came in quietly and handed Laura her tea. "Is there anything else?"

"No, we're fine, Tuan," David replied. When he was gone he said to her, "I talked to my lawyer today about setting up a trust for the baby."

"Why would you do that without talking to me first?"

"I'm talking to you about it now. We're not married yet and if something were to happen to me I want to be sure our child is taken care of."

She slid into his lap. "Nothing's going to happen to you."

His hand rested on her belly. "Probably not. But life is unpredictable."

The two of them were silent, watching the fire burn slowly down. "Is this about what happened to you when you were a child? Or is there something you're not telling me?"

He chuckled. "I'm fit as a fiddle as my grandfather used to say. It's just a precaution for you and the baby." David kissed her forehead as he held her in his arms. "Your great-grandfather must have loved his wife very much."

She nestled into him. "He did. It nearly destroyed him."

CHAPTER 39

Libourne

"It is your move, Michael," Adrien said with a grin. The two men had been playing chess for over an hour at Café Pascal. Marie was watching intently.

He was trapped and knew it was only a matter of two maybe three moves before he would be in checkmate. Michael tipped over his king. "The game is yours."

"Bon, bon, que je gagne a nouveau." The old vintner laughed so much that he began to cough. "Do you want to try again?"

"It is time for your medicine, Grand-pere," Marie reminded him.

"Being with the two of you is medicine enough for me, mon chérie," he replied jovially as he kissed her cheek. "Marcel," he called to the waiter, "Cognac, s'il vous plait for my son and me. And one more hot chocolate for Marie."

"Tout de suite, Adrien," the elderly waiter replied. Marcel Bouvier wanted to ask Elleanore for coffee and knew that to do so he had to move carefully without irritating his friend. The two men went to school with one another and had even talked of going to America together. But Adrien went alone while Marcel stayed. Marcel had been married young, had three children still living, and eleven grandchildren before his wife passed on. That was ten years ago, and he'd been alone ever since. Ellie was the first woman in all that time who had caught his eye.

They were sitting inside; the day was cold with a light snow falling outside as they set up the game once more. Adrien had been cooped up for several days with his cold and this was the first time Sofia had allowed him to leave the house; he'd protested but his displeasure fell on deaf ears. This was also the first day of Marie's holiday break from school and two days before Christmas. Adriana had driven into Paris for a business meeting before picking up Reina and Daniel at the airport. And Michael was aware that his wife had decided not to come. He hadn't been sure he wanted her to.

A small middle-aged man with a bushy mustache was playing acoustic guitar, accompanied on accordion by a rotund gentleman and a thin woman who sang moody alto vocals while playing the piano. Michael made his first move as Marcel brought their drinks saying cautiously as he put them on the table, "How is your lovely wife, my friend?"

Adrien reached for his pawn moving it two squares ahead toward the center of the board before looking up at the waiter. "Sofia est tres bien, mon ami."

"And your daughter. How is she?"

Adrien knew exactly what his friend was getting at but played along just the same. "She's gone to Paris."

"For work or pleasure, my friend?"

Michael countered by moving his pawn to face Adrien's. Adrien took a sip of cognac. "She's gone to pick up my granddaughter and her boyfriend from the airport." He moved another pawn one space ahead to rest diagonally behind the first to protect it.

"So, Reina is coming back," Marcel replied as he looked over Adrien's shoulder. "She's a wonderful girl, you should be very proud."

"I am," he said while observing Michael's next play.

The waiter hesitated a moment before saying casually, "Did Elleanore go with her?"

"Non, mon ami, she did not. Ellie is at home with Sofia."

It was Marie who suggested innocently, "You should ask her to dinner or a movie, Monsieur Bouvier. I think Mamie would like to go out don't you, Grand-pere?"

Adrien glared at her. "I think your grandmother is beyond such nonsense and you should mind your own business."

It seemed obvious to Michael that Marie's feelings were hurt and replied, "I think it was a nice thought, Marie. But your grandmother has a mind of her own. If she wanted to go anywhere at all I'm sure she would."

Hurting his granddaughter was the last thing that Adrien would ever intend. Yet he was irritated with the conversation and Marcel for bringing it up. He came to the café once or twice a week to play chess and spend time with Marie; he had very little patience for Marcel's desires. Adrien leaned over and kissed Marie's cheek. "Je suis desole ma douce." He then carefully wiped a bit of hot chocolate from her upper lip with his thumb. "Je t'aime, Marie."

She smiled once more. "I love you too, Grand-pere."

Michael's impressions of Adrien before arriving were that of a child. But during the time he'd spent with him, here in Libourne, he realized the depth of his sensitivity. It provided a knowledge of the profound difference between his birth father and Roger Strickland.

Adrien abruptly turned to the waiter and asked, "Are you going to spend the holiday with your family, Marcel?"

"Non, mon ami. Unfortunately, I cannot."

"You will come to our house then, Marcel, for supper on Christmas Eve," Adrien insisted. "Sofia and Elleanore will be pleased."

"Merci, Adrien. You're sure it's not too much trouble?"

"Not at all, my friend."

Sofia and Elleanore had spent the day getting the house ready for their guests and putting the finishing touches on the fir tree they'd decorated. "At midnight on Christmas Eve," Sofia told her, "we have a special meal to celebrate the beginning of Christmas Day. We call it Le Reveillon de Noel."

Elleanore was happy that her granddaughter was coming for the holiday but disappointed for her son. Her daughter-in-law had become increasingly distant over the years, taking less and less interest in the family. And once Reina graduated from college that distance had increased significantly. Ellie had tried several times to talk to Michael about it but the loyalty he felt toward his wife prevented him from opening himself up to her. She felt responsible for not acting as a better example. And she often wondered how much different it might have been if she'd simply left Roger when Michael was small. The decision she'd made, as Ellie looked back on it, was cowardly.

When Ellie hadn't said anything Sofia finally asked, "Why are you so quiet today?"

"I'm worried about Michael."

"Because of his wife?"

"Yes."

"This might be the best thing for both of them. It will give them a chance to decide how they want to spend the rest of their lives. Living half a life is not truly living; you know that better than anyone."

Ellie wanted that to be true, but it didn't erase the guilt she felt. "I should have done a better job with my children."

Sofia smiled. "They are nice people. That was no accident."

"But neither of them has found someone to truly love. Michael's marriage to Erica seems to be nothing more than an agreement made when they were young. They have been living this way for so long that they've stayed together out of habit." Once Elleanore had begun to speak about the worries that had been festering inside it was as if a dam had burst within her. She suddenly sat down by the fire and began to cry, saying, "Adriana is so unhappy."

Sofia came over to sit beside her, holding her hand. "Your children have made their own choices. Just as we have." She took Ellie's face in her hands saying, "Look at me. You are not responsible for what they choose to do."

Ellie kissed each of her hands and held them. "It doesn't feel that way. When I came here I wanted to find peace again with you and Adrien. But it seems that all I've done is bring the troubles I've created and dumped them on your doorstep."

"It's good sometimes to shake things up." Sofia smiled as she patted Ellie's hand and stood. "Adriana had her problems long before you arrived," she said while walking over to the buffet beside the dining room table; she poured each of them a glass of cognac. She brought the drinks back and handed one to Elleanore. "Because you had the courage to come to us Adrien was able to meet Reina for the first time. And even now he is building a relationship with his son." She took a sip of the liquor. "All of us are going to spend Christmas together, which is a miracle. Try to see your blessings, Elleanore, and let the past stay where it belongs, in the past."

Ellie took a drink, wiped the tears away, and replied with a forced grin, "You were the best thing that happened to me when I lived at Strickland House. I don't think I could have made it without your friendship."

Sofia chuckled. "Abigail was a real bitch. But Roger gave you two wonderful children. How about them?"

"Neither of them like me very much I'm afraid."

Adriana had gone to Paris to attend a business meeting with the new creative director of the Baudelaire Group, Henri Chausson. His firm was her most important client and in the past she'd had a close working relationship with Chausson's predecessor, Elaine Duval. During the ten years they'd worked together the two women had become close friends. And at times when Adriana came to Paris she would stay with her. She'd never met Chausson.

His secretary, a nice-looking twenty-something young woman, emerged from his office in a conservative dark business suit, and glanced at her sitting just outside the door saying rapidly, "Monsieur Chausson vous verrez dans un instant." Adriana took one look at her and self-consciously began to survey the way she was dressed for the meeting; she should have rethought the jeans. But it had been a long trip by car, and she wanted to be comfortable. Her top had navy and white stripes with a straight neckline and three-quarter-length sleeves. The wool blazer she'd worn for a coat was folded neatly on the seat beside her. She put it on and undid the barrette that held her hair back, letting it fall to her shoulders. The secretary watched from the corner of her eye and smiled.

Precisely fifteen minutes later the secretary rose from her chair and stood by the door saying, "Madame Forche, Monsieur Chausson vous verrez maintenant."

Adriana stood and smiled. "Merci."

Henri didn't look up from his desk at first as she walked in; his eyes were focused on the latest numbers from an ad campaign they'd been running for several weeks for a perfume manufacturer. He wasn't happy with the results and it irritated him that his day should be interrupted by a freelance artist. It wasn't something he normally would have done but his predecessor insisted it would be worth his time.

He would make the best of it, he thought, as he rose from his desk and saw her for the first time. Henri was suddenly mesmerized by the dark brown eyes that looked back at him and stumbled boyishly over a greeting. "Bonne apres-midi, Madame Forche." He walked around his desk and shook her hand. "It's a pleasure to meet you at last. Please"—he gestured with his hand toward two upholstered chairs on the far side of the room— "have a seat." She did as he suggested, and Henri sat beside her.

She'd been taken aback at first glance; he appeared to be much too young for the position he held. But as the minutes passed by it became clear to her that Chausson was one of those individuals whose boyhood image remained much longer than most. For him, she thought, this persistent appearance of youth must have been an obstacle in the business world.

Rather than send her latest work by computer Adriana had brought the original sketches with her in a black leather portfolio. Her initial conversation with him was light, and she'd completely forgotten she'd brought them when he asked, "Is that some of your work?"

Adriana nodded saying, "Oui, I thought you might like to see the originals."

"I would very much," he replied. And as he looked through them Henri began to understand why Elaine Duval insisted they meet. Adriana was too good for advertising; the work belonged in galleries not magazines. Henri looked at his watch. "Have you had lunch, madame?"

"Non, I arrived from Libourne this morning and came right here."

"Bon," he replied with a smile as he stood, "we'll discuss your future with us at a nice little café I know. It's close by." And with that said he began escorting her toward the door.

She really didn't know how to reply as he swept her away, out of his office into an elevator and down to the street below. The attraction was mutual yet Adriana was cautious; the internal walls she'd created to protect her heart still held fast.

The café he chose was equally as charming as the man who sat opposite her. Conversation between them was never strained but flowed easily from one subject to another. The lunch stretched from one hour to two. She told him about Marie, her father, mother, Sofia, and the Stricklands; she confessed to him the dreams and hopes she'd had that were lost over time. He listened intently, fascinated by her courage.

For Henri his heart was unexpectedly captured by this young woman who had carved out a career for herself despite the obstacles that confronted her. His life, in contrast, appeared to be made up of one success after another; he'd risen quickly in his profession, was financially successful at an early age, and seemed to have no set limits ahead of him. His personal life was a different matter entirely. He'd spent so much time building his career that any attempt at a private life was sacrificed. The single lengthy relationship he'd had was with a fashion model that ended ugly; she was as fixed on her career as he was with his and neither of them were willing to compromise.

The truth as he believed it to be was that he'd simply never found anyone who moved him to such an extent that he was willing to give as much as he received. Suddenly and quite unexpectedly this had changed. But for him such a thing was so new he hadn't had the time to reflect on the possibility that love had indeed come crashing into his life.

The magic of the moment was interrupted abruptly as she looked at her watch in panic saying, "I'm late," and started to stand.

"Wait," he replied, "when will I see you again?"

Spontaneously she bent down to kiss both his cheeks. "Pardonnez-moi, que je dois y aller," she said, handing him a card, "call me, please."

Before either of them could think clearly, he stood and took her in his arms, kissing her lips and saying softly while holding her, "Where are you staying? I'll call you later at your hotel."

With regret she began pulling herself away from him. "The Pas de Calais on the Rue De Saint Peres." When their fingers finally separated from his she said apologetically, "I've got to go to the airport." And suddenly she was gone.

Henri stood there watching her leave, knowing that life for him had altered significantly. But he was still a bit overwhelmed by the experience. His mind was so flooded with thoughts and feelings that the world could have stopped altogether, and he wouldn't have given it a second thought.

CHAPTER 40

Paris

When Laura told Daniel that Reina could have the time off it was with the understanding that she would be back in St. Helena before New Year's Eve, one of the busiest times of the year. The two of them were exhausted as the plane began to descend at sunset over the coast of France. It was dark by the time they were through customs and began making their way toward baggage claim.

Adriana was waiting for them, embracing Reina saying, "Bonsoir… I didn't expect to see you so soon." She glanced at the young man with her; he was a bit unkempt, but handsome she thought, with the eyes of a gypsy. "You must be Daniel," she said while kissing each of his cheeks. "Welcome to France." And while locking arms with Reina she laughed gaily. "Let's go get your bags."

Reina had forgotten how fast her aunt drove as they made their way from the airport toward the hotel. And then all at once the Eiffel Tower came into view, a beacon rising above the streets of Paris, that marked for more than a hundred years the age of Monet, Cezanne, and Degas. The lights from multistory buildings, streetlamps, storefronts, and more automobiles than you could count were shining upon a city forever linked to humanity's vision of romance. Daniel was captivated by reflections that lit up the surface of the Seine as a dining barge passed by. He whispered to himself as much as to them, "This is surreal."

Adriana during all the years she'd lived in France had never really gotten over her initial response to the vision they were seeing now. She could easily say that this was where she was meant to be and believed that one day soon she'd return, to live in Paris permanently. And the dreams that were once at her fingertips would finally be realized.

It was after eight by the time they were checked into the hotel. Adriana had made reservations for two rooms and intended to acquire them earlier in the day but her time with Henri altered that plan.

Once they were settled into their rooms she took them to a relatively quiet restaurant on the Boulevard Saint-Germain within walking distance of the hotel. But this time of year it was crowded with a mixture of locals and tourists. The wait was over an hour, which they spent in the bar knocking off a bottle of Chateau Fournier Cabernet. And they ordered another as they were seated for supper.

Whenever Adriana drank more than she should, she smoked. As the evening wore on she became more animated. Daniel thought her charming, but Reina couldn't help but wonder who this woman was who somehow had replaced her aunt?

Once the waiter arrived the two women ordered poulet de Provencal, a chicken breast cooked with balsamic vinegar and browned mushrooms then topped with provolone cheese, and Adriana convinced Daniel to try the filet mignon with pepper cream sauce, a specialty of the house. For dessert they shared bûche de Noël, a chocolate cake rolled with chocolate whipped cream and decorated to mark the holiday with confectioner's sugar.

The three of them had coffee and brandy afterward while the crowd within the restaurant gradually dispersed bringing with it a welcome calm. Daniel excused himself to go to the restroom and Reina finally had the opportunity to speak to her alone. "What is going on with you tonight? You seem different."

Adriana took a drag off her cigarette, the third of the night, and took a sip of brandy before asking, "What do you mean? How different?"

Reina shrugged. "I don't know… just different."

She knew exactly why her mood was light but wasn't prepared to share it with her niece. Adriana smiled. "I had a very successful meeting today. And, my darling niece, it is wonderful because you are back with us again." As Daniel sat back down she took his hand first, then Reina's. "I am so happy you've brought your young man with you."

"I didn't bring him; he brought me," Reina replied with a grin, kissing Daniel's softly. "And he is charming in a bohemian kind of way."

Daniel took one of Adriana's cigarettes from the pack lying next to her on the table, snickering as he lit it. "You two are getting absolutely wasted."

Reina gave him a gentle nudge. "I didn't know you smoked."

"I don't very often."

She took the cigarette from his fingers, inhaled a drag off it and coughed as she giggled. "Me either."

Adriana finished her brandy. "Il est temps d'aller a mes amis." She motioned for the waiter to bring them their check.

Dan asked, "What did she say?"

"She says it's time to leave."

"Does she always switch to French when she's drunk?"

Reina chuckled. "I don't know. I've never seen her this way before."

He reached for his wallet, but Adriana stopped him. "Non, chérie, this is my treat tonight."

They took their time strolling back to the hotel despite the chill. Adriana looked up at the stars. "I met someone interesting today."

Reina stopped suddenly; her breath was visible in the cold night air as she gazed at her. "Really? Tell us."

Adriana smiled, her mind picturing him. "His name's Henri. We had lunch today."

"You like him," Reina replied ecstatically.

"Oui, mon cher." Adriana took her niece by the arm. "Aller… allez move your derriere before we freeze."

Dan listened to the two women, less excited surely but amused at Reina's enthusiasm. Finally he said, "It seems to me it's a little early to start thinkin' about wedding bells. You've only known this guy what… a couple of hours? He could be an axe murderer for all you know."

"You are such a doubting Thomas." Reina bumped his hip with hers. "I knew you were the one from the beginning, that first night. It just took you a little longer to catch up."

"So you're saying it was love at first sight," he replied with a grin.

"Yes, I am. I knew right away."

He snickered. "You knew you had the hots for me is more like it."

"Well, there was that too... I admit it. But it was more than that and you can't tell me you didn't feel it too because I know you did."

She was right. He did feel it from the beginning, a connection, unspoken, before a word was passed between them. But for him there was a distinct difference between animal magnetism and love. Love, for him, was based on action; it was the way you treated another human being, the way you cared for them, and the concern felt for their well-being. It was beyond a romantic connection, much more, and had to be based on something other than the physical. Love, for him, was spiritual, no different than his art. And for that reason alone he'd guarded himself from opening up to the possibility of loving again. His experiences as a child convinced him just how difficult and troubled those waters could be.

When he didn't respond Adriana said quietly, "Daniel's right. The connection is one thing but loving someone is entirely different. And I have to be particularly careful because of Marie."

As they walked into the hotel Reina asked, "Is Marie excited about Christmas?"

"She's excited because you're here." Adriana smiled. "I'm still not sure how she feels about your father. I think he puzzles her."

"Why?"

Adriana pushed the button for the elevator. "Michael keeps his feelings to himself. All she's known from the rest of us is exactly the opposite. We're all up front; she knows how much she's loved because we tell her." She glanced at Daniel and winked. "And we show her."

"But the two of you seem to fight a lot," Reina replied.

As they stepped out of the elevator Adriana chuckled. "Marie's almost twelve. I'm still embarrassed about how I acted when I was her age." And as they arrived at her door she kissed each of them on both cheeks. "Bonne nuit à vous deux… I'll see you in the morning."

Dan hugged her. "Thanks again for dinner. It was great."

"Tu es le bienvenu, mon cher." She watched them a moment as they took those few steps hand in hand toward their room. As she opened the door she noticed a message light on her phone. Her heart began beating faster as she heard Henri's voice ask her to meet him for coffee in the morning.

The instant the door to their room clicked shut Daniel took her in his arms, kissing her mouth, her neck, his hands reaching out to caress her body. He wanted her badly but no more than she did him. Reina quickly kicked off her shoes while unbuttoning her jeans, kissing him again as they made their way hurriedly to bed. She plopped on the mattress giggling as he grabbed the cuffs of her pants and stripped them off both legs. In one swift move Daniel slowly kissed his way up her body from foot, to calf, knee, and thigh before taking her in his mouth to savor the taste. Reina's hips slowly began to rotate as his fingers found the sensitive flesh just inside, kneading it as his tongue gently flicked at the erect emergent bud sending waves of pleasure throughout her body. She reached climax quickly, then pulled him up her body to kiss his mouth, undoing his pants, and pushing them down enough for him to enter, filling the cavity that waited there.

They lay there in each other's arms afterward, his head resting on her breast. Daniel had never been so content as he listened to her heart beat. His fingers entwined in hers as he said softly, "I love you."

Adriana found it difficult to sleep thinking of Henri; she should have been exhausted the next morning except for the joyous thought of seeing him again. He'd asked her to meet him at nine at a small coffee shop on the Rue de Pontoise not far from her hotel, close to the river. She shoved a note for Reina under their door, asking them to have breakfast without her, and saying that she would return by eleven to check out of the hotel.

Despite the cold, the sun felt good on her face as she began walking to meet him, her excitement building with each step. Henri rose from his seat as she came through the door. She'd worn a white blouse under a navy blazer that hung casually outside her jeans with a multicolored pastel silk scarf about her neck; the image appeared sophisticated yet spontaneous. Adriana may have been born American, but she'd become a French woman and played the part to perfection. He kissed each of her cheeks, lingering a little longer than custom compelled, taking in her scent. "Bonjour, Adriana. I was hoping you'd come."

She smiled back, blushing slightly. "I was glad you called. But I can't stay very long. We're checking out of the hotel and driving to Libourne today."

"We must make the most of our time then n'est-ce pas?"

"Oui, Henri."

"Please sit," he replied. "What would you like?"

"Un café au lait et un croissant s'il vous plait."

Henri left her a moment to order from the bar, and she started to get nervous; the longer he was gone the more her anxiousness increased. She began to fiddle with items inside her purse, and finally pulled out a compact to check her makeup in the mirror. He returned, sitting next to her, and Adriana felt herself jump slightly. She smiled. "I feel like a schoolgirl on a first date."

"Je comprends tout à fait," he replied. "I changed my clothes three times this morning."

Adriana laughed. "Fortunately I had very little to choose from."

"You're beautiful." She lowered her eyes, blushing again, as he said, "I've been wanting to tell you that since we met. Je n'ai pas eu le courage."

"Merci, Henri." The waiter brought her order and she thanked him. Adriana took a sip of coffee. "I took my niece and her boyfriend out to dinner last night; it was late by the time we got back to the hotel, and I saw your message." She grinned. "I tossed and turned all night thinking about you. But I realized I really don't know that much about you. And you managed to find out all the gory details of my life yesterday."

He smiled warmly. "There's not much to tell. My father is a baker, so... we were never hungry. I grew up in Reims, my parents are still there. I studied creative writing at university and started in advertising as a copywriter." He shrugged. "I went from there into management."

"How about girls?"

"I was chubby in school," he replied with a grin. "Too many croissants. The girls were more interested in footballers. At university I spent my time studying." Henri paused briefly. "There was a girl… but it didn't work out. After that my career was the most important thing for me." He looked down, took a sip of espresso, and grinned. "Fini."

"Your life may be many things, Henri, but it is far from finished."

He took her hand in his. "And neither is yours n'est pas?"

She squeezed his hand gently, rubbing her thumb over his and chuckled. "I hope not. I want it to be much more."

"A woman with your talent belongs in Paris."

"I will be one day… but right now I have to think of my daughter."

"There are fine schools right here."

Adriana nodded. "Oui, there are… I've thought of that. But Marie wouldn't do well if she was away from her grandparents."

He grinned. "I've never seen Bordeaux… maybe you will show me?"

Sooner or later she knew the subject would come up and Adriana knew she had to tell him before it was too late. She gave his hand another slight squeeze, pulled it back, and took a sip of her coffee. "I've been seeing someone there for quite some time." The truth of it embarrassed her. "He's married… his wife lives here in Paris."

"Are you still seeing him?"

She nodded slowly. "Occasionally. It's become a habit between us now more than anything, the magic is gone." But even as she said it she wasn't sure how true it was for her.

Henri admired how straightforward she was, the honesty it took to tell him something so personal. He took her hand once more and kissed her palm. "I want to see you again; that is what matters."

CHAPTER 41

St. Helena

Mélange was slammed during the Christmas holidays, and Laura was shorthanded. Reina was in France; Alex had unfortunately come down with a cold and was sick in bed. The hotel was full of people and in a state of chaos with Michael gone. She took Isabella off day shift and had her replace Alex as her sous-chef during the evening. That was the one pleasant surprise during the entire week; Izzy was a fast learner with incredible skill. Laura began to realize that the day shift at the hotel restaurant had been running so smoothly primarily because of her leadership. She'd taken that effort for granted. It was a mistake that Laura had no intention of making in the future.

After twenty-two weeks she was beginning to feel fat; Laura had finally broken down and gone shopping for pants with an elastic waist and a prenatal bra. The upside was that she could feel the baby flutter periodically.

On Christmas Eve after the dinner rush she made an excuse and left Izzy in the kitchen to finish for the evening. Her back hurt: Laura stood up from behind her desk and stretched just as Izzy knocked on the door. She motioned her inside.

Isabella was concerned; she knew the workload was getting to be too much for Laura. "Are you OK?"

"Fine," she replied with a sigh, "just a little tired."

"Why don't you go on home? David's waiting for you in the bar and we're almost finished in the kitchen."

"How many people are left in the dining room?"

"Two tables."

Laura felt the baby and without thinking rubbed her belly. "I still have to lock up."

"I can do that."

"You sure?"

Izzy replied emphatically, "Sí, I've watched Alex do it many times."

"How is he?"

"Such a big baby. You'd think he was the only one who has ever had a cold."

She grinned while putting on her coat. "He's a good man… a good friend."

"Sí, Chef."

"You two have a Merry Christmas," she said as she gave Izzy a hug. "I'll see you tomorrow."

"It's Christmas, Chef, you don't have to come in."

Laura smiled. "I don't expect anything from you I'm not prepared to do myself." When she opened Mélange it was with the knowledge that although it would be closed during certain holidays the hotel restaurant would stay open but close early. It was a decision necessary for hotel operations but in addition to that Laura felt it was important for people who had no other place to go.

David was having a drink as she walked up to kiss him on the cheek saying, "You're a welcome sight."

He stood and smiled. "You ready?"

She nodded. "More than ready." Laura took his arm. "How was your day?"

"Missing you," he replied as they walked from the restaurant, through the hotel and into the cold night air.

"When I lived in Prescott," she said as he opened the car door for her, "and then again in Paris when I was training I used to love it if there was snow at Christmas." She chuckled. "I miss it… but I suppose that's what I get for living most of my life in California."

"It snows here sometimes," he replied. "Rarely, but it does."

"When?"

"I don't know, maybe seven or eight years ago was the last time." David grinned. "Of course it was gone by the time I got dressed that morning."

"Well, I'm not going to hold my breath this year."

"Smart move. Besides if you want snow I can always take you to Aspen."

"Thanks, but the last thing I'd want to do on Christmas is spend it in a hotel."

He pulled the car to a stop in front of his house and said casually, "I've got a condo there."

"You have a condo in Aspen, Colorado?" Before he had the chance to respond she shook her head and snickered. "Of course you do."

As they walked up the stairs and he opened the front door for her he replied, "I bought it as an investment about twenty years ago. After I moved here I haven't been there as much."

"You're a real piece of work, Steele."

Tuan took off her coat. "Merry Christmas, miss."

"Merry Christmas, Tuan."

"You want some tea maybe, miss?"

"That would be nice, thank you."

Tuan had a large family when he left Vietnam at fourteen during the fall of Saigon. He was, as far as he knew, the only member of his family who escaped when the North Vietnamese Army entered the city. At forty-five he had no family of his own and had worked for David Steele most of his life. When he learned that his boss was going to have a child with Laura Patterson he spent countless hours reading about pregnancy, particularly about the mother's health. He altered his menu to compensate for her needs, meats were cooked carefully, never undercooked and he avoided any fish that might have high traces of mercury. Prenatal vitamins were always placed by her breakfast plate in the morning. When she'd had severe morning sickness he'd taken slices of ginger root and mixed it with boiling water to settle her stomach. He made special teas with high contents of calcium, magnesium, and antioxidants but consistently avoided giving her anything with caffeine. The care and attention he gave were so extreme that David made jokes about it. But to Laura, Tuan was a godsend she'd learned to rely on.

David and Laura were sitting by the fireplace, quiet for several minutes, with only the flame and the bulbs of the Christmas tree to cast light about them. Finally, she said softly, "I miss my parents." A tear slowly made its way down her cheek. "I want to see my mother."

He was drinking Bowmore single malt Scotch whiskey over ice and replied casually, "I'll take you any time you want. Just say the word."

Laura was thinking about the Christmas when Matt Stryker proposed to her. And how he'd surprised her by bringing her parents to San Francisco for the holiday. Matt was like that; he gave to others easily but always maintained control. David was the opposite; he didn't ever take her choices away. He never tried to control her. But right now, she felt as if she was drowning and needed someone to take over for just a little while. She was tired.

He asked, "What is it?"

She forced a smile. "Nothing, I'm just tired."

"You've had a long day. Maybe we should go up to bed."

"In a minute," she replied while watching the flames in the fire lick the air. "Have you ever wondered why you and I have remained single?"

"Not really."

"I have."

"And."

Laura kept looking at the fire for a few more seconds as if hypnotized. "I think it's because we're basically selfish people and marriage means giving up some of yourself. Being a parent is basically the same thing." She turned and looked at him. "I can already feel myself giving up part of who I am."

"Isn't that a good thing?"

"For most people yes, I think it is. But for as long as I can remember I've been working toward being really good at what I do. I used to dream of getting a Michelin star; Armand Moreau at Entretenir has two and has spent a lifetime trying to receive a third. I helped him get that second star."

David stood and went to the bar to refresh his drink. "You're still young. There's plenty of time for you to achieve what you wish, to receive your star if that's what you want."

"And what about you?"

He came back and sat down. "I've had my fifteen minutes of fame."

"I don't understand you."

"What don't you understand?"

Laura's response was accusatory and her tone sharper than she intended. "You sit up here in this house day after day and I'm still never sure exactly what it is you do with your time. You don't even have a television for crying out loud."

"I don't like television," he replied and forced a smile. "There's too big a chance one of my old films will come on."

"I'm serious."

"I know you are." He finished his drink and set the glass aside on the lamp table next to him. "How old do you think I am?"

She shrugged. "I have no idea. It's never mattered to me."

"I turned fifty-two six months ago." He'd surprised her; David could tell by the expression on her face. "I haven't been offered a leading role in almost ten years. My agent keeps trying to get me to play character parts, but the truth is I was never a very good actor. I had a pretty face and a good-looking body; that was the appeal. It's not that I didn't want more, I did. The day I realized that I would always be good but never great, was the day I quit." Before she could reply he said, "I'll be seventy years old by the time our child graduates from high school. At this point in my life I don't really want very much except to be the best parent and husband I can be. That's enough as far as I'm concerned."

Laura remained silent; she'd assumed there were ten, maybe a dozen years between them. But it was closer to twenty. She replied quietly, "I had no idea."

He smiled. "When you were attracted to me at first, I was flattered. And then it became more than that. I didn't expect it to, but it did."

She got up and went to him, settling herself into his lap. "I love you."

"You were right," he added quietly, "when you said I was selfish. I should never have let it go this far between us. You're still a young woman and should be with a much younger man."

"I want you," she whispered nestling into him. "I'm just being bitchy."

"I'll always take care of you," he replied while rubbing her belly softly, "and our child. You can work on getting your star."

The fire was beginning to die down, the light from it fading. She kissed his lips softly. "I'm lucky to have you in my life." The clock struck midnight and she kissed him again. "Merry Christmas, darling."

When David Steele woke the next morning, she was gone, and he had a hangover to beat all hangovers. It had been years since he'd had that much to drink. He put on his robe and went into the bathroom to brush his teeth before going downstairs. He found her thirty minutes later in the kitchen with Tuan. She was taking something out of the oven when he asked, "What are you doing?"

She looked at him and smiled. "Baking Christmas cookies." Laura set the flat pan down on the granite countertop and crossed the few paces between them to give him a kiss. "Merry Christmas."

He smiled sheepishly. "I feel terrible."

"Drink plenty of water and a little exercise wouldn't hurt… sweat it out."

"A Bloody Mary would be more like it," he replied as he took a bottle of vodka from the freezer. As he turned around Tuan was glaring at him.

While taking a flat rectangular cookie sheet out of the oven she said, "The last thing you need for too much booze is more of it. Besides we're having company later." She gave him an inquisitive stare. "You remembered didn't you?"

"As a matter of fact… I did not."

"Well we are but not till tonight. And I'm going over to the hotel later this morning to make sure everything is going as it should."

"Don't you ever stop for a minute?"

She gave him another quick kiss. "Rarely."

"When are we going to do presents?"

"Soon, darling… very soon."

It was eleven that morning by the time Laura finished in the kitchen and walked the two miles to the hotel. The day was beautiful, a chill in the air, but warm in the sun and she needed the exercise. David was working on his second Bloody Mary.

CHAPTER 42

Le Reveillon de Noel

A gathering of several friends was invited to the Forche home to help celebrate the early moments of the Christmas holiday. Ellie and Sofia spent countless hours decorating the house and preparing the meal for their guests. The dining table was covered with embroidered linen that Sofia's grandmother had sent her as a wedding gift from Mexico. A centerpiece was made from fir cuttings accented with holly and the polished brass candlesticks that were passed on to Adrien from his mother. A Yule log of cherrywood sprinkled with red wine burned in the fireplace with the warmth of candlelight accenting their home.

A buffet on the dining room table included a selection of roast chicken, baked ham with spiced apples, whipped potatoes, slender green beans, and an endive and walnut salad. Dessert included fruit, marinated goat cheese, shortbread cookies, palmier pastries, and macarons. Red and white wines were served from their private cellar, wines that Adrien personally collected during his entire career as a vintner.

Adriana, Reina, and Daniel didn't leave the hotel in Paris until almost one that day and it was six o'clock in the evening before they arrived in Libourne. Daniel's introduction to the family was brief; the last-minute preparations for the party were still hectically proceeding. Michael's acceptance of his daughter's new boyfriend was guarded at best. Adrien was aware of his son's discomfort concerning the young artist and did what he could to try to ease the situation.

Earlier that afternoon, before the three of them arrived, Michael confided in Adrien. "I was hoping that she'd find someone with a little more promise." The older man stayed silent, listening as his son continued. "Her mother and I know very little about him besides the obvious." Reina's father began to pace. "He lives in a trailer for crying out loud and travels about all the time! She could do much better for herself." When his father continued to stay quiet Michael said, "I've seen some of his work. It is good. But he'll never be able to support a wife and family. And Erica, I know her, she won't approve."

The two men were in the Forche's makeshift wine cellar while Adrien decided which reds and whites would be appropriate for the evening. Adrien took out a bottle of Cabernet from a rack and blew the dust from the label, smiling. "I bottled this my first year back from America. My pockets were empty, I had nothing when I first came back. The Fournier's were still unsure of me then but the first taste of this brought them to their knees begging me to stay. It is a truly magnificent blend." He placed the bottle back carefully in its rack. "I know it must be hard for you," Adrien began, "to accept him. But I think it's important to try to give your daughter the respect of choosing for herself. It will be impossible for you to control her or the situation."

"I've never tried to control her; she's always made us very proud."

Adrien continued to go through various wines, picking some, and holding others back. Rather than replying to his son's last assertion he said quietly, "This is my life's work. It's not much in the scheme of things but we can only do what we can and do it well. You know this I think." He grinned and patted his son on the back. "And a good bottle of wine isn't that different from a good painting." Michael was holding the case where Adrien was placing his selected bottles for the evening; he added one more. "Both require the artist to bring them to life, n'est-ce pas?"

The guests were scheduled to begin arriving at nine that evening and at precisely that hour there was a tentative knock on the front door. "I'll get it," Marie called out as she ran to answer it. Marcel stood there in his best suit with his hat clutched to his chest and his hair slicked back. "Bonsoir, Marie," he said quietly.

"Joyeux Noel, Monsieur Bouvier," Marie replied. "Please come in."

The waiter crossed the threshold hesitantly saying as he observed the lack of guests, "Am I early?"

Reina answered him as she came down the hall, "No, Marcel, you are just the first to arrive." She sensed his distress and took him by the arm. "I'd like you to meet a friend of mine from America."

"It is good to see you again, Reina," the elderly waiter said quietly as she led him into the living room with its attached dining area where the table was set. A beautifully lit Christmas tree stood in front of the window not far from the fireplace. "How is your family?"

"Everyone is fine, Marcel. I've missed coming to the café."

"We're very busy this time of year."

After being introduced to Daniel and listening to Reina his eyes wandered about the room in search of Elleanore. Finally, without seeing any sign of her he asked, "Where is your lovely grandmother this evening?"

Michael overheard him and replied, "She's in the kitchen, Marcel, with Adrien and Sofia. Would you like to say hello?"

"Non, non, later maybe," he replied obviously flustered.

There was a knock on the door that Marie dutifully answered and shortly after there was another. Sofia saw Marcel and came over to kiss both of his cheeks. "Joyeux Noel, Marcel. It has been too long since I've seen you."

"Oui, it has, Madame Forche… I've missed you." Marcel always felt at ease in Sofia's company. "I've asked Adrien to bring you to dinner at the café, but he never does."

She chuckled. "He's afraid you will sweep me off my feet."

He blushed. "I wish it was only possible, Sofia. I know Adrien is the love of your life." He shrugged his shoulders with a smile. "But one can only hope."

Elleanore and Adrien both came into the room with platters of food that they placed on the dining table. Ellie was wearing an iridescent burgundy dress she'd had for years; it was accented with a corsage made of holly. A lump gathered in Marcel's throat, an unease when he saw her that made Sofia smile as she said, "I hope you will come and see us more often, Marcel." And with that she left him there so she could greet her other guests.

As the room continued to fill, Marcel tried to build up the courage to approach Elleanore. But it was Ellie who noticed him standing alone next to the fireplace and came to greet him. She kissed his cheek lightly. "Merry Christmas, Marcel. I was so happy to hear from Adrien that you were coming." She noticed him grasping his hat nervously and took it from him gently. "Let me put this up for you."

"Merci, Ellie," he replied as he gazed longingly into her eyes.

"Would you like a glass of wine, Marcel?"

"Oui, that would be nice."

Elleanore had heard of stories of Marcel for years from Adrien. The two grew up together from the time they were boys. But until tonight she hadn't quite realized how good-looking he was. She reached out and gently placed her hand atop his. "Red or white, Marcel?"

"Rouge s'il vous plait, Ellie."

She smiled. "I'll be right back."

The main room was becoming crowded; Marie had lost interest in greeting new arrivals and was trying her best to retain Daniel's attention. She thought him mysterious and handsome. Reina had shown her pictures of his work and she thought them fascinating. When there was another knock on the door it was Adriana who opened it to see Paul Fournier standing there smiling. He handed her a bouquet of flowers and kissed both her cheeks. "Joyeux Noel, Adriana."

She was shocked at first and said bewildered, "I thought you would be spending the holiday with your family in Paris."

"Non, mon amour, pas ce soir," he replied. "My wife after all these years has decided; she wants to remarry and has asked for a divorce."

This news unsettled Adriana, particularly after her recent meeting with Henri Chausson. She wondered suddenly if Paul would expect their relationship to go to the next level once the termination of his first marriage was finalized. She wasn't ready for that and had no intention of staying in Libourne after Marie was ready to leave home. Adriana desperately wanted the dream she'd been denied, and the attraction she felt for Henri was quickly becoming a part of that.

Still recovering from her disbelief and not knowing what else to say she replied unsteadily, "Please, come in."

Adrien had never truly recovered from the cold that nagged at him that fall and winter. He'd consumed enough wine to forget about it for a little while and was in the middle of an animated conversation with Claude Bescond, a coworker from his days with Chateau Fournier, when he saw Paul Fournier at the door. His daughter's reaction to their guest and the flowers Paul had given her confused him momentarily; he excused himself and went to say hello.

He held his hand out to Paul as he approached. "C'est une agreable surprise, mon ami. I didn't know you were coming tonight."

Adriana used her father's greeting to excuse herself; she held up the flowers. "I'll put these in water."

Paul glanced at her as she walked away before turning his attention to her father. "I'm sorry for barging in like this... my wife and I are having trouble and I didn't think you'd mind if I stopped by."

Adrien was well aware of Paul's estranged relationship with his wife. "I hope it's nothing serious."

"We're getting a divorce," Paul replied quietly.

"Come in, my friend." Adrien patted him sympathetically on the back. "Let's get you a glass of wine. I'm very happy you came by tonight."

To say that Adriana was agitated by Paul's appearance in her parents' home was to minimize the extreme discomfort she experienced while trying her best to avoid him. After her meeting with Henri that morning Adriana had already committed in her mind to ending her relationship with Paul. She assumed, however, that this could be done quietly after the holidays. But as the evening wore on she could feel his eyes fixed on her.

It was Adrien who finally asked his daughter, "What is going on with you and Paul?"

Adriana did her best to fake innocence. "Nothing. Why do you ask?"

Adrien never had the patience for beating around the bush. "The way he looks at you... and the flowers."

"Don't be silly, Papa. I've known Paul for years; he's a friend, that's all."

"He's getting a divorce. Are you aware of that?"

"Oui, he told me tonight," Adriana replied. She was committed to staying as close to the truth as possible. "They've been separated for years and she wants to remarry."

The combination of his illness, the wine, and staying up much later than he was used to made Adrien dizzy. He stumbled, and Adriana caught him before her father fell. "Papa, are you alright!"

"I'm fine," he grumbled. But he didn't argue as she led him to a chair. "Don't make a fuss in front of our guests."

She knelt beside him. "Have you had anything to eat tonight?"

The old vintner shook his head. "Non."

"I'll get you a plate and be right back," Adriana replied as she stood.

Paul noticed when Adrien started to fall, excused himself politely from the group he was with and went to check on him. He grinned as he approached his mentor. "Pardonnez, mon ami. Are you feeling alright?"

Adrien forced a smile. "A little tired is all." He motioned to a chair close to him. "Please… sit with me a moment."

"I'd like that. It has been too long since we've had one of our talks."

"You were always a good boy, Paul, and a better man. Much better than your father if you don't mind me being honest about it for a moment." Adrien had never liked Constantin Fournier, Paul's father. The vineyards were nothing more to him than something that gave him prestige and paid the bills. He didn't have the same love for them as his son. "You have made Chateau Fournier into a world-class vineyard." Adrien chuckled, saying, "That is hard to do with the Americans breathing down our necks, n'est ce pas?"

"I could never have done it without you."

Adrien laughed. "We have had good times together, mon ami." He reached into his pocket for his pipe and tobacco.

"The doctor told you not to smoke, Papa," Adriana scolded as she approached. "It is time for you to have something to eat." She locked eyes with Paul for a second as she handed her father a plate of food. "I'll be back in a moment."

After she'd gone Adrien stabbed a bite of ham and said, "What's going on with you and my daughter?"

Paul shrugged. "I don't know."

"Don't bullshit me."

"I'm not," he grinned. "We are friends… and I have hoped that one day it would be more than that. But with my wife and our situation it has been impossible." Paul glanced at Adriana across the room. "When the divorce is final, then maybe, with your permission it will become more than friendship."

Adrien took another bite of food. "You, my friend, as always, give me too much credit. It is my daughter you must convince. But let me warn you now that she is a pain in the backside. That advice, mon ami, is for free."

Daniel had never liked parties or group gatherings of any kind. But being among a group of people he didn't know who were drinking and speaking to one another rapidly in a language he didn't understand was making him miserable. Reina was busy helping Sofia in the kitchen and Michael finally took pity on him. "It was nice of you to bring Reina here for the holiday," he said. "I wanted very much for her to come."

"It's no big deal," he replied after finishing his third glass of wine.

"I'd be happy to pay you back for whatever it cost."

Among other things, Dan was suffering from jet lag and wanted desperately to sleep. And he hated being patronized, which he felt that Reina's father was doing. He shrugged. "She wanted to come, and I had the money."

Michael could sense some hostility coming from him but felt it his duty to ask, "Are you serious about Reina?"

Daniel glared at him. "That's between the two of us."

"I'm her father."

"And she's an adult," he replied as he set his glass down on a nearby table and walked away. He went outside through the kitchen into the side yard that led to Adriana's house. The cold night air felt good.

Elleanore noticed him go and followed a few moments later; he was smoking a cigarette as she approached saying, "It's cold tonight."

He nodded slowly while taking another drag from his cigarette. "I stopped smoking years ago," he said with a shrug, "but when in France."

"Are you alright?"

"Exhausted," he replied with a reluctant grin.

She smiled. "My son can be a prude, but he means well. He loves Reina a great deal but I'm afraid he hasn't been a very good father."

"I get that."

Ellie moved closer to him and gently took the cigarette from his hand, taking a quick drag before putting it out in the grass. "He didn't have anyone to teach him. That was my fault I'm afraid." Suddenly the sound of those inside the house became louder and Ellie looked down at her watch, smiling. "Merry Christmas, Daniel."

CHAPTER 43

Reina

"He doesn't like me," Daniel replied while putting on his boots.

"That's silly. Daddy doesn't even know you." Reina was doing her best to put on makeup by looking in an antique mirror that hung over the dresser in Adriana's spare bedroom. "Shit," she said suddenly, "the light is awful!"

"I like your grandparents; they're nice."

"Birds of a feather," Reina mumbled.

Dan pulled a black cotton sweater over his head. "What do you mean?"

She snickered. "You identify with their bohemian nature."

"Why, because they choose to live a little differently?"

Reina gazed at him through the mirror. "You're attracted to the unconventional, darling. And I love you for it." She finished her eyes and began applying lipstick. "That's probably what attracted me to you in the first place. I was always closer to Elleanore than either of my parents."

He approached her from the back, his arms wrapping about her waist as he kissed her neck. "You're beautiful." Daniel's hand moved to her breasts, caressing each softly. "I've never felt this way about anyone before."

"None of that," she said while turning into him. "I promised Marie that she could show us"—she kissed him quickly— "particularly you, around town."

He pulled her close. "And what's that supposed to mean?"

"She has a crush on you," Reina replied while pushing him aside gently and moved toward the door. "Come on. We're taking her out for breakfast."

Between the celebration on Christmas Eve and the activities the day after the whole house was in the process of recovering. The congestion in Adrien's chest began bothering him again and he'd been spending more time in bed. Adriana hadn't said anything to her mother or Sofia, but she was beginning to worry about pneumonia. She'd read on the Internet that at his age, smoking, and excessive use of alcohol added to the possibility. When Marie asked if she could go with Reina and Daniel, she hoped the decrease in activity around the house would allow her father to rest.

The aging vintner was in bed reading the morning paper when his daughter brought his breakfast on a tray. When she set it before him he protested. "Non, non, non, Adriana. What is this?"

"Some tea, toasted bread, and a cup of broth," she replied.

"Where is my coffee?"

She smiled. "We took a vote. You get tea."

He became sullen and returned to his paper, ignoring her and his breakfast. Adriana finally said, "Don't be a baby. Eat something and if you begin feeling better, I'll get you something a little more substantial."

Once she left, closing the door quietly, he took a bite of toast, a sip of tea and made a face of distaste as he whispered to himself, "Only the British would believe this is suitable to drink." Suddenly his coughing began again, and he reached for his handkerchief before covering his mouth; a trace of pink stained the linen. He tucked the material away beneath the bedcovers. There was a light knock on the door, and he said, his voice raspy, "Entrez."

Michael stuck his face inside the door. "Do you feel like some company?"

"Oui."

His son had gone down to Café Pascal early that morning and had Marcel prepare a café au lait the way Adrien liked it. Michael came in and shut the door before handing it to him, then reached inside his coat and brought out a paper bag with a chocolate croissant inside. "Another surprise."

Adrien looked inside the bag and smiled. "Merci, Michael. Those women downstairs are trying to starve me."

"Would you like a game of chess to pass the time?"

The old man's spirits began to lighten. "Oui, my boy. You have outdone yourself this morning." As Michael set up the board, Adrien took a drink of his coffee saying, "C'est tres bien, Michael. Tell Marcel for me that I owe him one."

They played for the next thirty minutes before Adriana came back to her father's bedroom for the breakfast tray. She glared at him. "You didn't touch a thing. It's important for you to eat."

"Oui, oui," he replied but kept his concentration on his next move.

Adriana, holding the tray in her hands, noticed the paper coffee cup from Café Pascal on the nightstand. She was just about to say something when Michael picked up the cup saying, "Let me get the door for you."

"Don't bother," she replied as she started to leave. Adriana stopped at the door and looked back, her eyes moving from her father to her brother. "Don't let him get too tired, Michael."

He turned and smiled. "I won't."

When she closed the door, Adriana heard the two men break out in laughter and she shook her head saying to herself, "Little boys, both of them."

Adrien's laughter caused him to start coughing again and without thinking he pulled out the stained handkerchief to cover his mouth. Michael noticed right away and asked, "How long has that been going on?"

"Just since this morning, mon fils."

The two men locked eyes, the silence hanging heavy in the air between them, until finally Michael said, "You know you have to see a doctor."

"I won't go to hospital," he replied emphatically as if knowing that this would be a physician's verdict.

"You don't know if you'll have to. It will probably only mean taking a round of antibiotics."

"Do you think so?"

"Yes, Adrien, I do."

Reina borrowed Adriana's car and the three of them toured the surrounding countryside of Libourne before entering Bordeaux in time for lunch. Marie guided them to Belle Campagne, a small restaurant she was fond of not far from the river on the rue des Bahutiers. It was a small, unpretentious café with excellent food and wine. After lunch the three of them continued their car tour, which finally ended at Chateau Fournier in the middle of the afternoon for a wine tasting. Marie was feeling very grown up as she showed them around the winery where her grandfather had worked for so many years.

Paul had just returned from a long leisurely lunch when he noticed Adriana's car parked outside the chateau. His heart quickened as he hurried inside and finally saw Marie with Daniel and Reina. But Adriana was nowhere to be seen. He found it difficult to hide his disappointment as Marie waved at him. She ran to him, and Paul swept her up into his arms, saying, "What are you doing here?"

She hugged him. "I'm showing Daniel and Reina around. We went to Bordeaux and had tapas at Belle Campagne!"

"So, you're finishing your tour here, n'est ce pas?"

"Oui," she replied as he let her down.

"Where's your mother and grandfather?"

"Mama's taking care of Grandpa. He's not feeling well again."

As Daniel and Reina approached, Paul greeted them smiling. "Bonne apres-midi." He kissed Reina lightly on both cheeks and shook Daniel's hand. "It's good to see you again so soon."

Reina smiled. "Marie's been our guide today."

Paul nodded with a grin and said to Reina, "How is your grandfather?"

"I'm not sure; he can't seem to get over this cough."

Paul had been concerned about Adrien since Christmas Eve. "Let me know if there's anything I can do."

Daniel stood silently next to Reina until Paul finally held out his hand and said, "We didn't get a chance to be introduced the other night. I'm Paul Fournier; this is my chateau."

The two men shook hands and Daniel said, "It's beautiful here. You're a lucky man."

"Merci," Paul replied with a grin. "I'd be happy to show you around if you'd like."

Daniel looked at his watch, then at Reina. "Thanks, but it's getting late, and we promised Marie one more stop before going home."

"I understand, maybe another time." He knelt down to look at Marie in the eyes. "I hope your grandfather feels better soon."

"Merci, Monsieur Fournier."

He grinned. "You're so formal, Mademoiselle Forche. I thought we were on a first-name basis?"

Spontaneously she hugged him. "Merci, Paul."

Paul kissed her cheek once more. "That's better, Marie. Say hello to your family for me." He kissed Reina's cheek and held out his hand once more to Daniel. "I'd like to get together before you leave."

It was Reina who answered him. "We'll certainly try. But I have to be back at work by the end of the week."

After watching them leave, Paul walked back to his office and said to his secretary, "Please get Doctor Bernard on the phone. I'd like to speak to him as soon as possible."

Adrien napped off and on during the afternoon but was interrupted consistently by fits of coughing. By that evening Adriana took his temperature and it was higher than normal but not high enough to concern the family. He picked at his supper and fell asleep again by nine that night.

After Daniel and Reina arrived from Paris on Christmas Eve Michael moved his things from his sister's house to a spare bedroom just down the hall from Adrien and Sofia. He hadn't told anyone about the stains on Adrien's handkerchief. The promise he'd made to Adrien nagged at him. He promised himself that if there was no obvious change in his father's condition by morning he'd have to tell them.

The coughing in the next room kept him awake and shortly after midnight Michael got out of bed, put on his robe, and went downstairs. He poured himself a glass of brandy, turned on a light by a chair next to the fireplace, and sat down to read. Moments later he'd fallen asleep.

He felt someone shaking him, opened his eyes and saw his mother looking down at him. "You should go to bed, Michael."

"What are you doing up?"

"I could be asking you the same thing."

Michael sat up slowly, turning his head from one side to the other trying to work out a kink in his neck. "The coughing kept me awake."

She sensed his concern. "Your father's sleeping comfortably now."

"I was dreaming of him… and of Dad."

Ellie seemed to ignore the statement at first. "I'm making tea. Would you like some?"

"No thank you," he replied as he followed her into the kitchen. The water on the stove was just beginning to boil. Michael watched as she added tea leaves to the pot. "Why don't you use tea bags?"

Ellie snickered. "Abigail Strickland had her faults but making a great cup of tea wasn't one of them. Sofia taught me." She brought the pot and two cups to the table, then sat down next to him. "So, when you say Dad, I assume you're talking about Roger." Michael didn't respond. She poured the tea from the pot into a cup for each of them and asked, "What was it about… your dream?"

Michael shook his head. "I can't remember."

She sipped her tea and said to him frankly, "Why won't you let Roger go? You're still trying to please him, and he's gone. Whatever it is that you think you needed from him will never happen."

He gazed intently into her eyes for a moment before asking a question that had haunted him for years. "Why didn't you go with Adrien when we were children?"

She took another sip of tea and answered him bluntly, "I was a coward and spoiled."

"You could have been happy. Adriana and I knew that you were miserable; we just didn't know why. We thought that it had something to do with us."

"Times weren't the same then as they are now." She sighed. "Women have no idea how much more freedom they have today. I was raised to believe that I needed a man to take care of me. That's what my mother taught me. And Roger Strickland was quite a catch. I had no idea what I'd have to give up." She gazed at him, the man she'd given birth to. "I really am sorry that you and Adriana were hurt. I was trying to do what was best for you."

He looked into her eyes. "Adrien would have been a better choice."

"All of us make mistakes. Hindsight can be a curse, Michael, if you let it rule the person you are now."

"What I can't understand is why you've decided to come back here after all these years? Why not just let it be?"

There were times when Elleanore marveled at her son's inability, for just a moment, to stand in someone else's shoes. She shrugged. "There is Adriana and Marie of course; I had to try and make it up to them." Ellie poured a little more tea into her cup. "But the truth is, Michael, that I want some of what I might have had if I'd made a better choice. I love Adrien and Sofia; I need to be with them. And they want me here, particularly Sofia."

His response was more of a plea. "I love you too. Doesn't that matter?"

Elleanore was tired; her son had always been demanding from the time he was little. Adriana had always taken a back seat to those demands. She stood and began taking the dishes to the sink. "I'm glad you came here. You need to know your father, at least some of who he is. The two of you have a lot in common. But I'm afraid you will never know me… at least the way I've always wanted you to." She turned back toward him. "It's difficult to really love someone, Michael, if you don't know who they truly are."

"I don't understand."

She kissed his cheek. "I know. But if you would just try to stop thinking about yourself long enough, you might. You might find someone you really do love. Heaven knows it's never been Erica." Ellie could see by his expression that he still had no idea what she was talking about. She kissed him again. "I'm going up to bed; you need to do the same."

Michael watched her leave, then silently rose from his chair, turned out the light, and followed her.

CHAPTER 44

St. Helena

Laura was sitting on the edge of her bed and took several deep breaths before leaving the bedroom. It was spring, she was in her eighth month, felt enormous, and growing more anxious by the moment. During her entire life she'd felt in control; now her feet were swollen, the leakage from her breasts was irritating, and occasionally a sense of vulnerability rushed through her in waves.

Reina was sitting in the breakfast nook drinking coffee, saying as Laura walked in, "Good morning. The water's already hot for tea and I have plenty of time to make you something to eat."

Her smile was forced. "I can do it." This had become her pat answer for everything lately. But as each day passed by she'd become less sure of that.

"Why don't you call him?"

She added one teaspoon of strawberry leaf tea to a cup of boiling water, added honey and stirred. "I don't want to." Laura took a sip of the warm liquid as she sat down next to Reina and sighed. "I miss Tuan."

"You love him."

"Tuan?"

"You know who I mean."

"Mmm, loving someone's not always enough."

"Sometimes it's the only thing we have to rely on."

There was no argument from her on that one; the trick was finding the right person and Laura wasn't sure that David, or anyone else for that matter, fit. The funny thing was that it was unclear exactly what it was that made her leave. She remembered saying to him, "I need some space, some time by myself." He didn't argue or fight, but simply withdrew. That was the last time she'd talked to him; one day led to the next, she expected him to call but he never did. That's when she began to fear that he'd never really loved her at all, that he just felt obligated, and an obligation was not what she needed. She needed someone she could count on, no matter what.

Laura took another sip of tea. "Thanks for taking me to the doctor today."

"No problem, it's my day to go into the city anyway." Reina gave her a quick hug. "I just have to run over to the hotel for a little while, but I'll be back in plenty of time to take you."

The front door closed a moment later and Laura was alone.

Tuan watched as David poured himself a glass full of Scotch and with a touch of irritation said, "Miss Laura has doctor appointment today."

David let that pass; he knew that Tuan didn't approve of letting her go without him, letting her down was more like it. But, he believed, it was for her own good. He'd stopped drinking hard liquor three years before and stuck to wine in moderation or an occasional beer. He'd never checked himself into a clinic to dry out or go to AA; he found those meetings intolerable. He stopped drinking on his own. And with Tuan's help he'd stayed relatively sober.

He was a child when his parents died, and he went to live with his grandparents. They loved him very much, but they were in their fifties by then. David's grandfather tried but while other boys played catch with their fathers it wasn't the same between them. It was no one's fault, just a gap in time and energy between one life and another.

The front door closed quietly and a few moments later Tuan slid behind the wheel of David's Mercedes and started the engine. It took him less than ten minutes to drive to the cottage where she was staying.

Laura heard the car, and a moment later there was a soft knock on the door. She immediately thought of David, but it was Tuan who stood there waiting. He said smiling, "We go to doctor today, miss?"

She smiled and gave the Vietnamese butler a big hug. "I've missed you." Laura turned her head away and quickly wiped a tear away. "If David sent you let him know that I'm just fine and Reina is driving me into the city today."

"Mr. Steele not send me, miss." He couldn't help but see the disappointment in her face. "You are my friend."

As he came in she closed the door. "I was just about to fix myself something to eat. Would you like to join me?"

Tuan was not a large or aggressive man, but he was decisive and began walking toward the kitchen. "I fix, miss. You sit, please, and talk to me," he replied smiling.

It was true, she thought, he was a godsend, and did as he suggested. Tuan worked quickly and quietly; they spoke of several things but not of him until finally she asked, "How is he?"

"David drink too much I think, miss." He placed a beautiful omelet stuffed with vegetables on a plate in front of her with a glass of orange juice and a fresh cup of tea. "Eat now. We have to go soon."

Daniel's show was scheduled to open in three weeks, and he was putting the finishing touches on two of the pieces before taking them to the framer. With a little work and some extra cash, he'd turned the garage into a decent studio. Travis had been patiently lying all morning on his bed in the corner. The golden retriever stood up, stretched, and picked up his ball. He dropped it at Daniel's feet, giving his friend a gentle nudge with his paw. There was no response; his second nudge was not so gentle. Dan glared at him sternly. "You know I have a lot to do today." Travis glanced at the ball then back at him. "OK, but fifteen minutes is the limit."

Their time outside went by quickly and Travis was just beginning to tire when Reina drove into the driveway and parked beside the black Mercedes. The retriever caught sight of her getting out of the car and bolted in that direction. Reina was dressed in one of her best suits and held out her hands to protect herself as Travis greeted her excitedly.

Dan reached the two of them just in time and held the dog back before Reina was knocked off her three-inch heels to the ground. She laughed and kneeled down to pet him. "Did you miss me, big boy! I haven't been gone very long." She gave him a careful hug and stood up. "That's David's car. Is he here?"

"I don't know. We just came out for a little playtime."

The door to the cottage opened and Laura came out onto the porch; Tuan held on to her as she made her way down the porch steps. Laura waved and smiled. "Tuan insists on going with me today."

Reina replied while walking toward them, "If it's OK with you I'll go ahead. I have several appointments at the bistro today and Shelly wants to meet with me. But I'll make it to your appointment."

"Great," she replied, "I'll see you there."

Tuan helped her into the passenger seat and closed the door carefully before going around to the driver's side and getting behind the wheel. Reina said to Daniel as they watched them drive away, "David is really being an ass."

Daniel chuckled. "Don't hold back."

"Well he is." She kissed him quickly. "I've got to get going. I'll see you tonight."

He waved as she drove away then said to Travis, "It's past time that we butted into someone else's business. Come on, boy." And they began walking toward the hotel.

The month in France was one of the best experiences of Michael's life. But it took weeks for him to catch up with work at the hotel, at the Oak Tree Winery, and prepare his vineyard for spring. To complicate matters Erica had insisted on leaving once he arrived, and they were officially separated. He was speaking to the head of housekeeping when Dan came into the lobby with his dog and interrupted them saying, "We need to talk."

Michael glared at him and finished with his conversation before turning to Daniel. "What is it? I've got a lot to do today." He was still resistant to the relationship his daughter was having with Daniel and had a difficult time hiding it. It seemed to him that Reina was making the same kind of mistake he'd made when he was young. And he didn't want to do anything that might encourage it.

"David Steele's your friend, right?"

"Yes, we have been for quite some time." Michael was walking toward the door to go outside. "Why do you ask?"

"Do you know how he's been treating Laura?"

"No, I do not. And I suspect that you know very little about the matter. If the two of them are having problems, that is their affair and none of yours."

Dan's first impulse was to wipe the smug look off the older man's face with his fist, but he took a deep breath instead. "Forget it. I thought you might be some help. I guess I was wrong."

As Michael watched him walk away feelings of regret were already forming themselves. He hated how self-righteous he must appear to Daniel. That was not his intent. But the young man irritated him. And with that settled in his mind, he went back to work.

Rather than go back to the cottage and get his truck, Dan walked up the hill with Travis to the Steele house. It was good exercise for the retriever and didn't hurt him either. It took most of the way there to get over his anger at Reina's father. He didn't know what bothered him more, the complacency or the air of superiority.

Dan rang the bell and knocked several times on David's front door without a response. On impulse he tried the handle and found the door unlocked. He opened it slowly and called out, "Mr. Steele, are you here?" The house was quiet; he looked Travis in the eye and said, "Stay!" He found David a few moments later passed out on the couch. He had nothing on but a robe and boxer shorts; his hand gripped a half-empty bottle of Scotch.

Suddenly Daniel heard something behind him and turned to see Michael standing there. Strickland shrugged his shoulders and said sheepishly, "I changed my mind. Is he alright?"

"Just passed out. Help me get him into a shower."

It took all the strength both men could muster to get Steele up the stairs. The middle-aged actor grumbled several times asking for his bottle, protesting repeatedly, his voice slurred. "Let me be." And finally shouting, "Get out… get out of my house. This is my house."

Michael led the three of them toward the master bath; they stripped him, placed his body in the walk-in shower, turned on the water and closed the door. They ignored the screams that followed. Within the hour he was clean, and the two men were in the process of dressing him while David sat on the bed and begged. "I need a drink… please."

Dan met Michael's eyes and asked, "Should we call a doctor?"

"No… no doctor." David grabbed Michael by the shirt. "A drink will set me right."

"I don't know," Michael replied while ignoring Steele's insistence. "Maybe. I've never seen him this bad before. I could call Erica; she might know what to do."

"Do it then. I'll stay with him."

David tried to push both men aside and stand but fell back onto the bed mumbling quietly, "I'm no good for her." And with that said he passed out.

It was Erica's day off and against her better judgment she agreed to come over and look at Steele. Her response was direct and to the point. "He needs supervised care. Sobering a man of his age without it could be dangerous." She wrote down the name of a doctor and a facility in Napa. "This place is excellent. But he as to agree to go."

"He could drink himself to death," Michael reminded her.

Erica picked up her purse and started to leave. "Then call the authorities."

After she'd gone Michael said, "I'll stay with him until Tuan gets back. Maybe he'll have some idea of how to handle this."

Dan nodded and walked to the door before saying, "I'm not sure we did any good… but thanks. Call me if you need help." Travis was stretched out on the front porch waiting for him, the animal got up slowly, stretched and followed his friend down the hill. When they were almost back to the cottage Dan glanced down at the retriever. "Today is an example of why we mind our own business. Remind me of that in the future."

He hadn't had any lunch while they were dealing with David and later that afternoon Daniel was inside the cottage making a sandwich when the Mercedes pulled to a stop in front of the house. A few moments later Tuan came inside with Laura and began helping take off her coat and scarf. Dan walked out of the kitchen and asked, "How did it go today?"

Laura's smile was forced as she said with a sigh, "Everything's fine. But I'm exhausted. I'm going to lie down for a while." She hugged Tuan. "Thank you for taking me today."

"You're welcome, miss."

As she started for the bedroom and Tuan began to leave Daniel hurried after him saying, "Hold on a second." When they were outside he told him about what had happened that afternoon and Tuan didn't seem surprised.

Laura was looking out the window at the two men talking and when the Mercedes finally left she asked Daniel about it as he came back inside. "What was that about?"

"What was what about?" Dan continued walking toward the kitchen.

She followed him saying, "Don't avoid me."

He took a bite of his sandwich and started cleaning up his mess. "Michael Strickland and I went over to see David this afternoon."

Panic was the first thing that began to surge through her. "Is something wrong?"

Being a good liar wasn't something Daniel had mastered, but he tried. "It's nothing serious."

"Then tell me!"

"Apparently he's been drinking pretty heavily… I'm not sure, but it looks like he has a problem."

"What did Tuan say when you talked to him just now?"

He locked eyes with her. "Tuan wasn't surprised. Apparently this isn't the first time."

Laura had no idea that David had a drinking problem. They'd been seeing each other for almost two years, and she'd never seen any sign of it. But his behavior the last few weeks began to make sense. He'd gradually become more distant, closed off, and she recalled that he'd increased his drinking to such an extent that it had caused arguments between them.

He watched while Laura was trying desperately to understand what he was telling her. "Reina's mother came over and looked at him. She gave us the number of a place in Napa that could help him. But he'd have to agree to go. Tuan just told me he won't do that; they've already talked about it."

"We'll see about that," she said as she went to the closet and began putting her coat on again. "I can drive up there by myself, but I will feel better if you'd take me."

"There's not a lot you can do… he's pretty wiped out."

She glared at him. "Are you coming or not?"

"I'm coming."

CHAPTER 45

David

It was dark when he awoke, still dressed, and disoriented. David struggled to rise, lost his balance, and started to fall into the nightstand, catching himself but tipping over the lamp, which crashed to the floor. A moment later the bedroom door opened and light from the hall framed the silhouette of Laura in the doorway. He kept his balance by hanging on to the side of the bed.

She went to him saying quietly, "Let me help you." His eyes were bloodshot, and his face had two days' worth of growth.

David was embarrassed, angry and needed a drink desperately. "What are you doing here?" He didn't wait for her to answer as she tried helping him into the bathroom. "Get out."

Laura leaned against the countertop next to the sink while he relieved himself. "Why are you doing this?"

"I'm no good for you… or her."

"Is that why you're trying to drink yourself to death?"

He started to zip his pants and began to stumble, catching himself on the edge of the countertop. David's mind was clouded, unable to think straight; he leaned over the sink, splashing his face with cold water. She handed him a towel. "This is your child too. You can't run away from it or use alcohol to avoid the responsibility."

David sighed, took two steps toward the doorjamb and leaned against it. "I'll support her."

"Children need more than money."

He noticed Tuan come into the bedroom to put the lamp back on the table, and shouted at him angrily, "Get me a drink!"

It was Laura who answered. "He's not going to do that."

"I'll fire his ass if he doesn't." He yelled, "Tuan, now!" The butler left the room quietly and the desperation within David began to build. He started to weave about his bedroom, opening drawers, going through his closet looking for the stash of bottles he'd kept in case of emergency.

Laura sat on the edge of the bed. "You won't find what you're looking for."

David glared at her saying, "Leave," and began making his way from the bedroom to search the rest of the house. She followed as he clutched the banister while going down the stairs one at a time. He stopped briefly, wiped his mouth, and ran his fingers through his hair, shouting again, "Tuan!" When there was no response he mumbled to himself, "I don't need him."

She kept a step behind David as he made his way carefully down the stairs. "I'll get you a drink, but you'll have to do something for me."

At the bottom of the stairs he turned, catching his breath while leaning on the banister to snicker. "Bargains... damn women always want to bargain." He sighed as he asked, "And what would that be?"

"There's a clinic in Napa. You agree to go, right now, tonight... and I'll get you your drink."

"Not a chance."

"Fine," she replied as she walked to the closet for her coat and purse. "Let me know if you change your mind. But you won't find anything here and I've got the keys to all your cars so you're not driving anywhere." She opened the front door. "And the key to the wine cellar."

He sat down on the stairs, feeling beaten. "You don't understand."

"And what is it I don't understand?"

His head went between his knees for a moment before he looked up at her pathetically. "I'm sick... and I need a drink. Please... just one," he begged.

She came back toward the stairs and sat down next to him. "You agree to go to this clinic, tonight, and show up sober to see your daughter born. Then I'll get you your drink." Laura reached out tentatively and took his hand. "You can do this. It's important. And I promise that if you don't want the whole marriage thing it'll be OK. But you're going to be a parent and you must act like one. It's not just about you and me anymore." Laura took his hand and placed it on her belly. "It's about her. She'll need both of us."

He started to cry, silently. "I'll fail her." David shook his head. "She doesn't need me."

"All little girls need their fathers." She kissed his hand. "And you won't fail her. I know you... you're a good man. You just need to believe it."

David wiped the tears away with the palms of his fists and nodded slowly. "OK."

Laura called out, "Tuan, you can bring him a drink now and then move the car around to the front. We'll be leaving in a minute."

She'd never doubted her ability to persuade him and had already contacted the clinic late that afternoon. The doctor that Erica recommended agreed to meet them that night and be there while David was checked in. Laura made sure that his admittance would be strictly confidential. She was assured that the facility had several high-profile individuals as patients in the past and David would be free from any outside interference from the press.

Later that night, after admitting him, she was riding back to St. Helena with Tuan when a wave of sadness came over her. And after being silent for most of the trip she asked, "Are we doing the right thing?"

He didn't hesitate. "Yes, miss."

"How can you be sure?"

Tuan pulled into the driveway in front of the cottage. "I work for Mr. Steele, long time. He has demon inside, here," Tuan pointed toward his heart. "When he meets you I think maybe this will give him reason to live again. But the demon doesn't sleep, miss. It wants to be fed."

"What is it, this demon, Tuan?"

"I don't know, miss. We live in LA it was party all time… everybody like Mr. Steele. Then things change, no more work. He start drinking too much and then nobody call. No more work, no more friends."

"You like him very much. Don't you, Tuan?"

"Yes, miss. Mr. Steele very good to me. I was scared when I first came here. I not know anyone, very young. My family still in Vietnam. I not know if they alive or not. Mr. Steele give me job, help me learn English, become citizen. He is very good man."

Daniel, Reina, and Travis were sitting out front of the cottage on the porch steps watching while Laura finished talking to Tuan. Reina asked, "Do you think she got him to go?"

"I don't know." A moment later Daniel said, "I hated it when I was a kid… the unpredictability, the never knowing how it was going to be when I got home. When I walked into David's house this afternoon I was right back there, like it was when I was a kid. For years I thought that if I just kept moving it would never happen again."

She gazed into his eyes and even though it was dark she could still see the pain there. "But you did stop, and it did happen. You became involved again. That must have been hard for you."

"Yeah, it was. I like David. But when we were getting him cleaned up the fear in the pit of my gut was there again. My old man woulda knocked me around for tryin' to help. That kind of scared doesn't go away. I dream of it sometimes at night."

His pain hurt her as well and even though she had never been abused physically or mentally Reina knew what it felt like to feel alone. She cupped his face in her hands and kissed him. "I love you."

"That street goes two ways," he replied with a grin, letting his lips linger a little longer on hers.

Travis looked at the two of them and placed his head in Reina's lap with a sigh of contentment. She kissed the top of his head. "I love you too."

Tuan got out of the Mercedes and went around to the passenger side to help Laura. She kissed Tuan on the cheek. "Thank you very much for helping today. I couldn't have done it without you."

"Yes, miss," he replied with a smile. "I see you tomorrow, maybe."

"Yes, but we won't be able to visit David for a while."

"Maybe you move back to Mr. Steele's house now. I take care of you."

She took his arm and began walking toward the house. "I don't think I'll be moving back. But you're welcome to come here anytime you want."

"Cottage too small, miss."

As Laura approached Reina called to her, "Did he agree to go?"

"Yes, and the doctor said he should be finished with the program by the time the baby comes."

Tuan let go of her. "I go now, miss. See you tomorrow."

Laura smiled at him as she sat down on the steps next to Daniel. "Till tomorrow then." She watched as he drove away saying to herself as much as to her friends, "Tuan's remarkable."

Daniel grinned. "Walks softly with a bit of a big stick."

For several days Reina had been concerned about Laura being over an hour's drive to her doctor and decided to bring the subject up. "I was thinking that during these last few weeks it might be best if you and I moved back into your place in the city... so you're close to the hospital there."

"What about the restaurant?"

"Alex and Izzy are here. You can communicate with them by phone or computer and I'll help keep an eye on things. It'll just be until the baby's born."

It had been a long day for her and Laura was exhausted; there was nothing she wanted more than to simply close her eyes and rest. "Maybe you're right. But give me some time to think about it." She started to struggle to her feet. "Right now I'm going to get something to eat and go to bed. Everything else can wait until morning."

David had in the past tapered off his drinking, but he'd never stopped. And the withdrawal was worse than he could have imagined. His body was gradually starved of alcohol and although he was constantly monitored by medical staff, in the end the battle was a lonely, unforgiving one. He couldn't concentrate on reading, television, or anything other than the need that was forcefully left unfulfilled. After two days of hell he was able to get out of bed unassisted and make it to the bathroom by himself. Splashing water on his face, he looked in the mirror, and was shocked at the image staring back at him. This, he thought disgustedly, was the man he'd become, a shell of the person he'd been once. How, he wondered, could Laura have ever loved him?

By the third day, memories that had been diluted with alcohol began to come back to him in pieces. The pieces, as they began to fit together, started to form ugly images in his mind. He'd been running away for a long time, David could see that in his mind's eye. But he had no idea what he could possibly be running from. Laura, he knew, was only the latest abandonment. He'd destroyed his career. The stories he told about it were watered-down half-truths. The reality was that he was so afraid of being rejected by the public. And he'd found a way to escape from the possibility by ruining his reputation before that could happen. He'd become so unreliable that producers and directors no longer considered him worth the trouble.

In the rehab facility he felt like he was in a glass bubble with patients and medical staff staring at him, talking behind his back, judging him. And even when he was able to leave his room David chose isolation. During the end of his first week a young woman in her early thirties knocked lightly on his door and asked, "May I come in?"

David had been staring out his window and turned to look at her; she was pretty, he thought. But it occurred to him that she did everything possible to play down her appearance. She wore very little makeup; her hair was kept up off her neck and held there with a plastic clip. Her clothes were casual; she wore jeans and a Tom Petty T-shirt.

When he didn't respond right away she walked into his room and held out her hand. "My name's Alice Whitaker, Mr. Steele. We met the night you were checked in." His expression showed no sign of recognition. "I'll be your psychologist while you're here."

There was an element of surprise in his voice. "You're a doctor?" And then he smiled for the first time since being admitted. "I'm sorry if that sounded like a question. But if this was a movie your appearance alone would keep you from getting the part."

She chuckled. "I suppose you're right. Would you mind if I sat down?"

"Go ahead, Doc. I'm just visiting." She sat while he continued to stand, making it clear to her that there were still choices left up to him.

Alice sat with his file in her lap but didn't open it or make any sign at all that she was going to take notes. She noticed his hands shaking. "It's been a difficult week for you."

David nodded slowly. "That's putting it mildly." He put his hands in his pockets. "What can I do for you, Doc?"

"I thought I might be able to do something for you."

"Like what?"

"Why don't we start by telling me why you think you're here?"

He walked back toward the window to look out. "I made a deal."

"What kind of deal?"

"I promised Laura"—he glanced back at her— "my girlfriend, that I would be sober when our child is born."

"That's admirable. Do you normally have trouble staying sober?"

It felt like he was going to get the shakes again, took his hands from his pockets and began to rub his shoulders. Alice said, "Take a few deep breaths."

He did and felt the agitation decrease just enough. "During the last few weeks, yeah." David began to pace as she sat quietly, listening. "Usually I just have a couple of glasses of wine at night."

"That's two glasses of wine at night. Is that right?"

Impatience began to grow within him. "Not always, sometimes more than that if I have people over or go out to dinner." He glared at her. "Why all these questions?"

She smiled. "They help us get to know one another."

"So, I tell you about me and you tell me about you." He shook his head disgusted with what he believed to be at most a half-truth. "That'll be the day."

"You're right. It is more of a one-way street. But if there is something you'd like to know about me I'll try to share what I can."

"OK, Doc, why do this? Why spend your time with a bunch of drug addicts and alcoholics who'll probably be using again in a few weeks

after they leave here? Why not couples therapy or charging big bucks
to people so they can cry on your shoulder?"

Alice took off her glasses. "My parents are alcoholics."

The stark reply took him by surprise and he immediately regretted
asking her. He was intentionally being offensive, trying to challenge
her, but unprepared for her response. Clumsily he replied, "I'm sorry.
That's none of my business."

"Your questions are reasonable, Mr. Steele."

"Maybe, but I wasn't trying to be." Suddenly he was tired and sat on
the edge of his bed. "What else would you like me to tell you?"

"Anything you'd like."

He sighed. "I've stopped by myself before. With Tuan's help, he's
my butler… not just a butler, he's my friend."

She smiled. "Yes, we met the other night. He seems to care about
you a great deal."

"I thought I had it licked."

"Would you like to tell me why you were drinking to excess?"

"Yes," David replied as he nodded slowly.

ly ## CHAPTER 46

Laura

Laura took Reina's advice and moved back to the city at the end of her eighth month. It felt good being back in the city, she was home. Leaving Mélange was difficult, but she didn't have the energy anymore to contribute adequately. And Alex had proven himself time again to be more than capable of running the kitchen. David wasn't allowed visitors for a while, and in any case, she wasn't sure how she felt about him. She'd entirely missed any sign of alcoholism and felt foolish as a result. It felt to her as if he'd been lying the entire time they were together.

Reina insisted on staying at first. "It's just until the baby is born," she reminded her. "You can't be here by yourself."

"The answer is no," Laura replied emphatically. "Daniel's show is a few days away and he needs you even he won't admit it. You can act as a liaison between Alex at Mélange and Shelly at the bistro. That way I won't worry as much." Laura maintained eye contact as she asked, "Will you do that?"

"You're giving me the look."

"What do you mean?"

"It's the look you give sometimes when you're in the kitchen and it's really busy. And you want to make it clear to the staff that they should get their ass in gear." Reina gave a defeated sigh. "The answer is… yes,

Chef, I will do it. It'll drive me crazy worrying about you, but I'll do it your way."

Laura hugged her. "I knew I could count on you."

"Yeah right," Reina replied as she hugged her back.

Two days later Laura was taking a walk through Golden Gate Park, a few blocks from her house. The late morning sun was warm as she strolled along before finally stopping to sit on a bench by the children's playground. Laura watched the youngsters climb, swing, and slide, wondering how she'd let herself get into the mess she was in. There was no way, she decided, that she could count on David. She was sure that he meant well, he did love her and would undoubtedly help support the child financially, but she needed help with the day-to-day stuff. And Laura didn't believe she could count on him for that. He'd lied to her by omission and leaving her baby with an alcoholic wasn't an option as far as she was concerned.

Suddenly a soft voice asked, "Do you mind if I sit next to you?"

Laura looked up at a woman not much younger than herself with a stroller. She smiled. "No, it's quite alright."

"Thanks." She held out her hand. "I'm Kelly."

"My name's Laura," she replied.

"How far along are you?"

She felt her belly. "Going into my ninth month."

"The last few weeks are a bear aren't they." Kelly chuckled. "I thought this little one would never come," she said while reaching out to adjust her baby's blanket. She gazed back into Laura's eyes. "But it's so worth it. I was scared to death and didn't think I could do it alone." She looked back at her baby. "But the two of us are doing just fine, aren't we, little man."

The coincidence puzzled Laura. "Where's the father?"

The young mother's eyes began to water. "Bob was in the service, Iraq… he didn't come back." She held the tears at bay. "I learned I was pregnant right before he went overseas; he never did get to see his son."

"I'm sorry."

"We're doing OK. With the compensation we get from the service and what I make at work, the two of us get by just fine. I hate leaving him with a sitter though."

"How about your parents… or his? Can't they help out?"

"Not really. He wasn't that close to his folks and mine are separated. I haven't heard from my mom in a while. She remarried, and my dad moves around a lot. How about you?"

"Right now, it's just the two of us."

Kelly looked at her watch and started to stand saying, "Gosh I'm going to be late for work. My shift at Ghirardelli starts in a couple of hours and I have to still get my boy to the sitter."

"What do you do?"

"I wait tables. It's a nice place with a great view of the bay."

Laura opened her purse and took out a card. "If you ever need work come see me."

The young woman looked at it, didn't recognize the name of Mélange in St. Helena but said, "I've been to this place, the Bistro on the Bay." She forced a smile. "Bob and I used to go there on Sundays sometimes. Anyway… thanks, maybe we'll see each other again."

"I hope so. It was good to meet you." Laura watched as she walked away and wondered if she lived in the neighborhood. Somehow, speaking to her for a few minutes made her feel better. And then she realized that she'd been feeling sorry for herself.

Suddenly she heard a child cry nearby and looked around to see a little girl of four or five who was on the ground near one of the slides. Laura struggled to her feet and slowly made her way toward the child, kneeling down beside her. "Hey there," she said softly, "are you hurt?"

Tears were streaming down the child's face as she pointed to a skinned knee. "I fell down." She rubbed the tears away with the back of her hands, creating streaks of dirt on both cheeks. "I want my mama!" And with that she began to howl again.

Laura had a pack of Kleenex in her purse, pulled out two sheets and gently began to wipe the little girl's face and helped her blow her nose. "It'll be OK, sweetheart. Let's look around and see if we can see your mom." Laura saw two women chatting on a bench. "Is that your mama over there?"

The little girl shook her head slowly from side to side, her cries tapered down to sniffles. "No."

A woman came running up, obviously panicked. "Hannah, where have you been? I've been looking for you everywhere." All at once she realized that her daughter had been crying and knelt next to the child. "Are you alright?"

Laura interrupted. "She took a tumble, but it doesn't look serious."

"She's always running off," the mother replied, "thank you so much." And a moment later the mother and child walked away hand in hand.

Fifteen minutes later Laura was almost home when she saw David's Mercedes parked in front of the house. Her heart quickened and then she realized it was much too early for him to be out of rehab. A second later Laura noticed Tuan sitting on her front porch with a suitcase at his feet.

She tried giving him one of her severe I'm not happy to see you looks but was so overjoyed it was impossible to do anything but give him a hug. "Reina sent you down here."

"She say you need someone to stay with you. I say fine, I go."

Laura looked down at his suitcase. "And I assume you're moving in."

"Just until baby born. Reina say I help with nursery."

The nursery he spoke of was the second of her two spare rooms; Reina had been using the first and the other was mostly storage. She cupped his face in her hands and kissed his cheek. "Thank you." She fit her key into the front door lock and turned. "I'll show you where you can put your things."

David Steele sat across from Alice Whitaker; she was waiting patiently for him to respond. During his first ten days in the clinic he'd met with her once a day for the last five. She still held his file unopened in her lap as she did for each appointment. Inside of it Alice had her own notes and information about David that included public records. She knew where he was born, went to school, the deaths of his parents and a record of a police arrest for being drunk and disorderly in a Hollywood restaurant years before. But these were only the facts, a brief sketch of his life, void of personality.

She'd said, "Tell me about your parents."

"What do you want to know?"

"Let's start with your mother. What was she like?"

He sat back in his chair on the other side of her desk. "I don't remember much, mostly fragments." A few seconds went by before he continued. "I remember feeling safe with her… you know what I mean?"

"I think I do. How about your father? Did you feel safe with him?"

His response came much faster than he would have expected. "Not particularly."

"Why do you think that is?"

He shrugged. "I don't know; he was gone a lot. And when he was there things were different."

"How were they different?"

The memories he did remember seemed to be formed in categories of light and dark, colors that were warm, comforting, in contrast to those that were not. "I didn't see him much except at night and I was usually in bed by the time he came home." Suddenly a distinct memory came to him. "They fought… I remember waking up, they were yelling, and I went down the stairs. My father's hand was raised in the air like he was going to hit her."

"What did you do?"

"I ran to her… I think." These questions were making him agitated; David got to his feet and began to pace. "That was such a long time ago, I don't really remember."

Alice wasn't sure exactly how much to push him. "I know but it's important to try. Do you remember them fighting often?"

"No."

"How about the accident?"

"What about it? I only know what I was told." Images of the two of them in the front seat of the car began to flash through his mind. He shook his head to block them, to send them back where they belonged. "I'm tired," he said.

She smiled patiently. "We're almost finished."

David was suddenly angry. "I'm finished now!"

"In a minute." She shifted the subject. "How is group coming along?"

"I hate it. Listening to all their bullshit is a waste of time."

"All of us have our issues, David. Being able to step into someone else's shoes, only for a brief time, can help us gain a better perspective of ourselves. Isn't that what you want… to gain a better idea of who you are and what's brought you to this point in your life?" Alice stood and before he could reply she said, "We can take this up again tomorrow." She rested her hand on his back while opening her office door. "You've made progress today."

That night the dream came to him for the first time in years. They were in the car; he was in the back seat and his father was yelling at his mother. David yelled something to them and everything went dark. He awoke and sat up suddenly, sweat soaking his skin, breathing heavily, shaking. It took a moment for his eyes to adjust to the dim light in his room. As his breathing slowed, he lay back and listening to the pounding of his heart.

The first two weeks had gone by quickly since Laura and Tuan had taken David to the clinic. She put on fresh lipstick and looked at herself in the bathroom mirror one more time before leaving her bedroom. Tuan was sitting at the table in the breakfast nook and stood when she walked in the room. She grinned. "How do I look?"

He smiled. "Very pretty, miss." Tuan had been staying in the spare room and helping her convert it into a nursery. They'd put up new wallpaper, ordered drapes, and he was in the process of refinishing the wooden floors. "I think it time to go now."

It felt as if butterflies were dive bombing inside her stomach as Tuan helped her on with her coat and she picked up her purse. "I'm scared," she said suddenly as they were leaving the house. "Maybe he's not ready for visitors yet."

"David will be very happy to see you, miss."

"Are you sure?"

"Yes, miss."

She was silent as Tuan drove through the city, lost in thought and more than a little afraid of what would happen when she saw him.

Would he resent her, she wondered, for forcing him into the rehab facility? And she still wasn't completely sure how she felt about him. He'd lied to her indirectly and abandoned her when she needed him most. There were excuses of course and Laura had examined most of them. But she was raised to face her problems and solve them rather than quit or run. When she first found out that she was pregnant the thought of an abortion never occurred to her. It wasn't that she had anything against it and certainly knew that for many women it was a necessary choice. But Laura also knew that this might be the last opportunity for her to have a child. The timing wasn't the best but the people she'd brought into her life, Alex, Izzy, Tuan, and certainly Reina were there for her when she needed them. It was David who had failed.

Tuan was driving across the Oakland Bay Bridge when she asked, "Why do you stay with him?"

"When I live Vietnam my father work for Americans in Saigon," he began quietly. "He was afraid of what North Vietnamese would do. He say to me, Tuan, you must go, so our family survive. He put me on boat to come here… to America. I miss my family very much. David help me. I help him too I think."

Laura looked at his profile as he drove. "You're a handsome man, Tuan. Why didn't you ever marry and have children of your own?"

He hesitated not knowing exactly how to tell her, and then, after a moment he said, "I never meet right woman, miss."

"You'd make a wonderful father, Tuan."

"Thank you… Laura."

She smiled at the use of her given name, a minor victory she thought. "You've been a good friend… I know it's not because of David."

"Yes, miss," he replied but knew it wasn't entirely so.

They were quiet for the most part during the rest of the trip and as he turned into the parking lot of the clinic she said anxiously, "I don't know about this. It's probably too soon."

Tuan didn't reply but stopped the car, got out, and went around to open her door. She continued sitting there as he waited to help her; Laura breathed deeply and took his hand. A few moments later they were shown past admittance to the interior of the clinic; she was surprised to see that in many ways it reminded her of a resort rather than a medical facility. David was waiting for them in a large communal area outside, under a covered patio; he looked good she thought as they approached.

CHAPTER 47

David

As he turned to see her his heart began to pound; he'd been a shit and knew it. Tuan was with her, standing slightly behind, gracious as always. David's hands shook as he smiled at her saying, "Imagine meeting a girl like you, in a place like this."

Laura had stopped ten feet from him not knowing exactly what to do or expect. But once she saw the slight twinkle in his eyes her doubt eased enough to close the gap between them, wrapping her arms about him, resting her head on his chest. "It seems like forever since I've seen you."

"Sober at any rate," David replied with a chuckle as he kissed the top of her head. He didn't exactly push himself away but guided her to a table. "Let's sit down. You must be tired."

"I've been sitting for the last hour."

Tuan approached the couple and said quietly with an abbreviated bow of his head. "I wait for you in car, miss."

"You don't have to leave," she said hurriedly with a touch of panic in her voice.

David gave him a slight nod. "Thank you." He meant it for so much more than bringing her to the clinic. Once Tuan had gone he sat down next to her. "I suppose I should thank you too."

"Why?"

He grinned. "For blackmailing me into coming here."

She blushed and lowered her head. "I thought you were too far gone to remember that."

"I was drunk not dead."

Her expression turned serious. "I didn't," she began then hesitated. "I didn't know that you had a problem."

"You mean you didn't know I was a drunk." He snickered. "Well I've sort of been on the wagon for a long time. I thought I had it licked."

Laura took his hand from across the table. "I missed you."

"I missed you too," he replied as he squeezed her hand gently before pulling it away. His hands continued to shake, and he put them in his lap. "How's our little girl?"

It hurt when he pulled away from her, but she forced herself not to show it. And she noticed his quiver. Laura forced back tears and said with a grin, "She's restless. I think she knows it's almost time to come and say hello to her daddy."

"I want to be there," he began, then noticed Alice Whitaker come through the patio doors. He gazed back at Laura as he stood and said facetiously, "It looks like you're in for a treat."

Walking directly to their table Alice rested a hand on Laura's back and said to her, "I heard you were here and wanted to come and say hello."

Laura looked up. "It's good to see you again, Doctor. Won't you sit down for a minute?"

David spoke up. "I didn't realize the two of you knew each other." Then gestured with a nod of his head. "Please, Doc, have a seat."

"Thanks, I'd love to… but just for a minute. I have to meet with a patient soon." She did have a patient but not for an hour; she'd intentionally left this time slot open knowing that Laura was scheduled to visit. Alice took a seat and said with a smile, "Your little one should be on the way soon. The two of you must be excited."

He sat down again. "I was just about to tell her that my stay here might be longer than we thought at first."

"I'm sorry but David's right. I've asked him to consider a ninety-day stay with us." She immediately saw the disappointment in Laura's face and said quickly, "But he can still be with you in the hospital when the baby is born."

David added. "I'll just have to come back afterward."

Laura gazed into his eyes then looked at her. "Why? This was supposed to be a thirty-day thing."

The psychologist continued to hold her hand. "We're trying to deal with why David drinks. Alcohol or drug abuse can be a symptom of a deeper problem."

"What problem?" She sensed David becoming restless.

"We can't answer that just yet."

Finally, David spoke up. "Doc, give us a minute."

"Certainly," Alice replied with a smile and started to stand. "It was really nice seeing you again, Laura."

When she'd gone Laura asked impatiently, "What's going on?"

He hesitated a moment, looking away from her toward the trees on the far side of the grounds. "I've lived a lie for so long it's difficult for me to be real. That's probably why acting came to me so easily." His gaze returned to her. "I could just step into someone else's fictional life and avoid my own. But eventually things catch up and they did for me in Hollywood. I've told people a dozen different reasons why I came here, to St. Helena. Most of those reasons are partial truths. The real reason is it's easier for me to run away. I've become a master at it."

"And now?"

"I think I'm ready to figure it out. Part of the reason is because of you"—he glanced toward her belly— "and her. But it's for me too. I want to feel useful, and capable of being a good father. I think the reason I started hitting the booze again was that I knew deep down I wasn't ready to do that."

She knew he sounded sincere but then again, he always did. The bottom line for her was that while he was busy getting well, or at least trying to, she had to deal with everything else alone. Laura looked at her watch. "I want to stop by Mélange before we go back to the city."

She started to stand. "I'd better get started… I don't want to get back to the city too late."

"You just got here."

She sighed. "David, we've both got a lot going on right now. But to be honest I don't know when you're telling me the truth and when it's bullshit. I have a baby on the way and two restaurants that need to be dealt with." She struggled to her feet and started to walk away but stopped. "I do hope you solve your problem whatever it is… for your sake and our daughter's."

"I want to be a good father."

"Then just do it," she replied in frustration and left him there.

As she was walking through the lobby toward the main entrance Alice Whitaker stopped her. "Could we talk for just a minute in my office?"

Laura's first thought was to dismiss her, but she agreed. "Five minutes… Tuan is waiting for me in the car."

Alice escorted her into her office. "Please, take a seat."

"Thank you but I'd rather stand."

"OK then, let me ask you this. How much do you know about substance abuse?"

"Not much I grant you that." Laura felt the impatience in her voice and knew it wasn't like her. But she was tired. She wanted normal for a change; she wanted what her parents had between them for fifty years.

Alice took off her glasses. "For years alcoholism has been treated as a disease. People come to places like this to dry out… it works for a while and sometimes programs like AA are successful. But I believe that many people take drugs or drink to excess for a reason. In other words, drinking is a symptom of a problem rather than the problem itself. I try to reach the core of the patient's problem and if I'm successful there's no longer a need to drink."

"And you're trying your theory on David."

"I'm trying to reach that core within him, yes."

Laura sat down. "I don't know what to believe anymore. He's lied to me."

"He's ashamed of that I'm sure but it's one of the ways he's learned to survive. It was difficult for him just facing you today."

"Dr. Whitaker, six months ago I was dating what I thought to be a kind, charming man who wanted to be a part of my life and the life of our child. Since that time, he's intentionally withdrawn from me, physically and with alcohol. Recently I've found out that from the beginning he's lied to me or at the very least skirted the truth. Now I'm learning that he drinks because of some unidentifiable problem, which you are working on with him. And although he will be present when his child is born he'll still be separated from us for God knows how long." Before Alice could respond she continued. "Right now I'm not sure that's good enough. To be honest I wasn't sure of that when I came here today." Laura sighed. "I know he has problems and heaven knows I want him to work through them. But I have to decide what is best for me and for our child."

Alice nodded. "That's understandable. If you're up to it after the baby is born it might be helpful if the three of us could meet. It could help both of you work through this."

"I'll think about it," Laura replied as she stood. "Right now, I have to get going… there are people who rely on me."

Tuan could see by her expression as she walked toward the car that things hadn't gone well with David. He liked the two of them very much and the situation saddened him. He smiled as he opened the car door for her. "Is everything alright, Miss Laura?"

"No, Tuan, it isn't."

Her day finally began to turn around for the better when she entered the hotel restaurant. Several members of the dining room staff greeted her and when she went back into the kitchen Laura could hear Izzy barking orders to her staff. "Sí, sí, we're behind, vamos!" The activity within the room came suddenly to a halt, the volume of sound hushed when they saw her; everyone from the prep cooks to the busboys wanted to welcome her.

Laura gave all of them a moment before saying with a tear in her eye, "I missed all of you. But we have hungry people out there. Let's get to work."

Isabella began to cross the room wiping her tears away as she went and hugged her. "We've missed you."

"I know, me too."

The young woman took her hand. "Alex is in your office; he'll be so excited that you're here."

"How are you two getting along?"

She smiled. "Like an old married couple."

Alex had worked hard to pick up the slack after Laura had gone back to the city. But he hadn't realized how much was involved. Without Izzy and Reina, he would have been lost. He was in the process of going over the menu for the week while Reina sat on the other side of the desk paying bills.

Izzy knocked and opened the door in one quick movement. "I have a surprise with me."

David went back to his room after Laura left; he knew it was going to be bad after she was told. But he hadn't realized just how bad. She was gone. He'd done everything he could to push her away and now it was done. Why, then, did he feel empty? It was as if some essential part of him was cut away leaving only a shell in its place.

Alice knocked on his door. "May I come in?" He'd been staring out the window and turned to look at her. She tried to console him. "You've got to give her some time to digest everything she's learned today." Without a response she continued. "I explained to her what we are trying to do. And I'm sure that once Laura has had the time to think it over she'll realize you're doing the right thing."

He snickered. "It looks like my chickens have come home to roost."

"Do you want to quit?"

"No." He ran his fingers through his hair. "She thinks everything I've said to her is bullshit."

"I doubt that." Alice took a seat just inside the door. "But you have lied to her and that will take time to rebuild… to regain trust. I've asked her to meet with the two of us after the baby is born."

"And what was her response?"

"She said she'd think about it. But I think, given time, she'll agree."

He sat on his bed across from her. "I had the dream again last night."

"Tell me as many details as you can remember."

"It was exactly the same; he was driving."

"Your father?"

"Yes, and they were fighting the same as before but this time when she looked back at me it was Laura."

Alice should have been surprised but she wasn't. There was a given amount of symmetry about this development that she found interesting. "Are you afraid of hurting her?"

His gaze turned stern. "Why would you say that?"

She met his stare calmly. "Your mother was almost killed in that car. You were there; you saw it." Alice paused a moment, long enough to take that in before saying, "Laura is going to be a mother… the mother of your child."

"I didn't do anything to hurt my mother and I certainly wouldn't hurt Laura or my child!"

A few seconds passed by as the two of them stared into each other's eyes. Alice was considering his emotional reaction as she stood up. "No, David, you wouldn't."

Once she'd gone he felt it stir within him, the guilt. Why, he wondered, should he possibly feel guilty about the death of his mother? He was a child. But just the same he felt it and that was enough.

Tuan had gone to David's house to check on it while Laura was in the hotel. And he was waiting for her two hours later as she came out smiling. He opened the door to the Mercedes for her. "You look happy, miss."

"I am now," she replied as he helped her.

It was the middle of the afternoon when they started back to the city and early rush hour had already begun. Laura leaned back in her seat and closed her eyes listening to the radio. Alex, Izzy, and Reina were doing a good job; this eased her mind. For the first time since she'd moved back to the city she believed everything would work out.

Without the day-to-day responsibility of running both restaurants Laura had the time at her home in San Francisco to experiment with new dishes. Two of those recipes she gave to Alex to try at Mélange. And she began writing down all her recipes in her computer, recipes that she'd been collecting since she was a student in Paris. She thought she might publish them someday. Tuan had been cooking with her, sharing what he'd learned over the years and that too stimulated her creative process.

The traffic on the bridge was bumper to bumper; Tuan was quiet as he drove thinking that she was asleep when suddenly Laura said, "If David and I don't get back together would you consider staying with me… working for me instead of him?"

"Doing what, miss?"

"Help me take care of the baby. I can't take care of her the way I should and still do my job."

He paused. "David is my friend, miss."

There was disappointment in her voice. "I understand. It was just a thought… forget I asked."

"Is alright, Laura. I be happy to do this… David would want me to."

CHAPTER 48

Libourne

Adrien battled pneumonia for several weeks that winter. It was Doctor Bernard, who'd stopped by the house as a favor to Paul Fournier, who made the initial diagnosis and had him admitted to the hospital. The family kept the severity of his condition from Marie, but she knew just the same, and in her room each night she prayed silently for her grandfather to recover. He did and by Easter Adrien was strong enough to return home.

It was a Saturday in late May; Marie was playing chess with her grandfather while Marcel Bouvier watched. The elderly waiter was sitting between the two of them giving periodic unsolicited advice when Adrien finally said, "Don't you have work to do?"

"I'm on my break, mon ami?"

Marie moved her bishop, threatening Adrien's queen. Her piece was protected by a pawn, which forced the old vintner to move his piece or lose it. Adrien reached into his pocket for his pipe and took it out. Marie's response was immediate. "Non, Grand-pere. Doctor Bernard said you are not to smoke."

"Do you see any tobacco, my child?" He smiled at her. "The doctor didn't say I couldn't pretend just a little." He stuck the stem of the empty pipe in his mouth before moving the queen out of danger.

Marcel whispered to himself but still loud enough to be heard. "She'll put you in check."

Adrien, irritated, gave his friend a dirty look. "Is it impossible for you to be quiet? We are trying to concentrate."

"Check," Marie said as she moved her other bishop into place.

It was clear that his granddaughter would have him in checkmate in three, maybe four moves. Adrien sighed. "You've won again. I should never have taught you this game." He took out his father's pocket watch from his vest and looked at the time. This was the only thing he had of his father's; it was given to him by his mother at the end of the war. "It is time, my sweet," he said to her, "that we start home. Your mama will be looking for you."

Marie carefully put the pieces away in their wooden box and folded the board. "Don't you remember, Grand-pere, she went to Paris for the weekend."

He stood slowly, using his cane for support, and kissed her cheek. "Absolument, mon doux. I was testing you."

"Testing her my ass," Marcel muttered as he began to clear the dishes from their table.

Adrien scowled at him again. "Watch your language, you old fool. She's a child."

"Oui… oui, but not as much of a child as you think, mon ami."

She wasn't a child any longer; Adrien could see that. During the last year Marie had begun to blossom. He knew that before long she would no longer be interested in spending time with two old men. Her interests would shift to boys, who were already noticing her.

It took longer now for the two of them to make the walk back home, but Marie was patient. She'd been asked by her friends to a picture show that afternoon, which she declined; it was an American picture with Johnny Depp, one of her favorite film stars. But she knew that her grandfather would be disappointed if they missed one of their Saturday afternoons together.

They'd only gone about a block from the café when Adrien said to her, "You have better things to do than spend time with an old man like me, chérie."

She smiled as she held his arm, more for Adrien's benefit than her own. "Have you become tired of me beating you at chess, Grand-pere?"

"Non, ma fille chérie, it's not that," he replied seriously. "You always make me proud… but I know you could have done something with your friends today. I want you to spend time with them."

"If I did you'd have to play chess with Marcel."

He stopped walking to catch his breath and after a moment he chuckled. "But I would win."

Marie tried to change the subject. "Marcel likes Mamie Ellie, doesn't he, Grand-pere?"

"You know he does, chérie. What is your point?"

"Why won't she go out with him?"

They started walking again as he said, "You should ask your Mamie."

"I did… she wouldn't say."

Adrien tried his best to answer her indirectly. "Your life, my child, is ahead of you. There are unimaginable wonders for you to discover, full of joy and heartache, but wonders still. For us the greatest part of our lives is behind us. We have loved, and we have lost some of those we've loved. It is the way of life n'est ce pas?" The old man put his arm around her. "I suspect that your Mamie is doing exactly what she wishes to do with her days. And, my darling, it is time for you to do the same."

Later that night Adriana and Henri Chausson were having supper at Le Christine, an upscale restaurant close to his apartment. He refilled her glass of red wine. "You look beautiful tonight, chérie."

Adriana had been dating Henri for several months and she liked him a great deal. He was intelligent, sensitive, and they had the same interests. But she didn't love him. She was more in love with the idea of loving him. Adriana didn't know how to tell him the way she felt but only smiled. "Merci, Henri."

The waiter had just brought their entrées when she noticed Paul Fournier come in with several people. She'd been avoiding him since Christmas. Adriana was grateful to him for sending his doctor to treat her father but whenever he was near she became agitated. He didn't fit into the plan she'd made for herself once Marie was grown. She'd loved him terribly a few years before, but her love cooled once she accepted the fact that his wife would never give him a divorce.

Henri asked, "What is it?"

She took a bite of her salmon. "Nothing… why?"

"You've become so serious."

"It's nothing, Henri." Adriana glanced across the room and saw Paul staring back at her. He smiled, and she did the same with a slight nod.

Henri turned to see who she'd seen. "That's Paul Fournier. Do you know him?" And then the connection occurred to him. "Of course, you're both from Bordeaux."

Adriana wiped her mouth with a linen napkin and took a sip of wine. "Libourne actually. But yes, my father used to work for him."

"Would you introduce me? We've been trying to get the Fournier account for years."

She was about to tell him it wasn't a good time when Paul began making his way across the room toward them. Adriana took another drink of wine and muttered quietly to herself, "Shit."

Paul approached their table smiling. "Adriana, I had no idea you were in Paris." His hand rested on her back as he kissed her cheek. "I haven't seen you since the holidays."

His eyes seemed to burn into her soul for those few seconds before she said, "Paul, this is Henri Chausson."

Henri stood and shook his hand. "It's a pleasure, Monsieur Fournier."

"The pleasure is all mine I assure you."

Adriana's nerves felt as if they were unraveling quickly. "I work with Henri, Paul. He's the creative director of Baudelaire Group." Her heart was pounding in her chest. "This certainly is a coincidence."

Paul's attention shifted back to her. "Oui… it certainly is."

She had to do something, anything, to make the insanity of the moment end. Adriana glanced toward the people he'd come in with and said, "Your friends are becoming impatient."

He smiled. "It's my lawyer and a few friends, my divorce was finalized today." Paul took her hand, his lips lingering briefly as he kissed it. "You're lovely tonight, chérie." He let go of her hand reluctantly, then said to Henri, "It was a pleasure. Please forgive me for interrupting."

Adriana couldn't deny her feelings, the way her heart pulled toward Paul as he walked away. She'd convinced herself that it was over months ago but every time she saw him those old feelings seemed to rise to the surface. And it became increasingly difficult to push them aside.

"Are you alright?"

She set her napkin on the table beside her plate and started to get up. "Yes, Henri, I'm fine. Please excuse me for a moment." As Adriana made her way into the ladies' room, tears began to form. Paul had promised her for years that he would get a divorce and now when it was too late, when she'd found someone new it was finally complete. She stood before the mirror trying to compose herself, dabbing at her eyes, afraid that the liner would begin to run and muttered to herself, "Why now?"

A stylish forty-year-old woman came in, walked to the mirror and began freshening her makeup. She'd been one of the people who had come into Le Christine with Paul. Suddenly she said, "Excusez-moi. You are Adriana Forche, n'est ce pas."

"Oui."

The woman held out her hand. "Je suis Jacqueline Daladier. My husband is Maxime Daladier, Paul's lawyer." She smiled. "Paul's mentioned you several times over the years. I'm glad we've had the chance to meet at last."

Adriana didn't know what to say to her; she was still upset, confused and had no idea why Paul had confided in anyone about their relationship. "My father worked for the Fourniers."

Jacqueline leaned back onto the countertop, staring deeply into Adriana's eyes. "He cares for you a great deal. You're a lucky woman. It's about time that snotty bitch gave him a divorce."

"What makes you say that?"

She grinned as she took a cigarette out of her purse. "Do you mind?" And as Adriana shook her head she lit it. "Which part… you being the lucky one or about the bitch."

"Both, I suppose."

"Simone Fournier has been treating Paul like shit for years," she replied and blew smoke away from them both. "She was only after him for his money and the privilege of being Madame Fournier. Simone hated Libourne, too provincial for her. She's raised the children to be just as spoiled and narcissistic as she is." Jacqueline tapped her cigarette over the sink, letting the ash fall there. "You helped him through a bad time." She stubbed out her cigarette and started to walk out saying casually as she went, "I wouldn't wait too long if I were you."

Henri knew something was bothering her; he just had no idea what it was. They were friends, good friends, and he believed he was in love with her. The consideration of marriage for the first time in his life had begun to entertain his thoughts. But he'd sensed the chemistry between Adriana and Paul Fournier and that troubled him. When she came back to the table he asked, "What's going on?"

Adriana took a drink of wine. "Nothing. Why do you ask?"

"It's obvious he upset you."

She sighed and took another drink. "We were close once. It was over a long time ago."

"Are you sure of that?"

"Oui," she replied. But inside she wanted to scream that she wasn't sure of anything. "I'm tired, Henri. Could we go please?"

"Bien sur, Adriana," he replied and signaled the waiter.

The next morning Henri slept peacefully as Adriana got out of bed and quietly began to dress. He opened his eyes slowly. "Were you going to leave without saying anything to me?"

She'd slept poorly, still tired, and in no mood for a battle of words. "I have to get back. Marie has school tomorrow."

"I was hoping we would have time to talk. Your parents are there with her… stay, for a little while, and have breakfast with me."

Adriana sighed. "I can't."

"If that is what you wish," he replied, throwing the covers aside and getting out of bed. Henri started putting his pants on. "You haven't been the same since you saw Fournier last night."

She sat in a chair opposite him to put her shoes on. "That's not true." And then suddenly Adriana said, "It's not working between us, Henri. I was going to tell you that last night when Paul came in. And then everything got thrown off." The look on his face made it clear that she'd hurt him. She stood and began gathering the rest of her things, unable to do more than say, "I'm sorry... I do like you very much."

"I love you, Adriana."

"Please don't, Henri."

"Let me finish... please," he implored.

She sighed, unable to fight him, and sat down once more. "Say what you have to say."

He sat on the edge of the bed, opposite her. "I love you and I'd be dishonest if I told you I haven't thought of marriage because I have. But I like you, Adriana, and I know you're wasting your talent living in the country. You could be so much more here in Paris; Marie could have much more, good schools, friends, opportunities that she's been denied living in Libourne."

"I know that, Henri. But that is her home... the people she loves are there. I can't take her away from that; she'd hate me for it." A thought came to her suddenly, rising to the surface without warning. "It seems to me, Henri, that we are blessed with two lives; the one we might have had and the one we've chosen. I can't go back and do it differently. Right now, I'm not sure I'd want to if given a chance." She gazed at him intently. "For years, Henri, I've thought poor me, I could have done this or that if only this or that would have been different. When my father got sick this winter I was terrified of losing him and thought what if things had been different? I would never have been able to really know him, to share the things we've shared. Oui, Paul is a part of that, of my experiences there, but he is only a part. There is so much more. Maybe I'll feel differently once Marie leaves or when my parents pass on but until then I know I belong in Libourne."

He could feel the sick pull of his broken heart. "Why didn't you tell me this before?"

Adriana was exhausted; she'd tossed and turned most of the night trying to figure out how she felt about Paul. She'd played what Jacqueline had said to her over and over again in her mind. "I don't have an answer for you. I'm not even sure I really knew until now. I've been trying so desperately to change the past, to correct the mistakes I've made; I didn't see what was right in front of me. And the truth, Henri, is that I have some making up to do… with Marie, my father, and my mother. I've treated them badly at times, blaming them in some small way for choices that I've made."

"I see," he replied finally and got up slowly. "Let me help with your bag." And as they walked down the stairs to her car he said, "We're still friends."

"Always."

"And you won't let this interfere with our work."

"Non, chérie."

He put her bag in the back seat and held her door open as she got in behind the wheel. Before shutting the door, he leaned in kissing her cheek. "Take care driving back."

CHAPTER 49

The Bridge between Two Shores

Sofia took Marie to mass leaving Ellie and Adrien alone. Elleanore wasn't Catholic and Adrien was famously disdainful of the church and what it stood for. He'd been working in the garden all morning, a task that always managed to bring him a sense of peace. He felt the soil between his fingers, watched while the beginnings of life emerged from the earth. The effort was harder for him each year; his mind knowing what needed to be done while the age of his body fought the strain of physical labor.

He'd finished and came into the house to wash his hands; Ellie was sitting at the kitchen table with a full cup of tea that had grown cold. "Bonjour," he said and kissed her cheek. "Did Marie and Sofia go to church?"

"Yes, they left a while ago."

She'd been acting strange all morning and as he dried his hands Adrien asked, "What's going on with you today?"

Ellie was staring out the window trying to calm a sense of restlessness mixed with the fear that something bad was about to happen. The feeling had begun earlier that morning and continued to nag at her as she sat waiting. Suddenly the phone rang, and Ellie jumped, her heart beating rapidly in her chest as Adrien went to answer it.

He picked up the receiver on the third ring. "Oui," he said, "c'est Adrien Forche."

She waited patiently for him to finish with only the sound of silence between them as he listened. He nodded once, twice, then replied, "Oui, oui, un moment s'il vous plait." Adrien hurried to one of the kitchen drawers for a pen and paper then went back to the phone. "Oui, allez-y." He wrote something down, repeated an address into the phone and said, "Merci," then set the phone down quietly onto its cradle.

As he turned, his eyes gazing into hers she said, "Adriana," and he nodded.

It was difficult that spring for Michael to find the time to take care of his vines, and the hotel. Reina was doing her best to help but with Laura's time getting closer by the day she was spread too thin. She was in her father's office going over the receipts for the weekend when the phone rang. It was her grandmother asking if Michael was there.

"No, Grandma, I think he's outside."

There was a long pause as Ellie tried to collect herself before saying, "Reina, tell your father there's been… an accident." The tears began again, and it was difficult for her to continue.

Finally, Reina said, "Grandma, I can't understand you. Who's been in an accident?"

Ellie took a deep breath. "Adriana… in her car. Tell him she's in the hospital." The crying began again and the next few words were indistinguishable.

"Slow down, Grandma. Can you tell me what hospital?"

"Bordeaux University," she replied. "She's in intensive care." It felt to Elleanore as if all that she'd done in her life and all that she wanted to make right was lost, suddenly, without warning. After a moment's hesitation she took another deep breath and said quietly, "Tell him he should come."

Reina found him in the field behind the hotel checking the vines. Her father had spent the week before maintaining the poles and wires that supported each plant. Michael loved spring, the time when the buds first began to break. This simple sign of life that sprang from months of winter dormancy always lifted his spirits. He'd just begun walking back to the hotel when he saw his daughter running toward him. The seriousness of her expression told him something was wrong, and when he asked, "What is it?" She began to cry.

His arms gathered about her as he said softly, "Tell me."

She looked up into his eyes. "There's been an automobile accident. Adriana is in intensive care in Bordeaux and Grandma says for you to come."

Michael was confused at first, trying to make sense of what she'd said but realized quickly that there was no sense to it, only the cold reality. He knew without asking that if his mother wanted him to come then Adriana's condition was a matter of life and death. He kissed his daughter's temple. "I have to go and pack. Call the airlines for me please."

Laura went into labor early that same morning; she'd been walking in the park with Tuan when her water broke. Reina was driving Michael to the airport in San Francisco when her cell phone rang; it was Laura's cell. She said quickly, "Hi, Laura, listen something's come up. Can I—"

Before she could finish Tuan interrupted. "Miss Laura is in hospital. Her baby comes now. She want me call you."

"I'm on my way into the city now, Tuan. I'll be there as soon as I can."

"She want me ask you to pick up David."

"Shit," Reina whispered to herself, then said, "Tell her I'll get him there."

Daniel's show at the gallery had been a success; he was in the process of finishing three more pieces to replace the ones that were sold. He ignored the phone when it rang the first time knowing that Reina was on her way to the airport with her father. He didn't really want to stop and talk with anyone else. When it rang the second time he put down his brush and reached for the phone in his back pocket, saying impatiently, "Yes."

"It's Reina."

"I thought you were on your way to the airport."

"I am… but I need a favor, a big one." She told him about Laura and asked him to pick up David and take him to the hospital. Before she hung up Reina said, "And just one more thing. Would you tell Alex and Izzy about Laura?"

"Sure, no problem."

"I owe you one."

He grinned. "I'll collect later."

"Daniel," she replied, "we're on speakerphone."

Knowing he was already on shaky ground with Reina's father he said, "Have a safe trip, Mr. Strickland."

Michael's feelings for Daniel were gradually beginning to soften. But he enjoyed keeping the young man off balance. "I'd appreciate it if you would help Reina out as much as possible while I'm gone."

"I will, Mr. Strickland." After he'd hung up he turned to Travis. "You up for a road trip?" Travis got up, stretched, and began wagging his tail as Dan grabbed his backpack. "Let's go then."

By the time Daniel reached the clinic, Tuan had already called Dr. Whitaker and told her that Laura had gone into labor three weeks early. David was packing a small bag in his room when Alice knocked on his door to say, "Your ride is here."

He zipped up the bag. "Thanks."

"Are you OK?"

David forced a smile. "About what exactly?"

"This is a big day for you."

"You're right about that." He looked about the room and took a deep breath. "I'm ready."

She grinned. "Come on. I'll walk you out."

As they made their way down the hall toward the front of the clinic David said, "I feel like a kid on his first day of school."

"I'll see you the day after tomorrow. You can give me all the details."

His nerves refused to settle as they reached the front entrance; he could see Daniel waiting for him outside, leaning against his truck. He looked at Alice, hesitated briefly, then said, "I want to thank you… for everything."

"You make that sound final."

"I hope not."

Her tone turned serious. "Come back, David, and finish what we've started."

He held out his hand to take hers. "The day after tomorrow and I'll tell you all about it."

Travis had his head sticking out of the open window of the truck and when he saw David coming toward them he seemed to be smiling. Dan started the truck as he opened the passenger side door. "You look good," he said and shifted the gear into first.

David gave Travis a pat as he slid into the seat. "Thanks... better than the last time we saw each other."

"I didn't figure you'd remember that."

"I'm working on my denial issues."

Dan grinned. "You ready, Papa?"

"Ready as I ever will be."

Tuan was relatively calm while he took Laura to the hospital and while he made the few phone calls she'd asked him to make. But the waiting was difficult. They'd taken her into a small birthing room that looked more like a small bedroom; the medical equipment was hidden from view and there was a rocking chair in one corner. Laura insisted that Tuan stay with her.

They'd been there over an hour when a male doctor Laura had never seen before walked into the room smiling. "Hello, Ms. Patterson. Doctor Singh is on vacation and I'll be looking after you today." He turned to the nurse. "How far apart are the contractions?"

"Every six minutes, Doctor."

He took Laura's hand and gently gave it a squeeze. "We've probably got some time yet but let's take a look."

While she was being examined Laura turned to Tuan and asked as another contraction began. "Did you call my folks?"

He hated being helpless just sitting while she was in pain, but he answered her. "Your mother say they come."

The doctor finished and covered her once more. "We have some time. Try to keep yourself as comfortable as possible, drink plenty of water and empty your bladder as often as you can." He smiled. "You'll be fine. Try to relax, breathe, and rest when you can."

Reina arrived at the airport and parked in front of baggage check-in outside of Air France. "Are you sure you don't want me to go to the gate with you?"

Michael kissed her quickly on the cheek. "Too much hassle. Besides you have to get to the hospital."

As he got out and was about to close the door she said, "Call me, Daddy, and let me know how she's doing."

He lifted his bag out of the back seat along with his carry-on. "I will as soon as I know anything."

She watched him briefly, before putting the car in gear once more and driving away. For the first time all day she had a few moments to herself to consider how much had happened that morning and how quickly it had happened. Reina thought of Marie and what she must be feeling, of Laura, and her grandparents. She'd never heard her grandmother this upset. Life went on from one moment to the next, one day moving into another without any real change and then suddenly there would be a shift. She'd felt that shift when she met Daniel for the first time so many months ago and she felt it when she knew that she loved him. And she felt that shift today.

By the time Reina found Laura's room she was in the middle of a contraction and Tuan looked panic-stricken while pacing about nervously. Reina set her purse on the floor and immediately took Laura's hand saying calmly, "Breathe... yes, that's it."

A moment later it began to ease, and Laura gasped, "It's almost over." She took a few more quick, deep breaths. "That's better..." With a sigh she collapsed back into her pillows. "They're coming every five minutes or so now."

Reina pulled a chair close enough to Laura's bedside to be near her. "Can I get you anything?"

Laura pointed to the nightstand. "Water please."

She replied with a smile, "Is that all?"

"You're here. That's enough."

Tuan was still nervously fidgeting about the room as Reina said to him, "Why don't you take a break for a few moments? We'll be fine."

He practically ran for the door. "OK I go watch for David."

When he'd gone Laura asked, "Where is he?"

Reina took her hand again. "Daniel is picking him up at the clinic. They should be here soon."

Suddenly Laura gripped her hand and began breathing rapidly. "Another one is coming!"

David was silent as Daniel drove toward the city and finally the young artist asked, "You worried?"

"Of course, I'm worried," he barked. "She's early by three weeks."

"She'll be fine. Take it easy."

He'd been out of the clinic for less than an hour and David wanted a drink so much that it hurt, just one to even out the anxiety that raged within him. "Why are you doing this?"

"You mean taking you to the hospital?"

"Yes… but not just that. You helped me get sober."

Dan snickered. "All I did was help get you cleaned up."

"You got involved and you didn't have to. Why?"

"Laura's a decent person; I like her." He paused. "And Reina asked me to get you to the hospital."

David studied his profile; Daniel was so young and not anything like someone he'd imagine Reina might find attractive. His demeanor was moody, innocent at times, wounded at others, and angry. But deep down he was kind. What was it, David wondered, that wounded him? Whatever it was, he thought, Daniel didn't let it run his life. And David had been the opposite. No wonder Reina was in love with him.

Rather than drive into the parking lot Dan stopped the car in front of the hospital entrance. "This is your stop."

"Aren't you coming in?"

He grinned and shook his head. "There's probably already a cast of thousands in there. Besides I want to stop by the gallery. I have a couple of pieces in the back that I need to drop off."

David held out his hand. "You're a good man… thank you."

"I had to come into town anyway."

"I don't mean just for the ride."

There was a small, almost imperceptible nod and then half a grin as he took his hand. "Good luck."

CHAPTER 50

Elizabeth

Tuan had shown David to Laura's room five hours earlier and she was still in labor. Reina could see the strain of worry and took him quietly aside. "Take a break for a little while. Get something to eat or a cup of coffee. If anything happens I'll come and get you."

Laura was exhausted and she could see that Reina had no idea what to say or do. As a contraction began to ease she closed her eyes in relief. She felt a cool cloth on her forehead and smiled at Reina. "Thank you."

"Try to rest."

"I want you to call Lia… my cousin," Laura said as she suddenly reached out and gripped her hand. "We're more like sisters really." Her breathing was fast and shallow with a tinge of urgency to her voice. "Tell her I want my baby to have our grandmother's name, Elizabeth, and Emilia after her. And tell David and my folks, OK?"

"Lia… like the musician?"

"Yes. I haven't had anyone call her yet. She lives in Hawaii. But her address is in my book at the house. I want you to call her… promise me."

"I will." Reina forced a smile. "Let's just get this little girl born first."

"Good idea." Laura smiled reluctantly, then closed her eyes.

As the hours passed by it seemed to Reina that Laura was monitored more closely by the nursing staff. The obstetrician came and went several times to check on her; he always seemed positive, but Reina sensed concern.

During the middle of the afternoon Daniel arrived at the hospital; he found David and Tuan in the waiting room. He patted David on the back and joked flippantly. "You passin' out cigars yet?"

"She's still in labor," David replied nervously.

Tuan was silent. His mother had given birth to two boys and three girls in their home with a midwife. None of them had taken this long.

Daniel sat down and asked, "Is Reina still with her?"

David nodded and stood up again to pace the room.

Helen and Sean Patterson were childhood sweethearts. They'd been married for more than forty years, had three children and five grandchildren. After the cancellation of Laura's wedding to Matt Stryker, Helen had given up hope that her daughter would ever find love again or have a child. When they found out she was pregnant it was one of the happiest days of their lives. They'd made plans to fly out to San Francisco when it was closer to Laura's due date but when they received the call from Tuan that morning the earliest reservation they could make was at three o'clock that afternoon.

They were both in their late sixties and traveling for them had become increasingly difficult. Sean was driving the speed limit on Interstate 17 down the canyon toward the Phoenix Valley and Sky Harbor Airport. Helen looked at her watch saying nervously, "We're not going to make it."

Sean did his best to calm her. "There's plenty of time." He took his eyes off the road momentarily and glanced at his wife. "What's wrong?"

"Nothing," she replied emphatically. But all morning she'd felt the opposite. A feeling of dread had been nagging at her from the time she'd got out of bed that morning. When Tuan called she was afraid that feeling was somehow tied to Laura and a sense of urgency began to grow. She'd tried her best to convince herself that there was no danger. This was the United States for heaven's sake, she thought to herself, with some of the best medical care in the world.

She looked at her watch again. "Can't you go any faster?"

"The important thing, my love, is to get there in one piece." He paused for a moment, gave her hand a gentle squeeze and said, "She's going to be fine."

David was standing by the window in the waiting room looking west toward the sea as the sun continued to descend toward the horizon. Reina tapped him on the shoulder and as he turned she said, "Laura wants to see you for a minute." He nodded and followed Reina toward the delivery room.

The contractions were coming faster now; Laura closed her eyes for a minute to rest. A moment later David took her hand and sat down saying softly, "Hi there."

She opened her eyes slowly, his face lacked clarity for a second, and once she'd focused Laura made every effort to smile. "Are my folks coming?"

"Yes. Tuan talked to them this morning and they said they'd try to get here as soon as possible."

She felt another contraction coming and cried out urgently, "Call them again. I want to see them."

"I will," he replied but just as the words were spoken Laura cried out in pain once more. Reina hurried to her side as David backed away.

The flight was delayed and landed finally at five thirty that afternoon; by the time the Pattersons made their way through baggage claim, found a taxi, and traveled at a snail's pace through rush hour traffic it was after seven when they arrived at the hospital. Helen was beside herself and Sean had done everything he knew to try and calm her. They were shown to the waiting room but didn't know anyone there. It was Reina who recognized them from pictures on Laura's desk and said hurriedly with tears in her eyes, "Laura gave birth a little while ago."

Helen was crying now. "Are they alright?"

Reina lowered her eyes. "I think so... the baby's fine. You can see her in the nursery." There was a moment's pause before she said, "After she was born the doctor asked me to leave. He said there were complications."

"What complications?"

"I don't know. There wasn't time for me to ask."

Thirty minutes later the obstetrician came into the waiting room. He was introduced to the Pattersons and sat down to talk to them while the others listened. His face was grim. "Your daughter has an uncommon condition called placenta percreta. It's rare but it happens when the placenta becomes embedded deep within the uterine wall. In Laura's case the placenta has breached the wall. I'm afraid it's caused severe bleeding."

Helen was gripping Sean's hand as her husband asked urgently, "What are you doing about it?"

"Laura's in surgery now. We're giving her transfusions, but she may need a hysterectomy." His gaze was serious and steady. "We're having a problem stabilizing her heart rate. Has she had any problems with her blood pressure in the past?"

Both of her parents shook their head and Helen said weakly, "She's never said anything to us about it."

The doctor stood. "As soon as we know anything more the surgeon will come out to talk to you."

There were still the last fragments of light on the western horizon as they all waited on edge. David had gone back to the window and was looking out toward the darkened sea. Sean Patterson approached him saying, "Excuse me."

David turned toward him. "Yes."

"We haven't really been introduced." Sean held out his hand. "I'm Laura's father."

He shook the older man's hand. "David Steele."

"Yes, I recognize you from your pictures." He hesitated briefly. "Laura hasn't told us very much about you. As a matter of fact, it was your Vietnamese friend who told us you were the father."

This came as a total surprise to David, but he gave no sign of it. "I see," he replied. "I just assumed you knew."

"Yes, well… Laura keeps a great deal to herself. She always has, even as a little girl." Sean was thinking that Steele wasn't making this easy for him but felt he had to ask, "Are the two of you planning to get married?"

"We've discussed it. But I think Laura's been having second thoughts." David wanted to change the subject. "Have you seen Elizabeth?"

Sean was confused at first and then remembered that their grandchild was his mother-in-law's namesake. "Yes… Helen and I just got back from the nursery. She's a beautiful child."

Reina was sitting beside Daniel holding his hand and noticed Helen was by herself. She said, "I'll be right back," and went to talk to her.

Helen saw her approaching and forced a smile. "You're Laura's friend."

"Yes, I am. Do you mind if I sit down?"

"No, dear, it's quite alright." Helen was grateful for the distraction. "Have you known Laura very long?"

"Almost two years now."

"Laura's always been the go-getter of the family; she takes after her father. For the life of me I don't know why she chose cooking as a career."

"She told me her grandmother taught her."

Helen nodded in agreement. "I suppose so… Mama taught all of us or tried to." She grinned nervously. "My sister is a horrible cook."

"There's something that Laura wanted me to do but I haven't had time."

"Is it something I can help you with, child?"

"Yes, you might," Reina replied. "Laura wanted me to call your niece… Lia. She told me the phone number is in an address book at her house. But with everything that's been going on today I haven't had a chance to go and look for it. I thought you might have her number."

"Not here, dear… I'm sorry. But it's still early in Hawaii. I can call her mother and she can tell Emilia what's going on if you'd like."

"That would be great, thank you."

Sean came back after talking to David and Reina introduced herself. They spoke for a few minutes before Reina excused herself and went back to sit with Daniel. The minutes seemed to crawl by as they waited until gradually the activity within the hospital began to slow down. Reina finally said, "I need to get some air." She patted Daniel on the knee. "You up for a walk?"

"Sure," he replied and pulled her gently to her feet.

There was an open courtyard between the wings of the hospital. They walked outside and Reina rubbed her hands together. "It's cold out here."

Daniel looked up to the sky above. "The stars are beautiful tonight."

"Yes, they are," she replied with a shiver.

He put his arms around her, drawing her close. "I love you."

She kissed him. "Why tell me now?"

He shrugged as he pulled her close. "The last few months David could have been spending time with Laura. And he didn't. He let all his bullshit get in the way. It's sad."

A sick feeling, a feeling she'd been nursing all day took hold of Reina. "Do you think she's going to die?"

"No, but we don't have any guarantees." He held her tight. "What's going on between us is something special. I know that."

Reina continued to nestle herself into him and said quietly, "I think I've loved you from the first moment I saw you."

"Really?"

She smiled. "Yes really."

A few moments later they were making their back to the waiting room and passed David walking quickly toward the front entrance to the hospital. Reina stopped to watch him. "Where's he going?"

Daniel was looking in the other direction toward the waiting room and saw the surgeon speaking to Laura's parents. Helen was sitting down weeping as Sean stood beside her listening to the doctor. Daniel instinctively wrapped Reina in his arms.

She turned her head and glanced into the waiting room to see the surgeon leave as Sean took Helen in his arms to comfort her. Both parents were sobbing. Reina gazed at Daniel with tears in her eyes. "This can't be happening." And she tried to pull away to go to them.

He held her forcefully in his arms saying, "Give them some time."

Tuan had left the room as Laura's parents were grieving. He felt numb as he walked back toward the hospital nursery and stopped to look through the window. He glanced at one crib after another until his eyes settled on Laura's child sleeping peacefully, innocently unaware of the tragedy surrounding her. His hand reached out and rested on the glass as he whispered, "I always be here."

It's difficult to accept why one person survives in a given situation and another passes. Some of us search desperately for answers and others find comfort in faith. Reason doesn't enter into it and the search for blame is hollow. David was at a loss. He didn't know how long he walked that night through the lonely streets and didn't care. Eventually his thoughts were interrupted by the sounds of laughter inside a bar; he stopped to look in the window and after a moment's hesitation opened the door to go in.

CHAPTER 51

Adriana

It was late Tuesday afternoon by the time Paul Fournier returned to Libourne and was told of Adriana's accident. He immediately went to the hospital and found Adrien there. The old vintner appeared tired and emotionally worn. Paul put a hand on his shoulder. "I just heard, mon ami. How is she?"

There were tears in Adrien's eyes. "She's in intensive care. Elleanore is with her now."

"What happened?"

"She ran her car off the road." Tears started running down his cheeks once more. "Adriana does nothing but lie there."

It seemed incredulous to him; Paul had just seen her three nights before at Le Christine. He'd made up his mind after seeing her with Henri Chausson that he would tell her how he felt and try his best to win her back. He'd planned to call her when he returned to Libourne.

Paul sat down next to him. "How is Marie?"

"Not well. She's at home now with Sofia."

"Would you mind if I went in to see Adriana for a moment?"

Adrien began struggling to get up with the help of his cane and felt Paul take his arm as he answered him. "Come, I'll talk to the nurse."

A few moments later when Paul came to her room Adriana still lay there silently with Ellie sitting beside her. She was beautiful, he thought, peaceful, but completely lacking the fire that burned within her so intensely. He kissed her temple lightly, saying in a whisper, "Je t'aime."

Adrien watched him and knew what he'd suspected for years. He touched Elleanore lightly on the shoulder. "You should go home for a while and get some rest."

Ellie shook her head silently from side to side. "No, I've failed Adriana too many times already. I'll see her through this."

He kissed her cheek. "I'm going home to check on Marie and Sofia. I'll bring you back some supper."

"Don't bother. You need to get your rest… I'll get something here."

Adrien, with her back to him, ran his gnarled fingers lightly down the contour of Ellie's face to her shoulders, then kissed the top of her head. "I'll see you soon." He nodded toward Paul. "Thank you for coming."

Paul had pulled up a chair next to Adriana's bedside and was holding her hand. His eyes gazed into Adrien's and both men knew that there was no longer any reason for pretense. It was too late for that. Paul was incapable of hiding his feelings and Adrien accepted what he'd intentionally ignored for so many years.

Elleanore watched the silent exchange between the two men and when Adrien finally left she asked him, "How long have you been in love with my daughter?"

There was a moment's hesitation as he thought of the years off and on that they'd been together. "A very long time, Madame Strickland."

"Then why haven't you done anything about it?"

He was still holding one of Adriana's hands in his. "My wife is Catholic and refused to give me a divorce. We have children."

"But you're here… tonight."

"I'm finally free," he said as his voice broke; his eyes began to well up with tears. "And I may be too late."

Ellie sighed. "We always seem to think we're doing what's best for our children… don't we. Tell me… are your children better off because you remained married?"

He shook his head guiltily. "No, madame, they are spoiled and angry. I rarely see them and when I do…" His words ended there for a moment until at last he admitted, "I feel as if I've failed them."

"We are alike… you and I."

"How is that, Madame Strickland?"

"Please stop with the formalities. I'm too tired," she replied as she looked back at Adriana lying silently next to her. "When she was a child I almost lost her completely because I stayed with someone I didn't love. I thought I was doing what was best for her and Michael, but it turned out that I was a fool."

Paul understood completely; he hadn't stood up to his wife when he should have. He should have demanded a divorce when she left him originally and then try his best as a single parent. The results would not have been worse than the way it eventually turned out to be. And in the process, he'd lost, maybe forever, the love he might have had. "I too have played the fool, Elleanore," he said sadly.

Sofia was in the kitchen cooking supper when Adrien returned home. She heard the front door open, the shuffle of his steps, and tap of his cane as he walked down the hall toward her. There was a second of silence between them before she asked, "Is there any change?"

He shook his head. "Non. Where is Marie?"

She nodded her head toward Adriana's house. "Next door."

"She can't continue to stay there alone."

"I know… but she wants to believe that nothing's changed."

"I'll talk to her."

"Be gentle," she said while setting the table. "And tell her supper is almost ready."

As she took the bowls down from the cupboard he said, "Ellie isn't eating with us."

"I didn't think she would. I'll take her some stew after supper."

Adrien glanced through the window toward Adriana's house. "I'll go talk to her now."

Sofia was exhausted from worry and ill-tempered as she raised her voice, "Then go!"

Before Adrien had the time to respond there was a knock at the front door. Tears formed in Sofia's eyes as she stared at her husband. "I'll get it."

Michael stood there as she opened the door; Sofia embraced him, kissing both cheeks. "I'm glad you're here. Come in, come in." She called out, "Adrien… Michael is here!"

Adrien came as quickly down the hallway as he could and wrapped his arms around his son. "Thank God you've come."

"How is she?"

"There's no change. Your mother is with her now."

"I should go there."

Sofia took his arm and led him down the hall toward the kitchen. "Nonsense, you'll eat first and then we'll take your mother some food."

Adrien put on his hat and coat. "I'll go get Marie. She'll be happy to see you again, Michael." He left by the kitchen door and walked across the yard toward Adriana's house. When he knocked there was no answer. He knocked one more time and went inside calling out to her, "Marie!" There was no answer and even though it was spring the house was chilly. He began to climb slowly up the stairs and tapped lightly on her bedroom door with his cane. "Marie… are you in there?"

He could barely hear her answer as she said quietly, "Leave me alone."

"It's time for supper, chérie."

"I'm not hungry."

He opened the door a crack and peeked inside. "You must eat something." She was lying on the bed with a blanket covering her. Adrien sat on the edge of the bed and said softly, "Your Uncle Michael is here."

Her head peeked out from under the covers and there were tears in her eyes as she sniffled. "Really?"

"Oui… and we're all going over to see your mother after supper."

She tossed the blanket aside and said as she blew her nose, "I'm ready."

Adrien stood up and looked at the streaks on both cheeks. "It might be best to wash your face first."

Marie went into the bathroom and when she came back she asked, "Can Uncle Michael stay here with me?"

They'd planned for her to move into the main house with them, but Adrien reconsidered. "I'll have to ask Sofia and Ellie first. But yes, I think it might be best."

"Are Uncle Michael's brother and sister coming?"

Elleanore had called her oldest children; she was unable to reach Jane, and Roger was out of town on business. Adrien shook his head. "No," he replied, "they're not."

She thought that odd but didn't say anything. And as they began walking down the stairs Marie suddenly asked with a quiver in her voice, "Is Mama going to die?"

Her grandfather stopped on the stairs briefly, trying to think of what to say, then started down again. "None of us know what God plans for us. We can only keep our faith and do the best we can."

"I didn't think you believed in God."

"What a silly notion… where did you get such an idea?"

"You never go to church, Grand-pere."

"Well, I might not be religious, but I do believe in God. I just believe he is all around us and not to be worshiped only one day a week."

"What if God isn't a he?"

They reached the front door and as he opened it Adrien smiled for the first time in two days. "Then so much the better."

There was no change in Adriana by the time the family arrived at the hospital; she continued to lie there silently with Paul on one side of her and Ellie on the other. Adrien was surprised but grateful that Paul was still there. Sofia was not surprised and had brought enough food for them both. Michael had tried to prepare himself, but he was taken aback once he came into her room; she was alive but so incredibly still it was unsettling. His relationship with his sister had always been combative and now she appeared small and frail. Marie went to Paul immediately and he wrapped his arms about her saying, "It will be alright, chérie." She hoped that was true, but the doubt was frightening.

It was approaching midnight; the family had gone long ago leaving Ellie and Paul once more. He'd told Adrien that he was only going to stay a few minutes longer, but those minutes stretched into hours. His mind was fixed on one thought: that if he stayed there long enough her eyes would open and she would know how much she was loved.

The pain was the first thing she was aware of; Adriana tried to focus but it was dark except for the light from the hallway. She turned her head and could just make out the form of her mother sleeping in a chair beside her. She began to move slowly, her fingers at first, then the feel of the breathing device frightened her, and she began to panic. A moment later the lights in the room flashed on and a nurse came in followed by a doctor. The physician was a woman and began speaking to her softly, "Try to stay calm. You've been in an accident and are in the hospital. We had to insert an endotracheal tube to help you breathe. It will just take a minute for us to get it out."

Adriana was trying to calm herself when she felt her mother take her hand. "I'm here with you, sweetheart."

She gasped for breath once the tube was removed, and her throat felt raw. Adriana tried to speak, to ask what had happened but the words came out in a raspy whisper. Ellie sensed what she was trying to say and replied, "You ran off the road in your car."

The next word was clearer. "Marie?"

"She's with your father and Sofia." Ellie smiled with tears streaming down her cheeks, saying rapidly, "Michael is here. They all went home for the night, but we've all been here with you."

Suddenly Paul appeared in the doorway; he'd been in the chapel to say a prayer and was walking back to her room when he saw the rush of activity going on. He panicked at first and hurried to her room and stood in the doorway watching as the medical staff did their jobs. And then she turned her head and saw him standing there gazing down upon her. Adriana raised her hand slowly in a silent plea for him to come to her. He crossed the few feet between them and took her hand, kissing it softly, weeping.

She saw the tears in his eyes and said in a whisper, "I'm sorry."

"Sorry for what, my darling?"

"For not seeing what's important… for doubting you."

He kissed her lips tenderly. "We've both been foolish."

Adriana tried to smile. "I must be a mess."

"You're beautiful."

Ellie watched them and knew that everything would be alright. Her daughter was safe and had found herself. She kissed Adriana's cheek. "I'm going to go and call your father. He's probably not sleeping anyway, and the news will be good for him, for all of them."

As Ellie turned to leave Adriana said, "Mama."

"Yes."

"Thank you."

"For what, sweetheart?"

"For everything."

CHAPTER 52

Libourne

It felt as if she'd just fallen asleep when she felt someone shaking her. "Marie." The voice was soft and gentle. "Marie, wake up."

She rolled over to see her grandfather and rubbed her eyes. "What is it, Grand-pere?"

He smiled at her. "Your mother is awake."

She immediately scrambled out of bed while rubbing her eyes. "Je serai prêt dans l'instant, Grand-père."

The old man chuckled as he watched her dash about, then stood and began to leave her bedroom. "Take your time. We'll wait for you." But before Adrien reached the bottom of the stairs Marie had already caught up to him.

The drive to the hospital in Bordeaux seemed to take forever. Marie felt that until she saw her mother, and held her, the reality of recovery was nothing more than illusion. And once they arrived at the hospital her anxiousness began to build. She feared that somehow between the time they received the news of Adriana's recovery and the time it took to get to the hospital something bad might happen. But when they got to her room Adriana was smiling and holding Paul's hand. Marie broke away from her grandparents and ran to her, crying, "Mama!"

The tears of relief poured from Marie as her mother held her while she sobbed. Adriana stroked her hair, saying softly, "It's alright now, my darling." But the words seemed to fall unheard as the little girl continued to cling to her, releasing all the worry and fear that she'd kept concealed from everyone. Her mother kissed the top of her head. "I love you."

Paul began to get up, to move away so the rest of her family could come closer to the bedside, but Adriana held on to his hand saying, "Don't go… stay with me." And he did that night, the next day, and the next until she was scheduled to be released.

Adriana absorbed the shock of the collision with her right arm; it was broken along with her collarbone. But she was alive and free to go home by the end of that week. It was Paul who volunteered to pick her up and take her home from the hospital. Adrien was about to tell him it wasn't necessary, that he could do it, but Ellie stopped him by saying, "I think Adriana would like that, Paul. Why not take Marie along with you? She would love to help."

"Merci, madame," Paul replied. "I'll ask Marie."

After he'd gone Adrien protested but Ellie argued, "He loves her, you old fool. Can't you see that?"

"I do, Elleanore… but I am still head of this family, n'est ce pas?" Before she could answer he turned to leave the room, mumbling, "I am no fool."

Ellie called after him, "Speak up… what are you saying?"

He looked back at her and replied impatiently, "I say yes, Elleanore, I am old. And I don't need to be reminded of it."

She walked up to gaze into his eyes. "I'm sorry… it was a bad joke. I love you… we all do. You are, my darling, the heart that beats for all of us."

Adrien grinned. "So… you've become the poet now."

She smiled back at him. "You bring out the best in me… you always have."

"That, my darling, is a two-way street." He started to leave again. "I will tell Sofia that Paul will be having supper with us."

"I expect she already knows."

He shook his head and laughed. "Of course she does."

The pain and discomfort Adriana felt on the way from the hospital in Bordeaux to her home in Libourne was difficult to deal with. But being in a car again was upsetting; the memories of the crash were gradually beginning to come back to her. The only positive distraction was the sun, the blue of the sky, and the smell of fresh air for the first time in days.

She'd been careless and almost died because of it; this thought had been nagging at her since she regained consciousness. Life was too precious to be taken for granted and she unknowingly had done just that. She'd been so busy feeling sorry for herself and planning for the future she'd lost contact with those she loved the most. And Adriana regretted it deeply.

Marie was talking incessantly from the back seat of Paul's Mercedes. What Adriana might have felt about her jabbering in the past felt different now. There was joy and comfort in the sound of her daughter's voice.

Paul sensed her uneasiness and took her hand from across the console. "Are you alright?"

Adriana squeezed his hand lightly. "Yes. Everything is perfect. Thank you for picking me up."

The car finally stopped in front of her parents' house and Adriana breathed a sigh of relief. Marie got out of the back seat as fast as she could and opened the passenger side door for her mother. Adriana smiled. "Thank you, darling." But as the little girl reached in to help her get out she said, "Let me do it please." She took a deep breath and carefully swung her legs from the inside of the car to the pavement and used her good arm to help herself stand. She could tell by the expression on Marie's face she was worried and tried to console her. "I'm fine, sweetheart."

Paul had just come around the side of the car when the family came out to meet them. He put one hand on the small of Adriana's back and the other on her good arm protectively to support her. The family was excited to see her, but Adriana was very tired; she forced a smile and made her way slowly up the walk to the house.

She let her family fuss over her for several minutes before confessing, "If you don't mind, Papa, I think I'd like to lie down for a while."

"I thought it might be better if you stayed here with us rather than your house," Adrien replied.

She shook her head. "Thank you, Papa, but I've been looking forward to my own bed for days now."

Ellie was concerned for her and tried to insist. "Are you sure, sweetheart? You might need us."

"If I do I'll call."

Michael interjected, "I'll be there and so will Marie. She'll be alright."

"You see," Adriana said with a grin. "I have my daughter and brother to look after me. But right now, I need a nap." She turned to Paul. "Would you see me home please?"

As they were walking across the yard toward her house Adriana said, "I want to thank you."

"What for?"

"For being there with me... when I needed you most."

He stopped and took her gently in his arms. "I love you... and never want to let you go."

"Are you sure?"

"I've never been surer of anything in my life than the way I feel about you." He paused briefly. "I want you to marry me... and live here in Libourne and forget about Paris. We could be so happy together."

She looked into his eyes. "I had a lot of time to think while I was in the hospital. And one of the things I'm absolutely sure about is you. I want us to be together the rest of our lives." She raised her good arm, letting her fingers caress his cheek, then kissed him softly on the lips. "Yes, I'll marry you."

Ellie watched the two of them from the kitchen window, smiled to herself, and when Marie started to open the door to go home she said, "Wait, darling. Your mother needs to be alone with Paul for a minute."

"But why?" Then as curiosity got the better of her Marie peeked outside and saw her mother embracing Paul. "They love each other... don't they?"

Ellie put her arm around her granddaughter. "Yes, my darling… I think they love each other very much."

Michael received a call from Reina and was told about Laura's death and knew he had to go back as soon as possible. Later that night after Marie had gone to bed Adriana came into her brother's bedroom and saw him packing. He looked over his shoulder and saw her standing in the doorway. "I'm sorry I have to go back so soon."

Adriana came in and sat down on his bed. "I am too." She continued to watch him for a moment then said, "I'm sorry about your friend."

He nodded. "Laura was more of a friend to Reina. I really didn't know her that well."

"But you worked together every day."

"You know how I am." He closed the lid to his suitcase zipping it shut.

"Distant?"

Michael smiled half-heartedly. "To say the least."

"You're a nice person, Michael. If anything, you've always been too nice… too forgiving."

He knew she was thinking of their siblings. "Roger and Jane can't help the kind of people they've turned out to be."

"That might be, but their father might have helped just a little bit."

"He was our father too."

The two of them had circled around this same debate for years and hadn't found common ground. "Stepfather. And not a very good one at that."

"She cheated on him… remember?"

"Mother simply wanted someone to love… and someone to love her."

"If that's the way she felt she should have left him. She should have gone away with Adrien and all of us would be better off."

Adriana was getting tired again and exasperated. She stood and kissed his cheek. "Goodnight, Michael."

"You're mad at me again."

She shook her head. "No. I'm not really. It's all water under the bridge anyway… the damage was done long ago."

Just as his sister reached the door he said. "She was an artist."

"Who, Michael?"

"Laura. She was the best chef I've ever known. Cooking was an art to her… no different than your own or Daniel's."

"Like making wine is for you and Adrien?"

"Yes, just like that."

The next morning after his goodbyes were finished, Ellie walked her son to his car. "Please come back for Adriana's wedding… and tell your brother and sister I wish they would come. I know they've been distant with her but it's important for all of us to be a family once again."

"I'll try, Mother… but no promises."

"I liked her," Ellie said at last. "Laura I mean. She was everything I hoped to be when I was young." She kissed her son. "Tell Reina how sorry I am."

"Are you sure you won't come back with me?"

"No, Michael, this is my home and I'm happy here. The happiest I've been in years."

Hours later as he flew through the night sky, thoughts of his sister and Laura kept returning to him. Life was as fragile as it was precious; the vines should have taught him that. But he hadn't paid attention. Michael finally closed his eyes and moments later he dreamt of the old oak tree by the cottage, of the swing with its splintered wooden seat hanging by ropes from a limb above, and the man who pushed his child high enough to touch the sky.